T0322493

THE SAVED

By Liz Webb

The Daughter
The Saved

THE SAVED

LIZ WEBB

Allison & Busby Limited
11 Wardour Mews
London W1F 8AN
allisonandbusby.com

First published in Great Britain by Allison & Busby in 2024.

A CIP catalogue record for this book is available from
the British Library.

First Edition

HB ISBN 978-0-7490-3013-1

Typeset in 11/16 pt Sabon LT Pro by Allison & Busby Ltd.

By choosing this product, you help take care of the world's forests.
Learn more: www.fsc.org.

Printed and bound by
CPI Group (UK) Ltd, Croydon, CR0 4YY

For all my brilliant writer friends.
Especially my writing group: Jo Pritchard, Katherine Tansley,
Marija Maher-Diffenthal & Sarah Lawton.
And my writing mentor, Sarah Clayton.

'There is something at work in my soul
which I do not understand.'

Frankenstein by Mary Shelley

NOTE ON THE LOCATION

There are 94 inhabited Scottish islands. I've made up a 95th island called 'Langer'.

Any positive things about Langer are based on the wonderful Scottish slate islands of Seil, Luing and Easdale, 'the islands that roofed the world' with their slate industry. Any negative things about my island or its people are entirely fictional and based on my warped imagination. While inspired by reality, I've taken creative license with the landscapes, buildings, ferries, weather, whirlpools, religion and churches.

CHAPTER ONE

I lean forward on the icy ferry rail, as the white coils of mist slowly unravel ahead of us.

And finally . . . there it is. The island of Langer. Our new home.

All the other passengers on this little ferry have stayed in their cars, safe from the intense cold. Calder and I are the only idiots watching the approach from outside, clearly newcomers. Well, I am. Calder was born here, but left twenty-odd years ago. I look up at him, his long black hair flapping in the wind, his cheeks ruddy and his forehead scrunched, with little lines puckering at the corners of his eyes. Is that from the cold? Or from memories of his childhood here?

'You OK?' I call, pitching up over the wind.

He nods, not taking his eyes off the island.

I glance down and notice a fat seagull bobbing on the

surging water below us. Aren't its feet freezing in that cold sea? Yet it looks totally unperturbed, all puffed up and full of itself.

The A4 typed timetable on the quay noticeboard said that the journey to this slate island off the west coast of Scotland would take fourteen minutes. That sounded short, but it feels much longer in this bitter buffeting. How can it be this sunny and yet still so brutally cold? Our rental car is parked in the base of this little ferry, cleverly packed in with five other cars by the burly man in a tight brown jumper who waved us on. But we've come outside to the metal ramp on the side of the boat, at my insistence. I want to enjoy every moment of our approach, however glacial it is.

The fat seagull abruptly dives down, instantly invisible in the grey depths. I wait for it to resurface, but it's nowhere to be seen. I keep on scanning the water, but it doesn't come back up.

'Where's that bird?'

'What bird?' Calder asks distractedly.

'A seagull. It was just there,' I say, pointing. 'I was looking right at it and it suddenly ducked under, and disappeared entirely.'

'Oh, Nancy, it'll be fine.'

'But how long can it survive down there? That water must be freezing.'

He turns to face me and raises an eyebrow. 'I sincerely doubt that some bird has decided to end it all just 'cos you were staring at it. Then again, you do have an impressive stare, sooo . . .'

'Yeah, all right,' I laugh. But as he looks back at the island, I drag my thin coat sleeves over my bitten fingernails to grip the railing, then lever myself over it as far as I dare, to scan the water.

'Hey, be careful,' Calder yelps, pulling me back.

'I'm fine,' I laugh. But where is that bloody bird? The poor thing must be dead by now. Though if it is, why hasn't its frozen carcass bobbed up yet? I inhale the cold briny air as I stare down at the ever-changing pattern of fine lines on the surface of the water. Can it have swum down deep, right under the ferry? I turn and look back. No sign of it. Only the furrow of white frothing water the ferry is leaving behind in its wake, just as we're leaving behind our old lives. And everyone in them.

Oh please, come back up, you stupid bird. This is surely a bad omen for our move.

But there's no sign of it. It's dead. Of course it is. Life is so fragile. If you don't stay alert, hold on really tight, boom, it's gone in an instant.

Suddenly the bird pops up right in front of me, shaking itself free of water, all jaunty and smug. Oh, thank God. It cocks its head and locks its beady eyes on me for a moment, regarding my relief with a withering look. Then it merrily bobs off on the undulating water. Everything's fine.

My breath puffs out into the icy air as I return to watching the island coming into view. The mist has now curled around and re-formed behind us, erasing where we've come from. But the white coils up ahead have completely cleared, to present the island to us in all its glory. Before I met Calder, I'd heard of the Hebrides, Skye and Mull but always assumed that there were only about twenty or thirty islands dotted along the coast of Scotland.

But I now know that there are over nine hundred. Ninety-five of them populated. Some with a few thousand people and some with less than a hundred, like this windswept beauty. It's long and tapering, comprised of endless curves and planes of different angles and painted with every gradation of grey, green and brown imaginable. It looks like a dappled sleeping monster, half submerged in the grey sea and basking in the sun. To the right of the small bricked dock ahead is a slate beach, which hardly fits any category of 'beach' I've ever known or imagined. It's an awesome expanse of glinting angles, endless jagged grey shards, as if this huge gunmetal sea all around us had risen up into the air, frozen, and then exploded all over the shore.

'It's amazing,' I whisper.

Calder takes a sudden breath as he snaps out of his strange trance and looks down at me. 'Excited?'

'Totally,' I laugh. 'No mortgage, no boss, no commute. Just . . . all this.' I gesture at the stunning rugged island. 'What's not to love.'

'We'll be our own bosses now, so I hope we're easy to work with.'

'Oh, I intend to be very lax indeed.'

He laughs. He's starting his own loft extension company up here having been an employee in one for years. I'm swapping the hectic stress of being a BBC radio drama producer in London for the hassle-free simplicity of being an online film script editor. He's asked me so many times if I'm sure about this move and I so am. More than he can possibly know.

The boat judders and goosebumps flare across me. I hadn't realised quite how bizarre it would feel to be crossing a huge surging sea to get to our new home. Fantasising about moving to an island and actually moving to one are very different things. I'm only just now grasping that once these ferries stop running in the evenings, we'll be totally marooned here. Which is exciting. As if we're entering some magical guarded realm. I breathe deeply and the rush of cold air makes me dizzy. My giddiness is probably heightened by the fact that I haven't slept for about twenty-four hours: including seven and a half hours not sleeping on the sleeper from London to Glasgow, three hours not sleeping on the local train from Glasgow to Oban, where we picked up our hire car, and half an hour not sleeping on the drive from Oban to the coast. And now we're on the final leg, the fourteen-minute ferry ride to the island, and no one could possibly sleep in these arctic conditions. It was thrilling to get single tickets all the way. At first, I couldn't find the option on the Trainline booking site, only returns, as if the site was saying: *Single tickets to Scotland and not just to the mainland, to an isolated island, are you absolutely sure?* I was. And I am. This is a completely fresh start with the only person who really matters to me any more.

'Five pounds!' comes a shout. It's the burly man in the thick brown jumper who waved our car on. He's approaching us with a black shoulder bag of money and holding a grey card-reader.

'Of course,' Calder says, pulling out a note from his overstuffed wallet.

'Calder, isn't it?' the man asks.

'Yes, that's right. Hi Mr Mullins, I wasn't sure if you'd recognised me.'

The man snorts. 'Aye, course I did. I wouldn't forget you, you gobshite.'

I tense, but Calder laughs.

'And anyway, we've been warned to keep a look out for you. You're the talk of the island, coming back to take over your mum's place. Not many of our lost children come back here. Welcome home.'

They share a knowing nod.

'Oh, and this is my girlfriend, Nancy.'

'Pleased to meet you,' the man mumbles, then turns and his retreating footsteps clang on the metal steps.

'Lost children?' I ask, once the man's out of earshot.

'It's nothing sinister. It's just the dramatic way they talk here. Lots of the young people born on the island get bored by the time they're teenagers and leave as soon as they can. But the islanders have to guilt-trip us by making it sound sad and suspicious.'

A blast of cold air buffets me and I shiver.

'You OK?' Calder asks.

'Yes, just excited – and a bit cold.'

He pulls off his huge black coat and wraps it round me. 'We need to get you a thicker jacket.'

'But now you'll be cold.'

'Pah, I'm made of hardier stuff.'

'Pah?'

'Yeah, pah!'

I've only been here once before, on a flying overnight visit in the summer, to finally meet Calder's formidable mum Isla. It had been endlessly sunny that day, warm with glorious clear blue skies, and I didn't factor in how shockingly extreme the winter weather would be when we decided on this move. But this bracing cold is oddly exciting, underlining how new and different this life will be. When Isla had an unexpected heart attack two months ago, her will insisted on an unattended cremation, but she left Calder her cottage here. We were burnt out with our pressured London jobs, struggling with high rent and mounting bills, and wondering if there could ever be more to life than our relentless rat race. So, we made the snap decision – crazy decision, according to all our friends – to move to this sparsely populated, inaccessible island off the far western coast of Scotland, with a population of eighty-three, one pub and one shop.

'I can't wait to go out on the water again,' Calder says, pointing at a small white-sailed boat that's slicing through the water in the opposite direction to us. 'I used to love sailing, but I haven't been out since I was sixteen.'

Oh. I hadn't factored in him going out in boats. Stupidly.

'Don't worry,' he says, patting my shoulder. 'Sailing's just like driving for me.'

Since I don't drive and lost both my parents in an awful car accident, that's hardly reassuring, but I guess Calder is an excellent driver, so . . . time for one of my resolutions for this move. To stop my ridiculous over-worrying. I will be a new improved me here: calm and meditating, eating healthily while doing Couch to 5K running, and . . . baking bread, probably in a headscarf.

Calder looks down at me and strokes a fluttering strand of hair off my face. 'Nancy, I . . .'

'Yes?'

He shakes his head. 'Nothing. I'm just getting that weird

feeling you get when you return to where you grew up.'

'I know what you mean.' I move my hand along the rail and entwine my fingers with his.

He frowns. 'Do you think there'll really be enough of an appetite for my loft conversion business here?'

'Totally. You said this place is all one-storey cottages. You'll be a bloody fox in a henhouse.' In London he was just a cog in a large glossy-brochured company. His best mate Hamish, who left the island with him, set up and was the smooth-talking, client-facing side of their loft extension company, gratingly named 'Lofty Ambitions'. No, I mustn't dwell on the past. Calder's gruff honesty will work just fine here. His more prosaically named 'Loft Rooms' is going to do just great. I nibble at an annoying lump of hard skin down the side of my thumbnail. That's the downside of love. Now Calder's worries are my worries. Worse than mine. Whenever he's stressed or hurt, I'm wounded and I'll do anything to diffuse his worry or try to change what's hurt him.

As we near the island, the little ferry overshoots the dock and slows, the engines straining, the boat juddering. What bad driving. Except . . . it's on purpose, I realise, as the boat does an awkward little dance of turning and then backing up to the quay. I see that it's actually a very skilled manoeuvre, requiring timing the engine thrusts with the distance to the shore and in relation to the speed and angle of the current. I was doing a similarly awkward little dance over my last few months in London, trying to keep my life together despite work pressure and rising anxiety. I bite the hard skin of my thumb again, then gnaw it right out of the nail bed. The stinging groove floods with blood.

There's a loud clanking of chains and I look up to see the boat's wide metal drawbridge being lowered. It scrapes onto the concrete as we clamber back into our car. The vehicles are waved off one at a time, and our car finally creeps forward and clunks over the metal lip of the bridge onto the concrete.

'We made it,' Calder announces. 'Welcome to your new home.'

'Hurrah!' I shout, staring at everything greedily as we drive up the steep slope and round to the top of the beach. I touch Calder's hand on the steering wheel. 'Can we stop for a moment, so I can get a piece of slate?'

He laughs, turning off the engine. 'Yeah, sure, it's not as if it's in short supply here, since all the mining's moved to Wales.'

I get out, bow my head against the wind, and step onto the slates. They knock together with a strange, woody, Jenga block sound under my unsteady feet. I pick up a long shard. But it's freezing and sharp in my numbed hand, so I throw it down and it bounces and rolls.

'Are you trying to smash it?' Calder calls as he gets out of the car.

'No. This stuff looks unbreakable. No wonder they use it on roofs.'

'Every piece has its weak point, however big and sturdy-looking,' he says, pointing to the boulders at the curve of the bay. 'That's how they cut it, by making a little groove and tapping along it, till they find the fault line.' He picks up my piece and throws it. This time it splits in half. 'See.'

I reach down for the two pieces and fit them back together again. 'Two halves of a whole. Like us.'

'Ah. That's a bit cute,' he laughs. 'But look, some bits have sheared off. Smashed slate can never be mended they say.'

'Who's they?'

'*They* do,' he says, lifting his hands like a ghoul. 'Ooh.'

I laugh.

'So, d'you want to explore the beach some more or shall we drive straight to the cottage?'

'Let's get to our new home.'

After ten minutes driving along glorious coastal views, we're crunching down a stony track. Isla's squat, white block of a cottage hunkers alone on a cliff edge, above an even more dramatic slate-strewn beach. It looks out on a stunning, shortbread-tin-lid bay, and has the majestic arch of a steep hill behind it. Calder fumbles with the keys, but finally unlocks the door and pushes. It creaks open, straight into the kitchen, which smells musty and feels even colder than outside. It's hard to see much, as the small deep windows in the thick walls give so little light.

Suddenly, there's an ungodly growling from the gloom.

'What's that?' I yelp, backing out.

Calder picks up a chair and pokes it towards the sound.

There's a creaking in the blackness.

A snarl.

And then a large black cat shoots past us and out the door.

'Christ.'

'It's OK, it's a good omen,' Calder laughs. 'Black cats protect fishermen at sea.'

I thought a black cat crossing your path was a bad thing?

He flips the switch for the overhead light.

We both gasp.

The room is like something in a horror film. Chairs are knocked over. The old gas cooker is caked in grease. And there's debris, cobwebs and thick dust on every surface.

'God, look at this place,' I say, as I step in.

'It's OK, don't panic. Just needs a good brush-up. We knew there'd be work to do after it being left empty for a while.'

'Yeah, course,' I say, trying to hide how appalled I am. 'I guess we just need to gird our loins.'

'Let's get our bags out of the car and I'll pop back to the village for cleaning stuff and supplies.'

'Sure,' I nod uncertainly.

'Then more of these loins of which you speak,' he grins.

I laugh and recalibrate my expectations for our first days here. I put my slouchy shoulder bag down on the kitchen table. Next to a dusty wooden box. 'What's this?'

Calder wipes the dust off the slate lid, narrows his eyes, then jolts back. 'Oh, for God's sake.'

'What?'

He shakes his head. 'It's Mum.'

'What d'you mean?' I say, peering over to read the engraving he's uncovered.

ISLA CAMPBELL 1956–2022
Come to me, all you who are weary and burdened,
and I will give you rest.
Matthew 11:28

'It's her actual ashes?' I ask.

He's frozen for a long moment, staring at the box.

'Calder?'

'Guess so.'

'That's a bit of a bleak quote. Who . . .'

He swipes the box up. 'I'll put it . . . her, away,' he mumbles, shoving it into a low kitchen cupboard and slamming the slatted door.

'There? Shouldn't we find somewhere more meaningful?'

'Once we're settled,' he snaps. 'I'll find a proper place for her then.'

I touch his arm but he shakes me free. 'I'm fine, Nance. Let's get unpacked. We've got lots to do.'

I glance at the slatted cupboard door as we unpack. I know it's only Isla's ashes in there. Literally dust. Yet although Calder's busying himself lugging in our stuff, I can feel his inner bristling and sense his body turning imperceptibly away from her presence.

But of course, that was weird for him, discovering her like that. What sadist left her ashes there, for him to find? He's just a bit wrong-footed. He'll be all right. I need to get on with organising our new life. I stride towards the door, but trip over a dirty mud-scraper that's bolted to the floor. God. I must watch out for that. It's lethal. I walk out, shaking myself into action and out of my silly sense of foreboding. I'm just indulging in my usual habit of catastrophising.

Aren't I?

CHAPTER TWO

Oh my God. I'm awed by the huge paperweight of blue sky in front of me, pressing down on the carpet of silvery sea below it. We've been stuck in the cottage cleaning for three days straight, so this morning Calder left at first light, eight-thirty-ish here, to have a ride around the bay in his mum's small boat. Standing on the edge of the cliff, I scan the horizon for him. But all I see are these glorious slabs of colour, rubbing together and blending at the horizon.

It's mesmeric, but the cold's crawling into me, and I don't like being so close to the triangular pile of slates on the edge of the cliff which mark the spot where Calder buried Isla's ashes. I'm glad they're out of the cottage, for Calder's sake.

I go back to his mum's – our – cottage, to the warmth of our new plug-in radiators, which Calder bought for us until we can get more oil canisters delivered for the heating. This room looks clean and sort-of-liveable now. And there's a half-full gas canister to keep the cooker working till more supplies arrive. It's so alien to me that all the energy here, except for the electric, is delivered. But I'll adapt.

I glance at my open laptop. I've got enough files downloaded to be getting on with my work, which is just as well since there's no internet here yet. And luckily, I have a dog-eared copy of the text I'm working on, lying splayed on the worn kitchen table. My first freelance job is editing a contemporary film script which is a modern re-imagining of *Frankenstein*. Yawn. Why does everything have to be re-imagined? This wonderful book was a metaphor about science having gone too far and a truly scary story to boot. But in this trite retelling, called *No Firewall*, mankind has gone too far with social media. A pretty tech genius called Victoria (a young, modern, female Dr Victor Frankenstein) has created an online version of herself, which has morphed into an out-of-control monster, wreaking havoc on her life and loved ones. I guess it's a fair enough modern parallel, but this script is superficial and silly and in making the monster an internet being, it loses the horror and fascination of the re-animated body parts in the original. But hey, I'm getting paid shedloads to sleek up this tech-y confection, so, onwards. I open the novel to Chapter 3, where Dr Frankenstein's mother is dying: *I will endeavour to resign myself cheerfully to death, and will indulge a hope of meeting you in another world.* Ugh. Who resigns themselves cheerfully to death?

I glance through the small kitchen window at the empty bay and feel a sudden whoosh of panic. Where is Calder? Is it safe for us to live in this isolated cottage? Am I up to this bottled-energy living? Will this quieter life really help me to get pregnant? And how will I cope with working alone at my computer day after day? What if I turn into a bleak barren lump chained to her laptop, while her attractive windswept husband roams the seas like a pirate?

Then I hear the crunch of footsteps and see Calder strolling over, flicking back his unruly black hair.

'All right,' he says breezily, as he comes through the door.

'All good,' I say, fake-typing industriously. Everything's fine. I'm just catastrophising, as usual. Nothing is ever as bad as in my imagination.

'Had a great motor round the bay,' he says, as he bustles around the kitchen. He knocks open the bread bin and pulls out the heavy soda bread I made yesterday, trying to fulfil my resolution of cooking from scratch. But I found Isla's oven hard to control and the bread's rock-hard.

'You don't have to eat that,' I laugh.

'Oh, but I want to,' he smirks, hacking off two massive wedges. 'I'm man enough for the challenge.' There's a volley of tiny gunfire, as his mum's gas grill sparks to life, then he opens the fridge-freezer. 'This fridge's massive, four times the size of our old one. And the freezer. My God. Without the shelves I could stand in it. See.'

'Oh, my cooking's a challenge, is it? Keep saying that and you will be in that freezer. Permanently.'

'What I meant was. Your cooking is . . .'

I mock-glare.

'A gastronomic delight!'

'Hmm.'

When his toast's done, he slathers it with big lumps of butter.

'Hey. You'll have a heart attack. Think of your dad. Put that back in our icy coffin,' I laugh as I reach out for the butter, but he catches my hand.

'Let go,' I say, playfully.

He squelches my palm down, smothering it in butter.

'I'll just have to work the calories off, won't I,' he mumbles as he lifts my hand and licks the butter off my palm, smirking. 'We need to christen this table,' he laughs, as he lifts me onto it. I inhale him as he bends his shaggy head over to unbutton my dress down its front and runs his hands over me, while I pull up his shirt and grasp his flesh. We kiss deeply, then pull back to the faintest lip graze, before surging in again. My hip knocks over a half-drunk mug of tea and the caramel liquid slithers between the wooden grooves of the table, filling and obliterating every space.

When we've finished, we're hazy and loose-limbed. He picks up his toast, which is now soggy with melted butter, and folds the entire piece into his mouth.

'Look, you made the papers,' I say, lifting a tea-stained copy of the local *Langer Times*, which he brought back from the local shop yesterday. 'You're the headline: LOST CHILDREN RETURN.'

Calder reaches for the paper, but I swipe it away. 'Listen: "Langer has always suffered with an exodus of young people, which has decimated our numbers and broken our hearts." Nice OTT prose there, I'd have my red pen out. But there's more: "Now, not only are second homes being snapped up and full-time newcomers arriving, but some of our lost children,"' – I point dramatically at him – '"who left us for the mainland as teenagers, lured by the bright lights and big city, are returning to settle here once more. As adults, they have come to appreciate our quiet beauty and sense of community. With Christmas approaching, we are especially thankful to open our arms and welcome back Martin Ferguson, Jean Connolly and" come on down "Calder Campbell".'

'Ah, what a lot of tosh, we all left for very different reasons,' he says, glancing towards the sea.

'Like what?'

He waves his hand dismissively. 'Everyone had their demons.'

I seize. Why did he say that? He can't possibly know about my demons.

Can he?

'That's a funny word to choose,' I say lightly, tidying his plate into the sink so he can't see my face.

'You know what I mean. Teenagers are headstrong, full of hormones and secrets.'

'Oh, so mysterious,' I say, washing up to cover the rush of blood to my face. 'And remind me, what was your reason?'

'To find a sophisticated city-dwelling maiden to carry back for the yokels, of course.'

'But all you got was little old me.'

'Ah well, I'll have to make do,' he laughs, buttoning up his jeans and putting on a jacket. 'I need to get on now, I've got three appointments for new lofts. Why don't you go over to the "metropolis", start meeting the locals? D'you want a lift?'

I smile at our silly name for the tiny village over the hill. 'I'm fine, I'll have a walk on the beach I think.' I need to calm down alone, after our talk of 'demons'.

'Well, wrap up, lots of layers, remember you can get five weathers in one day here.'

We hear a mewing and frown at each other. Calder cautiously opens the front door. And there's the black bruiser of a cat who freaked us out when we first arrived, sidling in as if it owns the place.

'Come here, hun,' I invite, brightly.

'Go to Mum.' Calder laughs as it rubs its head on his leg.

I grip the table. He doesn't mean anything by that flippant label of 'Mum', but it pricks me after our two years of failing to get pregnant. But perhaps we've made a baby just now? A buttery ball of baby. I so want to make a family. My parents were kind, loving people, but were both killed instantly in a collision that concertinaed their car when I was fourteen. I was an only child, in foster care for four years afterwards, then a messed-up hard-living secretary who worked her way up to being a producer at the BBC, till I met Calder at the age of thirty-two, and he became my family and my place of safety.

'All right, hun,' I say, picking up the cat and trying to soften its rigidity with stroking. But it scratches me and leaps away.

'More like Attila the Hun, though it's a she,' Calder says, pointing between its legs. She lets Calder pet her and I rub at the scratch down my neck. 'You OK?'

'I'm fine. You get on.' I worry that the cat somehow intuits that I'm the outsider here and Calder is the true islander.

'OK, I'm off,' he says, picking up his bag and striding out. 'Love you.'

'Love you.'

I hear our rental car pulling away. Having always lived in London, I've never needed to drive, but I'll have to bite the bullet here. There are no other cottages on our bay. We don't have Wi-Fi yet. The landline's out and there's not even a decent mobile signal. I would be totally stranded here without Calder.

I walk through to the back bedroom, still finding it bizarre that everything's on the ground floor in these one-storey cottages. As I pull on extra layers, I feel Calder's recent touch on every part of me. Sex has always been intense for us, but also intuitive and easy. It gelled us instantly, despite our violent first meeting.

I was drinking too much that hot afternoon five years ago by Regent's Canal back in London. Stepping onto a patch of vivid green grass, I was instantly submerged in water, thrashing, gulping, sinking. As I was blacking out, my arm was yanked, I was dragged upwards and my slimy carcass was dumped onto the bank, where I vomited water.

'It's not grass, you idiot, it's algae,' this tall man barked, as he turned away.

'Hey,' I coughed at his departing figure, 'who are you?'

'Calder,' he grunted.

'What?'

'Calder. It's Scottish. Means "wild water".'

'Like this?' I coughed, gesturing to the canal.

He snorted. 'That water's not wild. You are.'

I grinned. 'So, Calder, just how wild are you?'

29

We clicked in bed instantly, matched in our feral greed. We were the same age, but very different people – me small, highly educated and verbal; him tall, left school at sixteen and practical – but our instant sexual click bound us together for long enough for us to find a deeper connection. After the procession of self-obsessed actors and writers I'd dated before, feeling endlessly not good enough, going out with someone who adored me was . . . like landing on solid ground and being able to look around for the first time. I can't ever imagine not being with him now. And five years on, I'm living with him in his mum's cottage on this tiny isolated island, totally surrounded by truly wild water.

I catch my reflection in the wardrobe mirror. My geometric black bob is starting to grow out, brown sprouting at the side parting and the sheerness of the cut disintegrating daily. Good. I want to leave that severe black-haired me behind. No. I won't dwell on the past. New place, new me. I need to get out of here and appreciate that truly wild water out there. As daylight only lasts from eight-thirtyish till four here in late November, I better hop to it. I pull on my boots, my coat and my shocking-pink woolly hat, which looked edgy in London, but seems touristy here.

I feel better as soon as I'm off. Out under this massive blue sky. Moving. Crunching along the path. Air filling my lungs. As I step out onto the slates on the beach, I'm a newborn calf, tottering and unsteady, then slipping and throwing my hands out onto slimy green rocks for support. All my jittery focus is on staying upright. I snort as I remember paying £135 back in London for a curve-based balance board. This jagged assault course is way better. The lighter dry slates are manageable, but the dark, glossy wet ones are treacherous, especially those spray-painted with lurid green seaweed.

'Hey,' a voice calls out suddenly.

I jerk my head up, to see a dark shimmering shape in the distance. As I shade my eyes and peer directly at the sun, I make out a tall spectral figure in long grey ceremonial robes. It moves eerily fast across the slates. As if propelled. But as it gets closer, I see that it's really a tall thin bloke in a long grey raincoat, with a bald head, strong features and piercing blue eyes. He's got to be well over six foot, in his fifties maybe, with an intense energy, like an ageing basketball player who still stays fit. I look around. Is this safe? I'm totally alone here. He's staring at me intently, extending his hand. I can't run away on these slates, so I plaster on a tight smile as I reach out my hand. But as I step forward, I slip. His hand shoots out and catches me in a firm, steadying grip.

'Careful, these slates can be very slippery,' he says in a deep voice.

'Thanks,' I say, extricating myself from his sweaty grasp.

He gestures backwards. 'I knocked at your cottage, but there was no reply, then I saw you down here on the beach.'

'Can I . . . help you with something?'

'More the other way around.' He grins, as if I should understand.

'Oh?'

'Yes, Mrs Campbell.'

He knows who I am? Was he also warned to look

out for us, like the man on the ferry? Calder and I aren't actually married, but I don't clarify for this disconcertingly charismatic stranger.

'I'm Arran,' he says, extending his hand again and forcing me into shaking it boisterously.

'Like the jumper?' I blurt.

'Like the jumper, but with an extra R,' he grins, flashing his intense blue eyes. 'It means "island dweller". I'm proud of the name. I love this island and its community. And you, Nancy, are its newest, very lovely addition.'

OK, this guy's a bit weird, I need to get away. 'Well, nice to meet you, but I better get on.'

'I'm the pastor of the church here.'

Oh. I'm so not religious but I know that Calder's parents were, his dad a church elder, his mum cleaning the church and doing the flowers, so I need to be polite.

'Of course. I've heard about your famous church.'

He smiles, making too much eye contact.

'I gather you have a slate altar,' I falter on. 'I read about it in a guidebook?'

He stares at me. I blink back, unnerved by him but unable to break the connection.

'Indeed we do,' he says eventually. 'A notable tourist attraction. But I was hoping that you and Calder might come to an actual service. We're all very excited that he's returned to us.'

What is this weird sense of ownership they all seem to have of Calder?

'Oh, yes, well, I'll certainly suggest it to him.' I can't see us attending church. Or do we have to get involved on such a small island?

I register him clocking my reticence.

'Calder's mother Isla was very committed to the church,' he says. 'It was a great sadness to her that he dismissed it as a youth.'

I balk at his implied criticism of Calder. 'Was it you who left her ashes in the middle of our table?'

He inhales sharply. 'It was what Isla wanted. To return to her cottage.'

'But didn't you think it would be upsetting for Calder to just find her there? No warning.'

He frowns. 'Oh dear, I wasn't thinking. Is Calder all right?' he says, touching my arm.

'He's fine.' I shift a step back, but my foot slides on some seaweed and he catches me again.

'Be careful.' He grips my arm firmly and pulls me up and into him. 'Will he be about later? I should apologise for leaving Isla's ashes like that. It was thoughtless.'

'I'll tell him you called,' I say, taking a deliberate step away.

He bends down and picks up a piece of the moss-covered slate, holding it out to me. 'Clean the slate, God, so we can start the day fresh.'

'I'm sorry?'

He wipes the moss off the slate as he stands. 'Keep me from stupid sins, from thinking I can take over your work. Then I can start this day sun-washed, scrubbed clean of the grime of sin.'

'Err. I don't—'

He grins. 'Psalm 19 verse 13. It's a modern version, but I'm a sucker for the slate imagery.'

'Oh, right.'

'Have you ever wished for the chance to wipe the slate clean, Nancy?' he says, barely blinking.

'I—' Can he see directly into my thoughts? I turn away abruptly and look up at the cliff behind our cottage to hide my eyes, which are filling with tears.

'Are you OK?'

'Just admiring that sheep on the hill,' I choke out, pointing towards a tufty animal balanced on the almost sheer hillside, looking very precarious. 'It's amazing they never fall.'

'Oh, sheep do fall from up there. More often than you think.'

His portentousness is really grating on me. 'Come on, that's just some biblical metaphor, isn't it?'

'No, they do actually fall. And die.'

I swing back to him. 'What, so "sure-footed sheep" is just some meaningless phrase?' I say, glaring at him. Can't he just stop all this ominous posturing and go away.

He smiles at me for a long moment. 'When I sprained my ankle last year,' he says eventually, 'all I noticed were people walking around easily with healthy ankles. We see the meanings around us which fit in with our concerns. You seem especially perturbed by that fallen sheep metaphor?'

'Oh, I'm a sheep now, am I?'

'We are all God's flock. My title pastor derives from the Latin noun meaning "shepherd", itself derived from the verb *pascere*, "to lead to pasture". If you need any help being led—'

'I don't,' I snap.

He shrugs. 'Well, I'd best get on. Do tell Calder I called. And I look forward to seeing you both at church.' He walks away, effortless on the precarious slates.

Damn it. What a total disaster that was for my first solo islander interaction. I'm bristling with annoyance but regretting shooting my mouth off. He wasn't meaning anything with his religious rambling. It was just an unlucky coincidence him talking about clean slates, and I assumed he could somehow read my thoughts. It's like what happens with horoscopes: I read my own star sign and the message resonates; yet if I read any of the others, they resonate too.

But he was uncannily accurate.

I am a fallen sheep.

Three months ago, I had a drunken one-night stand when Calder was away on a job. My chest falls in with self-disgust at the memory. I know it happened, but I still can't believe it did. However drunk I was, how could I? What pathetic black thoughtlessness possessed me. I close my eyes, wanting to turn myself inside out to escape being me. I've tried to 'be kind' to myself. To tell myself what I would say to a friend in this much agony: *It was a terrible one-off mistake, made when you were extremely drunk and despairing; everyone makes mistakes; you need to forgive yourself; try to move on with your life.* I'm always giving that kind of advice to others. But now I know it merely feels good to give, but so useless to receive. I deserve to suffer. I cheated on the love of my life.

Afterwards, my anxiety spiralled, my work suffered and I was at breaking point when I jumped at the chance of this move. I couldn't lose Calder, my safe harbour. If I'd told him, I would have compounded my sin by destroying him and then us. But now he doesn't fully know me. Well, I just have to tough it out. After my parents' mangled bodies were pulled from the wreckage of that awful accident, I learnt to dim the white noise of anxiety in my head, push down thoughts I couldn't face, and focus on the next thing I had to do, in the here and now. That's all I can do now. Keep embracing this new life here, and hope that it will become a habit and I can somehow move on.

OK, onwards. There's only one shop here, one pub and a load of boat stuff.

Shouldn't drink. Hate boats. Food shop it is.

The shop is on the other side of the island in the 'metropolis', reachable by following the coastal road round in either direction. But there's a way quicker route up over the hills, which I walked with Calder during our previous visit. It's such a sunny, calm day, and the climb will get me out of my head.

So, I leave the beach, skirt our cottage and start up the hill. I make my way up the shallow brush land, to the narrow track, barely five inches across, which hugs the hill. If it were chalked out on flat ground, I could run along it with abandon, but the drop makes it vertiginous. Calder advised me last time. 'Don't focus down, look across and lean into the hill.' So now I virtually lie on the hill as I inch across, pigeon step by pigeon step, and finally, I reach the rocky outcrop and the small climb upwards. At the top, my ragged breathing slows, and I take in the stunning views: the churning Atlantic, the rough rolling grassland, and the hazy green, brown and lilac hills.

This cliff-edge area, with its sheer drop to the sea, must surely be the highest point on the island. The ground is uneven and boggy and I have to step back from one of the crumbly fissures Calder showed me, which had opened up during the hot summer. I feel like I'm on top of the world here. The vibrant blue sky with its streaks of cloud is so vast. In London, I barely registered that such a thing as 'sky' existed, beyond being a space between buildings, as conceptual as the blue swipe in a child's painting. Here, skies dominate. A shaft of light suddenly breaks through the clouds, lighting up the hill, and I am consumed by an oddly religious sensation. Ha. Arran would be pleased. I'm in a natural cathedral, at some strange nexus point between man and the heavens. Perhaps I can finally forgive myself here.

The shaft of light is suddenly extinguished, and thick clouds start to descend quickly. I have to lean forward and brace my legs against the incredible force of wind. What fills the sky now isn't the gossamer streaks of earlier, but a crushing wodge of greys and purples, lowering like an alien spaceship and blocking out the light. The wind's an invisible battering ram, charging, then pushing me sideways. This weather could kill me. Easily. I must hurry.

Icy rain is driving straight at me as I make my way down the wider path on the other side of the hill. I place my feet carefully as I descend. I'm sure that Arran was lying about sheep falling from up here, but I can't stop imagining being one now, bleating as I plummet.

I see the ferry just pulling out below me. It connects not to the mainland, but to the larger more populated island next door, which is connected to the mainland by a single bridge. Apparently, there was much debate when the bridge was suggested. Not joyous support for it as I would have expected, but vehement arguments against it. The locals protested that 'it would destroy our island status', 'anyone could come over' and 'no one will know where the children are'. After all that talk about 'lost children', I wonder whether the islanders were really trying to trap their children here.

I finally reach the 'metropolis', which looks like a toy town from a children's book. There are two long rows of squat white cottages on either side of the single road running between them. At the end of one row is the pub, constructed out of two of the white cottages, with the addition of a rickety annex at the back. Many of the buildings here are constructed out of these squat white cottages: the pub, the local shop and the boat office. I feel like a rat in an experiment, being watched to see which white cube I'll scurry into next. Only Arran's prim church seems to be purpose-built, small, formal and decorated, of course, with grey slate. I thought it would be Church of Scotland, but it's some sort of home-grown Christianity, quite old school from what Calder tells me. Even more not our thing. The church perches on a small hill which overlooks the road in, so its censorious cross casts its chilly shadow across me as I pass. I don't believe, yet I still feel judged. I guess that's why people go to church: to repent and move on. Some people live with so much worse than I've done, with ongoing affairs, crime, violence, even with murder. Yet they watch TV, go to the shops, kiss their loved one and manage not to implode. How do they do it?

Icy pricks of rain needle my cheeks. I haven't used the expensive heavy moisturiser that Hamish's wife Gina gave me as a farewell gift, and I'm raw and smarting by the time

I reach Janey's Shop. I love that that's the actual name, painted in capitals on a board outside. Calder says we'll do our big shops on the mainland, but this post office slash grocers is for immediate needs. He said that Royal Mail tried to take away its licence because of the tiny population, but this Janey whipped up a local campaign and kept it open.

The doorbell jangles as I enter the stuffed shop. I see a tall, rangy woman with long grey hair and direct brown eyes, dressed in army trousers and a tie-dyed top with a yin–yang fish symbol. She's surrounded by sweets, gum, fishing accessories, scratch cards and cigarettes.

Right, I'll try harder with this second islander. I can't afford to fall out with anyone else in this small population.

'Morning, Nancy,' she says, as I enter. 'Sorry, small-town knowledge – you're Calder's wife aren't you? We're all so pleased that he's back. What can I do you for?'

I don't correct her about the wife thing. 'Janey?'

She nods. 'Aye.'

'Hi. I'm just browsing,' I say over-brightly.

She purses her lips theatrically and then gives me a huge grin. I burst out laughing. Obviously, no one 'browses' in this shop. 'Browsing' is so London.

'Browse away,' Janey says.

Suddenly there's an enormous crash from the room behind her. But Janey doesn't flinch.

'Everything . . . OK back there?'

'Yeah, why?'

'Umm, didn't you hear that?'

The door behind her opens, and a small balding man with warm twinkly eyes looks out, grinning.

'Just knocked over the—' He sees me. 'Oops, sorry,' he mumbles, then grimaces at Janey and turns away. I notice that he's got a tattooed capital C on the back of his neck.

'Should I go?' I whisper.

'No, no, it's just my friend Rob. He was fixing my plumbing.'

I smile and she goes bright red.

'I mean actually fixing the plumbing. Well . . .'

I smile. 'I'll go.'

'No, no, just give me a moment.'

She moves back. Through the half-open door, I see her embrace him and then he leans down, gently kisses her on the lips and caresses her cheek. It's such a tender private moment between two people who are clearly in love, that I feel bad for staring and move to the rear of the shop. Then I hear a door closing and she returns. 'Have a wee cup of tea with me. I need one.'

'If you're sure?'

'Come on back.'

'But the shop—'

'I'd like to see someone try to steal from me.'

I walk through to a low square room, with a fire going in the grate and a worn L-shaped settee facing it, covered in brightly coloured throws and cushions.

'Take those boots and wet trousers off and wrap that blanket round you,' she orders. She puts my wet clothes in the dryer as I snuggle into her comfy sofa. I like her already. She radiates warmth. Perhaps I can unthaw in her glow.

'I know this seems an odd thing to ask,' she says as she returns with mugs of tea, 'but is it OK if you don't mention

Rob to anyone? It's a "delicate" situation.'

'Okaay?'

'He was, well technically he still is, married to Alison, a woman who lives on the island.' I swallow. Arran was right – I see my guilt everywhere. 'He's separated, but when you've got a bairn, you're never really separated, are you?'

I shrug non-committally. But she's right. As I know only too well.

'They had a particularly nasty split, all sorts of unpleasant lies and rumours. He's a great bloke, but I don't want to cause more trouble so we keep things on the down-low.'

'Don't people see him around on the island? It's not very big.'

'We usually meet on the mainland, but very occasionally he comes over in his boat after dark and leaves at first light. He slept in this morning. Please don't even tell Calder. Or is that tricky?'

'No problem.' I never thought I'd have any secrets from Calder. But what's one more?

'So,' she says, shaking out her lovely grey hair, 'are you getting settled in all right up there?'

'Getting there, cleaning and mending. We've even got a cat, I think. A big black thing.'

'It's probably from that feral litter Isla was feeding year before last. She found them being nursed on an old rucksack in her shed. I'm surprised, feral cats rarely trust anyone.'

'She seemed to trust Calder instantly.'

She nods, as if to say *Of course! He's an islander.* 'Have you named her?'

'Attila.'

She inclines her head. 'Interesting for a female.'

'I called her "hun", then she scratched me, so Calder said "more like Attila the Hun".'

She laughs. 'Well she's a tough cat to have survived up there, so it's a good name. Attila was a fierce man, only lost one battle. Though he did die mysteriously.'

'Oh?'

'Aye, took a second wife and was found dead on the morning after his wedding, his mouth full of blood. No one knows what killed him: drinking too much, a freak nosebleed – or perhaps his new wife?'

We sip our tea.

'So have you met many of the locals yet?' she says eventually.

'Just one. And I think I rather made a mess of things when I ran into the local pastor earlier.'

'Arran?'

'Umm, I was kind of abrupt and I think I offended him.'

'Oh, Arran's all about forgiveness. For some, anyway.'

'Sorry?'

'He means well, but he's quite a control freak. Thinks he knows what's best for everyone.'

'He's pretty intense. But I want to fit in. Get to know as many people as I can.'

'Look, I'm sorry I didn't introduce you to Rob. I know that was awkward. But his ex, Alison, said she'd kill him if he set foot here again. Also, I thought it might be awkward, what with him being Caitlin's dad and all.'

'Calder's old girlfriend, Caitlin? Oh yes, he mentioned her. Said she left the island just before him.'

'Umm. Same year as Calder and another boy called Hamish.'

'Oh, I know Hamish. He and Calder set up a loft company together in London.'

'Yes, we heard about that.'

'So, all three of them were some of those "lost children" from the papers?'

'I guess. Rob took it really badly when Caitlin left. He moved to London to look for her. But she broke all contact with everyone, including her parents – only ever sends one postcard a year to Alison, on the anniversary of her leaving. It's the only time Rob and Alison speak. It upsets him every time.'

'Is that why he has that C on his neck?'

'Umm.' She gives me a small smile then looks down as if drawing a line under the subject. How strange to try to remember your own child by getting a tattoo on your spine, one of the most painful places to have one done? But I don't feel I can ask more.

'Anyway, how are you two doing?' she asks brightly, sipping her tea.

'Oh, Calder's taken the move in his stride. I'm . . . getting there.'

'Calder's an islander. You—'

'I know. I'm an outsider.'

'Don't be a daftie. You're Calder's wife.'

I nod, still annoyed by her assumption that we're married, but I don't want to appear too 'alternative' on this traditional island.

'Are you planning on having children?'

Now I look down.

'I'm so sorry, that was rude of me. None of my business.'

I smile weakly and wave away her embarrassment. 'We can't get pregnant,' I mumble.

Janey puts down her tea and pats my hand. 'You're just not pregnant – yet,' she says pointedly.

She's so warm, so intuitive, so nice. It's making the full truth slide up my throat. But I mustn't say it.

'I could help you,' she says gently. 'I'm a homeopath.'

Oh no, not that hocus-pocus.

'It's not hocus-pocus,' she smiles. God, is everyone here psychic? 'Well, not until the advanced sessions by moonlight, when we bathe in the blood of virgins. Oh my God, your face. I doubt there are many virgins on this island. It's freezing, the Wi-Fi's shit and we have to make our own entertainment.'

I laugh.

She touches my hand. 'You feel . . . cold.'

I knew it was hocus-pocus. I'm sweating in front of her fire, under her blanket.

'I'll give you some ginger tea to warm you up. Don't worry.'

'Oh, I'm a total worrier. I'm hoping to relax more here. Though as soon as Calder went out in his mum's boat, I was instantly catastrophising.'

'Well, of course.'

'Why "of course"?'

She frowns. 'Because of his father.'

'Douglas?'

She blinks, clearly registering that I have no idea what she's talking about.

'It means "black water",' she says, looking out towards the sea.

'What does?'

'Douglas. It's from the Gaelic *dubh* meaning "black", and *glas* meaning "water".'

'Oh, so water names are a family thing then? 'Cos I know Calder means "wild water".'

'Yes, that's right. But with you worrying about Calder out in Isla's boat, I thought you meant . . . because of what happened.'

'Why? What did happen?'

'Douglas drowned.'

CHAPTER THREE

'They want London spec, but with Highland prices,' Calder groans as he washes his hands in our deep kitchen sink.

'Umm,' I mumble.

Attila is rubbing at his legs, having ignored me entirely since I got back.

'It's a new couple who've bought the old Sullivan cottage at the edge of the village as a second home. Not popular with the locals, but hey, if they want a full loft conversion with a balcony, who am I to judge?'

'Umm.'

'What have you been up to today?' he asks, turning to face me as he catches my monosyllabic answers.

'Nothing much,' I say lightly, a balsa wood construction holding my smile in place. 'Oh, I did have a little walk over to the metropolis.'

'Good,' he says, checking on another doorstop of bread on the grill.

'You'll spoil your dinner,' I say dully.

'Oh, I've worked up quite an appetite,' he says with a wink.

I watch him opening a bottle of red wine and pouring it into squat tumblers for us. I knock mine back to pull the pin on my grenade of tension. Why the hell has he lied about his dad's death for all these years? He said it was a heart attack.

'I had a cup of tea with Janey earlier,' I say abruptly.

'I said you'd like her.'

'She mentioned your dad.'

Calder's suddenly bristling, like Attila with her fur up. 'You OK?'

'Yep.' He opens our coffin of a fridge and pulls out the cow-shaped butter dish.

'What's the matter?'

'Nothing,' he mumbles.

'She said he drowned?'

The smell of burning toast assaults us. Calder lurches for the grill.

'For fuck's sake,' he blurts, dropping the grill pan as blackened toast skitters across the floor.

'Your father drowned?'

He starts to butter a burnt lump, getting black crumbs all over the pristine butter.

'Calder? Did he drown?'

He drops the knife. 'Yes. Oh God. I was just about to tell you.'

'But why lie about it at all?'

He wipes his hands. 'I didn't actually lie.'

'Well, you didn't exactly correct my assumption of a heart attack.'

He slumps down in one of the chairs. 'Look, when we first met, you'd nearly drowned. And you were so freaked by it, seemed really phobic about water, so I didn't want to bring it up early on. Then time went by and it seemed . . . unnecessary. I knew I'd have to tell you once we were here, obviously I would, in fact I nearly told you on the ferry, but then I decided to wait till we were properly settled in.'

'But you knew I thought it was a heart attack. I've talked about those cholesterol-lowering drinks, got that heart-health cookery book for you.'

'I'm so sorry. I—'

I walk over and drag open the front door to stare at the roaring sea. 'You must have had a good laugh playing games with me.'

'No. God no!' he cries as he joins me. 'I guess I avoided it because I try not to think about it at all. It destroyed my mum. But of course you're right, I should have told you.'

We stand in the doorway, the freezing air sluicing us. He reaches out to touch me, but I flinch away. He blinks at me like a little boy.

'I hate secrets,' I blurt, wincing at my hypocrisy.

We listen to the roar of the waves and the violent dragging of the stones.

Whoosh. Drag. Whoosh. Drag.

I feel my vice of anger washing away. It was an explainable, understandable lie. Everything's fine.

I grunt.

'What?'

'The tinkling of the stones is making me want to pee.'

He laughs. 'Must be a monster pee.'

I burp up a laugh and feel our safe click of connection again. He reaches out and I slap his hand playfully. He laughs and pulls me back into the kitchen, shuts out the cold and hugs me to him. He stares down, his lovely eyes so honest, his face so open and kind. I can't stay angry at him. I know he'd never wilfully hurt me.

'Give me a second,' I say, untangling myself.

When I return from the toilet, he's sitting at the table, pouring more wine. 'Nance, I really am sorry.'

'And I'm sorry about your dad,' I say, sitting down and putting my feet on his lap. 'What happened?'

'I was away at secondary school. You know I boarded four nights a week on the mainland.'

'Oh yeah. Is there still only a primary school on the island? For if we ever . . .'

'Yep, same set-up. Primary on the island, secondary on the mainland. It was a Thursday night, so I was away when it happened. His boat washed up. Isla said he'd gone out drunk and must have got into trouble.'

'How old were you?'

'Fourteen.'

'But that's the same age I was when I lost my parents.'

'I know. When you told me about what happened to them, I knew it was the time to tell you about Dad, but I felt like I was muscling into your tragic story, so I waited again. I'm sorry. Do you forgive me?'

'Of course.'

He nods and starts massaging my feet.

'Is that why you buried her ashes on the cliff?'

'What?'

'Your mum. Overlooking where your dad drowned.'

'Oh, err, I guess.'

'They're together at last. Like my parents. You remember I showed you where their ashes are sprinkled in Bloomsbury Square, where they met.'

'Umm.' He's so quiet, but that's usual for him. I've learnt that he doesn't like to talk much about difficult stuff, so I know to let this subject drop. For now. It took me ages to piece together what a difficult childhood he'd had, with his strict religious mother and his gruff dad. But they were a strong couple, like my parents. I've always thought we were alike in both trying to create that kind of lifelong bond, but now I realise that we also both experienced tragedy when we were fourteen. With all his honesty, my secret chokes up my throat, but I swallow it down. 'I didn't cook,' I say, to cover.

He stares at me in mock horror.

'I was like, *If he thinks I'm making tea for him, he can spin on it*. Attila was quite unnerved. She thought I should perhaps tone it down a tad.' I reach down to pet her but she coils round Calder's legs.

'Good old Attila,' he says, rubbing under her chin. 'I'm sure we can bodge something together for dinner.'

We pull out dried pasta and Calder unseals a jar of pasta sauce with a pop. He reaches over to pour more wine and I see him hesitate over a bottle of his mum's whisky, like he's looking at a long-lost friend. I'm rocketed back to our early heavy drinking sessions. Loved up as we were, we had drunken arguments. I was a fast drinker. Calder, I gradually realised, was a marathon drinker, often drinking from midday but showing no signs till much later in the evening. While he was working for Hamish's loft firm, they would often have lunch at the pub. For the first month of our relationship, I thought that the 'office' phone number he gave me was an actual office, and was embarrassed by my naivety when I discovered it was a dingy pub. I drank because of my crushing insecurity after my parents' sudden death. Was his father's drowning why he drank? Why he left the island? I can't process all this yet. But I know it will make us even closer eventually.

'You should be proud of me making an effort with the locals today,' I say, trying to lighten the mood. 'And not just with Janey – I also talked to Arran, the pastor, though he was a bit harder going.'

He rolls his eyes. 'Ah, the pretty pastor.'

'What?'

'That's what all the boys used to call him, "the pretty pastor", 'cos he was good-looking and such a favourite with the ladies.'

'I had a bit of a go at him for leaving Isla's ashes on the table here.'

'Oh, Nance.'

'Well, it was a bit creepy. I mean how did he get in here?'

'I'm sure the church had keys, to help her when she was sick.'

'Oh. Now I feel bad. He said he was looking forward to seeing you, us, at church.'

He makes a face. 'Oh, I don't think so. But he was there for Mum after Dad died. She never got over his death. She . . . hardened. The church was all she had. She got Arran to keep tabs on me, which I resented. But I was glad they were there for her after I left and in those final months.' He falls silent and bites at his lip. I catch him glance over at the whisky again.

'Do you want some?'

He sighs. 'I always want some. But I'm better without.'

'Look, could you drop in on Arran tomorrow, to prove to him that I told you that he came looking for you. And to say I'm really sorry if I offended him.'

'Ah, do I have to? He's such an overbearing arse.'

'Please. I really want to fit in here.'

We're silent except for the glug as he refills our wine glasses. Is it all too much for him, coming back here? Did I force Calder here because of my need to get away?

'Are you sure you want to live here?' I say eventually. 'If you're having second thoughts, we've still got our nest egg in your company account. We could sell the cottage and move anywhere in the world.'

He shakes his head. 'Arran is annoying. But I'll go and see him and smooth things out – anything for you. It's gonna be great here. I'm a different person from the tearaway teenager I was before. And now I'm with you. My wilful, non-cooking lover.'

'Everyone here keeps referring to me as your wife. It's OK, I know we both said we don't want . . .'

'Never say never.'

I raise my eyebrows. And he raises his back. Then he grins and takes another gulp of wine.

Oh my. I thought it might only be me. Neither of us have felt the need to be married before to know we're together for life. But here on this traditional island, it suddenly does feel right to me. And now perhaps for Calder too?. We are going to be fine here. More than fine.

We eat too much pasta and laze in front of the TV watching a film, my head on his shoulder. Attila curls up on Calder's lap; she won't have anything to do with me, but she's besotted with him. I'm still a bit thrown by his revelation about his dad. But Calder has only committed a minor sin of omission by not telling me about an understandably difficult memory. I've committed a far bigger sin of commission. But hopefully, I can have a clean slate here, like that 'pretty pastor' said.

I squeeze Calder's hand, and breathe into the peace that his touch, his smell, his solid presence gives me.

'Promise me one thing,' I whisper.

'What?'

'That you'll never go out in your boat drunk. Or in bad weather. That you'll always be careful. I couldn't bear it if anything happened to you. You're my whole family.'

He hugs me to him. 'I'll be careful.'

'Promise?'

'I promise.'

CHAPTER FOUR

I'm brittle with cold, hunched on our hard, unfamiliar mattress. There's a strange drilling sound to my left. I reach out for Calder's warm body, but feel only icy, rumpled sheets. As I sit up and blink at the thin light coming through the tiny window, I realise that the sound is rain horizontally bombarding the glass. I grab my little square alarm clock and squint. 9 a.m. He must be having breakfast.

'Calder,' I call, as I pad towards the kitchen, my toes curling on the freezing stone floor.

But the kitchen's empty.

'Calder, come back to bed.'

The bathroom and lounge are cold and silent too.

So, he's gone out on a job already and didn't want to wake me? I search for his note by the kettle, which was where we always left notes for each other back in London. Nothing. He must be outside, doing one of the many jobs we have to get on with to make this place liveable. I need a strong mug of tea before I make progress on my list, so I lift the kettle to check for water. Why's it cold? Calder always has tea as soon as he wakes. I pull open the front door, but rear back from the sheeting rain.

Our car's still there. So, he must be somewhere close. I shove my feet into my walking boots, pull my coat on over my long white nightdress and step out, getting instantly drenched.

'Calder!' I shout, but the wind sucks up my voice. I trudge all the way round our squat cottage, my wet nightdress sticking to my legs, hair splattered across my face.

Where on earth is he?

I squint, expecting to see his huge black-coated figure at any moment, but the rain's making it hard to see any distance. I remember his mother's chunky binoculars on the nail inside the door and clomp back in for them, tripping over the stupid mud scraper as usual. As I lift the leather strap, I see his coat isn't on the hook and his walking boots are gone from the wooden rack beneath. So, he is outside. Pulling my hood forward, I step out again and use the binoculars to scan up the steep hill behind the cottage.

But there's no sign of him.

'Calder?' I shout as loudly as I can. 'CALDER!'

OK. Logically, where else? The beach? My breathing's getting shallow as I approach the cliff edge, my feet crunching on the gravel. Careful to plant my boots well back from the drop and crouch against the wind, I peer down.

But there's only the empty expanse of grey beach, with gigantic waves smashing onto the shore in a carnival of spray.

I pan the binoculars up one side of the bay and then the other. As I swing back, I realise that Isla's boat isn't tied up where it should be. My chest seizes. No. He wouldn't go out in this weather. Would he? It's only been a few days since he promised me he'd be especially careful on the water. I know he's a capable sailor, but the vast grey sea is surging wildly. My fingers are frozen and clumsy as I fumble to focus the binoculars and swing them across the churning water, willing him to appear on his way back to shore.

Come on, come on, come on.

The lenses are blurred with rain, so I wipe them off and pull my hood further forward. As my next sweep reaches the horizon, I see the dark hull of an upturned boat.

Oh my God. No. Surely that can't be his boat. But it is a boat. And ours is missing. Christ. What do I do? I need help. But I'm totally alone here on our secluded bay.

I rush back into the cottage, gulping breaths, and lunge for my phone, which is charging on the counter. No bars of connection. Jesus. But I have to get help. Right now. I run back to the bedroom, my voice cutting into the silence. 'No. No. No.' I drag on my clothes from the floor, struggle my sodden coat and boots back on and run out, leaving the front door swinging. Why did I never learn to drive? God, hurry up, hurry up. Every second counts. The road route to the village would take too long on foot, so I race round the cottage and launch myself at the hill behind, snorting and stumbling, blinded by the rain. After running up the lower slope, the narrow path lies before me. Mind over matter. Ignore the drop. It's just a chalk-marked path on flat ground. I throw myself forward, across the worn grassy track. I cannot fall, or Calder is lost.

I dash across, breath held, and then suck in a freezing lungful of air as I land heavily on the other side. No time to rest. I launch myself upwards, my icy hands sliced by the sharp cold rocks.

'Help!' I scream as I hurtle across the top and then down the path on the other side. Gulping cold air. Falling forward. Splattering shingle.

Don't think. Don't imagine. Just do.

The freezing rain sears my face as I approach the village. Ahead, I see a tall figure in a long grey raincoat inside the bus shelter. It's the last person I want to see, but I need anyone right now.

'Arran!' I scream.

He jerks his head up, and blinks at me.

'Have you got a boat?' I shout.

He stands, raising his palms in confusion.

'A boat!' I scream, as I approach.

'The ferry's not back yet. It'll be at least half an—'

'Not the ferry. I need someone who's got their own,' I pant.

'I've got one, but—'

'Take me out!' I shout.

'I don't think—'

'Now. A boat's floating upside down in the bay and Calder's is missing.'

'What?' He darts out of the shelter to look towards the sea.

'Not there. On our side of the island, I saw it from the cliff. Come on.'

He's suddenly galvanised. 'Exactly where?' he says, striding through the village towards the smaller of the two docks ahead of us.

'At the right curve of our bay!' I shout, pointing.

'The current's pulling it out. Did you see Calder?'

I shake my head. 'Only last night when we went to bed, but now he's missing.'

'Oh Lord. I'll call the coastguard on the way.' We simultaneously charge along the small pier, till we reach a dark blue and white boat.

'I'll show you exactly where,' I say, as he jumps down and starts untying a rope.

'No—'

'I'm coming!' I shout.

He opens his mouth, then nods. 'Put that on and follow all my orders,' he barks, chucking me an orange life jacket from beneath the seat.

'Just go!' I shout.

Arran starts the ignition and we're instantly shooting across the water. He calls out to me. 'I only saw him yesterday. He was so full of plans. Why would he go out in this weather?'

'I don't know. Please hurry.'

This boat's bigger and sturdier than Calder's. Its off-white detailing is stained, and it has scratched wooden seats around the edge and a small covered area at the front with grimy windows. But it's sturdy. Why did Isla leave us such a stupidly small boat? Oh God. This is real. Not one of my made-up fears. Yet it feels utterly unreal. Calder is . . . a burst of the truth of what's actually happened sweeps into me and I feel the cold hollowness of it. Calder is . . . then I snap my head inside out and shove myself to my edges, to focus on the next thing to do.

Arran's talking into a black snaking radio set, explaining what's happened to the coastguard. The boat bumps and thuds over the waves, icy sea spray splattering me. The rain's lifted but the air's arctic. As we round the headland, I see a family of seals lolling on the rocks. Big-eyed and fat, they regard us with disinterest. How is any of this real?

I swing round wildly, scouring the water for a sign of Calder. He must be OK, he must be. He's a strong swimmer, he's a strong man, come on, come on. Any second, I'll see him. But there's only endless lurching water.

Suddenly I catch a glimpse of the dark curve of the boat's hull.

'There,' I yelp.

But then the boat leaps.

'It's just a porpoise,' Arran calls.

And he's right. A dark curved body is scything rhythmically through the water, heightening the unreality of all this.

I suddenly realise that the water around us is swirling and bubbling, like we're in a cauldron.

'What's happening?' I shout. It's like some huge water god is about to rear up out of the waves and crush us.

'It's the whirlpools.'

'What?'

'Whirlpools. When the tide changes, and there's a build-up of water flooding in or out between the islands, it creates a whirling effect here, 'cos of a giant rock pinnacle on the ocean bed.'

'D'you think Calder got into trouble here?'

'Very unlikely, it isn't dangerous if you're a sensible sailor.'

'There!' I shriek. 'Over there.' And this time it's definitely the oval of Calder's upturned boat, the dark rusty paint glinting.

'Got it.' Arran slows the boat and circles. We both scour the water. 'He could be under it,' he says darkly.

I move to dive in, but he grabs my shoulder.

'Don't be crazy. The current's strong and the water's freezing. It'll kill you.'

No. Because if that's true, Calder is already dead.

Suddenly the upturned boat starts to move towards the widest arc of the bubbling.

'What's happening?' I scream. Calder's tiny boat circles like a toy in a bath, pulled further and further into the whirling.

And then it's gone.

'No,' I cry.

Arran crosses himself. 'I'm sorry,' he mouths. He moves towards me and put his arms around me.

I'm rigid and blank for a moment.

Then I struggle free. 'That can't be it. It can't be.' I swing round to scan the churning water again.

Then I see something in the distance, a coloured patch of blue and orange. 'There! Calder's coat is blue.'

'And life jackets are orange!' Arran shouts, turning the boat.

'CALDER!' I scream. 'We're coming.'

But he doesn't respond.

As we get closer, the picture coalesces and I realise that it is him, but that he isn't moving. At all. He's just hanging in the water, supported by his life jacket. Has he passed out? Been knocked out? The water's shifting so much I can't see his face.

Arran cuts the engine when we're still several feet away.

'Get closer!' I scream.

'I can't. We'll hit him. I've got the wind on the starboard side, we'll float in.'

It takes an eternity. Come on.

As we finally reach him, I see Calder's eyes are wide open. Staring up.

Then something spears past my head. I lurch back as a huge hook catches on Calder's life jacket and Arran drags him towards us. I see the awful greyness of Calder's lovely face, his eyes blank. Come on, my love, breathe for me. Please breathe. I'm dragging at his sodden blue jacket as a rope flicks past me and Arran reaches down into the water to secure it round Calder's body.

'Don't fall in Nancy, but kneel closer to the edge so we can drag him on board together. He's going to be very heavy, brace yourself.'

I'm nodding furiously, reaching down. The water's freezing. Calder's freezing. We're both leaning out, scrabbling to get a grip. Arran reaches round Calder as if embracing him as I link my frozen hands around his thighs.

'On three,' Arran calls. 'One, two . . . THREE.'

And we drag.

The weight and cold is impossible, but I don't let go.

My right shoulder is ripped apart, but I don't let go.

The sea tries to suck him back, but I don't let go.

'AAGH!' we both scream as Calder rises up out of the water, water cascading off him. Then we drag him up over the side of the boat, and he falls onto us. He's ice-cold, a gash across his face, not breathing. His face is bleached white as if drained of all blood. And his lovely eyes are just staring up, his pupils huge black counters, like a doll's.

I'm pinned under his . . . dead weight.

CHAPTER FIVE

'Mouth-to-mouth!' I shout.

Arran lurches up and rolls Calder off us, onto his back. He's so still, his face slack, his eyes staring.

'Do you know how to do it?' I demand.

'Yes. But I think CPR is more important, oh God, but I'm not sure for drowning.'

I push him forward. 'Come on, do something.'

He leaps into action and starts pumping hard at Calder's chest, counting out loud to thirty, then lifting Calder's chin, pinching his nose and breathing two breaths into him. He repeats. 'I think that's right – can you take over. I have to get us in.'

'Thirty and two breaths?'

He nods as I get into position and start pushing.

'I'll notify the coastguard and get us back. Push harder, both hands, more than you think.' He gets on the radio.

'Wake up, please wake up,' I sob as I pump his chest. 'Come on. Calder. Please come back to me.'

'They're sending the emergency helicopter from Oban!' Arran shouts.

I'm ramming all my weight down, staring at Calder's bruised, cut face. *Push*, *push*, *push*. My shoulders are killing me, my hands numb, my breathing short, but I keep thudding away, tears pouring down my face.

'We're nearly in,' Arran calls after an eternity, and I look up to see he's bringing us into the dock. There's a small group of fishermen gathered, with dark expressions.

'They'll land the emergency helicopter on the field above the beach,' Arran calls, pointing. 'We'll keep trying. We won't give up.'

The assembled men haul Calder's body up onto the land. And for an agonising eternity, Arran and another bearded man alternate breathing into his mouth and pumping his chest. As the other man gives me a weak smile, I realise that it's the burly ferryman who collected our fares on the way over. No one speaks. After two more changeovers between the men, the ferryman looks around, as if asking permission to stop. Then his eyes reach mine and he pumps again.

Suddenly we hear a rapid smacking sound above us and stare up at a bright orange helicopter that's straight out of a children's TV programme.

'Carry him to the field!' Arran shouts, sweat pouring down his face. The assembled men move Calder onto a length of tarpaulin and carry him up the incline, through the gate and onto the field where the helicopter is settling. The ferryman continues CPR as the helicopter doors swing open and two green-uniformed figures with white helmets race towards us, carrying huge padded bags. They drag off their helmets and a woman fits a bag over Calder's mouth and starts squeezing it. Simultaneously the male paramedic fits electrodes to Calder's chest and stares at the attached monitor. He shakes his head at the woman.

'All clear!' he shouts, and they stand back as Calder is jolted.

The paramedic shakes his head again.

'All clear!' he shouts as he turns the switch again.

He shakes his head at the monitor.

'All clear,' he repeats, but I feel the energy sucking from his words.

The paramedics look at the monitor and then at each other.

'Don't give up on him!' Arran shouts. 'Keep trying.'

'Yes, my God, don't stop,' I beg. 'Please keep trying, please.'

'We'll transfer him to Glasgow,' the woman says. 'We'll keep heart compressions going. We're not giving up.'

I see that Arran has his hands clasped and is silently praying.

Several others have bowed their heads.

'Please, let me come,' I say to the woman. 'I'm his partner, I—'

She nods. Then she says the strangest thing. 'Don't give up on him. He's very cold. You're not dead, till you're warm and dead.'

We're being beaten by the rhythmic slaps of the helicopter blades, in this physics-defying tin can. I twist round to see Calder shaking on his gurney, despite his restraining straps. Calder's body is being shaken, I remind myself. He hasn't moved. This noise is ridiculous, even with the heavy ear protectors I'm wearing. With my head banging, my guts twisting and my body numb, I am utterly outside myself, existing somewhere beyond my extremities. From the moment I saw Calder's body in the sea, a bomb went off inside me, leaving me disorientated, reaching around, all senses blanked. How is he right there, right next to me, but not alive? The paramedic is still giving heart compressions and a bag is pushing air into his mouth. But there's still no actual heartbeat. No thoughts flickering across Calder's brain. It's been too long. Way too long. We are transferring his body for confirmation of what is obvious.

If only.

If only I hadn't slept in. If only I'd never agreed to moving here. If only I hadn't cheated in London, pushing me to move here to hide it from Calder. If only I'd thought more about every choice I've ever made, considered the consequences of my every decision, I could have stopped this.

My fault.

Finally, we crash down with a massive jolt. The throbbing of the blades is even louder as the low back door of the helicopter is wrenched open and men in overalls and ear protectors pull Calder through the arse of the machine. But I can't release my bloody seatbelt.

'Get me out of this!' I scream. The pilot shoves my hands aside and releases the mechanism. My body slices through the freezing air as I fall out of the helicopter door onto the grey tarmac of the hospital helipad. My eyes smart in the thudding air as I stumble after Calder. A group of people in green and blue scrubs surround him, like scavengers hungry for prey. One leaps on top of him and straddles him, continuing heart compressions, and the undulating mass is absorbed into the hospital. As I fall through the doors, I catch sight of his gurney being whisked down a long corridor and through distant swing doors. A woman in blue scrubs stops me as I reach them.

'I have to go with him,' I beg, trying to shake her off.

'I'm sorry, but no unauthorised personnel are allowed beyond this point.'

'Please, I have to.'

She grips my shoulders. 'You need to let us take over. I know this is scary. We've been fully briefed about your husband's condition and our team is standing by to help him. I have to go. Every second counts.' She gestures to a row of chairs in the small waiting area.

All the loud frenzy of the rescue, the paramedics' attempts and the helicopter ride have been sucked through those swing doors and I'm left here alone. Like a stupid doll flung out of a tornado. I slump onto a hard seat.

It's so quiet. I'm the noisy one now, my heart thudding loudly. Deep in the burrows of the hospital, my lovely, warm Calder is so cold. Surely trying to get him back now is science fiction, the realm of corpse re-animation, of Frankenstein.

The floor is a hard grey plastic. I lift my boot and it unpeels gelatinously. I do it again. And again. I have to know. I don't want to know.

After an eternity, a tall white-coated man with a huge

forehead is directed towards me by the nurse and I bound up.

'Mrs Campbell?' the Klingon asks.

I'll never be that now, but I nod.

'Your husband is on full bypass now, as his heart isn't beating on its own. The machine is moving his blood and inflating his lungs—'

'But he's had no heartbeat for hours,' I blurt.

He's nodding.

Don't agree with me.

'So, he's . . . dead.'

He hesitates a fraction. 'Clinically dead, yes. But we still have a chance.'

'I–I don't understand.'

'Normally, even a few minutes without oxygen to the brain and organs and the patient would be beyond hope of recovery. But your husband didn't drown, he stayed afloat with his life jacket, and his heart stopped because of the extreme cold. He's hypothermic, his metabolism slowed right down and his organs needed a lot less oxygen. We're raising his temperature very slowly, one degree every ten minutes, gradually feeding warmed oxygenated blood back into him and hoping his heart will restart.'

'So, he's . . . not dead?'

He speaks slowly and deliberately. 'In cases like this, we clinicians have to expand our concept of death. The boundaries of what we used to define death by are . . . loosened. I don't want to raise your hopes, but there have been cases, a number of well-documented cases across the world, where hearts have stopped for several hours, when the patients were very very cold, and their hearts were successfully restarted.'

'You're not dead, till you're warm and dead,' I say slowly. 'That's what the paramedic in the helicopter said. But I didn't understand at the time.'

'That is a phrase we use,' he says with a thin smile.

'But how long can he stay on this bypass thing? If his heart doesn't start beating?'

He frowns.

'Weeks? Days?'

He's silent.

'Just hours?'

'We need to get his heart to beat as soon as we can. I'm sorry, but I have to get back. This is my first case like this, but I'm in contact with others who've dealt with this kind of situation.' He takes my hand and gives it a firm squeeze. 'I promise you we'll do our very best for him.'

I try to imagine Calder, his frozen system thawing, the spreading tree of his veins, arteries and capillaries draining of cold blue blood, filling up with all that rich red warm blood. But it sounds so wildly far-fetched. Like Frankenstein's monster being brought to life. Why do I have to be working on that stupid book about re-animation of body parts right now. I feel like I've somehow willed this tragedy into existence by thinking of it.

Please God, let Calder's heart start beating.

My brain is a wall-space that's been injected with expanding foam. I sit on the hard plastic seat in the glass-partitioned waiting area; I swing my legs in sync, then out of sync, then in figures of eight; I smash my ankles together harder and harder; I alert the nurses if I go to the loo in case they need me; I walk up and down, up and down, endlessly counting my steps and faltering each time the swing doors open. But it's never for me. Time has got stuck, juddering on the same second.

How long has Calder's heart been stopped? Half an hour of me running over the hill and getting Arran, half an hour bringing his body back, fifteen minutes on the shore, half an hour in the helicopter and I've been waiting here for – I check my watch – well over two hours. That's at least four hours since I saw his boat. And how long was he in the water before that? How early did he go out? If it was first light, that's eight-twenty or so. So, he could have had no heartbeat for five hours or more. Why did he even go out? Alone in that weather, when he promised me he'd be careful. Without even telling me?

I must call someone. But who? Normally I'd call Hamish's wife Gina, once my best friend, but she feels so distant now. I want her loud, brightly dressed, overweight, generous energy. I felt so safe in her orbit. Until she and Hamish had four children in quick succession and Calder and I hid our despair that we couldn't get off the starting blocks. God, that pain of childlessness was so stupid. How was I ever so self-indulgent? This is genuine pain. I've wasted so much time with Calder, worrying about things that didn't matter.

I try Janey's number.

'Oh, Nancy!' she cries.

'Hi,' I say quietly, afraid of making all this real with words.

'Oh, my dear, I've heard all about it. What's happening?'

'It . . . doesn't look good.'

'I'm so, so sorry.'

No. I don't want her sympathy. I want this reality to be shaken loose and everything to be all right again. Make it stop.

'Did he say anything?' she asks.

'Who?'

'Calder, has he said what happened?'

'How could he. He's . . .' I can't say the word for what he is. For what everyone knows he is.

'Nancy?'

I disconnect the call. I can't say it out loud. And make it real. I shove my hands to my chest. *Thump. Thump. Thump.* My heart is sarcastically showing off: *Look how easy it is to beat.* How do hearts beat at all? It's some weird magic. If he's warmed up, will his start? But it's not a wind-up toy. Can he possibly be restarted with a buzz of Frankenstein-esque electricity?

I saw an actual heart once. I was eight, shopping with my mother in an old-fashioned butcher's. White and blue tiles. The butcher standing proudly behind his meaty counter in a white coat, like a pretend surgeon. Ugh, those slippery dark skeins of liver. Then I looked along the fleshy array in the glass cabinet to a large dull lump sitting on a marbled block, labelled *ox heart*. It was nothing like the bright red curvy heart that I'd cut out at school for Mother's Day. This was a big folded lump of browny-red flesh, fat yellow tubes poking out the top. The poor ox from which it had been ripped was dead; his sad cow wife was alone. Now I'm that sad cow wife. Not even that, as we're not married. I'm not even a widow.

I approach Calder's heart in my head, slamming open the swing doors, speeding along the corridors, falling into the room where the blue and green worker bee medics are buzzing around him. I slip between their jostling shoulders to see Calder on the bed. I sink down to touch his cold skin, then melt through it, swerve between his ribs and finally arrive in his chest. And there's his heart. Motionless. I reach out and clasp it, feeling the wet meaty texture as I squeeze it, rhythmically, in time with my own.

God, those footballers I've seen on news reports, flat out on the pitch surrounded by their teammates, everyone around them distraught and wide-eyed, but the running medics got to them so fast, in time to jolt their hearts back to beating. Surely Calder's is past such hope, like that ox heart: dead meat.

I swipe up my phone, googling heart attacks and cold. The high-foreheaded Klingon was right: there are all these cases across the world – skiers trapped under ice, children who fell into fjords, hikers trapped on snowy hilltops – who all came back. These people's hearts stopped for hours, but the varied array of youths, men and women now all look normal in their smiling photos, in the awkward interviews, walking, talking . . . even laughing. It's possible. I drink up each story. *Miracle. Unbelievable. One in a million.* Or are these just the rare flukes?

I need to talk to someone from before this terrible move up here. I switch to my phone contacts and tap *Favourites* – where straight after Calder is Gina. I press the green button as I walk over to the window and look out on a grey car park, rain splattering down.

She picks up after the second ring.

'Hey babe, long time no speak, I was just thinking I must ring you . . . hello? Nancy. Can you hear me?'

'Calder,' I blurt.

'What's happened?' she says, instantly serious.

'Accident,' I manage. 'He's—'

'Injured? What? Nancy?'

I make a strangled sound.

'He's dead?'

'No heartbeat.'

'What?'

'His heart isn't beating. But he's so cold, so they can maybe bring him back. It's impossible, isn't it . . .' I start crying, wailing, gasping for air.

'Jesus. I'll come straight up.'

'No,' I squawk. 'There's no point. It's a twelve-hour journey up here. There's nothing you can do. I just have to wait.'

'OK. Breathe. That's it. Can you tell me what happened?'

'I don't know.'

'Yes, shepherd's pie,' she says in a tetchy voice away from the phone. 'Sorry, Nancy, hold on. Hamish is away on a last-minute business trip. Let me get the nanny up to speed.'

'I'll go, it's OK—'

'No. God no, stay right there.'

I stab my finger on the disconnect button.

Calder's accident is karmic payback for my sins. The man I had the one-night stand with was Gina's husband Hamish. And now the universe has stolen my happiness in return. I worry about everything, all the time, imagining that worrying somehow stops things happening. But now the worst has actually happened. I can't feel. I can't think. Flashbulbs have exploded right in my face and there's just glare.

Dead.

Calder's dead.

What can that possibly mean? I exist. He doesn't. I can't understand the concept. I stagger back from the window and clatter into the chairs. I touch the rim of the grey plastic seat. I see my hand and register that it's feeling the plastic. There is a real world. Outside my thinking. I'm in this world. But he's not?

Calder. Is. Dead.

My phone rings and I turn it off completely.

I lean sideways to lie across the line of chairs. I look up at the bright strip lighting. I want to just stay here. Frozen. Pulled in. I don't want to know for definite.

Suddenly, the swing doors bounce open again.

No.

No.

No.

The Klingon doctor is striding towards me.

Beaming.

I swing round and stand up.

'We've got his heart started,' he says triumphantly. 'We got his temperature up to thirty degrees and started it with a defibrillator. It started on the second attempt.'

I stare at him, then grip his arms. 'Oh my God. Really?'

'Yes. It's an amazing feat,' he says, his eyes full of wonder. 'I cried when we saw the monitor respond. He's a strong man, your husband. And my team has done so brilliantly. Would you like to come to see him?'

I'm nodding furiously.

Calder's alive.

I'm finally walking through those forbidden swing doors. And it's just a normal hospital corridor like on my side, not a dark winding path that this doctor has travelled down, to pluck Calder back from purgatory.

Calder is alive!

My body is re-stacking itself, rebooting, filling out with space and potential.

I'm given a gown and told to wash my hands.

'This is the ICU,' a nurse explains. 'We have to be extremely careful.'

I scrub at my hands and think of Calder doing the same motions in our kitchen less than twenty-four hours ago. All I want is to be back there, in our little cottage. I love one-storey cottages now. I love isolated living now. I love slate churches and creepy pastors. I will never take anything for granted ever again. I pull on a mask and follow the Klingon through the swooshing doors into a large white room. Ahead of us is a hospital bed. There are so many people around it and there's so much machinery snaking in. Calder's face is obscured by a contraption over his mouth. He has various clear bags of liquid attached to drips and has electrodes all over his bare chest, all attached to monitors. I stare at the green line on one of the monitors, seeing its glorious regular peaks.

But my lovely Calder is so white, so still, livid bruises all over his face and torso. He almost looks worse than when Arran and I dragged him out of the sea.

'He looks so terrible,' I say through the muffle of my mask.

'He's been through a lot,' the Klingon says. 'This is all very invasive.'

'But he will . . . wake up?' I falter.

He hesitates to answer.

'What are you saying? Do you mean he'll be OK – or that he's back with a heartbeat, but . . . brain-dead?'

The other medics share glances. He gestures for us to move back and speaks quietly.

Oh no – I remember this kind of silent hesitation after my parents' car accident, those pitying looks, the halting words.

'You mean this is it?' I blurt.

'Slow down. It's a huge thing to have got his heart beating again after such a long time. He's in a coma right now, his lung function is erratic and we're monitoring his other organs.'

'Please be honest with me.'

He nods. 'We've checked his brain function and our initial analysis is positive. But he's been through an awful lot. He has to find an equilibrium, and then we hope that he'll wake of his own accord. Which has happened with other patients, though the results have varied.'

'As in some people . . . don't wake up?' Oh God.

'We are in rarely charted territory here. He could retain full function. Or there could be some mental impairment. Or some physical problem with lungs, kidneys, digestion, neural pathways to the extremities, it's too soon to tell. But there have been a number of cases where these kinds of patients have woken up fully and returned to normal life.

This is now a phase of wait and see.'

I thought we'd been in the phase of wait and see. But now I realise that was just the first rung on a long ladder. The Klingon is buzzing from the medical miracle of getting Calder's heart beating. But I need Calder back. I so wanted his heart to start beating. But it's not enough. Nowhere near enough. I need him to wake up.

'What happens next?'

'We monitor and support his system. And wait and see.'

'But what do you expect?'

He shrugs. 'I understand you want definitive answers. But this isn't an exact science. No medicine is, but this is especially experimental and unpredictable. This phase could take a while. You should get some rest, Mrs Campbell. We have your contact details. I promise you we'll call you if there are any changes.' He gestures towards the doors.

'But I can't leave him,' I cry.

'You must look after yourself. He'll need you . . . if he comes back. We'll keep you fully informed.'

I'm shepherded out, twisting to catch a last glimpse of Calder's still body, so much equipment beeping and flashing around him.

If he comes back?

CHAPTER SIX

Minutes tick by glacially. Hours pass like a drunken blackout. Then days merge and waking and sleeping become vague blurry states. In physics GCSE lessons, I survived the mind-numbing boredom by drawing little stacks of dashes, each representing five minutes, and doggedly crossing them off. I'm doing the same now, in an exercise book I've bought in the hospital shop. Sometimes I blank out for a few hours and have a frenzy of black crossings to make up, or five minutes go so excruciatingly slowly that I have to stop myself from screaming by drawing half marks.

How have three days passed since the accident? I can't hope. I can't not hope. That initial euphoric high when Calder's heart miraculously started beating has fizzled with every hour he hasn't woken up. Before, he was a body with no heartbeat. Now he's a body with a heartbeat. I've been blurring through, eating small amounts and grabbing short sleeps at Janey and Gina's urging. The high-foreheaded Klingon, who I now know to be called Dr Andrew Viner, keeps saying 'early days yet'. He tells me that Calder's brain scans 'look encouraging', but that we have to 'wait and see'. All these endless platitudes. It feels like he's playing a game, seeing how far he can push me before I call his bluff.

He's dead, stop it, I'll eventually scream.

Ah damn, you got me, he'll laugh. *Congrats on not calling me out sooner! High five.*

Gina and Janey have been phoning and messaging me at regular intervals. It's so much easier to talk to Janey, even though I've only known her for a week and Gina for five years. But of course, sleeping with Gina's husband caused that. Also, Janey is less OTT than Gina, less exhausting. For five years I've loved Gina's hard, sarky say-it-like-it-is way of communicating, but now, in this deadly serious void, we have no shared language and her version of solicitousness feels embarrassing and formal, even cruel with her 'tough love'. I put the phone down on her this morning. My voice had been shaking, as I explained yet again that there was no change in Calder.

'You're making yourself ill,' she said, sounding almost annoyed. 'Who does that help?'

'I can't help it,' I snivelled. 'I thought the worst was over but now there's a new "terrible" to deal with.'

'I know this is hard, darling. But maybe it would help to change your perspective, to accept that we all die eventually – all of us. We have to build death into our perception. Living in fear of it all the time is impossible.'

I cut her off.

Her prosaic realism is too much for me right now. After the loss of my parents, losing Calder seems so unfair. But life isn't fair. There are no cosmic scales.

I sit at Calder's bedside, wearing my gown and mask, staring at his flickering eyelids. I reach out and touch his cold, still hand.

'Calder, it's me, I'm here. Please come back to me. I love you so much.'

I play music he likes on my mobile phone: Arctic Monkeys, Dave, Eminem. I even give him a blast of Ed Sheeran, who he hates, to try to get a sarcastic reaction.

Turn off that shit, I want him to bark as he reaches over and switches to the Foo Fighters.

But nothing happens.

Hope has been dangled in front of me, only to be swiped away. *You thought the pain of him with no heartbeat was the worst; try this, heartbeat but with no consciousness.* I'm like my lovely Calder watching his beloved Rangers getting a late winning goal, only for Celtic to score twice in the final seconds, taking him from ecstasy back to utter despair. I used to find his football agony painful. Now I yearn for such pantomime upset.

My phone shudders in my pocket, on silent, and I see it's Janey calling.

'Hold on,' I whisper, carrying the phone out of the ICU. 'Right, OK.'

'Any change?' she enquires gently.

'Nope.' Don't any of them think I'd be letting them know if there was? I sit down on the shiny floor in the corridor. I want to lie down here and close my eyes.

'How are you holding up?'

'You know. Waiting. What else is there?' I say dully.

There's silence from the phone. I feel the reverberation of the aggressive bleakness of my tone, but I'm too tired to apologise or care.

'Why would anyone sail near them,' I mumble.

'Near what?' she says gently.

'Those whirlpools.'

'They're really quite safe. And a huge tourist attraction. What with all the stories – the Norwegian prince and the impure maidens.'

'What? Impure maidens?'

'Doesn't matter. Sorry. It's just a stupid folk tale.'

'No, tell me. Anything for distraction.'

'Well, the story goes that this prince was trying to show his love for the daughter of the lord of the isles. Prove his worth. So, he tied his boat up by the whirlpools for three nights. But you don't want to hear all this.'

'Keep going.'

'OK. Well he tethered himself with three ropes: the first night the hemp rope snapped; the second night the wool rope snapped; but he thought he'd be saved by the rope made of maiden's hair. But the third night it snapped too, and he realised that the maidens hadn't been so pure as he's hoped.'

'What?'

'It's just a stupid story. Bit misogynistic really.'

Not stupid at all. I'm an impure maiden. This *is* my fault.

I can hear her footsteps on gravel. 'Where are you going?' I snap.

'I'm walking towards the church. Arran's holding a

special service for Calder. We'll offer up prayers for his swift recovery.'

'What's the point?' I snarl. I hadn't realised it was Sunday. I've lost all sense of time.

She takes a breath. 'Well, we'll think of him, and of you, and try to hold you both up during these difficult times,' she says, unfazed.

'Ha. What God would have allowed this?' I spit out. 'Unless it's some sort of punishment.'

I glare up at a passing nurse's glance. She averts her eyes.

'No one's being punished,' Janey says gently.

'I could be. You lot are always going on and on about sin.'

'We just consider our sins and get washed clean. And then our pure prayers can reach God more easily. You'll see. You'll feel the entire congregation holding you at eleven, when Arran will give his special prayer.'

'Sure. Yeah. Thanks. Gotta go,' I mumble, as I disconnect.

I've never believed in her God – in any God. I was a common or garden atheist when I met Calder and he had an impressively vehement dislike of religion, having been dragged to the formal services on the island. Isla was very devout, so when Calder and I visited her, we weren't allowed to sleep in the same bed.

'Though shalt not commit adultery, Exodus 20 verse 14,' Isla clarified as she explained the rules of her house, Calder raising an eyebrow at me behind her back. 'I've put you both in the sitting room, but I've taken precautions.' Ah, those two camp beds against the opposite walls, partitioned off by sheets strung over a long cord.

We were in our thirties, but her word was law. I feel tears falling and wipe the snot across my sleeve. We sneaked beyond those white, blue and flowery sheets only when she went to sleep.

'Fancy committing adultery?' Calder whispered, sticking his head through the cotton wall.

'I don't actually,' I teased.

He frowned.

'Oh no,' I giggled, 'I've just borne false witness, so what the hell.'

'Well, I've stolen, murdered and coveted my neighbour's ox already today, so in for a penny, in for a pound.'

How was there ever a time when we were so simply happy?

The forbidding, the sneaking, the shushing were all an aphrodisiac, not that we needed any. But Calder wouldn't fully defy his mother's rules. He would always return to his side of the curtain afterwards to sleep. In case she caught us 'in sin'.

'It's all such bollocks,' I used to laugh.

Yet after three long days of this endless waiting, with these bloody beeping machines, and Calder so still, I want his mum's God to be real. I want miracles. If he wakes up, I'll go to church every week. I'll never be lazy. I'll do good. I'll embrace our new life, I'll be a perfect wife, and I'll never look back to our old life again.

I shift my watch on my wrist. Calder gave me this small gold watch on the first anniversary of us meeting. It's ticking off the minutes, hours and days. It says twenty to eleven and I can picture everyone approaching that little judgemental church on the hill back on Langer. A clean slate. Do they really believe that their arbitrary idea of a God can give them that? That he'll hear them more easily after their confessions? But what do I know? Who am I? Millions of people admit their sins and seek forgiveness. I need to be Dr Frankenstein and force life back into that husk that is Calder, whatever it takes.

I am standing. Moving. Approaching a nurse.

'Is there a chapel here?' I ask.

She nods, her eyes kind as she reaches out and touches my arm. 'Second floor, take the lift and there are signs from there.'

I'm in the lift. With a bustling Greek family. 'No, Daphne said she'd make the lasagne.' 'What about Ava?' 'Oh, who knows what she's bringing, as long as she brings the kids.' A big family. What's that like? Calder is my only family. He's my everything. What am I without him? I'll do anything, *anything*, to get him back. I get out on the second floor with signs for X-RAYS and OUTPATIENT CARE, but follow the black arrows marked CHAPEL.

I stop where the arrows do, at a pale wooden door. I take a deep breath and push it open to find a square room with matching pale wood pews, facing a stained-glass window showing a white dove, above a small wooden altar. There's a nervous-looking priest, wearing a grey suit with a white priest's collar, who's arranging a pile of small dark blue books.

'I need to confess,' I blurt.

He looks up and blinks at me. 'What? Oh. Hello. Well, I'm not a Catholic priest, so I'm afraid I don't take official confession.'

'But you could hear my confession, couldn't you? Please. You have to.'

'Well . . . I guess. If you need to unburden yourself, I'm here for you, of course.' He so doesn't want this, looks horribly nervous, but forces a kind smile.

'Good, so let's do it,' I say, striding over.

'Right now?'

'Yep.'

He gives a weak smile as he lowers his pile of books. 'Shall we sit down?'

No wonder Catholics do this in dark booths. It's better not to be seen, but who cares about anyone or anything now – my nerve endings are totally cauterised to embarrassment.

He blinks at me, smiles and then opens his mouth to speak, but I cut him off. 'I cheated.'

His face flushes, failing to rein in his shocked reaction.

'Not just that. I cheated with my partner's best friend, Hamish. And I got pregnant by him.' I'm gabbling, but I can't stop. 'And now my partner's lying in the ICU upstairs. His heart's beating, but he won't wake up. Is that a punishment from God? How can I make it right? How can I be forgiven?'

I see the priest forming reactions and discarding them.

'I'm sorry, I know this is mad, I'm fully aware that I'm being ridiculous, but I need help. Please. I've never believed. But I will, I'll do anything.'

He blinks back, patting my hand. 'I'm so sorry for your partner's troubles, and for the enormous stress you're under.'

'I don't matter,' I blurt, tears dripping down my face. 'I

know this is all beyond desperate of me. But I can't help him and I feel like this is all my fault.'

'It's OK,' he says gently. His kindness just makes me cry more.

'It's not OK. What can I do? Now I've confessed my sin, will God let him wake up?' I lean forward and moan in agony.

'Let it out,' he says, stroking my hair.

When the wave passes, I take a deep breath and stand. 'I'm sorry, I know I'm being beyond ridiculous. I'll go.'

He catches my hand. 'No, please stay. God's not holding your partner's soul hostage, my dear,' he says, reaching into his pocket and presenting me with a pressed white handkerchief. 'He doesn't work like that. He isn't the God of the Old Testament, smiting people. He's the God of forgiveness and kindness. His ways are mysterious and hard to understand. But your partner's trials are not your fault.'

'But he won't wake up. He's stuck halfway back. And I don't know what to do. How to help him.'

'You mustn't blame yourself. But sometimes these trying moments help us see what really matters to us. You needed to unburden yourself, and you have, and if you are truly sorry, God has already forgiven you.'

'But that doesn't help Calder, does it. Sorry, I know I'm asking for a miracle.'

'I can't tell you God's plans. But miracles do happen – every day. All you can do is pray for one.'

I stare at his wide-eyed open face. He means well, but he can't help me or Calder. No one can. I'm exhausted and deflated. What am I doing? Making this stupid scene isn't helping. I'm embarrassing and pathetic.

'OK, well I better get back to him,' I say flatly. There's no burden lifting. No freedom. Putting my 'sin' into words has just crystallised it and confirmed it. I can't help Calder. He's lost. Erased. And I'm alone now. For ever. 'Thank you for your kindness,' I mumble, holding out his hanky.

'Oh no, you keep it. I'll be praying for you both.'

What use is that? I nod, feeling utterly stupid for coming here. For my selfish histrionics.

As I leave the chapel, I glance at my little gold watch. It's eleven precisely. The island congregation is assembled in their church, all staring forward, all focused on Arran as they pray for Calder. They should be judging me. Condemning me. That priest is wrong. This long, drawn-out horror of waiting, of hoping and then of hope being dashed, is an Old Testament punishment. One that Calder's mother would have approved of.

How were we ever so simply happy?

I remember Calder pushing up the stiff little bathroom window of our fourth-floor flat in London to throw out my contraceptive pills. We'd laughed as they tumbled down onto the huge restaurant bins in the alleyway below. We thought we'd be pregnant immediately. But as the months passed, I realised that my cavalier youth of heavy drinking had destroyed our chances. Gina and Hamish had had three kids in the five years I'd known them, as if Hamish just had to look at her to get her up the duff. One or both of us were clearly infertile. After two years of failure, I was resigned and bleak. Jesus, how did I think I was so unhappy then? How stupid and frivolous I was. How did

I take our happy life so easily for granted?

I wince remembering my childish joy when my period was finally two weeks late. *The memory is hard to access and as I run it in my head, it's like I'm playing a jolly little film of simple happy folk – bright, tinkly Christmas movie happy folk.* Calder is in Birmingham for a big loft conversion. I'm planning on getting a pregnancy test on my way into work and effervescing with the thought of phoning him after I confirm the positive result. I'm grinning on the Tube in, so much so that people keep smiling back at me and making me laugh. I'm so ignorantly, stupidly happy. As I stand to get off the train, a large woman is nodding at me. I'm beaming back. *What a dumb idiot I was.* She's frowning and nodding. I'm laughing. Then she's pointing. Down. At my white skirt. I look and it's fine. But she's spinning her finger. I pull the back of the skirt into my eyeline. And it's stained with a rusty smear. My period's come. I've bled right through, like a stupid little girl who knows nothing.

My little film's now showing on an old-fashioned projector and as I tie my cardigan round my waist, the film starts stretching and distorting: I avoid the eyes of every commuter as I trundle up the escalator, to Oxford Street to buy sanitary provisions in Boots, new pants in M&S and a new dress from Zara. I chuck my bloody skirt in a big black bin and fall into the revolving doors of Broadcasting House.

I fast-forward through my little film, which is getting ever more blurry, as if Vaseline has been smeared over the projector. I'm on autopilot through the final day of a very tricky radio production. It's a big series that's been a total headache with compliance issues galore and problems with rights; today's timetable is chaotic to accommodate the commitments of my original star's replacement, multiple actors have script problems, my main studio manager is sick, and there are still acres of script to finish.

The film plays at normal speed as we finally wrap the damn thing and Calder rings me. Thank God, I so need to see him.

'Where are you? I really need that drink.'

'I'm still in Birmingham. I can't get back tonight. I have to stay one more night to finish this project. I'm so sorry, Nance.'

'Oh no worries,' I say fake-brightly. I can't tell him over the phone about our dashed pregnancy hopes. 'Then I think I'll go straight home.'

'No, no, you should still have a drink, you deserve it – meet up with Gina and Hamish like we planned.'

And the film freezes as I step out of Broadcasting House. That was the moment.

The moment when I could have made a different decision. I could have stopped everything that happened next. I want to push that frozen me back into the revolving glass door, but the film plays again, disjointedly, but forward.

I arrive at All Bar One and down a pint. No bloody point in being abstemious now there's no baby. Hamish is sweeping in, flashing his winning smile, his orange hair slicked back, his stylish blue suit jacket flapping open to reveal his tightly sculpted white shirt, the kind that Calder and I always laugh at.

'Just me, I'm afraid,' he says. 'Gina's had to go home for some emergency.'

'Oh, well Calder's still in Birmingham, so let's ditch the drink then. Do it another time when they're both here.'

'Ah no, Nancy, I've had a shit week. Please. I'm begging you.'

And I'm knocking back pints. Laughing. Finding Hamish's easy banter so relaxing and calming. *I want to shout at that old me, with her sharp black bob, her tired face, her silly idea that not being pregnant is the worst problem in the world. Get up, you fool. Go home! But the film continues forward.*

'So, what's so bad about your bad week?' I slur.

'Ah you know, same old same old, shit clients, the kids are getting to be quite a handful – oh and did Gina tell you, she's preggers again! What are we thinking having four! I envy you two, still living the high life. Cheers.'

I'm draining my pint, numbed and blurred and knocking back whisky chasers that burn my throat.

My little film finally stretches, distorts and then burns as the screen goes blank.

The memory of the next morning starts with a series of overexposed prints in harsh colours.

Me in bed, naked.

Hamish asleep next to me, naked.

Rumpled white sheets streaked with blood.

Calder's text on my phone: 'See you later. So sorry about last night. Love you x.'

Next, I'm in a horribly clichéd black and white kitchen sink drama.

I'm staring at the kettle as it boils.

'Christ. What have we done?' Hamish says, his face in his hands at our little kitchen table.

'Where does Gina think you are?' I spit out, burning my hand slopping boiling water.

'Oh God,' he mumbles. 'I sometimes stay up in London if I can't get back to Whitstable, so she won't suspect.'

'It's not about if other people know. We know!' I shout, slamming a mug in front of him.

'I know,' he says, touching my arm.

I spring back. 'I love Calder.'

'And I love Gina. This was a terrible mistake.'

'You have to get out of here and we can't mention this ever again. It would destroy them both.'

The last part of the memory plays out like an overdramatic nightmare sequence in an experimental film: I'm with Gina at Sadler's Wells weeks later, watching the Pina Bausch dance company in *The Rite of Spring*. She's smiley, so Hamish hasn't confessed. The stage is dark; the jumpy music jars; the dancers are all in skin-coloured dresses with one caressing a red cloth; the music rises to a horror-film crescendo. I feel faint. Surely Gina can see my grubby story being played out on stage?

As a dancer rubs the red material across her belly, I double over in pain.

'I have to go,' I whisper.

But Gina insists we go to Accident and Emergency.

Cut to a dazzling white clinic: 'It's probably just a bad period,' the starched nurse says as she removes her plastic gloves after examining me. 'But I'll just run a couple of tests.'

An hCG blood test confirms that I've just miscarried.

The nurse hands me a tissue. 'Did you want to be pregnant?'

'Yes, absolutely, but how long was I pregnant?' I'd avoided sex with Calder after Hamish, but we'd just had sex that week . . . ''Cos that's when I last had sex since my period a month or so ago. And obviously you can't get pregnant during your period.'

'I'd say a month sounds right,' the nurse says. 'It's rare, but yes, you absolutely can get pregnant during your period.'

Especially, of course, if you've slept with Mr Fertility himself.

Cut to the teen drama coda of me whispering to Gina on the top deck of a bus: 'Please don't tell Calder, it would really upset him. Nor Hamish 'cos he'd tell him. Promise me?'

'If that's what you want.'

And finally, the projector splutters off.

I've tried over and over to burn this ugly film from my memory. But it's indestructible.

I'm walking up the corridor, back to my waiting area, which I now realise I will only finally leave when accompanying Calder's coffin out. Because of course no God would ever allow him to come back to me, as that is my punishment.

I am the impure maiden who caused the whirlpool drowning.

Then I hear a flurry of footsteps and look up to see a nurse running towards me. Shouting.

'He's awake!'

CHAPTER SEVEN

Calder's eyes are wide open, blinking furiously as I peer through the glass of the door. He suddenly lurches up, yanking a needle from his arm, and blood spurts across the white sheets. That new warm oxygenated blood.

'What's happening?' I cry as I push the door open, but no one registers me.

'Don't panic,' Dr Viner is saying, getting into Calder's eyeline, as another doctor holds his shoulders down. 'You're in a hospital in Glasgow – you had an accident. Try to stay still. You've got a breathing tube.'

Calder's thrashing lessens a little as he stares up.

'Hey, Calder. I'm Dr Viner. We're going to give you a muscle relaxant to help you cope with the ventilator.' The nurse injects something into one of the lines connecting into him. 'Don't panic, you're fine. Keep focused on my eyes.' He's gripping Dr Viner, locked onto his eyes, but falls back onto the bed. 'That's right.'

I step further into the room. The doctors all speak in short, tight sentences, their activity conducted by Viner. They are a host of bees around their queen, all in sync, all focused and knowing their role. Dr Viner smiles and nods. 'Good, Calder. We're so excited to have you back with us.'

Calder gives a low animal moan.

'No, don't try to speak. Can you blink to register that you understand me?'

I can't quite see what's happening, but clearly, he's reacting given all the flicking glances the hyper doctors are exchanging between themselves. There's such a wild crackling energy in the room. Thank God for all these capable strong men and women who have pulled him back from wherever he's been. Not alive. Not dead. I feel weightless, my head flipped open, my skin dissolved, my blood effervescing out.

He's awake. It's impossible. But he's awake.

'Good. That's good, Calder,' Dr Viner is saying. 'Now we're removing your breathing tube, OK. I know it's uncomfortable. I want you to relax. Blink if you understand. Good.'

'Thank you, thank you, thank you,' I mumble, over and over. Everything I've begged for, had given up on, thought I didn't deserve, is coming true. That crazy slate cleaning, confessing my sins, the church's prayers. It all worked. How can I be this lucky?

Calder is coughing and sputtering, finally free of the machine.

'That's it,' Dr Viner says, 'you're doing brilliantly.'

The medical staff continue to buzz around him. I can

see that Calder is breathing on his own and that the lovely block of a heart monitor is beeping away, the green line sure and regular.

He has come back from the dead.

To me.

'You've been asleep for a few days and it's wonderful to have you back with us,' Dr Viner says. Calder stares back. Dr Viner puts his hand on his shoulder. 'You're OK now, try to relax, we're all here for you. You're OK.'

As the frenzy settles, Dr Viner looks over and beckons me. 'Just for a moment,' he whispers. He looks back at Calder. 'There's someone here who's very excited to see you.'

I creep forward, feeling almost formal as I move into his eyeline, in front of all these grinning staff.

And there's my Calder. Thin. Bruised. But awake. His eyes are flicking back and forth. It hurts how much I love him. He finally focuses on me.

'Calder, oh my love.'

Then he closes his eyes.

I reach out, but a nurse moves in front of me and gives him an injection and another adjusts his bag of medication.

I'm holding my breath, backing away.

'Is he . . . all right?' I say to Dr Viner.

'Don't worry, he's only just regained consciousness. He's going to be pretty out of it for a bit, and we have to sort his pain medication and keep him sedated. But this is a huge step. Huge.'

There's such a buzz in the room. Many of the nurses have tears in their eyes. People keep glancing at me, shiny-eyed, glowing. I keep up my crazy nodding and smiling. I feel numb but I have to match their excited energy. Calder's back. It's a miracle. All I have is splodges of thoughts, like plops of paint dropped into water, coloured in the air but dissipating as they hit me, so I can't quite feel them or believe them. I so want to embrace Calder, to kiss him, to keep him safe with me for ever.

Dr Viner walks back to me and I fling my arms around him. 'Thank you, thank you so much.'

He's laughing as we pull apart. 'I know,' he says, beaming. 'It's all a lot to take in. This is an amazing moment for everyone. We've never had a case like it. To bring someone back whose heart had been stopped for possibly six hours is historic. But now, he needs lots of rest and support.'

I make my way back to my familiar waiting room in a daze. Everything is the same, yet it all looks so different. Clear. Exact. Bright. He's back. I feel unworthy of this second chance, but so grateful. I've been holding myself in for days, away from what I thought had happened, and I'm scared of letting myself feel relief. I have to tell someone else to make this real outside of this hospital.

I think of phoning Gina, but my 'confession' has split her even further away from me, so I call Janey.

'He woke up!' I scream down the phone as soon as she answers.

'Oh, thank God. Oh, Nancy my dear, I'm so happy for you.'

'It's amazing. I didn't believe it was possible,' I gabble. 'I'm sorry I've been so tense with you. That I was so rude about the church, about—'

'Nancy, it's OK, take a breath. What you've been

through was unbearable. I handled it all wrong with even mentioning the church.'

'No, no, I get it now,' I babble, 'the idea of prayers, of a community holding you up, and of confessing. Please thank everyone for me.'

'Of course I will. How's Calder doing?'

I'm relieved to still feel her warmth after my snideness. 'Well, it's still a long road ahead. But his heart's beating strongly and the biggest hurdle was him waking up. And he has. Look, I better go, in case they need me, but I wanted to say thank you. Thank you so much.'

'I didn't, we didn't, do anything. It was God's will that Calder came back.'

'I'll come to church when we're back,' I blurt. 'I'm going to be part of the island now, embrace everyone, even Arran, especially Arran.' I've offered to go to church! Fine. Good. Where has my tight, tense, protective nature ever got me? 'How's your lovely Rob doing?'

'Oh, I haven't seen him this week. Now you go and look after that lovely husband of yours and yourself.'

I know I should ring Gina next, but I can't face her yet. Don't want to tip the good luck away from me again. I sit in my familiar waiting area, revelling in this new reality. Calder's clearly got a long recovery ahead. I sense but don't let myself explore the concept that he might be impaired, physically or mentally. But I know from all the stories I've read that some patients who've been brought back after long periods with no heartbeat have been affected mentally, or had problems with mobility. I know I'm ungrateful, but now, I don't want the small win on the slot machine, I want the all-singing, all-jangling, total-jealousy-from-all-the-other-punters jackpot. But I'll cope, whatever the outcome. I'll do everything I can to help him. I know how to deal with these jittery nerves now that there's hope – find a goal, take action, move forward. I never thought I could get over my parents' deaths, never escape that black hole, but things do pass if you keep moving forward. I need to do what I eventually did then, to focus on what I can do: get my health in tip-top shape, question Dr Viner, research what Calder needs and do everything I can for him.

But I know there's one thing I shouldn't put off. I pull out my phone and go to my Favourites and press the button for Gina. I'll keep it short so as not to let the bad luck back in. She answers after one ring.

'He's back,' I blurt, before she can speak.

'Oh, Nancy, oh my God.'

'It's a miracle. Not a miracle miracle obviously – but you know what I mean.' I feel guilty that I'm undercutting my earlier conversation with Janey to be sarky with Gina.

'Oh, honey, it's a big fat "loaves and fishes" fucking miracle all right,' she laughs. I laugh along with her, but feel awkward. 'Hamish!' she shouts away from the phone, 'Calder's woken up.' There's some hushed whispering and then the phone's passed over.

'Nancy?' says that voice I never wanted to hear again. 'He's back?' Hamish asks.

'Yes.'

'Oh, thank God.' I choke down my annoyance that he would speak to me, trying not to begrudge even him some joy on this marvellous day. 'Nancy – are you there?' he calls down the phone.

'Hi, yes, Calder's awake again.' I'm so aware of Gina in the background listening to us and am nervous what to say. 'It's great news. Now Calder and I can really move on with our lives up here.'

'Yes, of course,' he falters. 'I . . . understand.' I feel so guilty about this subtext in his wife's hearing.

'Can you put Gina back on?'

'Oh . . . of course. I'm thinking of you. Both.'

The phone is passed back. 'Sorry darling, he was desperate for news,' she gushes. 'He's been going off his head worrying, asking me for news every second of the day and night.'

'Of course,' I say dully, knowing that it was Hamish's guilt propelling him.

'Oh, honey, you sound so exhausted,' Gina says. 'You need lots of pampering with cocktails and massage. I'm coming up there to take care of you.'

'No,' I bark.

There's silence on the other end.

'Sorry, I didn't mean to snap like that. I'm really overwhelmed with everything. I'm OK. I just need to focus and I can't deal with being something for anyone else.'

'Okaay.' But I know I've hurt her. 'You must look after yourself, get a hotel room, eat properly, get some sleep. I know I'm being a mother hen, but you can't help Calder if you're a wreck.'

I get rid of her after promising to take care of myself. Her intense fussing is too much to deal with. I've really needed Janey's mellower energy during all this, even if it's not my natural speed. Or wasn't. Perhaps I'm changing, loosening, and can gradually move from my fast taut

'Gina me' to a newer softer 'Janey me' on the island. Most importantly, I'll soon be my safe warm 'Calder me', once he's fully back to health.

The nurse says that Calder's sedated for at least the rest of the day and that they're 'working on him'. It sounds like he's a robot they're rebooting. God, I have to stop analysing every word. His heart's beating, he's awake – the next step will be walking out of here.

I google hotels by the hospital and book a room in a nearby Premier Inn. After telling the nurses exactly what I'm doing and giving them all pieces of paper with my phone number on, I sweep out. I find the nearest supermarket and load up on healthy foods, supplements and cheap clothes. I take my haul to my hotel room, and relax into the familiar clean lines and simple greys and purples that I know from old work trips. I shower in scalding hot water, scrubbing all the agony of the last few days off me, wrap myself in big fluffy towels, drink a bottle of water and sit on the bed.

The padded headboard is slate grey. I ram my fingers hard into the sponginess, then watch as the indentations are slowly erased, as the foam fills back out.

Calder woke up. So, my sin is finally forgiven.

Isn't it?

CHAPTER EIGHT

I'm as excited as when Calder and I had our first proper date. I'm back at the hospital the next morning on the dot of visiting hours at 9 a.m. I can't sit still, keep patting down my hair, checking if anyone's coming, bouncing from foot to foot.

Finally, I'm called in.

But he's asleep and I'm told he'll be sedated all day again. I see his chest rising and falling, the monitor bleeping. Patience. I sit with him for a while, but when the nurses come in to do tests, I wander down to the canteen.

A thin woman with frizzy hair, wearing a crumpled coat, approaches me as I'm sitting at a table stuffing a blueberry muffin into my mouth.

'Hi, you don't know me,' she says, 'but one of the nurses just pointed you out to me. You're Calder's wife, aren't you?'

'Umm, partner, yes.' I munch and swallow, scattering

crumbs as I stand. 'Has something happened?'

She catches my arm.

'No, no, I'm not a member of the medical staff.'

'Oh,' I say, turning back to her.

'You are here for Calder Campbell?'

'Yes. Who are you?'

'How is he?' she says with intense interest.

'He's . . . good. I mean, it's a long process, but he's back.' I return to my table and sit down. She sits down facing me, eyes wide, fixed grin plastered on. 'Who are you exactly?'

'Sorry. I'm Fiona Loughty. I'm from a local Glasgow newspaper. I was here at the hospital covering an oil rig accident patient and someone told me about Calder. It's an amazing story. Could I just have a few words? I'm recording.' She shoves a phone in front of my face, full of bouncy smiley interest, and I can't leave her hanging. What harm can it do?

'Oh right. Well, it's wonderful, a miracle. His heart wasn't beating at all when he was rescued from the sea, but this wonderful hospital got him back.'

'From the dead,' Fiona prompts.

'Yeah – I mean, sort of – whatever that is.'

She beams. 'Indeed. And that's the million-dollar question, isn't it. What did he see?'

'When?'

'When he was . . . dead. People talk of a light beckoning them?'

What? 'Oh, er, I don't know. He's only just recovering, so I haven't got into any of that yet.'

'But he's fully back – he's himself?'

I don't want to disappoint this puppy-like woman. 'Err, yes, he will be, I hope.'

'But what did his doctors say? Exactly.'

I don't want to jinx Calder by being too positive or bring bad luck on us by being too negative. 'It's all very positive but I don't know the details yet. It's early days.'

'Well, how do you feel?' She holds her phone up to my face.

I've seen journalists asking these stupid leading questions so often. Like when the Rangers' manager is asked whether he feels pleased with their huge win. And I always used to laugh with Calder: 'What's he going to say, I wonder!'

'I'm so happy,' I trot out on cue.

'And how did you feel when you thought he was dead?'

I stare at her, but she just smiles and nods, prompting me to give a suitable sound bite. Can she not hear herself? But however crass she is, it's like with the nurses – I don't want to disappoint. 'It was awful, of course it was. I thought I'd lost him. But he's back. It's a miracle.'

The word ignites her excitement further. 'Absolutely. A modern miracle in a secular age.'

'I guess.'

'And what's your name?'

'Nancy. Nancy Ryan.'

'And you're Calder's "partner" you said.'

'Yes.'

'Not wife?'

'No.'

'And what is it you do?'

'I'm a film script editor,' I say, instantly feeling like I'm lying, as I've only just started doing this.

'Oh,' she says, perked up by the hope that I'm famous. 'Would I know your work?'

'I'm working on a *Frankenstein* reboot at the moment. I . . .' Her face positively glows at this and I realise that it was stupid to mention it, given the sensationalist twist it could lend to our story. Everything's so fragile right now and I worry my words could bring Calder's delicate recovery crashing down.

'I'm sorry, I have to go,' I say, standing abruptly and walking away.

'Can I do a follow-up with you later?' she pants after me.

'Umm, yeah sure, I guess.'

I need to hold my knowledge of Calder's experience inside me, as if I am the only one who can keep him safe, as if others knowing, or me getting it wrong, will tip his heart off-kilter again. Everything's so fragile, I dare not put a foot wrong.

I'm tense with too much coffee the next morning as I walk to the hospital, unnerved at what I've set in motion with my chat with Fiona the journalist. That local paper piece she wrote got instantly picked up by the nationals and Calder's all over the internet. The hospital press office has got involved and I'm letting them deal with it all from now on. The headlines are all so over the top:

MAN COMES BACK FROM THE DEAD.
MIRACLE MAN BREATHES AGAIN.
TREACHEROUS WHIRLPOOL REGURGITATES MAN.

And the one I hate most is copied from Fiona's paper to one of the red tops:

FRANKENSTEIN LIVES!!!

Why did I have to mention my work to that woman. The reference doesn't even really work. Frankenstein was the name of the doctor in the book, not the creature. And anyway, Calder isn't some ghastly monster. He's my lovely husband; these hacks can't have him as their hyped-up horror story.

As I walk towards the hospital entrance, I see a group of journalists lolling outside and a camera crew. Fiona spots me and makes a beeline.

'Nancy, Nancy, over here.' This alerts the other journalists, who swarm towards me.

'Mrs Campbell!'

'Over here, Nancy.'

'What did your husband see on the other side?'

'Did his life flash before him?'

'What pulled him back? Does he have a message for us?'

I lower my head and force my way through, refusing all interview requests.

Calder is sedated all morning, so I huddle in my grey waiting area away from the circling vultures.

In the afternoon, I'm called in to him. I walk towards the door and see him through the glass. He's sitting up and his mouth's moving. Oh my God, he's actually talking with Dr Viner, being watched by several of the staff. Everything's going to be all right. I haven't jinxed him with my loose mouth.

I push the door and walk forward.

Dr Viner glances over to me, which makes Calder look.

I give him a tentative smile.

He sees me and gives a tiny nod, his eyes . . . wary?

'Nancy,' he says quietly as I reach him. To hear him say my name is incredible. But he's so fragile, so distant, like a rare elfin life form from *Lord of the Rings*.

'Hey, Calder,' I say, aware that everyone's watching us. 'I'm so glad you're back.' He almost seems to wince; must be some sort of muscle spasm.

'Are you OK?' I ask, feeling a weird formality with this man I know so well.

'I'm all right,' he rasps.

I shiver with the thrill of his lovely voice, gravelly though it is, and reach out to touch his hand, which is bruised and scarred. From all the drips? I don't remember the state of his hands when we got him out of the water. He frowns, stretching the yellowy-blue bruise over his right temple.

'I've been with you the whole time,' I blurt. 'Well, waiting out there.'

'Thank you,' he croaks, then looks down.

I look around and smile at everyone. I'm ashamed not to be providing some storybook moment of our first words for the assembled staff. Calder keeps looking down. I'm so deflated, I burst into tears. But now everyone else smiles. They must think I'm overcome with joy? God, that stupid confession I made to the priest – I feel like Calder has heard me and now can't look at me. No. That's ridiculous. He's gone through hell. How selfish that I'm thinking about me at this moment. He's back.

106

It's a miracle. I'll fulfil all my promises. I'll be strong and pure, totally focused on doing the right thing for him.

Calder suddenly moans and twists away from me.

'Does he need more pain relief?' I ask.

'Do you?' Dr Viner asks Calder, like an interpreter.

Calder shakes his head at Dr Viner, leaning away from me.

'You've been through so much,' I blurt. 'When Arran and I found you in the water—'

He sighs.

'But you're here now. I'm so happy.'

Calder makes a vague wave in my direction, as if to say 'enough'. He's so not one for public displays of affection, that must be what's happening here. But he was talking to Dr Viner when I came in, so it's disconcerting that he's monosyllabic with me.

'And thank God for these brilliant doctors who got you back.'

Calder slumps back and his eyes fill with tears. I lean down and caress his face, tears pouring down mine. He must be so happy he's back. Though he doesn't look happy. He looks . . . distraught?

The nurses are beaming at us. I'm finally creating the proper happy scene for them, but am I really connecting with Calder? His deep-brown eyes that I know so well are bloodshot, lined and yellow. But that isn't what's unnerving. His 'him-ness' feels so far away. Like I'm trying to see him down the end of a long pipe and I can't quite focus on him, as he's so far away.

I nod and smile at him, to try to find our click.

I think I see it for a moment and then his eyes flick down.

'I need to rest,' he mumbles.

I jerk backwards. 'Yes, of course. You must be so tired. I'll be here. Well, just out there. As soon as you're rested, you let me know, and I'll come back.'

He nods and looks back to Dr Viner.

'OK, Calder, we're going to do some more investigations on your muscles and neural pathways, I . . .' The swarm of staff re-form around him and I back away, clearly not needed.

I go back to my familiar waiting area and slump. Patience. He's back. That's the only thing that matters. Why did I think this would be some instant rising from the dead? Of course this is going to take time, but eventually, he'll come back to me.

Won't he?

The next morning, Calder's sitting up and looks more alert. And we're finally not being watched by any staff.

'Hey,' I say.

And he . . . sighs?

'Are you OK?'

He nods. 'You don't need to keep asking me that,' he rasps.

'Sorry, I'm doing it for me, I guess. It's just so amazing to hear you.'

He nods and looks down.

How are we so tongue-tied?

'Is there anything I can do? That I can get you?'

He shakes his head.

I squirm in my uncomfortable new cotton knickers which are cutting into me, pull up my badly fitting new jeans and scratch at the neck of my huge green and pink sale jumper, which isn't warm enough for outside but is suffocating in the hospital heating. I'm desperate to embrace Calder, to connect, and feel awkward perched on the side of his bed, with the nurses glancing at us through their glass window. Selfish again. It's brilliant they can see him all the time in case he needs them.

'Do you remember anything from what happened?' I blurt, instantly ashamed that I've let myself be prompted by those stupid journalists' questions.

'What?'

'Sorry, I just, I've been waiting, hoping, praying for so long. Did you – were you aware of anything going on through all that time? Could you hear the doctors talking?'

'It's all a total blank,' he says in an exhausted tone.

I nod furiously. What am I doing? 'Of course. Maybe that's for the best.'

He's silent.

'Sorry.'

'I'm sorry, Nance,' he blurts, 'I need to tell—'

'Could you move to a chair?' a nurse asks as she comes in. 'I have to do some tests.'

'Yes, of course,' I say, leaping up and feeling in the way.

She takes ages, reading his blood pressure, taking a blood sample, checking his drips. Finally, she leaves and I pull my chair up close.

'What were you going to say?'

'When?'

'Before? You sounded like you were going to tell me something before that nurse came in?'

He shakes his head.

'Was it about that morning? I guess you must have got up really early to go out in your boat?'

'I told you, I don't remember anything,' he sighs, descending into coughing. 'It's all a blank.'

'From when?'

He narrows his eyes. 'From when we went to bed the night before. Then nothing.'

I swallow. 'Dr Viner said you might have some retrograde amnesia about that last day. Because of the lack of oxygen to your brain.'

'I know.' He takes a huge, exhausted breath.

Oh God, he looks so frail. I want to transfuse my energy into him. I scratch a red patch of eczema that's flared on my neck. I haven't had it since my parents' deaths. 'I'm sorry, of course. I'm just trying to piece things together in my head.'

'It's all a blank,' he says dully.

We sit in silence. What was he going to say?

I want to distract him, to cheer him up, so I reach for the bundle of papers in my bag. 'You're a bit of a star, you know. You made the papers. With your miracle recovery.'

'Oh God no,' he sighs, waving me away.

I let my bag fall.

He's so exciting to the public, a hopeful story of survival against all the odds, Jonah from the belly of the whale. But the print story is so simple and clear: he died and then he lived again – the reality is so much greyer. I look down and pull at a thread from his sheet. What should I say? My lovely Calder. I want to reach him, to help him, but I know I'm being too much with all my questions.

'I need to rest,' Calder says. And he's closed his eyes before I'm even standing.

'OK. Love you. I'll be right outside.'

I lean down to kiss his cheek but he doesn't respond and I feel like a maiden aunt kissing an unwilling nephew. But he just needs rest. His health is my only priority. Yet I can't help the thought that's rumbling around my head, like a loose pound coin in a washing machine: why was he out on the water that morning, after he promised me he'd be careful? Why didn't he tell me he was going out? Leave a note? Obviously, I'm being obsessive. I've been given so much by getting him back. I have to let my confusion drop. He's clearly really unwell. I need to look forward, not back. Calder's needs are paramount, not my endless need for everything to be explained.

But that loose coin keeps jangling.

It's a week after the accident and Calder is propped up in a high-backed hospital chair, scrolling through his phone. He's able to shuffle to the toilet on his own now and sit up for several hours at a time. We're sitting in silence. How quickly ecstasy turns to everyday routine. I thought I'd be dancing on air for ever. Now I'm . . . a bit bored. Selfish again. He's lost a lot of weight and his cheekbones are heightened. His long black hair is loose around his shoulders and though he looks like himself when he's silent, when we talk I feel on edge and . . . so formal still. This quiet coexisting is easier.

A young woman in tight trousers and a white T-shirt flings open the door and bounces into his room, ponytail swinging.

Calder smiles at her.

Why doesn't he smile for me like that?

'OK, Calder, it's that time again,' she trills.

Calder smiles a 'doh' smile. With far more lightness than he's been aiming at me.

'Sorry, Nance, it's time for my physio. I have to go.'

'Hi, I'm Christy,' says the perky woman, giving me a half-hearted nod and then flashing her wide smile at Calder again.

'Oh, of course. Shall I come? Perhaps I can learn some of the—'

Calder waves his hand. 'No. It'll just be boring for you. You relax. I'll see you later.'

'Sure.'

They shuffle off and I walk towards my familiar cocoon, the grey waiting area.

Dr Viner stops me in the corridor. 'Hi Nancy. Calder's making excellent progress, Christy says he's doing brilliantly.'

'Yes, thanks. I guess everything seems to be mending?'

He nods. 'We're very pleased with his progress. There may be some ongoing minor injuries, but the human body, and in particular the brain, is surprisingly plastic and, if necessary, can make new neural pathways to get to the same place. He'll be home before you know it. He's made a truly stunning recovery.'

'Great,' I say weakly as he sweeps away.

I can't say it to anyone, but I'm nervous of Calder coming home. He still seems so far from himself. How will I cope? With his physical and mental needs. Is this going to be a case of us having to get to know each other anew, because his personality has changed so much? Which it so has. Everyone else seems to think everything's just fine and dandy, whoop-di-doo. I'm such a selfish cow to be ungrateful, but I know he's changed a lot. Maybe it's temporary? But even if it is permanent, I can adjust. Happiness is relative, I remind myself. I thought I was unhappy in London when we couldn't get pregnant – but compared to Calder being dead, that was bliss. I mustn't make the same mistake of wishing away these good times. Things might not be perfect – but they're amazing, stupendous, undreamt of, compared to when his lifeless body rolled onto my legs in Arran's boat. I focus on this sensible logic and try to lean into it, willing it to be enough.

Ten days after the accident and I'm sitting by Calder's bed while he sleeps. I need someone to tell me that everything's going to be OK. Dr Viner is positive but keeps parroting his 'wait and see' and 'outcomes are variable'; Janey has her airy-fairy slogans to 'manifest the positive'; and Gina employs work speak, saying I should 'embrace difference and change my parameters'.

With his eyes shut, he looks like my old Calder. His thin, veined eyelids suddenly flutter. What's he dreaming about? Am I in his dreams? I don't seem to be much in his thoughts during his waking hours. He seems almost . . . a stranger. I pull myself forward in my chair at the sacrilege of this thought. But the feeling is so strong. It's been growing with every day, trying to push forward from a sensation to a thought. And each day I scold myself and jump away from the idea: how dare I be dissatisfied with him?

Of course he's him.

He has the same brown eyes under those flicking eyelids. He has that same uneven chickenpox scar on his forehead. He has that same single curling eyebrow on the right which flicks up from the rest and which I used to always want to pluck, but which I have grown to love.

Of course he's him.

He has the same arching fingernails, with perfectly showing cuticles, that my stubby-nailed self has always admired. He has the same hairy arms that used to hold me so tight. He has the same broad shoulders that carried our IKEA furniture up four floors to our flat to make our lovely London nest of a home.

Of course he's him.

He has the same smell, that woody musk that relaxes me, makes me tingle all over and erases the physical boundary between our bodies as I melt into him. I lean forward, till my face is so close I could lick the tip of his nose, and try to breathe in the old him. It's sort of there . . . but there are such heavy notes of disinfectant, medicine and sickness overlaying his essence.

I return to my blurry phone scrolling, checking all the news feeds for more Calder stories, researching his condition, and investigating whirlpools. Was Calder's dad sucked into a whirlpool? If so, why wasn't Calder more careful if he knew about them? But I can't ask any of that now. It's hard to let go of what happened that night. Calder broke his promise to me just after making it, and it feels so out of character. I've always known that he is one hundred per cent 'in my corner'. We've bickered, of course, but that bedrock of trust was so absolute, and now it feels . . . cracked. I know it's only one small broken promise and then a terrible accident, but why did he do it? I read more about whirlpool myths and find one about a hag goddess of winter who washed her woollen tartan in the whirlpool 'washtub' till it was pure white, and then spread it to dry on the mountaintops as snow. That's exactly what's happened to Calder. His memory has been washed to pure white.

Suddenly, he opens his eyes.

'What?' he barks.

I realise I'm too close to him and staring. I jerk back. 'I was just checking on you.'

'I'm fine.'

Where's the 'him' in those eyes? I can't see him in there at all, can't reach him, can't feel our click. Maybe he thinks I'm annoyed about him going out in his boat when he promised me he wouldn't?

'This wasn't your fault,' I say quietly.

'What?' he croaks.

'I know you promised me you'd be careful. And then you went out alone without telling me. But I'm not annoyed, just so happy you're back.'

'I know. I don't deserve you.' He's getting choked up and I lean in to hug him.

Oh my God, finally some connection. 'I'm sorry. I didn't mean to upset you. I love you so much.'

But after a few seconds of clinging to me, he pulls back. 'Can you get me a tea?'

'Umm. Yeah, of course. From the canteen?'

'If that's OK?'

'Sure.'

That was so abrupt. Does he really want tea, or does he just want me out of the room?

* * *

115

As I'm walking back to his room, the paper cups scalding my hands, I stop for a moment to put them down on a low table covered in leaflets. I slump in the chair next to them. What's the matter with me? Calder's been through so much. He 'died'. He's been in a coma. Who knows where he's been? What he's experienced? I must try to help him.

'All right, Mrs Campbell, can I give you a hand?' a nurse asks as she passes.

'I'm fine, thanks.' I don't correct the usual marriage assumption. What does it matter? Or does it? I have to show Calder how much I love him. I pull my long scratchy sleeves down to protect my hands and make my way back with the cups. There's a whole big world outside us, but there was a massive rich world between us before, complex and infinite. And I want it back. Some greater power, God or whatever, gave Calder back to me and I need to push us into our future so we can outrun our past. Calder needs me to know I'm totally there for him, however different he is now.

He reaches out for a cup as I enter, but I put them down on the side table.

He frowns.

I go down on one knee and smile up at him. 'Calder, I love you so much. I know you've gone through hell. I know this is all really hard for you. But I'm here for you. I'll always be here for you. Will you . . . marry me?'

He just stares at me. Shocked. Horrified?

The moment stretches. Embarrassingly.

I feel ridiculous kneeling on the floor, the nurses peering through the glass, so I stand up and start gabbling. 'I'm sorry. Is this too much? It's just everyone keeps calling

116

me your wife and I want to be. I want to show you how much I love you. How I'm in this with you, whatever happens.'

He's crying. The nurses are looking worried.

'Forget it,' I blurt. 'That was really dumb.'

He shakes his head. 'No. We have to try to get through this,' he says dully. 'We have to at least try. OK. Yes. Let's get married when we're back on the island.'

I stare at him, disconcerted by his flat reaction, but I lean down and hug him. We're getting married. But I feel like I've forced him into this.

We have to try to get through this?

Through what? His recovery? The strange distance between us?

We have to at least try?

Breakfast is my favourite moment of the day now. So far, I've had nine breakfasts here at the hotel. I look forward to it when I go to sleep and miss it as soon as it's over. My hotel life is the only reliable, controllable thing in my life any more. This morning I'm eating early-served eggs, yolks still runny and rich, bright red plump tinned tomatoes which explode when pierced, two sausages, cheap and bready and which remind me of family breakfasts when my parents were still alive, one piece of fried bread, so greasy the oil dribbles down my chin, and two perfectly toasted toasts and jam, crisp and sweet with perfection. I savour every look, aroma, sound, taste and texture.

DEAD MAN TO MARRY is the headline on the top of my pile of papers this morning, after a nurse fed the vultures our happy news from yesterday. FROM COFFIN

TO ALTAR reads another. And in a third there's a picture of me looking exhausted in Fiona's rag, with the headline BRIDE OF FRANKENSTEIN. Cheers for that Fi. It's cheap and crass, and also wrong, as Dr Frankenstein's wife Elizabeth was killed by the monster after the doctor destroyed the female mate he was fashioning for him. It's unnerving to be compared to a bride who was murdered on her wedding night.

After breakfast, I wander back to my bedroom on the third floor, which is pleasingly tidy and calm. Everything is arranged and clean: my ever-increasing number of new comfortable clothes in colour and size order, my notebooks of research about Calder's condition and my growing to-do lists. I've finally mastered the thermostat in my square room and I lie down on my lovely square purple bed in a well-fed, well-heated stupor till it's time to nerve myself up for the hospital again.

The hotel is my favourite place now. My second favourite place is my grey-chaired, oh-so-familiar hospital waiting area. The room containing Calder, my future husband, is third.

'So, Calder, do you remember anything from when you were clinically "dead"?'

He's smiling as he's interviewed on a balcony at the hospital. It's a five-minute clip with him and Dr Viner that's gone viral and has already had half a million clicks and counting. I've watched it over and over. Staring at Calder's eyes. Listening to his voice. Trying to find 'him'.

Calder laughs. 'No. I guess that's what being dead is. Not being.'

'So, what's the last thing that you do remember?'

How come I'm not allowed to ask about that kind of stuff?

'Going to bed the night before – everything else is totally wiped.'

'And how are you feeling now?'

'I'm still a little unsteady walking, due to nerve ending damage,' Calder says, the camera panning back to show his whole body, 'but other than that I'm totally myself.'

How can he say that? Is he so lacking in self-awareness? Or am I mad?

'And it's all thanks to Dr Andrew Viner here.'

Calder smiles at Dr Viner, who smiles back as he comes into shot, looking stylish in a beautifully cut suit.

Why do your eyes seem to light up more for him than me, Calder?

'It was a very tricky procedure,' Dr Viner says. 'We were in uncharted territory. But we got him back.'

Oh, we're still in those strange waters, lads, you two are both just faking it.

'We used to think of death as a moment in time,' continues Dr Viner. 'But this kind of case makes us realise that death is a process, not a clear end point, like it used to be regarded. And if it's a process, we can step into and change the course. It's very exciting for medicine. This kind of case shows us that extreme cold can be helpful for anyone who has a heart attack or whose body stops functioning for whatever reason. They can be cooled down with ice blankets, and the extra time we buy while they're "in limbo" lets us try to help them back to health.'

Yes, yes, you and your processes. I know that Calder's recovery is a process – I'm living it with him every day. And I'm trying so hard to have patience, but there's more warmth in that doctor/patient bromance than between Calder and me nowadays. I feel like my Calder did have a clear end point. When his boat overturned.

And he never came back.

It's two weeks since the accident, and I'm back at my lovely Premier Inn the night before Calder is being sent home. I'm using my little complementary sewing kit to mend a tear in one of my T-shirts and I suddenly prick my finger. A perfect sphere of blood blossoms on my fingertip. Sleeping Beauty was put to sleep for a hundred years by a needle prick. Lucky cow. She got to wake up to her perfect prince. I wish I could zone out until Calder's properly back. Or is there no sleep long enough for Calder to fully recover? I must just accept that he's changed permanently. His oxygen-less blood was pumped out and he had a whole body full of new blood pumped in, which brought his body back to life. But not him.

Whose blood, I wonder?

I give up on my sewing and start scrolling the TV channels aimlessly.

'But he's not the same,' says a pretty young woman to a white-coated hunk.

I stop scrolling abruptly.

'Of course he is,' the doctor replies. 'He's just got a new heart, he's still your boyfriend.'

They both look down at a heavily bandaged man in a hospital bed.

What is this? I click the info button. *Change of Heart* is the title of the film: *When eighteen-year-old Dean is involved in a horrific motorbike crash, his life is saved by a heart transplant. But when he wakes up, his girlfriend Trish is convinced something is very wrong!*

It's US teen drivel, but I move down the bed, rapt.

Dean proceeds to strangle the family cat and terrorise the neighbourhood kids.

'It's like there's someone else in his body!' Trish cries. 'Why can no one else see it?'

I'm transfixed, on tenterhooks about how this film will end.

Trish finally has enough of Dean's smouldering dark stares and casual violence, and breaks up with him. Good for her. I was impressed at how long she stuck it out.

The following murder rampage is horribly addictive. Dean's once fresh face is gone: now he has sunken cheeks, has taken up wearing thick black eyeliner, and he licks his lips a lot as he narrows his eyes. He strangles a homeless man in the park with a thin red rope; he strangles his mum's best friend with it next; and then he does it in triplicate, killing three squealing high school girls in their dorm late at night.

The fat local police chief is totally baffled by the uncanny similarities between these recent killings and a string of solved murders.

'How can it possibly be the same killer?' the chief drawls. 'That killer's dead. Executed two months ago.'

'But it's an identical red rope – and we never released that detail!' his confused underling exclaims.

And of course, it turns out that it was exactly two

months ago that good old Dean got his new heart – cut from the body of that executed killer. The deranged killer is living again in Dean's husk and continuing his murder spree.

I work my way through three little wine bottles and four beers from the mini bar, as I stay glued to the race to find Dean before he kills again. The police finally catch up with him in the school gym late at night, throttling the captain of the football team. Dean's old self rises up into his consciousness and battles with the killer's heart inside him. There are lots of double takes from Dean, rearing back, rolling his eyes upwards and hitting himself. I bet that extract went on the actor's showreel.

'Kill me now!' Dean screams at the assembled police, who all have their guns trained on him. But the fools hesitate. The killer's heart takes control again and he escapes through a convenient open window.

The total annihilation of Dean is clearly vital, for the residents of the town, for Dean himself and for the strung-out viewers of this film who can't believe they're still watching this tosh.

I'm exhausted and relieved when Dean's best friend discovers him trying to garrotte poor Trish in her bedroom.

'Shoot him!' screams the girl who once adored him. And the best friend obligingly opens fire, shooting Dean in the head. His brain splatters across a propped-up photo of him from before the accident. The old him from before the heart transplant. The smiling, fresh-faced 'real' him.

CHAPTER NINE

It's been fifteen days since I first stumbled into this hospital, chasing after Calder's gurney, sure that he would never leave it alive.

Now we're walking out together.

Dr Viner and his staff line either side of the corridor. The physio has done wonders and his walk is almost normal, if slightly John Wayne-esque. I follow with our bags. The staff are all clapping and beaming as Calder nods at each of them in turn and smiles broadly. It's like we're on a political walkabout after winning an election. As we reach the lifts, Dr Viner takes Calder's hand and gives it a firm double-handed shake, beaming at him like he's his long-lost son.

Then he turns to me. 'So, you've got everything?'

'Yep,' I say, tapping my bag full of the pills and monitors. Everyone else is happy. I'm clearly exhausted and catastrophising. Everything's fine. We just need to be alone together, to find the old us, or a new us. He's back, that's all that matters.

'And we'll be seeing you in a month for a check-up,' Dr Viner says, turning back to Calder. 'Contact us if anything changes. Anything at all. Got me?'

'Thank you,' Calder says warmly.

'Oh, come on now, it's I who should be thanking you. I'll be publishing papers galore and dining off you for years. No, seriously, it's been an honour to help you. While I know you've been through hell, we've had the chance to push the limits of medicine to the very edge and I would be lying if I didn't admit it's been . . . exhilarating.'

Everyone laughs. Except me. Even Calder laughs. Then he gives them all the wave of a departing hero, and we push through the swing doors. Back to our new life. Well, our new life Mark Two.

We get a taxi from the hospital to Glasgow Queen Street, to get the train up to Oban. Calder is quiet as I'm checking train times.

'You OK?' I enquire.

'Umm.'

'You look familiar,' calls the grey-haired taxi driver, looking at Calder in his mirror. 'Are you an actor?'

Calder glances at me, then lowers his eyes. His picture has been all over the papers, but I get he doesn't want any fuss.

'No, no, we were just here for . . . a brief visit, a little city break,' I say brightly, 'but we're back up to Oban and then to our home in Langer.'

'Bit of a trip ahead of you. But that's a great train

journey, amazing scenery. The wife and I try to make it at least once a year.'

'Yes, it's magical,' I agree, smiling at Calder.

But he's looking down.

It feels so bizarre to be out of the hospital on our own. I can't quite believe we've been let out and left to our own devices. Calder's been so heavily monitored every single day of the last two weeks, so assessed, so cared for, so protected. And I've become so used to the routines and rules of the hospital. Now I feel unsure of how to behave on our own.

I remember when I went to pick up Gina when she left the hospital with her first child.

'How are they letting me leave?' she'd cried. 'I don't know how to look after this fragile bird. I'll kill it. Thank God for nannies.'

That's how I feel with Calder, but I have no nanny, no support whatsoever. He's deemed OK to be with me alone, no carer needed. I feel weak at the responsibility, though Calder is physically fine. I'll probably never know that feeling of having a baby to look after. But thank God I don't have one, given what's happened. Calder will need all my attention.

At the station, I deposit Calder on the rigid seats facing the information boards and get us both coffees. Our train is up on the silver boards, but there's no platform number yet.

'I'm going out for a smoke,' Calder announces.

'You're smoking?' He hasn't smoked for two years. Since we started trying for a baby. 'Is that sensible?'

'Leave it,' he grunts as he walks off. He did all those

broad smiles for the hospital staff, but for me, grunts?

He comes back holding two packs of Benson and Hedges and smelling of fags. Seems stupid, but I must have patience. This is way more difficult for him than me; I must put his needs first.

Finally, Platform 4 comes up and then we're on the train to Oban. Stopping at so many unusually named stops along the way: Garelochhead – Arrochar and Tarbet – Ardlui – Crianlarich – Dalmally – Loch Awe. When we visited Isla that one time, we flew to Glasgow and hired a car. We've only done this train journey once before, when we moved here. But we're so different from that carefree couple. As if we're acting out the same scene, but in a different genre of film. We did the first journey in a romcom – bright colours, lots of funny dialogue, hugging and kissing. Now we're in a dark hyper-realistic indie film, everything grey and shadowy, silence, no contact, dour.

Calder is sitting opposite and absenting himself from me. He's not just being tetchy, he's utterly withdrawn, almost physically shrinking away from me.

'Bleak weather compared to last time,' I say, looking out at the overcast sky.

'Umm.'

The silence hangs between us.

'This must all feel so strange after your weeks in the hospital.'

'Umm.'

'Are you OK?'

'Umm.'

I catch an older couple sitting across the aisle from us

sharing a glance. Are they noting Calder's rudeness and detachment? Or do I seem like a henpecking wife? Is it him or is it me?

'Are you hungry?' I ask, as the woman looks down. 'The trolley's coming.'

'Three ham sandwiches,' he says to the concessions man. 'D'you want anything?'

'I'm fine.'

I watch him take apart the sandwiches, putting three lots of ham into one sandwich and eating the lot. I don't comment. Perhaps he's craving protein for his recovery?

'I'm just going to close my eyes,' he then murmurs, before slumping down in his seat.

'I—'

He closes his eyes immediately, so I look out the window. On this part of the journey last time, we took so many photos of each other against the stunning calendar-ready backdrops: the rolling hills, the regimented lines of firs, the fluffy sheep and the magical watery inlets. Calder had delighted in my awe.

We stop at Loch Lomond and the difference is especially extreme here. At this point in our earlier journey, Calder had hugged me tight as we stared at the glistening water together. Now he's hunched in his seat opposite, not beside me, with his eyes closed. There's a little island in the centre of the loch. It had looked so idyllic on the way up – now it looks cut off, isolated, like me.

My phone rings. It's Gina. I disconnect the call. I can't deal with her on top of everything.

Maybe Calder doesn't want to look at water as it reminds him of his accident? Even I can hardly face it, remembering plunging my hands into the sea to drag his lifeless body out. But we survived it all. We've been given a second chance. Of course Calder is closed off. I can't know what he's going through. I'm a person who sees red and green. Calder has red/green colour blindness. I was so shocked when he first explained that he sees one colour where I see two. How could his reality be so demonstrably different to mine? And now it's not just colours. I can't possibly know what he's been through, or see the world as he sees it. All I can do is be patient.

Under this overcast weather, the countryside is dulled. Even to me, it doesn't seem as picture-perfect as last time. I notice things I didn't see before: the wire netting holding up the banks, the power towers, the dark grooves between the undulations of the hills. Before the colours were sables and coffees, now they're grubby blacks and dried poo. The trees seemed ethereal and proud last time. Now they look twisted and grasping. The hilltops were sharply defined and snow-sprinkled, now they're blurred and shrouded in mist. As the train trundles on, I notice churned blackened earth, cut timber strewn like bodies and freshly planted trees with supporting sticks. Which look like war graves.

We're met at Oban station by Janey. She's waving frantically, at the far end of the long last-stop platform. She really is going above and beyond to help us. I only met her in the flesh once before. But maybe this is that island community warmth everyone goes on about.

'I'm so happy to see you both,' she says, beaming at us then hugging me. 'Calder, you gave us quite a scare.'

He nods, but doesn't speak.

'Come along then,' she says, leading us to an unfamiliar saloon car. 'I borrowed this from Arran,' she explains. 'I wasn't sure if Calder would need to lay out?'

'I'm OK,' he mumbles. 'But it would be good to lie down on the back seat, and have a kip.'

Janey busies herself getting Calder settled amongst all the pillows and blankets that she's brought, then I sit up front with her. We talk in hushed tones, although I don't think Calder's asleep. She glances at me, picking up the tension but staying upbeat.

'I'll drive you straight to the cottage, get you settled. We've got it all ready for you, stocked the fridge, given it a wash and brush-up.'

'We?'

'The church.'

'Oh right. Thanks. How did you get the keys?'

'Arran used his.' Of course he did. I'm embarrassed and put out that anyone's been in our cottage and that they thought it still needed cleaning despite all our efforts. But it will make our return easier. That's the plus side of a close community, I guess.

'How's things with . . . you know,' I whisper, thinking jealously of the obvious warmth I witnessed between Janey and Rob.

She shrugs. 'Ah, we had a bit of an argument the same night of Calder's accident. A lot of an argument. I didn't want to burden you when you asked before. But things have gone cold since then. For good, I think. But enough of us. This is your day of celebration.'

'I thought . . .'

'It's done,' she says with an uncharacteristically dark tone. They seemed so close when I saw them together. But what do I know about relationships any more?

She gives little glances back at Calder as we fall into silence. The drive takes half an hour, and then finally we're over the arched bridge and onto the island where we get the ferry. The burly men at the dock all nod at us with gruff warmth.

'Does everyone know what's happened?' I whisper.

'God yes. Calder is *the* subject of discussion on the island. In the pub, after church, on the local radio phone-in. He's a star.'

'Oh, cool.' I think of female peacocks and how dowdy, brown and small they are in comparison to the males with their massive tail displays. Of course, I'm the little brown peahen. That's as it should be. But I somehow feel even less chance of being accepted as an islander now. As we drive through the 'metropolis', everything is as quiet and reserved as usual, the roads empty. Thank God there's no fanfare for our arrival. I couldn't deal with loads of people today. We need to get settled in quietly. We drive under the long shadow of the church's cross and I swallow at the memory of my promises to be the perfect wife. Of course, I'm going to help Calder in every way I can. Because I love him. But also because I've made my pact. If I fail, Calder will be taken again. It's irrational, but it feels so real. Arran is right, I'm making a truth with my focus. But I feel like I'm somehow part of something bigger than me on this island.

Finally, we round the last curve and the track becomes uneven as we crunch down the drive to our cottage.

And, oh God help me.

The cottage is hung with coloured bunting. There are trestle tables in front with bright red tablecloths, all groaning under the weight of acres of food. And lined up on either side of the cottage . . . are the entire village, with a row of older men in front dressed in suits. What fresh hell is this? Right, game face on. We emerge from the car and there's an enormous cheer. Calder is clearly unnerved, but he smiles and shakes hands with people. I turn away from his sudden switch in mood. This being upbeat for others is grating when he's so sullen with me.

'You OK?' Janey asks.

'I'm fine, just tired. Who are those old men?'

'The church elders,' she whispers. 'You're being honoured.'

I really can't face all this, but I must buck up and be grateful.

'That's . . . amazing. And thanks so much for collecting us from the station and doing all this. You've been so supportive of me all this time and you didn't even tell me you were having your own problems.'

'Oh but you were dealing with much bigger things. We were dealing with the same old same old.'

'What happened?'

She pulls me further aside. 'That night of Calder's accident, I told Rob I wanted to start being open about us on the island, 'cos I hate all the sneaking around. But, he was droning on about his ex, Alison, repeating that old crap about how she said she'd kill him if he set foot on the island again, and I lashed out and said I'd kill him if he didn't make it publicly clear he was visiting me here.

He said I was being just as manipulative as Alison used to be – which really set me off 'cos I'm nothing like that vindictive shrew.'

I'm shocked by the intense anger coming off this usually tranquil woman.

She glances at me and collects herself. 'Anyway. We went at it. He stomped off just before dawn and I haven't heard from him since.'

'Have you tried to call him?'

'No point,' she says darkly.

'I'm so sorry.'

'Ah well, maybe I was asking too much. Alison turned the island against him. And I think he's just too broken by her and losing Caitlin for a real relationship. There's no chance now. Oh watch out,' she squawks, looking beyond me. 'Saint incoming! I'll catch up with you soon OK.'

I turn round into the tall intensity of Arran.

'God brought him back to us,' he says, his blue eyes blazing.

'Well, you and me, and then the doctors – but yes all right, God too,' I say, feeling tears welling.

Arran smiles. 'It wasn't his time.'

We stare at each other, both remembering. I feel so connected to him. I remember breathing into Calder's lips after Arran had breathed into them as we tried to bring him back. I put my hand on his chest, recalling him telling the paramedics to keep trying. 'Thank you for not giving up on him,' I choke out. And without thought, I suddenly reach out and hug him. He's stiff at first and then he hugs me back and I feel the memory of what we went through jolt between our bodies. He's slimmer than Calder, yet he feels more substantial to me right now. We hold each other for several seconds and then release each other awkwardly.

'You were so brilliant out there. How can I ever thank you?' I gush.

He blushes, his fair skin blooming red. 'Ah no. It was God's will. D'you want a drink?' He gestures to the piled bottles and kegs.

'I – yeah.' It's not like Calder and I will be trying for a baby any time soon. 'Are pastors allowed to drink?'

'Are you kidding?' he laughs.

I take the bottle he offers me, and we clink and drink. The cool, dark liquid ignites my insides. Somebody starts playing a fiddle, and there is a growing hubbub of chatter. I see Calder surrounded by friends. Laughing. I guess he feels he must put in some effort for them?

'Another?' Arran asks, holding out a second bottle as I realise I've already downed the first.

'Totally.'

With his piercing blue eyes and weather-beaten good looks, he's a striking man. The pretty pastor. I register a wordless connection between us. I guess it's the shared bond of an extreme experience. It seems to highlight just how far I've slid from Calder.

'Anyway, I'm glad Calder's OK. Things were – pretty intense out there that day.'

'Yep.'

'Well, I better go,' he mumbles, 'tend to my flock and all that.'

'Thank you, Arran,' I say, squeezing his arm.

He leans in and kisses the top of my head. Then he nods at me abruptly and turns.

I walk over to the edge of the cliff and look out at the sea. As if in honour of Calder's return, the weather is now glorious. The scene is picture-perfect: the steep hills, the ins and outs of the coastline, no outline identical yet with a rightness to the lack of symmetry. And the sea is sparkling like it's been photoshopped for a Scottish tourist board ad.

Look at me, it seems to say, so perfect, so light, so innocent. But you know. Don't you?

Whoosh. Drag. Whoosh. Drag.

I hear the slates being dragged back each time the waves pull in from the shore. I'm momentarily alone in the sound, tuned out of the party behind me. Hearing is an act of will, of focus. I did a documentary for Radio 4 on the 'cocktail party effect' – the way you can be at a busy cocktail party and at first you hear a wall of sound, but gradually you can choose to tune into individual conversations around you, because there's a psychological choice to which of them you hear, and as you choose one, the previous one recedes. Calder has chosen to stop hearing me. He's tuned into everyone else's energies, but not mine.

I look back towards the party and once more I hear all the laughter, the clinking of glasses, the shouts of children.

If I can tune back into these sounds, surely Calder can tune back into me?

CHAPTER TEN

As the last car crunches up the drive, I am finally alone with Calder. Just us. No hospital staff, taxi drivers, train passengers or islanders. We blink at each other across the loud silence. This was what I dreamt of through those endless days at the hospital.

Calder turns and walks into the cottage and Attila trots after him, tail waving, to stake her claim on him.

'Yep, Daddy's home,' I announce.

But she stops dead, as Calder reaches down to her. She arches her back and hisses, fur standing on end. Then she slowly lowers to the floor, razor-focused on Calder.

'What's up with her?' I ask.

Calder frowns as he sinks into a kitchen chair. 'She's just annoyed I've been away.'

But Attila shifts her weight back and forth, on high

alert, her ears flattened back like she's in a wind tunnel, making a low gurgling moan.

'What's she doing?'

'Silly thing,' he says, rubbing his fingers together. 'Here, I'm back now.'

A yowling erupts from her as she springs, paws outstretched. She lands on his arm, sinking her claws and teeth into his hand.

He yelps as he shakes her off, and she bolts out the front door.

'What the fuck?' Calder shouts, rubbing the long red scratches on his arm as he moves to the bathroom. He closes the door and, for the first time in the five years I've lived with him, he locks it.

What just happened? Attila loves Calder. Or she did, *before* the accident.

So, it's not just me that senses it. Attila knows he's changed too.

Eventually Calder walks out, drying his arm.

'Shall I put some antiseptic on that?'

'Don't fuss,' he mumbles, turning away.

I start unpacking one of our bags. 'God, it's such a relief that we're finally alone together,' I say.

'I need to lie down,' he mumbles, stumbling back to the bedroom.

I follow and notice how tidy the bedroom is. Not a speck of dust anywhere, freshly laundered bedding, clothes washed and folded. Calder pulls off his trousers and falls onto the bed. A shaft of light falls on the bedside table, across an artfully arranged pile of slate pebbles. Whoever put them there moved my little glass waterfall sculpture back. It's a silly tourist knick-knack, but I love it. On our first weekend away together in the Lake District to visit some famous rapids, Calder caught me eyeing them in a shop that overlooked the water.

'Oh no, they're tat,' I'd laughed.

'I'm tat, and you picked me,' he'd smirked, as he took it to the till.

'Sleep well,' I murmur now, as I lean down to kiss him. But I can't reach his mouth, which is pressing onto the pillow, so I kiss the side of his forehead awkwardly.

Returning to the kitchen, I register new curtains and that the windows are now scrubbed clean, the eye drawn beyond them to the sea instead of faltering on the grimy surface. I spin round. The pans are gleaming, the crockery spotless and when I drag it open, I see that our coffin of a fridge is stuffed with milk and juice, pies and flans, vegetables, yoghurts, sausage rolls and steaks.

Down the centre of the now scrubbed and oiled kitchen table is a long line of identically sized slate pebbles.

I stumble to the bathroom to splash cold water on my face. Every surface is shiny and clean. And along the edge of the bath is another row of slate pebbles. They're exquisite and someone has taken a lot of time arranging these slates all around the cottage. But to me, it feels like the cold sea has slithered into our home. I got Calder back from its clutches, but the waves have left their shingle everywhere, to remind us of their power.

I stay awake all night, occasionally creeping in to look at Calder, who I find sleeping next to our bed, on the cold hard floor. When he's stressed, he often sleeps on the floor. No cushions, nothing to ease him, as if he finds it soothing.

I sit in the kitchen, heaters blaring, watching Attila sleeping on Calder's stiff hiking rucksack, by the draughty door. She's draped herself across the lumps and folds of the angular blue bag, relaxing over the awkward zips and ties, melting into the sharp edges pushed up by Calder's files, as if it were the softest bed. Janey said that Attila was from a litter raised on an old rucksack. So, horribly uninviting though it appears to me, Attila must be comforted by it. Our hard, unforgiving floor must calm Calder similarly. Did Isla make him sleep on the floor?

I try to sleep in the lounge, but am so painfully aware that this should have been my first night sleeping with Calder again. Of course he needs space – but we're usually so physically connected and I feel, felt, such a wordless ease when I touched him.

I've barely slept as daylight breaks. Eventually Calder gets up, but he's monosyllabic. He eats a whole packet of bacon, barely frying it so it's fatty and gelatinous. What's up with all this meat eating? The morning crawls by. He chain-smokes and mainlines coffee. We always used to share a companionable silence together, my head on his lap as I read a book, while he watched one of his drug cartel or undercover cop shows with a million episodes, using his headphones. We would slide in and out of our connection, getting drinks, cooking, making calls, always pulled back into each other's force fields, slotting together again organically.

Now we sit in our austere lounge across from each other, him on the settee, smoking, me in the deep armchair, brooding. I don't like this separation. I uncurl, walk the few steps over to sit on the floor beside him, and lean my head against his thigh. We hold this position rigidly for a few unbearable seconds, then he eases his thigh out from under my head and walks to the kitchen.

I find him sitting at the table, bent over his laptop, his hair obscuring his face.

'What are you doing?' I ask, determined to connect.

'Just accounts,' he mumbles.

'But you're only just back from the . . . hospital.' I stop myself from saying 'from the dead'.

'I haven't been in contact with clients for ages. They'll go to someone else for their loft extensions if I don't keep in contact.'

'People will understand. And anyway, nobody else does them here.'

'They'll use the mainland. God, I can't find anything,' he snaps.

'Can I help?' I say, reaching for the laptop.

He slams the lid down, almost catching my fingers. 'Will you stop fussing?'

'I'm not fussing,' I say, my voice catching. 'But I can help you with admin. And I could get you decaf coffee and some patches for the smoking.'

'You are fussing,' he snaps. 'I don't want to stop smoking or to drink weak piss.'

He stands and for the first time since I've known him, his physical presence is daunting. He's bristling with anger, like he's having to hold himself back from hitting me.

'But your heart. Isn't it sensible to slow down, to be careful . . .'

'Stop it!' he shouts. 'Ever since my accident, you're doing

everything for me. I'm not a baby. It's so claustrophobic.'

I feel like I've been slapped. 'I know it's been hellish for you. Well, I don't know really. But I've been there through it all, by your side. I know it's been a billion times worse for you, but I'm so worn out by the horror of it all. I thought you were dead.' I burst into tears.

He shoves his laptop aside and steps towards me, towering over me. Then he blinks. It's like the moment at the end of that stupid heart transplant film, as if the old him is battling with the new him. 'I know it's been awful for you. I know that,' the old him says, his voice cracking. 'I—' But then it's like the new him takes over and he's walking past me towards the door. 'I'm off to the village,' he announces.

'OK, I'll get my stuff,' I say, wondering why he's calling it the village when we always used to call it the metropolis.

'No. Just me.'

'Oh.'

'I need a bit of time to myself,' he says quietly. 'Is that all right?'

'I . . . yes, of course.'

He scoops up his keys.

'But should you be driving?'

'God almighty. Why shouldn't I?' he barks.

'Because you've just been in hospital for two weeks. You nearly died.'

'But I didn't die,' he says darkly. 'Thanks to you.'

I freeze at his accusatory tone. 'What does that mean?'

'Nothing. See you later,' he says, as he slams the door.

He resents me for saving him? What's wrong with him? Dr Viner may have warmed up his blood, but he's

140

still frozen inside. I remember the feel of Calder's cold dead flesh as he rose from the sea. He was dead. Till they changed his blood. It's like that stupid film, as if that other blood has put a new person inside the body and face that I loved.

I wrench open the front door and rush outside, gulping fresh air. I have to move, to feel, to get away from that memory of Calder's cold dead flesh. I follow the path down to the shoreline and finally lower myself over a steep rock to get to the water, pulling off my socks and sinking my pasty white feet into the cool sea.

Everything is momentarily bright, clear and present. I wriggle my toes, thrilling with the sudden cold. I force my feet to stay in and run my hand over a vividly green patch of seaweed. I poke at the almost fluorescent slithery mass and pull a bit free. It shifts and spins, like a green water sprite, dancing and somersaulting as the sun plays on the water. The salty air enters my nostrils. The sun burnishes me. I just am. Beyond thought.

Then my phone ringtone slices through the thick silence. Thank God. Calder's ringing to say sorry. But the screen says it's Gina calling. I don't want to speak to her, but I can't keep avoiding her.

'Hi, I've been meaning to ring you,' I say brightly.

'It's me,' says that voice.

I tense. 'Hamish? Why are you ringing from her phone?'

'She asked me to call you and I didn't think you'd answer if I rang you.'

'Is she listening?'

'No, she's bathing the kids.'

'We shouldn't be talking,' I say, closing my eyes.

'How's Calder?'

'He's . . . I don't know. He's physically well but . . . not himself. Why's Gina getting you to ring me and not doing it herself?'

'She's upset. Says she's trying to reach you but you won't take her calls?'

'I've had a lot on,' I say brusquely.

'I know. But I had to check if you were avoiding her because . . . of us?'

'You think?'

'Look. I'm so sorry. I take all the blame. I still can't believe that happened. I'm so, so sorry. I'm a terrible person. Scum. But you and Gina were so tight. She doesn't understand what's happening. I . . .'

'Have you ever submerged your feet into cold sea water?'

'What?'

'I'm doing it right now, trying to find some bloody moment of peace in all this. It feels like I'm being punished.'

'No, not at all. That's ridiculous, Nancy. Calder's accident wasn't connected to what we did. Just . . . bad luck.'

'How do you live with the guilt? I thought I could escape the feeling up here. But then Calder had this accident – and when he came back, I thought I'd been forgiven, but I seem to have lost him anyway.'

'What do you mean? Can I help? I'll do anything you need.' I can feel his genuine concern, his warmth, his care for me. So different to Calder nowadays.

'Oh God, Hamish, this all feels like a punishment for what we did.'

'What can I do?'

I'm appalled that I'm even finding it easier to talk to him, of all people, than to Calder. 'You're the last person who should help me.'

'But . . .'

I want to talk to him. To confide. But I can't jinx Calder's recovery.

'No. Please, Hamish. Go away.'

I disconnect the call and wriggle my toes frantically in the cool water. But the momentary sense of release has evaporated.

We all came from this cold sea, after years of evolution in response to the shifting climates. The sea is where we all started. And the sea took Calder back, but I dragged him out. Did I somehow break the natural order of life and death?

Whoosh. Drag. Whoosh. Drag.

The waves are taunting me: *I returned him to you. But you're so ungrateful. So willing to sin again. Do you want to throw him back?*

CHAPTER ELEVEN

There's a strong smell of frying meat as I stumble into the kitchen the next morning after dozing all night in the lounge again.

And there's Calder sitting bolt upright at the table. He's so thin, his cheeks hollowed out, his chest shrunken, his knuckles poking up on his sinewy hands. But most shocking is that he's wearing a dark suit, a shirt and tie. I've never seen him in a suit before. The most formal thing he'd usually wear is a jacket with an open-necked shirt.

'Is that your dad's?' I ask tentatively. 'What are you—?'

'I'm going to church this morning,' he announces as he stands, his eyes oddly glazed.

'Yeah right,' I laugh, turning away to fill the kettle.

He's so silent, I turn back.

'I'm going to the eleven o'clock service,' he says stiffly.

'Oh, OK, I guess we should show our faces – to thank them, you mean?'

'I can go alone. Don't come.'

I stare at him for a beat, expecting him to break into a grin and shout 'Psych!', but he looks down.

'No, I'll come. Give me a sec to get ready.'

I race upstairs and drag on my best jeans and a beautiful cream shirt that I save for posh parties. Of course he wants to go to church. He wants to thank the community for all they've done. I'm selfish for wanting to spend our first Sunday morning alone together. I should thank the community too. And there's my pact to be fulfilled.

A Cherokee thing from a Radio 4 documentary I made suddenly leaps to mind. About the battle between the two 'wolves' inside us all. One is evil: anger, envy, jealousy, regret and guilt. The other is good: joy, love, hope, compassion and truthfulness. 'Which wolf wins?' 'The one you feed.' I am feeding my panic about Calder. I need to get on board with this new life and feed a positive belief in him.

As I walk down the stairs, I see Calder glance up and frown at my outfit.

'What?'

'It's fine.'

'It's clearly not fine, what's wrong with this?'

He makes a face. 'It's really old-fashioned round here. Jeans? I don't care, but why cause ructions?'

'Sorry, I'll change.'

I feel stupid and told off. My only two dresses are scrunched up and unwearable. I pull out one of Calder's mum's flowered dresses from the packed boxes.

As I walk down, Calder nods as if to confirm 'better', like I'm an obedient wife.

As we approach the church, it's like we've rocketed back in time and entered a sepia photograph of the islanders from the last century. All the men are in suits. All the women are in dresses. Janey steps out from a group and embraces me.

'That dress is lovely on you,' she whispers. 'Isla would have been so pleased.' We walk up the steps and into the church. In the plain vestibule, I see rows of long grey raincoats, like I've seen Arran wearing – but all together, they look like ceremonial robes. Which was exactly what I thought the first time I saw him in the distance on the beach. As we push through the inner doors to the body of the church, I see that the men are all sitting on one side and the women on the other. I am shepherded over to the women's side. Calder moves to the men's side and sits staring straight ahead.

I haven't been to church since I went to Hamish and Gina's wedding, which was a grand affair in a pretty country church. Then, Calder kept digging me in the ribs at all the laughable religious talk in the ceremony. Where is that man now?

This church is much more austere but it has a simple beauty, with rows of dark pews, a dark wooden beamed ceiling, and hundreds of slate pebbles embedded along the walls. At the front is the famous altar, which is a massive piece of polished slate, topped with a huge slate cross. Above the altar is a stained-glass window of a wave, to one side is one of the Virgin Mary and to the other, Jesus in a boat at sea.

Arran steps to the front, dressed in a real long grey robe.

'Welcome to all.' He catches my eye and nods. 'We will sing Hymn number 124.' There is a long chord and then they start singing.

Eternal Father strong to save
Whose arm has bound the restless wave

Oh no – it's that 'peril on the sea' hymn.

Who bids the mighty ocean deep
Its own appointed limits keep
O hear us when we cry to Thee
For those in peril on the sea.

I can't sing, I'm totally choked. But on they go through the endless dirge till they reach the portentous end.

That evermore shall rise to Thee
Glad praise from air and land and sea

The long last note dies away. Then there's an eerie silence. I feel sick.

'Please be seated,' Arran says eventually, his vibrant blue eyes flashing. I glance over to Calder for his sarcastic smirk, but he's looking straight ahead. Rapt. I've only ever seen that look when we've been watching Rangers on TV.

'In accord with the flow of things,' I hear Arran saying,

recognising a phrase that Calder is always using, 'we return here each Sunday, and today our brother Calder has returned to us from the sea.' There is a moment of nodding and smiling as people turn to Calder, then back to Arran. 'Our community has lost many of our loved ones. Those who have left us for other places or have left us to return to God. We are but flotsam, floating on the sea, moving with the flow of the water. The sea took Calder, yet God, in his mercy, gave him back to us. We pray constantly to be saved from ourselves, from our sins. And now "The Saved" is here amongst us. Calder is a physical manifestation of God's forgiveness. We can all become "The Saved", if we are washed clean by the waves. Let us look to the slate cross and take a breath.'

Everyone stares ahead at the huge slate cross and breathes in. I can't stop myself complying.

'And we let it go.'

We all breathe out.

'And again. We shut our eyes and breathe in. Hold. And breathe out.'

I am swept along, feeling us all breathing as one, like a single organism.

'We breathe in with the wave surging onto the beach. And out, with the water dragging the slates back. The water washes over the slates. Cleaning them. In. And out. Feel the water washing over you. Surging onto the slates and washing them clean. Let us all have a moment of silent prayer as we feel ourselves being washed by God's mercy and being cleansed of our sins.'

Whoosh. Drag. Whoosh. Drag.

I feel heady and faint. He's talking directly to me.

I open my eyes. Everyone else has their eyes closed. Calder's hands are clasped in front of him, his fingers tightly entwined, his eyes screwed tight. He's praying? I'm embarrassed by his naked emotion. Affronted to be shut out of this conversation he's having with . . . God? How is my unmystical, prosaic boyfriend praying? It feels so dangerous. But how controlling of me that I can't bear him to have any kind of connection beyond me.

Finally, the praying comes to an end and Arran reads an interminable psalm about judgement and sin. I wake back up to the church as everyone is scrabbling in the backs of the pews in front of them.

'Take your slate and chalk and write down the sin you wish to be washed away,' Arran says, looking straight at me. I scrabble in the nook on the back of the pew in front and my hand catches on the sharp edge of a thin slice of slate. Everyone is scribbling away with their chalks. I find my chalk and hover it over my slate. What should I write?

The organ suddenly starts playing big heavy chords, and everyone stands up in unison. They file forward.

'I shouldn't,' I whisper to Janey, 'I'm not part of this.' But I see Calder walking forward ahead of me and then kneeling down with his slate. Calder kneeling? Janey pushes me in the small of my back and I shuffle forward, caught up in the flow. I glance at her slate and she's written anger. She senses me looking and surreptitiously turns the slate away.

'Your slate is bare, write something,' she whispers.

I scrawl IMPATIENCE quickly in capitals and shuffle forward. The row of kneelers in front of us stands up and my group takes their place. Arran moves along our row, pouring water on our slates and then wiping them clean with a white cloth – in a strange version of the communion service. I suddenly remember going to communion with my parents the day before their car crash. I remember the words the priest intoned as he poured the communion wine: 'The Blood of our Lord Jesus Christ keep you in everlasting life.' I remember all that new blood that Calder was given to bring him back to life. What happened to him that day?

I feel dizzy and look down. My slate is almost clean, but I see the curl of the final T still there. Not so easy to wipe away everything in one swoop, is it? 'Impatience' sounds like such a small sin. But I know just how big it can be. I feel faint, rocking on my knees as I remember my fatal impatience. My parents' crash wasn't an accident. I was sitting in the back of their car, bored and playing up: 'Are we there yet, I'm so hot!' I was shouting, swaying back and forth, hands aloft, and Dad took his eyes off the road to turn to me . . . and our car veered wildly into the path of an oncoming truck. I watched in slow motion as the front of the car folded in like foil. With my seatbelt on, I was untouched, amidst the screaming chaos. *My fault.*

A loud crash jolts me back into the church. People are throwing their slates into a large box and smashing them. Janey is in front of me. She raises hers high, slams it down and mumbles something. What can this gentle woman have to confess? This is all so strange and violent.

'The sundered slate can never be made whole,' Arran proclaims as he smashes his own slate. What did he write?

I'm next. I raise my slate. Arran nods. I slam mine

down and it explodes apart. My heart is beating so fast. What's happening? I feel pulled apart. Like I'm breaking open and a huge weight is being lifted off of me and I'm floating away. But it's not a relief. It's terrifying. As if I have no outline, no presence.

I stumble back to my pew, afraid that I'll pass out. I'm in a daze throughout the rest of the service and am relieved when it's all over. What is this religion? Why does this community need so much forgiveness? I've wanted to let go of my guilt about my parents for so long. But this feels . . . so disorientating, so dangerous.

As Calder joins me in the vestibule, I sense a strange calmness in him that I haven't felt since his accident.

'You OK?' I ask him.

He nods. 'I feel very clear now.' What did he write on his slate? What has he let go? And why do I feel so smashed apart, when he seems so serene?

'What do you . . . ?' But we've reached the door.

'It's so lovely to see you, Nancy,' Arran says, shaking my hand and staring at me like he can see into my soul.

'Yes, you too,' I say, unnerved by the pull of his strange charisma.

Next to him is a tall attractive woman with shiny blonde hair pulled back into an Alice band. She reaches between us to shake my hand.

'Hello,' she says in a breathy voice.

'Ah, sorry. This is Alison,' Arran says, 'our flower arranger, she took over from your mother, Calder.'

'Hats off to you,' Calder says. 'It's quite a job. Isla was a real perfectionist about those flowers. She had sleepless nights about them.'

'Yes, she was a hard act to follow,' Alison says. 'You're looking well, Calder.'

'Getting there.' Is he? What's suddenly changed for him?

Alison looks me up and down and then starts talking about flowers with Calder.

I see Janey behind her, flaring her eyes and nodding furiously at Alison. Oh. This must be *that* Alison, Rob's not-quite-ex-wife, the one who said she'd kill him if he set foot on the island. Funny to think that both these sane-seeming middle-aged women have threatened murder to that smiley harmless-looking man. Alison is in her fifties. She's a very good-looking woman even now, but must have been a stunner when she was younger. I wonder what her daughter Caitlin looks like? And I feel a stab of jealousy that Calder had such a good-looking girlfriend before me. But Alison looks rather emotionally pinched, and I would imagine that twinkly-eyed Rob has more fun with Janey than he used to have with Alison. I do hope Janey and Rob make up soon.

How do I compare to Caitlin, I wonder?

I still feel unmoored and need to get out of here and get a drink.

'Well, lovely to meet you, Alison,' I say with finality. 'Beautiful flowers.'

'Thank you. It's hard work, sourcing flowers here. But it's God's work,' she says, looking up at Arran adoringly.

He nods and pats her shoulder.

'Well, that was . . . interesting,' I say to Calder as we move down the steps, out of earshot.

'It really clarified my mind,' he says, sounding the most upbeat he's been in ages.

'Yes, I know what you mean, I feel uncomfortably . . . open, but it's all quite—'

'Quite what?' he snaps.

'I don't know. Culty? The men and women separated. All that sea stuff and the washing away of sins. And my God, so much bloody slate.'

He doesn't make any funny rejoinder, so I fill the awkward space.

'I mean, I get the whole idea of the letting go – but can you really let go of your sins like that?'

'I hope so,' he whispers.

What does that mean?

CHAPTER TWELVE

I must be hallucinating. As I walk back to our car, ahead of Calder, a figure is walking up the hill towards us. I squint into the bright sunlight and shield my eyes. Oh God. No. It can't be. But I know that confident gait. That bright orange hair. Those green eyes.

It's Hamish. And he's . . . waving at me? How can he possibly be here on the island? I only spoke to him yesterday. He must have left immediately after our phone call in order to get here so fast. Did he think I was actually asking for his help?

'Nancy?' he shouts, as he strides up the incline towards me. He's got a huge backpack strapped to his back, and is dressed in a denim jacket and many-pocketed cargo pants. He looks like an Australian backpacker. Is he staying here? He's barking if he thinks I want him here.

He grins, as he approaches. 'All right?'

'What the hell are you doing here?' I hiss.

'Hey, it's OK, I'm here to help.'

'Are you deranged? I didn't mean that I needed your help in that phone call,' I whisper, leaning in. 'How did you get here so fast?'

'I got the first flight to Glasgow this morning and then a taxi all the way.'

'That's crazy, it must have cost you a fortune. Why did . . . ?' I leap back as I see Calder approaching.

'Ah, you made it,' Calder calls, dragging on a cigarette.

'He knew you were coming?' I whisper to Hamish.

'Yes. Of course,' he says.

As Calder arrives, Hamish embraces him and frowns at me over his shoulder. How can we possibly ever have a clean slate with him here?

'Why did nobody tell me about this visit?' I demand, looking between them.

'Why should I tell you?' says Calder. 'Hamish has come up to help me with the new business while I'm recovering. How can I thank you, Hame?' He slaps him on the back.

'I . . . I don't understand,' I falter.

'Yes, Calder asked me to come up,' says Hamish. 'I thought he'd told you.'

'No, he certainly didn't.'

Hamish glances at Calder awkwardly. 'Well, I'm here now, and ready to help.'

'But there's no rush with the business,' I say. 'People will understand that things will take longer after what Calder's been through.'

'Nance, we need the money,' Calder snaps. 'I've got

contracts, expectations. We've already committed lots of money to projects that are just sitting in limbo now. I can't do it all alone in my weakened state. I was talking to Hamish, and he said he'd help.'

I glance at Hamish. 'When were you talking to him?'

Calder frowns. 'Why shouldn't I talk to him?'

'Hey, hey, don't fall out over me,' says Hamish. 'I promise I won't get in your way, Nancy. I'm not expecting you to put me up.'

'Ah, don't be ridiculous,' Calder laughs. 'You're doing me a favour. Of course you won't be in our way. He has to stay with us. Doesn't he, Nance?'

'Umm, well—'

'No no, I've already booked a cottage in the village. There were several to rent – guess no one fancies a holiday let in this freezing weather.' Calder and I stare at each other as Hamish rattles on. 'Look, I'm just here to help Calder and catch up with my mates.'

'When did you two arrange all this?' I demand.

'Yesterday,' Calder says. 'Is that all right with you?' Then he smiles at Hamish. 'You and me should have a pub lunch together and then we can get down to work this afternoon and make a plan.'

'Yeah, sure,' says Hamish, looking uncertainly at me and my exclusion. 'And Nancy can . . .'

'Ah no, let's make it a boys-only lunch, we need to focus.'

I'm too stunned to speak. We stand in awkward silence for a moment and then Hamish breaks the tension. 'Well, I'll just drop my bag off. I said I'd collect the keys when I arrived. I'm booked into the White Cottage.'

'That doesn't exactly narrow it down,' I snap.

'So, err, see you in the pub in ten, Calder, OK?' Hamish glances at me and then sets off towards the row of white cottages. We both watch him walking away, his massive backpack bouncing with each step.

'You were a bit rude there,' says Calder eventually.

'I was rude?'

'Yeah.'

'But you said when we came up here that you couldn't wait to do things on your own.'

'Well, I didn't anticipate nearly dying. I'm struggling and I need help.'

'But you've got me.'

He snorts, like I'm the last person who can help him.

'You're still so fragile. I'm just worried for you.'

'I have to get things moving. I've hired people to do the physical labour. But I need help with the business side.'

'But why haven't you discussed any of this with me? I already said I'd help you.'

He breathes heavily like he's dealing with a difficult child. 'Hamish is a whizz at the business side. I need to get on with managing the workers I've hired, but there's so much paperwork. He can help get everything streamlined for me. Then it's easy to take over.' He pulls out another cigarette. 'You wouldn't understand, with your fiddling around with scripts.'

I'm jolted by this overt rudeness. Calder has never been anything but supportive of my work.

He strikes a match and lights his cigarette.

'Is that sensible?' I snap, wincing at the flare of annoyance he gives me.

'If I want to fucking smoke, I'm going to fucking smoke, all right.'

I step back, unsure what to say, he's freaking me out so much.

He glares at me.

'Whatever,' I mumble. I'm trying really hard to keep a lid on my anger. I know it's not his fault that he's struggling, but this is off the scale.

He narrows his eyes. 'Nancy, we've been in each other's pockets far too much recently. We need a break. Don't you think?'

'What?'

'What?' he parrots back and I flinch at the sarcastic venom in his voice.

I widen my eyes at him but he just shrugs. I step in to touch him, trying to moderate my voice. 'Calder, what's happening?'

He shakes me off. 'We need a break from each other.'

'What?'

'I'll stay at Hamish's cottage for a few days and we can really blitz the work and you can get a break from me.'

'But I don't want a break. How could . . .' I touch his arm again and he pulls it away like I've burnt him.

'Well, I do.' He stares at me coldly.

'You need a break . . . from me?'

He shrugs again, like a petulant child.

I step forward again and this time he pushes me away. I stumble back, falling to my knees and grazing my palms on the gravel. I'm disorientated by his violence. I stare at him as he regards me with . . . open hatred.

I stand and march away, breathing shallowly, trying to

contain the sliding panic inside me. What is happening? As I stride along the rows of white cottages, I see Hamish exiting one.

'I'm just coming,' he calls.

I stop abruptly. 'Calder wants a break from me – and to stay at your cottage.'

'What? Does he know about—'

'Shh. Not here,' I say, glancing around. 'Follow me.'

I pull him in the other direction to the pub, down a secluded path, to the edge of the grassy football pitch with its worn goals and sagging nets. I check around us, but can't see anyone.

'What the fuck?' I ask, swinging back to Hamish. 'What are you doing here?'

'Calder asked me to come.'

'But you had to know that was the worst idea ever. He's in such a fragile state. You've knocked him off-kilter by coming here. He's sounding deranged.'

'I was trying to help. I rang him after I spoke to you yesterday.'

'What?'

'I was really worried. And he was in such a state when I spoke to him. Crying down the phone. Begging me to come up. I've never heard him like that.'

'Crying?' I sit down on a boulder. 'What did he say?'

Hamish puts his hand on my shoulder.

'You're freezing,' he says, taking his coat off and draping it around my shoulders. 'Nancy, I'm really worried . . .'

I leap up as we hear the crunch of footsteps. Arran is walking towards us and we spring apart.

'Hamish,' Arran says with a nod. 'I didn't know that

you'd come for a visit. It's been a while.' He glances at me and then back at Hamish.

'Pastor,' says Hamish, with a nod and a subtly combative tone.

'To what do we owe the honour?' Arran asks.

'I'm here to help Calder and to check up on my father's old boat trip business, which I still run from afar.'

'Of course. And very successful it is too.' Arran is tense, doing his all-knowing eye contact. 'And I suppose you know Nancy from London?'

'Yes. She and my wife Gina were, are, great friends.'

Arran glances at me again. 'That's good of you to help Calder,' he says, stressing the name. 'And where is he?'

'He's just booking lunch,' I blurt. 'I was updating Hamish about Calder's condition – about how fragile he is.'

'I think he's looking good. Really good. He seemed to enjoy the service just now. People do find it cathartic.'

'Well, that service will have washed even the blackest of souls clean,' I say sharply, feeling guilty about him catching me talking to Hamish.

'That's the idea,' Arran says, looking like he can see into my thoughts. 'It was such a pleasure to see you and Calder there. His return to us is indeed a miracle.' Then he raises his eyebrows at me pointedly and turns away. 'Good to see you, Hamish. I don't know if you'll be here long enough to fit in a service? I'll bid you goodbye.'

We watch him as he walks up the hill, glancing at each other like naughty schoolchildren.

'He's still got a stick up his arse, I see,' Hamish says.

'Shhh, he'll hear you.'

'He's not the Pope,' he laughs, doing up the buttons of his coat on me. 'Don't say he's got you in his thrall too.'

I stare after Arran, feeling like I've displeased him.

'What were you going to say, before?' I ask, pulling Hamish back up the alley, out of the sight of two young boys who've started kicking a grimy football around on the pitch.

'That I had to come, because Calder sounded so strange on the phone. I was worried for him. For you.'

'Strange? How?'

'I've never heard him cry. Though I know he's been through a lot. But it wasn't just that. He sounded so . . . I've known him all my life but he sounded so . . . different.'

I can't believe it. Someone else is saying it out loud. I don't even care in this moment that it's Hamish.

'Are you OK?' he asks.

'What do you mean, different?'

'He sounded like . . . sorry, you're going to think I'm mad.'

I shake my head. 'Tell me.'

He blinks at me. 'He sounded like a different person.'

I embrace him. 'Thank you, thank you.'

He pulls me tight. 'It's OK, I'm here.'

I pull away but cling to his arm as I babble. 'It's just such a relief to hear you say that. No one else seems to think anything's wrong. But then everyone here either didn't really know him before the accident or only twenty years ago.'

'What's happened to him? Is it moving up here?'

'No, he was fine for the week we were first here. This is the accident. From the moment he woke up, he's been so distant, tetchy, as if he's far away and I'm an annoyance.'

'So, then it must be some brain injury. Surely that's the logical explanation?'

'Maybe. The doctors said no. And sometimes I think I glimpse the old him. But I don't know any more.'

'Gina's worried about you. She wanted to come with me, said you've been sounding so stressed, but she couldn't leave the kids.'

I step away. 'Does she suspect anything? About us?'

'No, of course not. She's just worried for you. Said I should stay for as long as you both need me.'

I swallow and rub a piece of grit off my palm. Maybe he can help Calder, if I can't. 'Stay as long as Calder needs you. I'll cope.' Being huddled here with Hamish feels dangerous. 'You should go meet him at the pub.'

'OK.' He looks like he wants to say more, but just blinks at me.

'And if he does insist on staying in your cottage, you will look after him, won't you?'

'Of course. Look, you've got my number. Any time, OK?' I nod.

Hamish walks back to the pub. It's starting to rain as I reach the end of the village, and I don't quite know what I'm doing. I daren't go into the pub, I don't want to go home, I don't know anyone else except Arran and Janey. Arran's definitely out so I detour to Janey's shop. As the door opens, she swings round. 'Oh hi,' she says, sounding uncharacteristically brittle. She's ripping up empty cardboard boxes and stamping on the pile as she adds to it. 'All right?'

'Yep,' I say, unsure how to go on.

'So what did you make of Alison just then? Prom queen wannabe that she is.'

'Oh yes, bit uptight I guess, she's very in thrall to Arran isn't she.'

She laughs. 'And some. I don't know how Rob stood being with her all those years. She's such a princess, thinks she's better than everyone.'

'How is Rob?' I say, needing to talk about Calder, but scared to start.

'Ah we're totally done. Probably for the best.' She swallows. 'I get so angry with his refusal to go public with us, I don't recognise myself sometimes.'

'But why does he want to keep you a secret? 'Cos of Alison or the church?'

'Oh, Arran's all for people separating if they don't get on – he's very progressive about marriage – really changed his views from the early days of his ministry, when it was all about "the unbreakable knot" of marriage.'

'Then why? Surely she's well in his past?'

She squirms awkwardly. 'Well, all right, I'll tell you. There was this stupid rumour – that Rob was a bit too close to Caitlin.'

'Close close?' I say warily.

'Yes, it was ridiculous to suggest that there was anything sexual going on with his daughter. It was all a total lie that Alison made up 'cos she was so angry at him leaving her. Beautiful women like her don't take rejection well. But in these small island communities, that sort of rumour can stick.'

The doorbell jangles. Janey moves back behind the counter.

Arran steps in, his tall frame dark against the light. He walks over, water slithering off his long slate-grey raincoat, like he's some otherworldly being, materialising into our realm. He has such an intense energy, and I feel sucked in and reduced by it. As if my edges have melted and I'm being coalesced into his force field.

'Morning, Arran,' Janey says with a firm, upbeat tone that is consciously measured to cover its brittleness.

'Janey,' he says, but focusing on me. 'Nancy. You seemed as thick as thieves with our returning Hamish just now?'

How dare he police me. 'I knew him quite well in London. He's Calder's best friend.'

'You seemed to be almost *hiding* down that lane.'

'We were just talking.'

Janey has a fixed grin, so wide I can see her little pointy teeth further back in her mouth.

'What can I get for you, Arran?' she asks evenly.

He lingers a fraction longer on me, then turns his piercing blue eyes to her. 'A leg of lamb, potatoes, and whatever vegetables you have in. Alison says she'll cook for me tonight as I'm always so tired after the service, and she wants to make me my favourite.'

'Give Alison my best,' Janey says. 'The flowers today were magnificent.'

'I will indeed.'

Janey collects his shopping together and he pays with a card. It seems incongruous for this man who was just draped in long grey robes exhorting us to let go of our sins, to now be using a bank card.

'I'll see you next week hopefully,' he says to me as he

reaches the door. 'I could see that you were struggling during the service. You found it a difficult experience?'

'Just . . . different, I'm fine thank you.'

'My door's always open, if I can be of any help to you, or Calder.' He pulls up his grey hood and strides out. The door closes slowly on its sprung hinge. He's left a festering energy in the room.

'I should be easier on Rob,' Janey says. 'People here are so nosy. Arran's pretty judgemental and thinks he can butt his nose into people's business.'

'And he's clearly very close with Alison.'

'Umm. Rob's especially scared of him knowing he visits the island. Arran was very concerned about the rumours about Rob and Caitlin at the time – questioned Caitlin over and over and interrogated Rob, who was furious and denied everything of course. But Arran gave the rumours validity with his questioning and made Rob's life hellish. He means well – but he's so overprotective of his parishioners, and can cause a lot of trouble. He was the same with Calder after Douglas drowned.'

'What do you mean?

'Over-involved, overprotective.'

'Calder said Isla asked Arran to keep an eye on him.'

'Well, he certainly did that.'

Janey gestures me into the back and makes us coffee.

I dribble the last of the milk into our mugs and go to chuck the glass bottle.

'No. Put that in the recycling,' Janey calls.

'You do that here on the island? How do they take it all away? By boat?'

'Yes, we have to do what we can. Sea levels are higher

each year here. There's flooding and coastal erosion, which has a knock-on effect on the water supply, crops, the grazing animals.'

'Maybe it's already too late,' I say, feeling exhausted.

'We have to try,' she says sharply. 'However hopeless things seem.'

'But some things can't be mended,' I blurt, knocking my mug off the table, and the slate coaster that was stuck to the bottom smashes. 'I'm sorry,' I mumble. 'I know slate can't be put back together again and all that.'

She tilts her head, assessing me. 'Is something else broken?'

Tears start streaming down my face. She moves her chair round the table to sit next to me and takes me in her arms. I sob, great big ugly moans, soaking her tie-dyed top.

'Calder?' she whispers.

'I don't recognise him any more. He's this dark ugly presence, who pushes me away. Literally now. I think he . . . hates me.'

'He pushed you?'

I nod.

'Then you need to leave him,' she says immediately.

'Oh no, I can't, not after all he's been through.'

'You have to protect yourself.'

'I'm just being histrionic. It's totally understandable that he's struggling. I'm sorry, I'm babbling.'

Janey takes a deep, slow breath, like she's about to meditate.

'Has he ever been violent before?'

'No.'

She cocks her head.

'Well, I mean, he's fiery, he can lose his temper, throw things occasionally.'

She frowns.

'But I've thrown things too. When I was trying to get him to give up smoking when we started trying for a baby, I threw a full glass of red wine at him. To get our flat deposit back, I had to paint over the mark. Don't couples often get passionate?'

'Are you scared of him?'

'I wasn't before. Not ever. But since the accident . . . I'm scared that I don't quite know him. And just now, he pushed me, really hard.'

She shakes her head. 'Bastard.'

'He's not himself. It's not his fault.'

She slowly lifts her hand and pushes back her long grey hair, to reveal a jagged purple scar running across her scalp, previously hidden in the waves.

'Douglas,' she says simply.

'Calder's dad?'

She nods. 'Many years ago, we dated, before he married Isla. He was a grand lad sometimes, but the hard drinking that goes on up here can turn even the kindest soul. I got this when he pushed me into a wall.'

'I'm so sorry.'

'Ach no, it was a long time ago. I've made my peace. He was full of remorse, said he'd never behave like that again, but I got out. I don't know what happened with Isla, what went on behind closed doors, but I looked into her eyes for years and I knew.'

'Oh God.'

She tuts. 'And then Douglas died in that "accident".'

'What . . . d'you mean?'

'I'm sure he was violent to Isla. And she was a woman who you could only push so far.' She walks back through to the shop and starts pulling out more empty boxes.

I follow her. 'You mean, you think Isla . . .'

She shrugs and continues her folding and stamping. 'His body was never found. Only the boat. And that was destroyed soon after it was discovered. Afterwards, she became very religious. Arran's lapdog. Obsessed with getting the flowers perfect. Polishing that altar till it shone. Endlessly writing on confession slates and washing them clean.'

'But that's awful. What do other people here think?'

She shrugs as she wipes her forehead. 'They destroyed the boat, which was the only evidence of whatever happened. You'll soon learn that this island is a law unto itself.'

'They condoned her killing him?'

'They . . . turn a blind eye if they think justice has been done.' She clicks open a large Stanley knife and cuts down the seam of a large box, the cardboard juddering and then falling apart. I watch as she chops away at a thicker box with big violent strokes. I can't believe all this. But why would she lie?

'Calder hated Isla's obsession with the church,' I say slowly. 'D'you think he suspects?'

She shrugs. 'Perhaps he doesn't let himself.'

Why has Calder come back to this bloody place if it holds all these awful memories?

'He's never been at all religious,' I say, 'but today he

seemed strangely engrossed in that bloody service.'

'Maybe it helped him?' she says matter-of-factly, holding the knife up between cuts. 'Some people do find solace in the church.'

'Sorry. I didn't mean to offend you. It's just that I don't know what's going on with him. He's been acting so strangely since the accident. Withdrawn, moody, even cruel – and he's doing weird things like going to church, smoking, eating loads of meat.'

She frowns, putting the knife down. 'Benson and Hedges?'

'How do you know that?'

Janey swallows. 'You sound like you're describing Douglas. The moodiness, the meat eating, the smoking.'

'Hamish says Calder's different too. He doesn't think I'm being paranoid.'

She narrows her eyes. 'So, Arran was right, you and Hamish were hiding from Calder?'

She's guessed our secret somehow.

'Nothing suspicious. We were just talking about how to support Calder. He's here to help him. I'm probably being ridiculous about Calder and, with time, things will settle. I should go.'

'You're playing with fire juggling secrets with those two, be careful,' Janey says, walking out the back. What does that mean? Am I dismissed? I need to get out of here – there are forces on this island that I don't understand – and it's something to do with that church.

I'm just opening the shop door to leave when Janey returns with a small brown bottle. 'I'm not judging you, but you need to be careful.'

'I'm sorry? Are you warning me?'

'This is the homeopathic tincture of slate: it represents total breakage, something impossible to mend. This remedy helps people to transition from one state to another, allowing an opening where none was possible. It will help you leave Calder, if you need to.'

I take the bottle. I don't believe in homeopathy, but daren't refuse. Maybe I do need something to help me do . . . whatever I'm going to do.

I can't stop Calder staying with Hamish. I don't think I want to now. So I have to go home. Alone. I walk back round the island via the road, filling my lungs with the cold, briny air. This island seems so solid, has been here for ever, yet it's vulnerable to the weather, to climate change. Without our efforts, it will be re-absorbed by the sea. Nothing is safe, nothing is for ever, even this rock-hard island. As I near our cottage, I pause at the old flooded slate pit. Mining ceased here in the 1950s and all the pits have long since filled with water. It's a round expanse of utterly smooth black glinting water that is never refreshed by the sea. Impenetrable, like Calder. God knows how deep it goes or what is living in its stagnant depths.

CHAPTER THIRTEEN

Please leave me alone to work, reads the text. Calder won't answer any of my calls, just sends me the same message over and over. He stays with Hamish for three days, holed up in the 'White Cottage'. I don't want to call Hamish. So I have no choice. I spend the days alone in our windswept cottage, wound tight, with only Attila for company. And she merely coexists with me, accepting food but snarling if I get too close. I work on the *Frankenstein* script obsessively and it's starting to really take shape. The internet monster is causing utter chaos in its creator's life and like in the original, the destruction and murders gather pace, the monster justifying his actions: *I have love in me the likes of which you can scarcely imagine and rage the likes of which you would not believe. If I cannot satisfy the one, I will indulge the other.*

By the fourth day, I almost understand the monster's

desperation. I'm up before first light. I've had enough. I'm going to the village to make Calder talk to me. I march furiously round the island by the road route, unable to trust myself walking over the hill. But there's no response when I knock on the cottage door. I walk over to the pub to see if they're there, but I see a crowd gathered by the dock as I get closer. At the front is Hamish, who's dressed like a cartoon character – wearing huge yellow waterproof trousers, a bulky yellow waterproof top and talking into a headset. I mock-frown at him and he makes a 'what can you do' face. He's talking to a group of people, all wearing the same kind of gear that he is: a Chinese couple, four young men with sharp haircuts who look like they work for a US tech company, a large WI-type woman with tufty hair and an intense man with a lot of expensive silver equipment.

'Once you've all got into your waterproofs, you should take a life jacket from this box.' Hamish points. 'I'll come round and check they're done up correctly. Snap the clip at the front and then run the long strap between your legs.'

In front of an open van full of more bright yellow suits is a big sign reading 'MOTORBOAT WILDLIFE TOURS'.

'Want to come?' he calls over to me.

I look round, assuming he's talking to someone else. But he points at me and smiles.

Like I'd ever go out in a boat by choice again.

'Why are you running a boat trip?' I ask him as I approach.

'This is my company. Well, it was my father's, in much less snazzy boats. And when he died, I kept it on, but got people on the island to run it. Calder doesn't need me

172

today so I thought I'd check it all out. I'm not driving the boat – just doing the spiel, which I know off by heart from all the times I went out with my dad.'

'Where is Calder today?'

'He's gone to the mainland to talk with his building suppliers.'

'Is he OK?'

He shrugs. 'I guess. He's been pretty manic. Coffee and smoking all day and hard drinking at night. Utterly driven to get the company profitable.'

'Has he . . . talked about me?'

He shakes his head. 'I'm so sorry, Nancy, but I can't talk now. Come on the trip with me. No charge.'

'I can't. After that day I found Calder's body floating . . .'

'The weather's fine, the sea's calm. You don't want to let that terrible experience cut you off from the utter beauty of the sea. If you fall off a horse, what do you do?'

I laugh. 'I fell off a balance bar at school and the PE teacher said, "If you don't get back on, you'll never do it again," – and that was the last balance bar I've ever seen, except on TV!'

'I think I'd like your PE teacher. Come on. I would never let anything bad happen to you.' He looks at me so sincerely. I can't keep living in fear and I just want to feel something different.

'OK. Sure.'

'Attagirl,' he says with a huge smile. He gives me a pair of stupidly large yellow trousers which I struggle on, then holds out the matching top for me to dive into and pulls it down. He's so careful and kind, as if he can feel my nerves. I'm already regretting agreeing to go. I shouldn't be spending time with Hamish, but I'm going mad on my own. Next, he stands behind me so I can pull on the life jacket. I can't see him, but I can feel the care he's taking to stop me from having to twist my arms too much, knowing we both know that the other is thinking about that night together.

'Now you catch the strap dangling between your legs,' he says. Him not helping me with this part makes me more self-conscious at reaching between my legs. It's all strangely intimate.

We all trundle down the slope to a large bright orange inflatable speedboat alongside the concrete incline. It has rows of narrow seats with silver handlebars in front. They look like tightly packed frill-free fairground horses.

Oh God. Can I back out? I don't think I can do this. The WI woman smiles at me. In a strong Nordic accent, she says 'I did it yesterday – is wonderful. You'll love it.'

I can't just sit in the cottage. I have to do something. I must push through my fears. I clamber on, take a seat at the front and once everyone's on, we're off, shooting out across the water. An older man at the back is steering and Hamish is moving from front to back, talking about the island. The bumping over the water, the sea spray, the expanse of grey sea, all rocket me straight back to that ride to find Calder, and the journey back with his body. I grip the silver bar and scrunch my eyes shut. Make it stop. This is horrific.

And then I feel a hand gently settling on my shoulder. I open my eyes. Hamish is standing beside me, talking to the tourists, but steadying me with his touch.

'These were called "the islands that roofed the world"

174

because the slate mined here travelled all across the world to be used on roofs,' Hamish says. He's looking at the tourists who are all snapping away at the slate coastline, but I feel his attention all on me. I allow myself to breathe slower, to relax my shoulders and to look around. Today the sea is almost smooth, like ruffled grey silk, with ever-shifting lines of thread. I'm OK. I can do this.

'Look up,' Hamish calls suddenly, and we all jerk our heads up. 'That is the ultimate bird of prey – a white-tailed eagle.' And there, hanging in the air above us, is a majestic brown bird with a white head, a splayed wedge of white tail feathers and huge powerful wings. 'And if you look in those trees on the coast to our right, where there's a double bed-sized lump, that's their huge nest. Their courtship involves aerial displays culminating in the male and female locking talons' – he rams his hands together – 'and hurtling to the ground in a death dive' – he pulls his hands apart dramatically – 'separating just before they smash themselves to death.' He smiles at everyone's horrified expressions.

I laugh.

'In contrast, can you hear that chirruping?' We all tune into a strange squeaking sound, like rubber toys being squeezed. 'See there on the shore – those small black and white birds with thin orange legs – they're oystercatchers.' The much smaller birds have comically long orange beaks and are like birds a child would draw.

I laugh again, and Hamish grins.

'Glad you came,' he whispers.

I nod.

Once the tourists have snapped and filmed enough,

the boat revs and we're off again. The driver shows off a bit, banking the boat up steeply to the right and then the left. I hear a few cries from behind me. But I realise that this is all for show. Hamish is right, I'm quite safe. I start to fully appreciate the rugged beauty of the island as we shoot along beside it. The cliffs are steep, with dark caves sunk into them and jagged smashed layers of slate exposed to the elements. Then the coastline gets grassier and I hear Hamish, further back in the boat, as if he knows I'm OK now. 'On the island over there, you can see some red deer. You don't think of deer swimming, but this lot swam over and set up here. Of course, they have to be hunted to keep the numbers down or they'd eat all the vegetation – but the hunting is humanely carried out.'

That's an odd concept – humane murder. Though after what Janey said, I imagine that the islanders would be fine with it.

'And look there: a heron, cormorants and some shag.'

Someone sniggers behind me.

The tall long-legged heron is obvious, but the rest are all black dumpy birds.

'The cormorants have the white necks and are heavier than the shag,' Hamish continues. 'Evolution hasn't been that kind to the poor old shag as their feathers don't have the oils to make them waterproof, so they have to hang in the water with their heads tipped back for safety. They get cold very quickly and have to get out and sit on the cliffs.'

I look at the half-drowned little black heads peeping out of the water, and at the ones on the land, slender little black birds with long necks and snake-like faces, with an almost green gloss to their feathers and purplish glint to their wing tips. I feel for these odd little waterbirds whom nature has forgotten to make waterproof. I feel akin to them. Up here in this wild place and lacking the basic requirements for this life.

'You like shag?' Norwegian woman asks.

'What? Oh, yes, they're cool.'

Hamish catches my eye and looks away instantly.

It's getting cloudy and there's a sprinkling of rain, but a distant shaft of sunlight from the edge of the cloud creates a rainbow and we all 'ooh' and 'ah'. I feel like I'm in a children's story of magical animals and treasures at the end of the rainbow. I had assumed that these islands were desolate and empty – who knew that they were teeming with such beautiful and extreme wildlife?

And now we're passing the top of our bay, where Arran and I found Calder – dead. He was dead. Literally stone-cold dead. He's breathing again now, but he might as well be dead. I breathe faster and feel faint. Then I hear the swish of plastic trousers as Hamish approaches, sensing I need him.

His hand rests on my shoulder again. 'And there on the headland are two seals. One grey seal in the water and a harbour seal on the land. The harbour is more uniformly spotted, whereas the grey has the pale belly and darker back.'

I don't know if either of those are the seals from the day of the rescue, but I feel like they're watching me and saying, *Well there you are, and today is another day. Life goes on.* I feel my breathing slowing.

'Can the two species mate?' my Norwegian compatriot asks.

'No, they're too different,' Hamish says.

I think of Calder and me staring at yet another failed pregnancy test.

'And there to our left, you can see several porpoises swimming along with us.'

I see the glorious curves as their dark backs and low fins break the water. They're all leaping slightly out of sync, creating a cascading effect and I giggle with pleasure, replacing the memory of the porpoise I mistook for Calder's boat.

The blue sky has layers of cloud spread across it, whites, greys and purples, with sunlight darting down like spotlights, onto the craggy piled-brick-effect cliffs and the grey silky water. It's spectacularly beautiful. The sea, the land and the sky are so huge and I am so small. My emotions feel dwarfed, in the best possible way.

At the end of the trip, Hamish gives me his hand to help me out of the boat and then walks with me up the slope and helps me out of my waterproofs.

'I'll look after Calder, I promise,' he says. 'And if you need anything, anything at all. You've got my number. I'll come. Straight away.'

CHAPTER FOURTEEN

The sea is sparkling, the cold air bracing and I'm briefly just in the moment of striding along. But as I turn the corner, I see that the cottage window is open. And I can hear rock music and smell frying garlic.

I open the door slowly, my fragile ease evaporating.

And there's Calder, eyes bright, his clothes rumpled, with four days' worth of stubble on his face. And he's cooking.

'Are you hungry?' he asks, as if his days of absence haven't happened.

'I . . . yeah. I could eat a horse,' I say lightly, not wanting to set him off. But what's happening?

'Only prime beef today, I'm afraid,' Calder laughs, poking at two slabs of meat searing in the big metal frying pan. He's doing his signature steak and home-made chips. A meal we often had back in London. I think of our little fourth-floor kitchen, our happy life there, with a pang. Maybe he's somehow sorted out his head at Hamish's? I shouldn't mention anything negative, just play along.

I sit down at the table. 'Smells great.'

He pulls open the oven door and tips an enormous pile of chips onto each of our plates, and then lovingly slides on the two gargantuan steaks. They're browned, just how I like them.

But as I cut into the thick slab of meat, greasy blood slides out of the pink raw flesh. Yuck. 'It's raw,' I blurt. 'I can't eat it like this.' He knows I hate undercooked meat.

'That's how you're meant to eat steak,' he says in a strange steely voice. 'It's how Dad liked it cooked.' Why is he talking to me as if he's never met me? 'Are you going to eat it?' he demands.

'Umm . . .'

'Fine, give it here,' he barks, swiping the plate away from me.

'No, no, it's OK,' I backtrack.

He pauses, plate aloft, assessing me.

'Please Calder, I didn't mean anything by that. I want the steak. Give it back. Please.'

He slowly lowers the plate in front of me and gives me a nod. I slice an edge off, hoping that the slight searing on the outside will make it edible. He stares as I bring the chunk towards me. I manoeuvre it into my mouth and start chewing. It's so disgustingly fleshy, like I'm biting into my own cheek. But I keep on, Calder not breaking eye contact with me.

Finally, I swallow the lump down. 'So, Douglas liked cooking?'

'He always did the Sunday lunch for us. Roasts or steaks.'

I slice off another edge and manage to chew through this wodge of bloody flesh as Calder's attention turns to his food. He's sawing through his steak and eating it in huge lumps. With great relish.

We continue in silence, me working my way around the outside of mine, him devouring his.

All I have left now is the thick inner circle of bloody flesh. The greasy smell is overpowering. I don't think I can choke any more down. But I so don't want to break this fragile truce between us and I feel so guilty about spending time with Hamish today. Enjoying spending time with him.

Calder glances across at me. I smile and nod like a simpleton. 'Umm, delicious.'

'Good.'

I slice into the raw flesh, red blood oozing out and pooling on the plate. I think of Calder's blood being replaced by a stranger's in the hospital. I feel woozy. I need to do this quickly, so I hack off a huge bloody chunk and shove it in my mouth. I gag slightly, but cover it with a cough as I masticate the fibrous lump. I'm rocking with the effort, feeling saliva gathering in my mouth as I fight to stop myself retching. I have to spit it out or swallow. I throw my head back to propel it down, but the lump sticks in the back of my throat. I seize, eyes wide. I can't swallow. But I can't get it back up.

I moan and bang the table desperately, gesturing wildly at my neck.

'Jesus!' Calder shouts as he leaps up, getting behind

me and slapping my back hard. I flail out both arms and crockery crashes to the floor.

'Breathe, Nancy!' Calder screams as he smacks me harder.

I'm seized rigid, gagging, unable to breathe at all. I'm going to die here.

He drags me up out of my seat, kicking the chair aside, wraps his arms around me and gives my ribs a violent jolt, crushing me and forcing all the air up out of me.

The lump of meat shoots across the table.

We're both breathing fast, looking at the fibrous mass.

'Oh my God, you could have – Jesus.' Calder spins me round and stares at me, wide-eyed.

'Thank you,' I squawk. 'You saved my life.'

'What did you think I was going to do? Let you die?'

I realise that I thought he might have.

'Water!' he shouts, leaping to the sink and coming back with a glass. 'It's OK,' he murmurs as I sip. A cry escapes me and he puts my glass on the table and holds me. I cry into his chest as he strokes my hair gently.

We both simultaneously register this newly unfamiliar physical closeness. My skin flickers to life, goose-bumped and alert. I look up at him, seeing a glimpse of the old him, and we both lean in for the faintest of kisses.

Then he flinches. As if my lips are poisoned.

He sees me registering his withdrawal and he frowns as he steps back.

'Calder . . .'

He shakes his head.

I frown. Pleading across the chasm. We haven't touched like this since the night before his accident. Three long weeks ago – an unimaginable length of time for us.

I step in and kiss him. The physical click of recognition between us is intense, but everything feels off-kilter. As if our dimensions have changed since we last touched and now we don't quite fit together any more.

I think of his cold wet body as it fell onto me in the boat, and pull back from the kiss. 'Is this safe? For your health? I don't want to hurt you, I—'

'It's fine,' he murmurs.

'What did Dr Viner say?'

'I'm fine,' he mumbles breathily. 'Don't talk. Come on.' He takes my hand and leads me to the bedroom. I feel far more nervous than the very first time we slept together as drunken strangers. We've had sex so many times, but now I feel so shy. Scared even? He struggles to unbutton his trousers as I get my arm caught in my dress. In the past, we would have laughed at all this awkward practicality. But now we are both deathly silent, just doggedly ploughing on.

He pulls me to him and we both take a deep breath. I smell the grease and meat on his breath, but I still feel my body responding. We're both into this, our bodies connecting in spite of ourselves. He pushes me onto the bed and straddles me, then kisses me. Hard. His mouth is meaty and strange. His unfamiliar stubble sandpapers my skin. I want to pull away. But I don't want to ruin this fragile moment. I shift back slightly to try to make the kiss lighter, to find that frisson of play that we used to have. But he pushes down on me, grinding his face into mine, his tongue engorging my mouth. I make myself engage, matching his ferocity. We've often been wild, but we've come to it organically, building slowly from tenderness to passion. Never like this.

'Slow down,' I whisper.

He grunts and squeezes my right breast, hard.

'Ow,' I blurt. He pauses for a fraction, but I pull him back in. 'Don't stop.'

He lifts me and throws me further back on the bed and I scrape my leg on the edge of the metal base. I yelp as it shaves down my thigh, but he takes this as a cry of passion as he shoves himself into me. We're both into this but we're in utterly different rhythms, everything clashing and disjointed. I want to keep going, to somehow break through the wall between us and find each other again. His whole body is slick with greasy sweat. He doesn't smell or feel like him. I try to find our connection as he pounds into me. I'm squashed by his weight, my left leg stuck out at an unnatural angle. He's slamming into me, my hip aching, my breath shoved out of me with each thrust.

We've hardly started, when he shudders and slumps down on me. I'm breathing heavily. Slick with his oily sweat. My hip is in agony, but I daren't move him. He's obliterated.

'Are you OK?' I whisper.

He gives a small grunt.

'Calder?'

He grunts again, then rolls off me and stands. Without a word, he turns and leaves the room and soon I smell cigarette smoke.

I'm suddenly cold, the sweat drying on my skin, making me brittle. I pull the blankets over my nakedness.

Embarrassed. I haven't come, but all desire has drained out of me.

We always curled up after sex before, breathing each other in, totally meshed. This is the first time I've ever felt that Calder was having sex, and I was someone . . . merely present. He has totally changed personality. Oh God, that stupid heart transplant film. Calder had a huge blood transplant. I know it's delusional to think there's some parallel.

But what has happened to my Calder?

CHAPTER FIFTEEN

I've lied to Calder. Told him I've gone to Oban to 'have a pampering day to myself': a massage, a cinema trip and the simple pleasure of shopping in person in a supermarket. Ha! As if. I've got lies ready to cover the whole day. I've downloaded the film I said I was seeing onto my phone, to listen to on the journey back. I've booked a 'Click and Collect' from Aldi to pretend I've been indulging in shopping in person. And as for the outlandish concept of someone massaging me . . . I'd explode if anyone touched me, but I can imagine one if I'm called on my lie. Not that Calder will likely show any interest in my day or quiz me on it later. He's back to spending all his time with Hamish. But I don't want to get caught out.

As soon as my taxi dropped me off at Oban station, I got straight onto the train to Glasgow. And after arriving and a short walk, I'm finally here.

I swallow, raise my fist and knock on the wood.

'Come in,' calls a familiar deep voice. I put my head around the hospital door and smile at the tall figure of Dr Viner. Calder's saviour? Or a Svengali who used his dark arts to sell Calder's soul?

'Ah, Nancy, come in, come in.'

We embrace awkwardly. His office is so familiar: the stylish leather chairs, the high shelves stuffed with books, the large desk covered in papers, with dried rings on the wood. I'm rocketed back to when I sat here in a panic during those early days after the accident.

'Take a seat,' he says, gesturing to one of the two seats facing his desk, and then sits opposite.

'So how are you doing?'

'Yeah, you know.'

He inclines his head. 'I was intrigued to get your call. And a little unnerved.'

'Unnerved?'

'Because you asked me not to mention this meeting to Calder. Is everything OK?'

'I wanted to discuss some . . . delicate things and didn't want to upset him.'

Dr Viner raises an eyebrow. 'Go on.'

'I can't thank you enough for all you've done for us.'

He nods. 'But?'

'I don't want to sound ungrateful. I know you performed a miracle.'

He smiles. 'I'm a practical man, Nancy. Miracles are beyond my purview. But it was certainly very fortuitous that your husband's heart stopped in such freezing conditions, that he didn't drown, that you found him so quickly, that the helicopter brought him to my hospital, that I'd read about this technique, that I was on call that day and that I could reach more experienced practitioners quickly for advice. Some might call that series of events, happening together, a miracle.'

I glance at his framed print of Michelangelo's *Creation of Adam* painting on the wall behind him, God reaching out for Adam's hand.

'But you don't call it a miracle?'

'It's a synonym for right time, right place, a ton of scientific advancement and some dumb luck.'

I stare at God's hand almost touching Adam's drooping finger and remember when Calder and I saw the original in the Sistine Chapel, during a tour of the Vatican City in Rome.

'Yet you have that particular painting on your wall?' I say, pointing.

He turns to look at it. 'Yes, beautiful isn't it. It's said to represent the moment when God bestows the breath of life on Adam.'

'Do you think that you imbue life, Dr Viner?'

He laughs. 'Hardly. I'm . . . a mechanic. I get my patients' bodies to run as best they can, in their circumstances. I like that painting because of the characters and cloths around God.'

'What?'

'Some people think they represent the human brain. Michelangelo knew about anatomy. Look,' he says, getting up and pointing to the shape around God and the figures and material filling the space. 'See. The inner and outer brain, the brain stem, basilar artery, pituitary gland and optic chiasm. Astonishing accuracy. Nothing mystical.'

'That's amazing. But I don't believe in anything mystical. I just felt incredibly lucky that Calder came back. At the time. But now . . . I don't feel so lucky.'

'Why's that?' he says, sitting back down.

'When we left here a week ago, you thought that he was fully recovered, except for some peripheral nerve damage. You said his brain scans were normal.'

He nods, assessing me. 'I said that he'd made a brilliant recovery. Sounds like you're trying to catch me out?'

'No. Not at all. But you thought he'd made a good recovery?'

'Considering. But I also said that medicine isn't an exact science. So much of it consists of "wait and see" and recovery is a relative term, an experiential term. How does he feel in himself?'

'He says he's fine.'

'But you don't think so?'

'He doesn't seem . . . quite like himself.'

'Understandable, in the circumstances.'

'No. Literally not himself.' I purse my lips together in disbelief that I've said it out loud to this clever doctor. 'I know that's terribly unscientific, but I don't know how else to say it.'

'Go on.' He laces his fingers together and leans forward.

'OK. So. His personality has changed drastically. He's distant, cold, even cruel. He can hardly meet my eyes. He flinches from my touch. He even feels different physically when I do touch him. He smells different. I'm sorry. I know this sounds ludicrous out loud.' I'm sweating, but it's such a relief to get it all out. 'And now, another friend who knows him really well has said the exact same thing, so it's not just me. I know Calder's exhausted and certainly has some memory loss because he still doesn't remember that night. And God knows I'm grateful he's back. But he doesn't . . . feel back. I'm living with a stranger.'

Dr Viner nods. 'This is not unexpected.'

I feel deflated. 'Really?'

'I'd hoped that Calder would be back to full health after a period of recuperation. From a medical point of view, he's made a miraculous recovery. When he left us, his heart was beating strongly, he was breathing easily, all his organs were working well, and in particular his brain function was incredible, considering how long it was starved of oxygen. To us, the only obvious effect was the slight damage to his neural pathways, to the ends of his limbs, hence the physio he had. I hope he's keeping up with his exercises?'

'I–I don't know.'

He nods. 'Well, typical bloke if not. But he's moving around?'

'Oh yes, he's moving normally. Pushing himself if anything.'

'Good, as long as he doesn't overdo it.'

'But how long does recovery take?'

'We had every expectation of him making a full recovery. Eventually. But—'

I raise my eyebrows.

He sighs. 'Yes, there is a "but". I and my team don't know your husband. You know him best of all. So, if you feel that there's something going on with him, then that's important information. And we will, of course, bear it in mind when we're doing his follow-up. Which is in' – he consults his diary – 'three weeks' time. Unless you think I should see him now?'

'I don't know. I think he'd be annoyed if you called him in early.'

'So, Calder himself doesn't think there's a problem?'

'I . . . no.' God, I feel so stupid coming here.

He leans back. 'It's OK, Nancy. Your feelings are valid. Can you talk a bit more about what you think you're seeing?'

I don't like that phrasing. As if the problem is with my feelings, not what I'm observing. Not demonstrably and factually with Calder and his behaviour. I stand up and move behind my chair. 'It's not any one thing, though I could list many: the coldness, the distance, the monosyllabic communication, the way he kisses, the way he eats, the smoking, the drinking, the very way he looks at me.' Dr Viner looks at me with pity. 'But it's more than any one detail. It's like, no it is, that the person I used to know has disappeared. I used to love Calder. Now I don't even like him. Something's very wrong.'

Dr Viner flexes his long fingers and takes a breath. 'Let's try to take a step back from your panic. None of this is anything sinister, I'm sure. There could be small mental effects which didn't show up on our scans. These could resolve in time.'

'None of this is small,' I say too loudly.

He flinches. 'I didn't mean to belittle your experience. I'm saying there may be small neural problems which could resolve eventually – or even if not, as I said to you before, the mind is an incredibly plastic thing and new neural pathways can be made to reroute so that function is fully returned, so

191

there is a good likelihood of things improving.'

'So, I just have to wait it out?' This was a pointless trip.

'But that may not be the full explanation.'

'What d'you mean?'

'Calder's mental functions may be fine, and it may be that emotionally he needs time, and perhaps help, to deal with what's happened to him. People who go through near-death experiences do sometimes feel "changed" by the experience, they may sometimes exhibit behavioural or personality changes – quite extreme ones – which are not to do with any physical causes, but because of the patient having a different perspective on life. The extreme effect of a near-death experience can break down, or erect, certain barriers in their previous personality. This isn't my field and I don't want to stress you with this or make it sound bigger than it is, but you should be aware that Calder may be physically recovered but need time to mentally adjust and re-orientate.'

'But you think he will come back?'

'That's impossible to know. I'm afraid that some patients do make drastic changes to their lives after these kinds of extreme events. They change their looks, change the people they like to spend time with, change their jobs, they go travelling, have affairs, leave spouses – it's a reaction to nearly losing everything.'

'So, he's making a choice?'

'It may not feel like a choice to him.'

'But these are reactions – not permanent?'

He shrugs. 'I can't answer that. There are so many possible explanations. But whether it's physical or psychologically reactive, all you can do is look after yourself, and offer him help, if he wants it. Do you want me to ring him?'

'God no, don't tell him I've contacted you.'

He frowns. 'You're not . . . scared of him?' That's what Janey asked too.

'No. Just. Look, I know this is crazy but I have to ask . . .'

'It's OK, fire away.'

'Well, when you explained everything before, you said you'd changed his blood when you were warming him up.' I scrutinise his face for a sign that he knows what I'm talking about, but he stares back impassively. 'Is that like when someone gets a new heart and they absorb something of the personality of the donor?'

He smiles at me, sympathetically. 'That's an urban myth about hearts. And even more so about blood. Very quickly, there is only a very small amount of donor DNA in the recipient.'

'But there is some. It could still . . .'

'No, no, honestly, that is biologically impossible.'

What an idiot I sound. Now I'm saying it out loud, in this office, to this clever man, I feel so stupid. 'Of course, sorry, I'm clutching at straws here.'

'But anyway, to put your mind at rest, that isn't what happened with Calder,' Dr Viner says brightly.

'It isn't?'

'No. Not at all. It wasn't someone else's blood that Calder received. It was his own blood which was taken outside his body and warmed up.'

'What?'

'It's called an extracorporeal membrane oxygenation machine, known as ECMO. It took his blood, infused it with oxygen and warmed it up gradually, and then we re-introduced it to Calder's body and his own blood circulated again.'

'So, it was all him all along?' I say, realising how stupid I've been. 'You didn't introduce anything alien into his body – nothing new that could explain what's happening?'

He shakes his head and I catch a fleeting glance at his watch. He wants the crazy woman to leave. But I have to find some kind of answer. I can't go home with nothing.

'But how can he even feel so physically different to me, smell different?'

'Well, he's been on lots of medications. And is he eating differently? Sleeping differently? Smoking perhaps?'

I nod. All those things are true. How have I been so stupid?

Dr Viner looks at me kindly, but I can see him recalibrating his approach and putting on a professional demeanour to 'manage' me. 'I think that perhaps you need some support, Nancy. You've gone through an awful lot with the stress of him nearly dying and then his recovery. You've been changed by this experience too. You're a different person seeing him from the person you were before.'

'What d'you mean?' I squirm in my seat, seeing myself as he sees me. Delusional.

'It's not a criticism in any way,' he says gently, clearly very sorry for me. 'I'm not saying "don't trust your own experience", but you do need to step back from what you think is demonstrably real and be aware that what you're experiencing may not be coming from Calder. But from you. Calder will almost certainly be struggling, physically and mentally, but you may be extrapolating conclusions because you're so afraid.'

'You're saying that I'm the one who's different?' Oh my God, is he right? I can hear how mad I sound. No wonder he's treating me like I'm the sick one. I am.

'Look, this really isn't my field of expertise. But I've dealt with many families of people with severe life-changing injuries. And the whole family is changed by the injury, even after recovery, not just the patient.'

'I need help?' I falter.

'And we can get you help. Calder went through an extreme, near-death experience and you suffered through that process with him. You almost certainly have PTSD yourself. It would be totally understandable. I can give you a referral of a therapist near you, if that's helpful?'

'Err, yes, sure.'

'Well, I've got your email; I'll do some research and forward you the details. OK?'

'Thank you. I'm really sorry about all this,' I say, standing up.

'No, no, it's totally understandable. I'm glad you came to see me. And I'll see Calder in three weeks.'

'Would you mind . . .'

'Don't worry, I won't tell him about your visit.'

'Thank you.'

I back out and run down the stairs. I have to get back to Calder. I've got everything so wrong, made up outlandish explanations because of my desperation and selfish impatience. And I've been ridiculous in letting Hamish get so close to me because of my fears. I've let Calder down so very badly. Again. I have to find him and make everything right.

CHAPTER SIXTEEN

A huge Christmas tree has been erected in the square, ringed with circles of multicoloured lights. As I walk up from the dock, I hear fiddle music and see the light from the pub spilling out into the darkness. The faces of the drinkers idling outside swivel towards me as I approach. I nod at some half-recognised faces, but I don't see Calder.

'Nancy,' calls Janey, walking over. 'Everything OK?'

'Have you seen Calder?'

'He's here somewhere, has something happened?'

'No, it's fine. Everything's fine now. But I have to find him.'

I step through the low pub door and into the reek of beer, the cacophony of noise and the throng of people, all drinking, talking and laughing. The walls between the original rooms of the knocked-together cottages have been removed but without losing the supports, creating semi-walled-off areas. I turn endless corners, where people stare up at me, wide-eyed.

Calder's nowhere to be seen.

'Nancy,' I hear and turn to see Hamish, looking flushed. 'Where's Calder?'

'D'you want a drink?'

'No. Is he here?'

'Yeah, he's somewhere about – he seems OK tonight. Life and soul of the party.'

'Really?'

'Yeah. He's on top form.'

'Oh . . . good.'

I'm suddenly shoved up against Hamish by the throng and remember that night of drinking in London.

He pushes a strand of hair out of my face.

'Nancy,' he murmurs.

'Hamish, I've got it all wrong about Calder. I need to tell him, to help him. You and I – there is no you and I.'

I catch sight of Arran across the other side of the bar, staring at me standing so close to Hamish.

'I have to find Calder,' I blurt as I twist away from him. I push myself through the crowd. 'Sorry, excuse me.' It feels like the entire island is squashed into this place. How different they all are here from when they're in church. There, it's all clean lines, lowered eyes and silence. Here, it's chaotic merging shapes, leering looks and a wall of noise. I move into the rear of the pub and step out into the back garden. It's a freezing night, stars ridiculously clear in the inky sky. I miss the murky London skies, no stars, the blanketing of my old safe world.

And then I see Calder.

He's holding a pint aloft. Laughing. Huge full-body belly laughs. His beer is sloshing out of his glass. He's sweating, hair slicked back from his face, his body so relaxed and fluid. Seeing him like this is breathtaking. I step back into the shadows. It's like going back in time. Like the film of our lives has reversed: back through this last week of horror, the hospital stay, the accident, the move up here, my night with Hamish and now I'm landing slap back in London, in All Bar One in Oxford Street and Calder's meeting me after work, laughing uproariously about some shared joke. Calder and I loved to laugh, till drinks would spill and tears would pour down our faces. I'd totally forgotten that Calder, even though he existed only a few weeks ago.

Calder is fine. He is the old him. Right there in front of me. There's no brain injury, no psychological trauma. He's obviously just choosing to be vile with me. Specifically.

There's a huge cheer, as Calder downs his pint and slams the glass on the round wooden table. How has he been so awful with me all this time – so tense, so in need of special dispensation for his moods? When all the time, he's been capable of being like this. With them. But not with me. There was no ludicrous blood exchange obviously, but no physical injury either; he's just had the revelation that he despises me and wants rid of me. It wasn't in my imagination at all.

I circle round the very edge of the pub garden till I'm behind him. I take a small step in, head bowed, so I can tune into his conversation without him seeing me, my hood pulled over my head to avoid others noticing me.

'Ah, come on, she's not one of us,' he bellows at the

man on his left. It could be any 'she', but I know it's me.

'She's land-bound,' laughs a tall man in a khaki army jacket.

'Mainland-bound at this rate,' laughs a smaller man in a pork-pie hat.

Calder looks down.

'You need to get her bed-bound,' jacket-man continues. 'Busy with bairns.'

The men all laugh raucously.

Calder is shaking his head, silent. The group is suddenly awkward, glancing at one another.

'Sorry, didn't mean anything by that, just joking,' jacket-man says, slapping Calder on the back.

'We don't want kids, never have,' Calder says flatly. 'Another?' he asks, gesturing to the assembled men with his pint. They all cheer and he turns towards the pub.

I scurry back into the pub.

I'm halfway across the main room, the door ahead of me, when I stop dead. I swing round. And Calder walks straight into me. I pull back my hood.

'Nancy—' he mumbles, trying to focus.

'We don't want kids? Never have?'

'I was just—'

I swipe the empty pint glass from his hand. It slams onto the pub wall, smashing into a glass-encased stuffed fish, which shatters. Cries bounce off the walls as the spray of glass shards falls onto the customers below. They lurch backwards, chairs knocking over, wiping themselves down. It's now deathly quiet in this section of the pub as everyone stares at me; then the quiet spreads across the room, and across the whole pub. Everyone is staring and craning. Calder lurches slightly. I can see how drunk he is, but he can still see me down his tunnel of alcohol. He glances around at the appalled, excited drinkers.

'Oh no, am I being embarrassing,' I spit at him.

He reaches to touch me, but I swat him away.

'Fuck off!' I shout, the sound cutting across the quiet void. I'm shimmering with anger as I turn and sweep out, people dodging to avoid me.

I march out of the pub and along the road back to our cottage.

I glance back once. But no one's following me.

CHAPTER SEVENTEEN

When I reach the beach in front of our cottage, I want to throw myself into the freezing water. To experience first-hand what Calder felt that day. I lurch at it . . . but I can't. I can't face that cold submerging.

'AAGH!' I scream into the darkness, picking up handfuls of slate and chucking them into the water, hearing them plop in and then be swept up into the waves crashing and dragging on the shore.

Whoosh. Drag. Whoosh. Drag.

I can't feel what Calder felt. I never will.

My hands are raw and numb as I stomp back home, and I'm freezing by the time I shut the door. The cottage is arctic, frosty crystals on the inside of the windows. My toes curl on the floorboards, my hands ball into fists and I'm crouching over and shaking.

I know what happens with cold. Physiologically.

It curls around your limbs, sinks through your skin and settles deep into your flesh, till it scuds up against your organs. I remember the explanation from biology GCSE. Your body is trying to save the centre, to protect the heart so it can keep on beating, and sending out blood to those vital organs. To keep the centre safe, blood must cease flowing to the extremities, where the huge surface area allows a profligate loss of heat. As the cold takes hold, the tips start shutting down. 'The fingers, the toes, and the end of the nose,' my biology teacher Miss Summerbell recited in her sing-song voice, 'they're all cut off. Left to die at their chilly outposts, like foolhardy explorers.'

I thought I was cherished by Calder. Was one of his vital organs, his precious love, safe and protected above all else. But since that awful day of his near-drowning, I've become an expendable tip. I've been jettisoned by him, unnecessary for his survival. He's holding his centre. And I'm not in it.

I'm being cut off, frostbitten, till I drop away.

I slowly reach out and curl my fingers around the long silver freezer handle, and the door gives a sarcastic 'tut' as it opens. It is the embodiment of my mortal enemy: the cold, which Calder experienced out in the icy sea; and the cruel coldness with which Calder now treats me. I'm so sure that his physical coldness and psychic coldness are linked in some way, but I cannot unravel how. Does being frozen change you so totally? I have to know. I have to experience some tiny fleck of what he felt. Perhaps if I am frozen, I will be able to cut off from him and this pain will stop.

I pull out a big blue IKEA bag from my old London life and fill it with some of the frozen food, big solid hunks of meat, huge bags of vegetables and berries, icy chips, bagels, ice cream. I drag it into the bathroom and deposit it into our deep sarcophagus of a bath. I open the cold tap and turn the bulbous silver prongs as far as they'll go, then I drag off all my clothes. The water is already freezing as it gushes forth, but I let my meaty veggie ice-pops pull the temperature down even further as I make three more trips to the kitchen to bring in more frozen food, including the church-donated lasagnes, paellas and pies, and tip it all into my icy witch's brew.

The freezer alarm bleeps, because the door's been open too long. But I revel in the sound, leaning into it. Its desperate squawking perfectly expressing my desperation. Fuck Calder and the fucking mystery of whatever he experienced. It doesn't make him more special than me. It doesn't give him the right to discard me.

I am not nothing.

My naked skin is goose-bumped in preparation.

I test the water with my hand, and it's startlingly cold. Good. I step in and stand in the icy bath like a child paddling in dirty junk-filled water, my feet and calves smarting painfully. It's too cold. But I lower myself anyway and lie down flat amongst the floating packages, gulping air as the cold ignites my body.

Fighting my every natural instinct, I sink down beneath the surface and close my eyes, my head popping as the freezing water closes over me. I am iced, frozen and taken apart by the cold. I have spread beyond my physical form. Disembodied.

Is this what you felt, Calder? This but times a million, in that swirling freezing sea. Did you feel free of everything . . . released from yourself . . . escaping from me?

I need to breathe, but I stay down, ramming my heels onto the hard base of the bath. I open my eyes and they bulge into the iciness. I am made of searing pins and needles. I stare bug-eyed into the grimy water, registering the floating shapes and the white of the bathroom above.

Cold. Taken apart. Free.

Suddenly, a dark shadow looms over me. My wrist is clamped, and I'm dragged up out of the water. Rebirthed into the air.

'Fucking hell, Nancy!' Calder shouts as I hit the air.

'Get off me!' I scream, squirming out of his grasp and falling heavily, my shoulder smacking onto the rim of the bath. I scream in agony as I roll back under the water.

'Christ!' he shouts, lunging in and bear-hugging me to wrench me out. We both fall out of the bath, onto the cold tiled floor, my throbbing rubbery skin exploding off every surface I touch. I scrabble like Attila and crawl into the kitchen, my bare knees bruising on the hard floor.

Calder launches himself onto me and flattens me.

'I can't breathe!' I scream.

He lifts his weight but holds my wrists hard. 'Stop struggling and I'll let you go.'

'Get off me.'

'I can't let you hurt yourself. Stop it, Nancy.'

'Oh no, am I scaring you?' I shout, managing to pull one hand free and smashing it backwards at his head.

He yelps and loses hold for moment. I'm trying to get a purchase on the floor with my legs, to throw him off, but he's too strong for me and eventually I collapse down under his weight.

Trapped.

There's just my heavy breathing. In and out. In time with his. In and out. Like we're decompressing after a wild bout of sex. Our breaths slow together. I feel his spittle dripping onto my back.

Slowly, he releases my wrists, but I stay frozen.

'Get away from me,' I snarl.

He rolls sideways and stands up.

I roll over slowly and stare up at his hulk.

'What the fuck, Nancy?' he asks, daring to sound affronted. 'What were you doing?'

I painfully push myself up to sitting.

'Give me a towel,' I say, horribly conscious of my shivering nakedness, in front of this 'stranger'. He passes me a dressing gown from the bathroom door and I huddle it around me.

'I wanted to feel it,' I say in a low voice.

'Feel what?'

'What you felt,' I snap, raising my face. 'When you were out there. You're the one with the special experience that mere mortals like me can never know. The cold, the submerging, the whatever the fuck it was you experienced, 'cos you won't tell me. Will you?'

He is silent, motionless. I stand up and push him in the chest. 'Because something happened to you out there, didn't it? You're different. You've cut off from me. I can't reach you.'

'Stop this. We need to get you warm,' Calder begs, reaching for a towel.

I knock it out of his hands. 'No, I want to be cold. It's exciting,' I snarl. 'But then you'd know all about that.'

'I—'

'No, it's time for me to speak now. I've tried to talk to you. You chose not to engage. Fair enough. You don't owe me anything, just because of our past. I went to see your precious Dr Viner today.'

'What?'

'How dare you sound affronted. What do you expect me to do? You've cut me off.' I lift my hand to silence him. 'He was no help. Persuaded me that it's all my perception. But it's not. I saw you tonight, laughing, the old you. It's just me you loathe. Who you treat like dirt.'

'I—'

'I'm packing tonight and leaving here tomorrow. A clean slate for me!' I shout. 'While you've been doing . . . whatever it is you've been doing . . . I've stopped loving you.'

He doesn't react. Just stares down at the floor. 'Good,' he says eventually.

'Good?' I shout.

'I want you to leave me.'

It feels like the earth shakes.

'Because,' he continues, 'I haven't been able to leave you. But it's what must happen. I've wanted you to leave me, ever since the accident.'

Hearing him finally saying the terrible thing that I've silently feared is beyond bearing. I run at him, hitting his chest over and over. 'Who are you? What are you—?'

He catches my wrists and holds me tight. 'Nancy—'

'No!' I shout. 'Don't you dare. Tell me now. Who are you?'

He lets me go and I sink to the cold, hard floor. Defeated.

And then he speaks, 'I'm a murderer.'

CHAPTER EIGHTEEN

'What?'

'I'm a murderer,' he repeats dully, staring straight ahead.

I'm breathing heavily, sounding so loud in this silent room. 'I . . . I don't understand,' I whisper, my anger condensing into fear.

'I'm a murderer,' he says louder.

What is he saying? I inch my way back on the floor and stand up very slowly. He's staring at me, eyes wide, pupils huge and black – like when we pulled his body from the sea. I edge away from him.

He slowly brings his gaze to rest on me. Then takes a jerky step towards me. I step back.

He lifts his palms. 'It's OK, Nance.'

'Keep back,' I whisper, moving so the big table is between us.

I glance towards the door and he catches me.

'What do you think I'm going to do?' he asks incredulously.

'I–I don't know.'

'I'm not going to . . . hurt you. Is that what you think?'

'A murderer? I don't understand.'

I stare across at this man I used to know so well. What has he done? What is he going to do?

'Jesus, Nance, stop looking at me like that,' he says as he starts round the table.

I edge further round. 'I need some clothes. You stay there.'

I dart back to the bedroom, but he follows me and grabs me from behind.

'Listen to me!' he shouts in my ear, his smoky breath so close and suffocating.

'All right. But let go of me!' I shout, pulling free and running round the bed. Calder is glaring at me. 'Stay back!' I shout, lifting up a chair and brandishing it at him.

'What the fuck, Nance, I'm not going to hurt you. Christ.'

'You're scaring me. You need to keep back. What do you mean you're a murderer? Who did you kill?'

'Get in the bed,' he orders.

'What. No. Please. Please let me go.'

'To keep warm. Jesus, Nance. Look at you. You're freezing.'

I look down at myself, my gown flapping open to reveal my nakedness, and see that I'm shaking.

'I'll tell you,' he says slowly. 'I do need to tell you. But get into bed to get warm.'

I can't get past him and if I'm going to make a break for it, I need to warm up. So I pull on some trousers and a jumper from the floor and get under the covers. He moves to sit on the bed, but when he sees my face, he backs up and sits in the chair by the door. Blocking my escape?

The waves are breaking on the shore, dragging the slates.

Whoosh. Drag. Whoosh. Drag.

I stare across at him and I see my old Calder in his eyes. He's exhausted, agonised and spent. But it's him, as if the old him has settled back into his body. I know immediately that whatever he's saying, whatever he's about to tell me, it's the truth. Finally. And that there will be no going back from it.

We breathe in sync.

'Who?' I whisper. 'Who have you killed?'

'Robert Walker was his name,' he says dully.

'Who?'

'You don't know him.'

I shudder.

'You're freezing,' mumbles Calder. He gets a blanket from the cupboard and drapes it round my shoulders. I let him, unable to move. His face is so close to mine, his smoky breath wreathing around me. This man, who is admitting to . . . murder?

'But why?' I whisper.

He gives a small, gulping moan.

'I don't understand what you're—'

'Let me get it out.'

I nod.

He sits down on the bed. 'I killed him that day I nearly

drowned,' he says, looking up and back into his memory. 'I'd got up early that day, before daybreak. I opened the front door for some fresh air. But the second I stepped outside, I got this strong sense that I wasn't alone. I couldn't see anyone in the dark, but I knew someone was watching me, casing the cottage. They were careful, but I knew they were there. I called out to show themselves, but nothing. It was really pissing me off, so I decided to mess with them and I started round the cottage and over the hill.'

'In the dark?'

'I know it inside out and I thought they'd give up soon enough. But they kept on coming. So, I knew it was an islander. No mainlander could've dealt with that hill in the dark. I got up to the top of the cliff and the sun was just starting to come up. I was getting really narked. I crouched down behind a boulder and threw some stones ahead, to make them think I was further on than I was. And when they passed me, I tripped them up, and they went flying onto the cliff path.'

I'm appalled at the danger of being on the cliff in the half-light, but I don't stop his flow. He's talking so energetically, as if he's reliving it.

'I jumped on him and turned him over. I thought it was going to be one of the lads. We used to play so many stupid games up on that hillside. But it was . . . Robert Walker.' He takes a deep breath.

'But who is he? Do you – did you – know him?'

'He lived here when I was a boy. I haven't seen him for years.'

Some wordless knowledge is shifting inside me,

barrelling towards me. I don't want to know. But I have to.

'He left the island soon after me – to look for his daughter. When I turned him over, he was screaming, "Where is she? Where is she?"'

No. It can't be. Robert. An ex-islander. With a daughter. Who hasn't been seen since the night of Calder's accident? Robert. Rob. Janey's Rob? That gentle man with the twinkly eyes. 'Caitlin's dad,' I say slowly.

He frowns. 'Yes. How do you know that?'

Oh God. The smiley man from that morning at the shop – with the C tattooed on his neck. C for his missing daughter Caitlin. Calder killed Janey's boyfriend? Of all the things I thought he might say, I never ever imagined this.

'Nancy? How do you know that?'

'Janey mentioned Caitlin and her dad Rob.' I don't want to admit I've met him till I find out more.

'Caitlin and I dated in that last year I was here. I had all these plans for us. We talked about going to the mainland a lot that summer. I was so determined to get away from this claustrophobic backwater. But then she just left, without me.'

'But that night? With Mr Walker. What happened?'

Poor Janey is tying herself in knots thinking she's pushed Rob too far and destroyed their relationship – when he's been dead all along. Murdered the last night she saw him. By Calder.

'But why did you kill him? Because you do know where Caitlin is?'

He frowns. 'No, of course not. I haven't seen her since I was sixteen. She left a few days before I did and I've never known where she went. I thought Mr Walker had accepted that, but he obviously thought I was still hiding something.' Calder shifts on the bed and looks out the window. 'I was so shocked to see it was him. He was properly winded from the fall, and I was apologising for knocking him over. But he was screaming at me about Caitlin, said he'd just found out I was back and couldn't believe it.'

Janey must have told him. After he saw me in the shop.

Calder is glazed, staring back into his memory. 'He was so angry. "After all your big proclamations about what a shithole this place is."' Calder mimics him in a scathing tone. '"Filling my girl's head with all your nonsense about this big wonderful world out there, that was so much better than our life here. And then she hightails it without so much as a word to her mum or me." He went on and on about how her postcards told him nothing and that she was probably working as a prostitute or something down in London. He kept screaming at me. "Everyone here thinks I did something to her – but it was all your fault."'

'But how was it your fault?'

He shakes his head. 'I was obsessed with the mainland. I filled her head with it. But I thought she'd leave with me – not take off on her own.'

'OK. But what happened with Mr Walker that night?'

'He screamed that I didn't get to come back here as if nothing had happened. Kept saying "You must know something". Which I don't. Then he launched himself at me. And . . . I didn't mean it, I was feeling sorry for him, he was in so much pain, but he wouldn't stop attacking me and then he scratched my face, really deep and I . . . punched him. And he fell backwards. Off the cliff.'

'Oh God.' I think of that scar across his face when we pulled him from the water – not from being buffeted in the sea, but from Rob.

'He was there one second, hanging in the air, his eyes bulging, his arms scrabbling – and he was gone.' He slowly decompresses and lowers his gaze to me, and we stare at each other in silence. Then he gets up and walks to the window. 'I leapt forward but he was falling already. I saw his body bounce off the rocks. And then he fell into the water. And was gone.' He stares out at the sea.

'But it was an accident, wasn't it? A horribly unlucky punch. You read about that kind of thing all the time.'

He shakes his head. 'I knew where the cliff was. Maybe I meant to punch him off.'

'Did you?'

'No!' he cries. 'I don't think so. It happened so fast. I was trying to contain him – but in that split second . . .'

His agony is unbearable – but I can't make myself reach out to him across the void between us.

Eventually he turns towards me. 'So that's what happened,' he says dully.

'But how did you end up in the sea?'

'I'd seen him slam into the rocks but I thought that maybe there was a chance he was still alive, if he was just concussed, so I ran down and took my boat out to search for him.'

'In the storm?'

'I couldn't let it happen again.'

I stare at his back. 'Let what happen?'

He turns to the sea again. 'I couldn't let another man drown out there – where Dad drowned.'

'But you weren't on the island when your dad drowned. You had nothing to do with that.'

'No, but I know that's where it happened. The exact same spot. Mum told me.'

'So, you went out to try to save Mr Walker?' Finally, pieces are falling into place.

'But there was no sign of him, just endless grey thrashing water. Then it was suddenly a swirling cauldron 'cos I'd floated out to the whirlpools. I pulled on my life jacket, and the next second my little boat was thrown into the air and I was submerged.' Calder's eyes are wide and fixed, staring into the middle distance, back in the water. 'It was total blackness, this massive freezing water enclosing me, pulling me down. I was kicking and being pulled up by my jacket, but then it was worse when I broke the surface, the water surging and throwing me about like a doll. It was so fucking cold. I tried to swim towards the shore, could see the light of the cottage. I knew you were there, that I had to get to you. And then my chest started seizing and then . . . nothing.'

He looks back at me.

'But – I don't understand. Have you only just started to remember this?'

He shakes his head and looks down.

'But when? When did you remember?'

'As soon as I woke up in that hospital bed.'

'What?'

'I'm so sorry.'

I crawl forward towards him. 'You mean, you remembered all this and you didn't tell me.' Oh my God, the minutes, the days, the weeks of agony I've gone through, waiting, trying to understand. 'But why didn't you tell me? When you woke. Or any time after? Why didn't you explain? Did you not remember clearly? Were you confused?'

He shakes his head. 'No. I knew. From the moment I opened my eyes. Remembered the whole thing, like it had just happened a few seconds before, crystal clear. I couldn't believe it when Dr Viner said I'd been there a few days. It was like it had just happened. But I couldn't tell you.'

'Why not?' I cry as I step off the bed. My fear of him is now subsumed in my anger.

'How could I tell you what I'd done, burden you with this terrible secret? I couldn't bear to see your face, have you see me for what I was. A murderer.'

I step right up to him. 'But you left me totally confused – shut out.'

'If I'd told, I'd be arrested, imprisoned for murder. I wanted to escape that. I was totally selfish. In survival mode.'

'But you could have told me.'

He shakes his head. 'I couldn't lay this all on you too. I thought I'd be caught eventually – that Mr Walker would soon be missed. That someone would work out that he'd gone missing on the night of my accident. That I'd be questioned. But – nothing. Everyone was reacting to me like my return was a miracle. Like I'd done something amazing.' He suddenly slams his fist into the wall then hunches over in agony.

I am so angry at being shut out, it almost dwarfs the horror of what he's done. I'm not scared of him any more, but I feel so distant from this moaning heap of a man.

He crumples onto the bed. 'I was a murderer, a selfish coward and no one knew – especially you. I thought maybe I could bury it all down, as if it never happened. That I could come back to the island and it would gradually recede. That I could eventually meet your eye. Start up our life again. But you can't clean the slate like Arran says. God had thought of killing me in the sea, but then decided on a worse punishment – for me to have to live with what I'd done. Yes, I went to that stupid church, and that's when I knew there really was no hope for us, that I had to push you away and get you to go back to London so I could end things.'

I remember that weird peace he had after the service. But it wasn't peace, it was a stoic decision to drive me away . . . and kill himself?

'All I see every day is Mr Walker's face, just before he fell. His eyes, knowing I'd killed him. We couldn't go on. I had to get you away from me – so I tried to make you hate me, make you leave me. It was agony being nasty to you. I'm so so sorry.' Calder rocks back and forth, violently hitting himself.

'Stop it!' I scream. 'Stop it!' I leap forward to grab his arms, but he pushes me off and I slam backwards against the wall. He looks at me in horror.

'I'm OK,' I say, though I've jarred my back. 'But please calm down, Calder, you're scaring me. I can't take any more.'

My words, rather than calming him, seem to ignite something in him. 'Of course I'm scaring you,' he says, standing up. 'My dad scared my mum, terrified her, and now here I am doing the same to you.' He punches himself in the face.

'Stop it!' I scream, grabbing his arms.

'I always vowed I'd never be anything like my dad. He was a violent, horrible man. You had this idea of my parents as decent, God-fearing, a strong couple. But it was just the ridiculous pressure from the church – all this "unbreakable knot" stuff about having to stay together. And he was so big in the church, one of the elders, he would never consider splitting. My mother put up with so much from him. His irrational lashing out when he was drunk. Or just because he wanted to. He seemed to enjoy the violence. And then off to church on a Sunday to get forgiveness.'

'But you're not like your father.'

'I am!' he shouts and I rear back. 'See, I know that look in your eyes. I saw it in Mum day after day.'

I want to get away, but he's so wild with self-hatred, I'm scared of what he'll do. 'No. Your accident was a single moment of madness. That's not you. Rob provoked you. He attacked you. It was self-defence.'

He laughs. 'I was the stronger one. I could have wrestled him down. I was just so angry at being hit. And guilty, I guess, because he was right. I drove his daughter off the island. I've got a temper. In London, I felt like I'd escaped that side of me. With you. But it was always there. My darkness. It was stupid to come back here, to the memories of Dad. I was only back a week and I killed someone.'

'So, is that why you invited Hamish up here?' I say slowly, piecing the last weeks back together. 'To get me to go back to London somehow?'

He nods. 'I asked both Gina and Hamish to come. I was panicking. No matter how vile I was, you wouldn't leave. I wanted to get you away safely and then I could . . . but first I was really worried about money. I didn't want you to be left in huge debt. And I'd already spent so much. I thought Hamish could come up and make the business viable. We could make back the huge outlays. So you wouldn't be left with nothing, when I—'

'Killed yourself?'

'I'm sorry, Nance, I'm so sorry. But you're better off without me.'

'No. That's not true.'

This is all so impossible to take in. But the idea that Calder was going to kill himself is too awful. I can't leave him now. I have to pull him back.

He shakes his head. 'I'm a coward. An idiot. A murderer.' He walks towards the door.

'What are you doing?'

He pulls the door open. 'I'll do what I should have done as soon as I woke up in hospital. Go to the police.'

'No.' The word comes out without thought. After this awful revelation, I feel a strange lifting, because at last, I start to sort of understand what's happened. I grip his arm. 'I feel like I'm talking to the real you again. For the first time since the accident. Things make some sort of crazy sense. We have to think about all this before we make any decision.'

'Think about what?'

I'm warming up, stacking back together, and thinking about how Calder can get away with murder.

CHAPTER NINETEEN

'What was Mr Walker doing on the island at all?' Calder asks as we pack the salvageable frozen food back into the freezer. My hands are numb but I don't feel any pain. I hardly feel my body at all, as I've leapt from anger to fear to . . . what? We're fully dressed, heaters on, and we've been going round and round for hours. I've started organising because I can't sit still for a second longer or I'll implode.

'Go back to the beginning again,' I say, needing to anchor myself in facts. One moment I'm scared of Calder and want to get away, and the next I'm scared for him and can't imagine leaving him.

'Like I said, Mr Walker was just there when I went out that morning, waiting for me. I hadn't thought of him in years. I don't know why he came to ours that particular morning in such a state?' Calder forces a pack of frozen pittas into a haphazardly stuffed freezer drawer. We're acting out a grotesque parody of domesticity.

'Janey must have told him you were back,' I say quietly, passing him a column of rock-hard bagels. 'I saw him at her shop one morning earlier that week.'

'What?'

'She's been seeing him. I didn't want to interrupt you before to explain. She calls, called, him Rob. That's why he was on the island. 'Cos they're seeing each other secretly.'

'Oh my God.' He forces the freezer drawer closed, something plastic snapping with the force.

'She asked me not to tell you as she didn't want to stir up some old rumours about him and Caitlin.'

He sits down and puts his head in his hands. 'I've been racking my brains all these weeks, trying to work out why he came here.'

'He occasionally comes over in his boat in the dark to visit her.'

'Jesus, that's not easy here. It's hard not to be seen.'

'She said he wasn't welcome with most of the locals, due to him still being married to Alison, and rumours about him and Caitlin. Is that really why you fought?'

'No. That was all ridiculous gossip. Utter tosh made up by Alison 'cos she was so bitter when they split.'

'You're sure?'

'Yes, of course. I knew Caitlin better than anyone. If there'd been anything creepy from her dad, she'd have told me.'

'But how can you be so sure?'

'We had no secrets.'

I feel a stab of jealousy at their closeness. Does he still miss her?

'But she left without you? Didn't you think that was suspicious?'

He shrugs. 'She was very impetuous, always breaking rules.' I hate this admiration for his ex. His beautiful ex. And a true islander.

'So, you have no idea at all where she is?'

'No, of course not.'

I get up to put the kettle on the hob. I need coffee to think more clearly.

'Shouldn't I go to the police now?' he asks. 'How can you accept this, after all I've put you through?'

'I don't know if I can. But I think you made a terrible mistake. Did a momentary action with dire consequences. That's not murder. Manslaughter I guess?' I know I'm trying to balance what Calder's done on some scale with what I've done. His murder is obviously so much worse than my sleeping with Hamish – but was similarly done without thought or planning.

Now.

Now is the time to tell him about what I've done. I've cheated. He's killed. Surely my sin is less than his and he'll forgive me.

'Calder.'

'Yes?'

'I have to—'

'What is it?'

'I . . .'

The kettle starts whistling, screaming a warning.

I can't tell him. But maybe, by accepting what he's

done, I can accept what I've done for the both of us. I pour the water into mugs and add milk. 'Calder, I can understand a momentary awful action.' I sit him down and take his hands in mine. He looks down. 'No, look at me. Come on Calder.'

I can forgive myself, by forgiving him.

'I don't think we should tell anyone,' I say slowly.

'But . . .'

'No, listen to me. No one knows or can ever guess what you did. So why destroy our lives?'

He shakes his head. 'But what happens when his body washes up?'

'Well, it hasn't washed up yet. And it's been weeks.'

'But . . . Janey will sound the alarm eventually. Surely.'

'I don't think so. She thinks Rob's ended things with her after an argument.'

'But someone will register he's missing from wherever he's living now. People don't just disappear nowadays and no one registers it.'

'They might register someone missing, but it's not that unusual. Thousands and thousands of people go missing every year. Especially men. I've read about it – there's some crazy statistic like, someone is reported missing every ninety seconds. There are so many unsolved missing persons cases. The police are used to them. And Rob, Mr Walker, was a single man, living alone, shunned by his local community.'

'Jesus, listen to you,' Calder says, looking at me in horrified fascination.

'What?' I let go of his hands. 'You think I'm sounding hard? Well, I've become hard over the last few weeks.'

'I'm sorry, I'm so sorry.'

I take his hands again. 'We're here now. After my parents died in that . . . accident, I imploded for a while, but then I gradually accepted that you can't go back after terrible things happen – you are where you are, and you have a choice to make. To give up. Or to go on. I'm so sorry about poor Mr Walker. I so wish it had never happened. But we can't undo what's happened. There's no *Groundhog Day* rerun option. All we can do is accept it has happened – and make a choice.' I swallow, hearing my hard logic. But I can't back out of this. I'm over a canyon on a wire. I have to follow it through – save him, save myself.

'Oban, she said,' I blurt.

'What?'

'Oban. That's where Rob was living – in a rented room, I guess. So yes, eventually someone will notice. But why would they connect him to you? Even Janey doesn't know that he disappeared that particular night – just that she hasn't heard from him since that night when as far as she knows he left the island and went back to Oban. So, there's no connection with you whatsoever. So many people go missing, especially sad lonely people, so his disappearance won't arouse that much suspicion. We can be careful not to let the police make the connection with you. We can choose to not let your one terrible mistake ruin our future.'

I pull my chair closer and lean over to rest my head on his chest. I can feel his heart beating strongly. He nearly killed himself trying to do the right thing by saving Rob. And then I saved him. So now I'm responsible for helping him live with what he did. It was an accident. Intention is all. I have to believe that. For him and for me.

He pulls his cigarettes towards him.

'Is that why you started smoking after your accident? 'Cos you felt you were like your dad?'

He nods. 'Yeah. I smoked as a teenager and started again 'cos of all the stress after my accident. But every time I took a drag, I could feel Dad taking one. He was violent, I was violent. He'd drowned, I'd nearly drowned. Should have drowned.'

'But you're not him. I know you're not. The fact that you struggled with what you'd done, even though it was an accident, shows that you're basically good. I've lived with you for five years. I know the real you. You're a kind, caring, gentle man. One terrible mistake doesn't take all that away.'

'I started consciously trying to be him, so I could be cruel to you. Tough, smoking, eating meat. I had to make you leave me but I couldn't do it if I was me. But I could do it if I was him.'

Finally everything is making a terrible sense.

'Rob's dead. You tried to save him. You nearly killed yourself in the process. What good will it do for you to destroy our lives? You're not your father. You're not a violent man. Don't I get some say in this? If you turn yourself in, you're destroying your life, but you're also destroying my life.' I shake him. 'We can do this, Calder. Now you've told me, you can get beyond this.'

'But—'

'But now you've got me in your corner. You know how strong I am. With me helping you, you can get through this.'

He gives a little snort and pushes a strand of hair behind my ear. 'You think you can will anything into being, don't you?'

'I've been going out of my mind since your accident. Thinking you were injured, changed, possessed – whatever the cause, I thought you didn't love me.'

'I'll always love you,' he whispers. 'But how can you still love me?'

'I'm a lot tougher than you think.'

'Tough enough for living with what I've done?' He reaches for his pack of cigarettes then shakes his head. 'I can't put all this on you – I have to go to the police.'

How little he knows me. 'You think I can't deal with it?'

He nods then pulls a cigarette out of the crumpled pack. I take a match out of his box and strike it. It flares violently, but I don't hold it up to him. I just stare at it, as it slowly burns down and singes my fingers. I don't flinch.

'Stop it!' he shouts, knocking the match out of my hands. 'What are you doing?'

I calmly strike another match and it starts to burn down, but he blows it out.

'Stop it, Nance. Now you're scaring me.'

'Then stop spiralling and hear what I'm saying. I can, we can, survive this.'

I light a third match. He nods. And this time, I light his cigarette.

'I'm a lot, lot stronger – and tougher – than you think.'

He takes a deep drag, holds the breath and then we both watch the smoke as he breathes out. The grey curls hang in the air and then gradually fade away. Only the woody smell lingers. It reminds me of my father. I got myself through what I did to my parents by toughening up. I can get Calder through what he's done. And save myself in the process.

I reach up and stroke his face. He leans down and kisses me. It's finally my Calder kissing me. For the first time since the accident. And I feel like he's accepting me despite what I've done, because I'm accepting what he's done. He runs his fingers through my hair. I feel myself softening, melting into him.

'Come on,' I say.

He nods and follows me to the bedroom. He sits on the bed. And it's like we've stepped through a magic looking glass back into our old selves. I don't let myself think. Just lean into our connection. I slowly kiss his forehead along the long scar, kiss his cheek, his neck. I push him back and smile down on him.

'Are you OK?' I ask gently.

'Are you?'

'If you're OK, I'm OK.'

I reach out and touch his face.

Then I pull my dress over my head. It catches on my watch and we smile nervously as I pull hard and rip the seam. I try to unbutton his jeans, but the metal buttons are stiff in my icy fingers. And we laugh weakly, but like we used to. It's like we've stepped away from the awful real world of our actions and into our private safe place again. He reaches to touch me, but I push him down and run my fingers lightly across his chest, down across his firm stomach, and then between his legs. He's my Calder again. I feel powerful for the first time in weeks. I lie down next to him. We're desperate for each other, but we hold back. Everything is so fragile. Our bodies moving together feel so familiar; every subtle touch of our fingers across our skin, every press of flesh, every teasing pull back, and every tentative kiss feels so exquisitely known. Our bodies slide against each other as we kiss lightly and then deeply. Eventually, I can't bear it any more and I straddle him and guide him into me, and finally, finally, we are together again, lost in each other, utterly melded – and safe.

CHAPTER TWENTY

The arches of my feet are fitted into the soles of his feet, knees piled on knees, thighs against thighs, chests moving in sync, lungs inflating together, hearts beating as one. It's well into the morning, but I don't want to get out of this bed. My body is tingling all over. The slightest touch is intense. There is only this endless wordless connection. We've been alone together in the cottage for three days. Calder rang Hamish and told him to go back to London and that he'll sort the business out himself. Thank God I don't have to see him again. Now I'm helping Calder to accept what he's done and in doing so helping myself to accept what I've done. Of all the people who could understand this moral relativism, it would be Gina. But I can't ever explain it all to her. And hopefully will rarely, if ever, need to see her again.

I yawn, stretch and start to slide back into the safe blur of sleep.

But there's an irritating distant bleating sound.

'What's that?' Calder murmurs.

Everything is still brittle with us, but starting to make sense. It's like we've stepped off a swirling waltzer ride at the fair. We're disorientated, but now there's solid ground under our feet.

The sound again.

I shake Calder's shoulder. 'What is that?'

'Foxes probably,' he mumbles.

'The foxes don't usually come up near the cottage in the daytime.'

'Just ignore them,' he says, stroking his hand across me gently.

Then there's a loud knocking on the door.

We freeze.

'Who's that?' I whisper. Have they come for Calder? How do they know?

The strange bleating sound starts up again.

'What is that?'

'I think it's – a baby crying?'

'But who's coming here with a baby?'

More loud knocking, the baby shrieking now. We stare at each other in horror. We're not ready to face the world with our secret yet.

'What do we do?' Calder asks, sitting upright.

'We ignore it. They'll go away.'

More loud knocking and raised voices.

'I'll go,' Calder says, pulling on his discarded shirt and jeans. He bounds through to the kitchen, while I hover behind him as he pulls open the door.

And there, totally out of place, is the larger-than-life

presence of Gina, Hamish's wife, grinning at us and holding a bawling red-faced baby, with Hamish standing behind her, looking nervous.

Oh God, how's he still here? Has he told Gina about us?

'Darling, there you are, come here,' Gina laughs, melodramatically flinging her arms out for a hug, her long red hair swinging out. So he hasn't told her.

I step forward, pulling my dressing gown around me as I'm enfolded in a hug.

Their pudgy baby is screaming its head off between us.

'Hamish, can you do something with him?' Gina says, unhooking a massive purple carry-contraption from her chest and passing the baby to him.

He stares at me and mouths 'Sorry' behind her back.

'You two took for ever answering the door. Whatever can you have been doing?' she says with a smirk. 'If you're trying to make one of these, I advise against it!' She sees my horrified expression. 'Sorry darling.' She must think I'm offended about the baby comment. 'I'm just tired of the wailing. I hadn't quite appreciated what a long journey it was up here.' She's bustling into our little grey cottage, her expensive sunglasses on her head, wearing an oversized jungle print DryRobe with fuchsia lining. It's all her London colour and intensity that I used to love. But now I desperately want the last ten seconds of reality to rewind and for her to be picking up her bright detritus, reversing her steps and being sucked back into some mental image of a London that I can miss. I don't want London coming here.

'Calder, it's been a long time,' Gina booms, slapping him on the back.

'Have you brought all the children?' I ask, looking outside.

'Are you mad. My mum's got the other three and I got the early flight to Glasgow this morning and a taxi from there. This place really is at the end of the world.'

'A big surprise to me too,' Hamish says.

'Hey,' Gina laughs. 'You're a lucky, lucky man, and don't you forget it.'

'Obviously it was a lovely surprise.'

'I thought you were going back to London?' I say to Hamish, pointedly.

'I was just finishing up what I'd started for Calder's business. And then Gina announced she was coming to join me. But said not to tell. She wanted it to be a surprise for you two.'

'Oh well – it certainly is that.'

Gina's eyes are running me up and down. I must look a fright to her. Dishevelled, make-up-less, in a dirty dressing gown, so unlike the primped and plucked woman she knew in London just a month ago. Calder glances at me and I see him through Gina's judgemental eyes: his hair greasy and wild, his eyes bloodshot, a hole in his dusty shirt, stubble sprouting over his face.

'You should have let us know you were coming,' I exclaim.

'What kind of welcome is that, about as excited as my husband's was,' Gina laughs, but I see her taking us in and storing up questions. 'I've come to help. Now where can I change this squawking lump?'

I slept with her husband and miscarried his child. Now she's here with their baby while we're still trying to come to terms with Calder having murdered someone. Dear God.

'You see,' Hamish says, 'I said you shouldn't just rock up.' He flicks a glance at me and I look away.

'I've only got two nights here,' she announces, 'and then Hamish and I have to get back to the kids. If you don't need him any more?'

'I'm fine now,' Calder says. 'I already told you that, Hamish.'

'But you're very welcome,' I say brightly, aware how tense we're sounding. Gina frowns, not fooled. 'No really,' I say, embracing her. 'I'm just a bit shocked to see you two in our painfully unglamorous home. But it's lovely to see you. Come in and you can sort, God sorry, what's his name, I've totally blanked?'

'Mason,' Gina says. 'I know, it's the fourth. I should just give them numbers at this point.'

'Mason, yes of course. He's lovely.'

'He's a pain in the arse most of the time, aren't you,' Gina murmurs to her baby, then lays out a changing mat on the kitchen table and unpeels a stinking, poo-filled nappy. I've wanted a baby for so long, but the physical reality of one, right here right now, is so violent.

'We were waiting for you to get settled before we suggested a visit,' Gina says, 'then poor Calder's accident happened and you didn't want help – no, no, I can read the room, it's fine – then out of the blue, Calder invited us. But I couldn't get away till now.'

Hamish brushes against me as he walks in. I shiver but don't make eye contact, and sidestep him. Of course, I should never think things can't get worse. There's always a trapdoor at the bottom of the barrel you're scraping.

'Well, it's wonderful to see you,' I manage. 'Give me a moment.'

'That's OK, I—' Gina starts, but I'm out of the room, waving away her protestations.

'Come on, Calder, we should get dressed,' I call.

'I'm sorry,' Calder whispers as he closes our bedroom door. 'I should never have asked for their help. I thought he'd gone home.'

'We just have to act normal.'

'How can we possibly act normal?'

'I've been doing it for weeks with you,' I snap. 'You have to deaden off.'

'You two all right?' Gina asks as she sweeps in without knocking. 'Who's deadening off?'

'Oh, err, Calder has an ingrowing toenail. He's not good with pain.'

'I'll be fine,' Calder says, giving me a desperate look and walking out.

'I don't want you to go to any extra trouble for us,' she says. 'We'll sleep at Hamish's cottage and see you in the day.' The baby's now back in its purple contraption on her front, sleeping soundly. 'Was this a huge mistake coming here? Hamish said you might not want me here.' *Did he?* 'But you've been sounding so out there on the phone – when I could get hold of you.'

I'm violently tucking the bedsheet.

'Hey! Nancy. Stop for a second. It's me. What's up with you?'

'I'm fine. Just a bit knackered with the move and then Calder's accident,' I say, finding clothes. 'But it's great to see you. I mean it.'

She frowns, but the door flies open and Calder bursts back in. 'I've decided to help Hamish give Gina a tour of the island. He's never brought her here. Give you some time to get some food in for our visitors, Nance.'

'Umm, yeah, sure,' says Hamish, looking over Calder's shoulder. Why didn't he leave when we told him to?

'That's a good idea,' I say, nodding my thanks at both of them.

'I'd rather stay here with you,' Gina says.

'Oh no,' I blurt loudly. 'You must see the island and then I'll be more sorted for guests. Will the baby – will Mason be all right being carted around?'

'Oh God yes. He sleeps a million hours a day. At this stage, it's just like carrying around a large poo-ey watermelon in a sling. All right, if you're sure. We'll get out of your hair and catch up properly later. OK?'

'We'll have a feast tonight. I'll do my coconut chicken.'

Gina puts on some ridiculously expensive walking boots that she's clearly bought at the airport and sweeps out with Hamish looking sheepish.

Calder steps back in and catches my arm.

'I love you,' he whispers.

'Be strong,' I say, squeezing his arm and hoping he can hold things together.

As Janey glances at my ingredient list, I stare at the door frame behind her, remembering Rob's bright eyes and his gentle caress of her face, right there, only a few weeks ago. Calder killed the poor man. Talking about toughing it out when we were in our private little cocoon was one thing. Lying directly to Janey is another. How can we possibly live here? We'll have to relocate.

'I can get you anything with enough notice. I'll see what I've got.'

'How are you doing?' I ask, trying to sound light.

'I'm OK, muddling on – but I think it really is over with Rob.'

'Oh, that's a shame.' *God I'm vile.*

'I've heard nothing from him at all. Total radio silence.'

I widen my eyes in a pathetic parody of affront. 'That's a bit mean of him.'

'That's what I thought at first. But now I'm getting annoyed, as he's completely ignoring all my calls.'

'Well . . . maybe he's going cold turkey to deal with the break-up?' *I'm going straight to hell.*

'But that's extreme, isn't it? He's not a cruel man. And anyway, I've looked at all his social media and he hasn't been active on it for weeks. That's so not like him: he's always reposting stuff about missing people, commenting.'

'Does sound a bit strange. But people do take breaks from their socials when they're overwhelmed, don't they?' *I'm not going to hell – I'm there already.*

'I think I'll drive over to his Oban digs soon. To have it out with him.'

'Good idea,' I say brightly. Oh God, the net's closing in on us.

She starts checking my list and collecting ingredients. 'Anyway, enough of my sad dating life. How are you and Calder doing?'

'Oh, things are a bit, a lot, better. I'm sorry I went on before. I gave you the wrong impression 'cos I was a bit overwrought. We're fine.'

She narrows her eyes. 'I'm here if you need me. Take your time. But . . .'

'I'm really fine. Honestly.'

'OK. Right, let's finish this list: chicken breasts, chicken stock, fresh coriander, coriander seeds, cumin, turmeric, cardamon, onion, garlic, olive oil, coconut milk, limes, almond shards and coconut flakes.' She makes a face. 'I've got everything except the chicken breasts, a couple of the herbs and the last three. But I've got thighs and the rest. Can you manage?'

I leave with a bag of some of the ingredients and a sackful of shame.

I want to text Calder about Janey's plans to search for Rob in Oban, but I daren't risk eagle-eyed Gina reading my message.

As I walk back from the shop, along the row of white cottages, I see a tall slim silhouette approaching in a long grey church raincoat, with two huge baskets of flowers: Alison. She's poised and radiant. If she knew about Rob's murder . . . would she be distraught or not, given what Janey's said? But how can I talk to the not-quite-ex-wife of the man Calder killed? I start to turn away but she's seen me and is giving me her fixed smile as she approaches.

'More beautiful flowers, Alison,' I manage to say, in what I hope sounds like a normal voice. And they are beautiful, glorious reds, whites, and purples and a cascade of dark green foliage. 'Arran's very lucky to have you doing his flowers.'

'Thank you, I've been scouring the mainland markets and as well as the obvious holly I've got irises, red winter roses and snowdrops. I see you've been shopping at Janey's?'

'Yes, I've got a dinner party tonight.'

'Janey's is hardly the place for dinner party ingredients,' she says with a sneer. No wonder Janey and Rob didn't want this tense, judgemental woman knowing about them. But who am I to judge her when Calder killed her husband, and propelled her daughter to leave the island.

'We've had some London friends turn up unexpectedly.' I feel like I'm acting in a play.

'My daughter Caitlin lives in London,' she says abruptly.

'Oh, lovely,' I say stupidly.

'Well, I don't know really, we're not in much contact. Just the odd postcard.'

I nod. 'That must be hard. Well, I better get on, I—'

'Calder and Caitlin dated, you know,' she says, with an odd smile. 'That last year she was on the island.'

'Yes, he said.'

'Oh? What did he say about her?' she says sharply.

'Not much. Just that she was one of his girlfriends.'

'Hardly "one of",' she says, narrowing her eyes. 'They were very much an item. I thought he'd marry her eventually.'

'I suppose they were quite young then.'

She purses her lips and fiddles with her flowers. 'They were very smitten. Has he never mentioned meeting up with her in London?'

'No, never.'

She inclines her head, assessing me. 'All her postcards are postmarked from a Central London sorting office. Perhaps he didn't tell you about meeting up with her there?'

'I don't think so.' It's so disconcerting to be accused of one untrue secret while hiding a worse true one. 'Whereabouts does she live?'

'Central London I presume,' she says sarcastically. 'She's a secretary, I know that, very busy, happy – but I have no way to contact her.'

'That must be upsetting.'

She scrutinises her flowers and snaps off a frond she finds wanting.

'Anyway, I should—'

'Whereabouts did you live with Calder in London?'

'Russell Square – it's near King's Cross.'

'The very definition of "Central London".' She smiles. 'Yes well. I'd best get on, get these flowers into the fridge.'

'The fridge?'

'It keeps them fresh. I have a separate fridge just for them, because some food, especially fruit, gives off ethylene gases which harm them.'

We're just talking about flowers but there's some subtext that I can't get a fix on. 'You put a lot of care into your flowers.'

'I've learnt how to preserve them,' she says in a steely voice. 'I need to cut these stems, get them well watered, remove excess leaves' – she snaps off another leaf – 'and get them on my proprietorial blend of sugar, pH-levelling acid, and a bit of bleach to reduce the bacteria.'

'Wow. You're a real expert. You'd think it would be too cold for them in a fridge.'

'Oh no, it works for a couple of days. But you can't freeze them. I tried that. Catastrophic.'

* * *

Our kitchen table rocks as I thump down my string-bag of produce. I lay out Calder's mother's utensils, which are worn but sturdy, including a set of dangerous-looking yellow-handled knives.

I tip the chicken legs onto the chopping board and they roll everywhere. I prefer using breasts, but Calder likes legs. 'Legs have more flavour,' I remember him saying once, back in our little London flat, when he was parodying a cook we'd just watched on *MasterChef*. He tucked a tea towel into his jeans, ripped off an oily haunch and did a great impression of the guy's exuberant manner: 'The legs are more muscular, gorgeous browned skin for flavour, and then there's all that lovely bony richness.' I think of Calder's muscular body that I love and must protect at all costs, of Hamish's fair freckled skin that slid against mine on that drunken night together, and of Robert's bones, somewhere deep in the sea, waiting to come back and destroy us.

Without all the ingredients I don't bother following my usual recipe and so I'm 'winging it', making some kind of spicy stew. I'm an instruction follower, so out of my depth in this situation so far beyond my control.

No one knows Calder's secret, except me. I can keep it, but can he?

Hamish knows part of my secret. I can keep it all, but can he?

Can I hold myself together and keep these two men from revealing everything?

I unwrap a stock cube. Dark brown, sharp corners, dusty stink. Before I met Calder, I would have bought a lump of resin this big to smoke, to get me through the week. For the first time in years, I wonder how to get some here on the island. I pour hot water over the stock cube, hoping for a mouth-watering transformation. But it hunkers at the bottom of the glass measuring jug, defiantly not dissolving. I bash it into smaller chunks with a wooden spoon. I finely slice two onions, speed-slamming the huge knife down over and over, enjoying the release of the smarting tears, till I have an onion mush, which I fry. Then I brown the chicken legs, but have to look away from what look like sizzling baby limbs.

Every phone bleep makes me jump. Calder texts me with pointless updates of their tour of the island, and says they're stopping for a pub lunch. He's giving me time to compose myself, while unable to stop himself from reaching out to me. I'm dazed and jittery. His revelation was so outlandish and I'm trying to process, to justify, but how on earth can I pretend to be the hostess with the mostess when they return?

When they bundle in at four, throwing their stuff about and declaring how 'totally knackered' they are, I suggest they chill in the lounge. But they all hover in the kitchen, Gina giggly and secretive.

'What? What is it?' I ask, looking from one to the other. Calder looks sheepish. Hamish looks annoyed.

'Please someone tell me what's happened?'

'Daa, da, da, daaaaa, daa, da, da, daaaaa,' Gina sings, clearly tipsy.

That's the wedding march.

'You are our very own Bride of Frankenstein,' she laughs. 'We were so happy when we read the headline.'

'Oh, that stupid newspaper. Well, yes, eventually, once Calder's back to full strength,' I stammer.

'It all kind of happened very quickly,' Calder mumbles.

'Yes. Well, your accident showed me what was important in life.' Now I understand his horror when I asked him to marry me in the hospital.

'No, he means, things happened quickly this afternoon,' Gina smirks.

'What happened very quickly?'

'You're getting married.'

'Eventually, yes.'

'Not eventually!'

Gina is fizzing with her news, while Hamish and Calder both look embarrassed.

'What's going on, please will someone tell me?'

'Arran was in the pub,' Calder says warily. 'He came over when Gina insisted on buying champagne.'

'What a lovely man,' she says, 'wonderful eyes. I explained that my best friends were getting married soon, and he knew all about it of course from the press coverage when you were in hospital. I said something about not knowing if I could get back up here for whenever the wedding was going to be and he said, no problem, we could have the wedding while we're here.'

'What?'

'Tomorrow in fact. I don't know why you two have waited so long.'

'No.' I look at Calder who shrugs helplessly. 'It's not possible. Not that I don't want to. But there'd be too much to organise.'

'You know I love organising,' Gina says, 'I've got loads

242

of people in the village on it already.'

'But it's just not feasible. We haven't even registered the marriage yet.'

'That's all done,' Calder says.

'What? By who?'

'By the groom,' Gina shrieks.

'What?'

He shrugs. 'Just before my accident I went to see Arran. You asked me to.'

'When?'

'You remember. You wanted me to tell him that you'd passed on the message about his visit. And when I was with him, I suddenly thought what a great surprise it would be if I . . . registered our wedding. I was about to ask you before the accident.'

'But . . . the groom and the bride have to both be there to register, surely?'

'Arran was so excited he said he'd waive that requirement.'

'But—' I flail desperately, searching for more impediments. 'The banns! We haven't had them read. Isn't that a thing?'

Gina laughs. 'That Arran is a controlling monster. Man after my own heart. He told us that when he read about you two getting engaged when you were in hospital, he started getting the banns read in that dinky little church of his.'

'What?'

'And they've done three weeks' worth during the evening services, not telling you in case Calder wasn't ready, so, you're good to go.'

I stare at everyone, Gina all hyper with her plan, Hamish looking stunned, Calder looking scared.

'What right did Arran have to post our banns without us, to push for this wedding?' I shout, incensed by his meddling. Janey was right about him. Why is he pushing this at such speed? Is he trying to head Hamish off at the pass or something?

'All right. Calm down,' Gina says. 'Arran said tomorrow was the perfect day. Because it's the shortest day of the year, the winter solstice, the day of rebirth apparently. All very pagan and magical. I love it.'

'Why is everything so bloody symbolic for that man?' I snap.

'Nancy,' Calder warns and I realise that they're all staring at me.

'Don't you want to get married?' Gina says suspiciously.

'She doesn't want to be rushed,' Hamish says.

'You don't have to,' Calder says. 'Let's forget it.'

I look around at their questioning faces. I desperately wanted to marry Calder before, might want to again one day, but not like this. Not with all I have to get my head around, with Calder only recently teetering on suicide, and definitely not in that judgemental slate church, with that control freak pastor presiding and reaching into my soul, and with Gina and Hamish looking on with their bloody baby. Oh God.

'Come on, Nancy, embrace the moment,' Gina laughs nervously. 'That Arran was positively champing at the bit. And some woman called Alison said she'd got lots of flowers for the solstice theme.' Of course Alison stuck her nose in . . . Gina nods encouragingly at me. 'Come on,

Nancy. You get to marry the love of your life in that cute little slate church you're always going on about. How can you not?'

I don't reply.

Gina frowns – she's confused by my hesitation.

Hamish frowns – does he have the wrong idea about us?

Calder frowns – is he losing faith in my belief in him?

'It's just shock,' I say. 'But.' I have no choice. 'Yes!'

CHAPTER TWENTY-ONE

It's my wedding day.

The kitchen is a chaotic mess from last night. Discarded bowls of my disgusting dried-up stew lie untouched. Wine bottles, glasses and snack remnants are strewn everywhere. I'm ignoring the screeching brakes inside my head telling me to call this wedding off. I think of my parents in those final seconds before their car careered off the road into oncoming traffic. They had no chance to save themselves as that lorry drove straight at them, its headlight blinding them, its huge wheels crushing the life out of them. I do still have a chance to save myself, but I'm paralysed as the arrangements career along.

Arran, Alison and the congregation spent yesterday afternoon and evening decorating the church in the winter solstice colours of red, white, green and gold. The Heritage Centre was opened specially for us and we bought wedding rings from a local craftsman there. After Gina rifled through my wardrobe and dissed everything of mine, she insisted that I also buy a long white tunic-style dress from a local designer, along with various expensive gold accessories: a rope belt, embroidered slippers and long entwined rope earrings. She's in full party-planning mode, like an unstoppable avalanche.

Yes, the timing is wrong, so very wrong. But if Calder and I have any hope, I have to jump in with both feet, don't I? Doing this will show that I believe in him, and have accepted what he's done. I feel a surge of nausea and rush to the bathroom. Last night I drank past my old safety valve of four drinks and then stopping was a non-concept. The tension had been building all evening. All of us crammed together into this bloody cottage, the salty meal and the brittle socialising, Calder and I hyper-aware of everyone, me analysing every word, glance and modulation of tone.

I spew putrid vomit into the basin, then run the taps and try to force the reeking mess down past the slats of the plughole. When I finally stand up and look at myself in the mottled mirror balanced on a shelf above the sink, my left eye flickers back at me. I lean in to try to find myself in my reflection, but the 'me' in my eyes is unmoored. It's not just the hangover. I've held everything together since the accident, reached breaking point, come back from the edge, but then last night I was penned in with the very people I have sinned against and sinned with, and my cheap acceptance of Rob's murder now feels so gross.

Last night's late dinner is a drunken fog, with only snippets of memories breaking through.

There's Gina, forcing me to try on my new outfit. 'With your hair in plaits, I think this will work. Feels very pagan and blood-sacrificey!'

There's Hamish, joining me outside to look at the sea.

'Are you sure about this wedding? You don't have to go through with it just because Gina's pushing it.'

There's baby Mason, asleep in their carrycot, an innocent whose parents I could destroy so easily.

And there's Calder, laughing with Hamish as they arm-wrestle at the kitchen table, Calder's huge muscles bulging as he slams Hamish's finely boned hand onto the wooden table. I didn't dare tell him about Janey going to Oban to look for evidence of Rob's whereabouts.

And then finally there's Hamish and Calder walking off in the dark to stay at Hamish's cottage, because Gina said it was bad luck for Calder and me to see each other on the morning of the wedding.

I knead my brow, trying to dissolve my eye twitch. I adjust the mirror and it tips forward, catching the edge of the sink with a sharp crack as it falls. Ha! Seven years bad luck is the least of my problems. The final memory of last night was my future husband, a murderer, walking off into the dark with the man I cheated on him with, and got pregnant by.

Will they even be at the church this afternoon?

I have Calder's long black coat over my sacrificial gown, and extra trousers and boots beneath, as I sit next to Gina in the taxi, baby Mason strapped to her front. She and the baby stayed at the cottage with me last night and this morning, she made up my face so that I positively glow now, with gold burnishing my eyes and cheeks and blood-red lips. My hair is tightly plaited with gold thread running through it and clamped in place by long gold pins, which pull at my scalp. As I was changing, she'd noticed the bruise on my shoulder from when I fell in the bath fighting with Calder.

'Slipped on the slates,' I'd explained. If I press it, it aches. I should be heeding the warning pain, but I'm on autopilot.

As I get out of the taxi in front of the church, I see a group of islanders waiting near the door, the men in dark suits, the women all wearing red, green and gold. Janey comes running over in a dark green dress, her hair wild, with dark circles under her eyes.

'Can we talk?' she begs, glancing at Gina, who is dressed in a bright red kaftan-like dress which she got special-delivered over from the mainland at wild expense.

'This is my friend Gina,' I explain. 'The one who arranged this crazy wedding.'

'Hi,' she says distractedly. 'I'm sorry, but could I just have Nancy for a moment? Alone.'

'Well, she doesn't really—' Gina starts.

But I can't say no. 'Yes, sure, a quick chat and then I need to get to the church.'

'Sorry, but this is urgent,' Janey calls to Gina, pulling me aside.

'Are you OK?'

'No. I went to Oban, to Rob's flat first thing this morning. The neighbours said they hadn't seen him for weeks. I thought he must have had a terrible accident and be lying in there dead. So, I called the police, and they eventually took me seriously and broke the door down.

But it was empty. No sign of him. Everything was tidy, like he always keeps it. No sign of foul play.'

'What did the police say?'

'They didn't think it was suspicious. Said he could be away on a trip. Which is stupid. He'd have told me if he was going away.'

'Would he?' I see Gina beckoning me in the distance.

'Of course he would.'

'But if it's over for him, he could be off licking his wounds somewhere.'

She falters. 'Well, yes, I suppose. But would he leave all his stuff?'

'Perhaps he's gone to clear his head somewhere, then he's coming back for it?'

'I guess . . .' She's looking at me strangely. I must be careful that I don't appear too dismissive of her fears.

'Can you contact any other family or friends?' I manage to ask. How is this cruel lying not the worst omen for a marriage.

'He is a bit of a loner,' Janey concedes. 'But I called Alison, which was tricky, given how much she hates him. I made up some tosh about post coming to the shop for him. She said she hasn't heard from him for ages. She said he didn't even ring to check whether this year's postcard from Caitlin had arrived yet – which it did, two weeks ago. He's never missed calling about that before. Not once.' This lovely, calm woman looks so strung out and it's all our fault. 'I don't know what to do. I think something really bad's happened to him.'

'Probably not, but I get how worrying this is,' I say hoarsely. I hug her as she cries quietly, looking over her shoulder at Gina, who is motioning at me furiously to be careful with my dress.

'I'm sorry,' she mumbles, lifting her head. 'I shouldn't be saying all this now. It's your wedding day. And you're probably right, he's holed up somewhere licking his wounds.'

'It's OK, I can stop all this right now. If you need me.'

'God, no.' She wipes her cheeks. 'Of course not. I'll get myself presentable and see you in there. I'm sorry I've been so caught up with Rob – I should have been checking on you and what you're feeling about Calder. Are you sure you want to go through with this?'

'I . . .' Now's my chance to stop this. But I suddenly see Calder and Hamish walking up towards us between the white cottages. Calder nods at me and I nod back. 'No. We're fine now.'

'Sure?'

'Yes, absolutely.'

'Then I'm happy for you. I really am. And you're right, Rob's OK, there'll be an innocent explanation.'

'I'm sure he is, Janey. And I promise we'll talk more soon. OK?'

'OK, you're probably right, I'll get on. Good luck.'

Gina comes over as she scurries away. 'What was up with her?'

'Her boyfriend's missing. Look, I don't think I can go through with this.'

She tuts. 'Don't be ridiculous. It's just wedding jitters. Come on. Calder's just gone into the church.' I have to plough on – for Calder. Stopping now would raise suspicions.

I watch the winter-coloured congregation moving like a flock of exotic birds into the church and finally, it's just me and Gina left outside.

'Get those trousers and boots off,' she barks.

I scrabble out of them, my skin goose-bumping up my legs as I pull on the gold slippers. Gina hugs me, takes off my coat and marches in ahead of me. I'm bloody freezing on the outside, but churning and hot within. Like an inside-out baked Alaska. What on earth am I doing? I should run. Now.

But I step forward, on autopilot.

Alison is standing inside the empty church vestibule in a long purple dress, holding a white bouquet of roses with a single red Christmas rose at the centre.

'For you,' she says, extending the flowers to me. 'Your bouquet.'

'Thank you, it's beautiful.'

'Blood on snow.'

'What?'

'That's the name of the arrangement.'

I grab them and walk towards the inner church door but she grips my arm. 'I always thought that Calder would marry my Caitlin, that I'd be making her wedding bouquet.'

'That was a long time ago,' I mumble.

'Yes, and he's moved on, I know that. I hope she has too, wherever she is.' She lets go of my wrist and walks into the church. I look round the empty vestibule, decorated with grey slate, lined with all the long grey raincoats. The grey accuses me with my secret sin.

But here we go. For better or for worse.

I pull open the inner door to the church.

The music swells with the wedding march. The whole community is here, all smiling and nodding. We are catching the very last of the daylight, but the candle-design-lights give everything a warm glow. Alison has filled the church with a wild array of white and red roses (presumably fresh from her morgue of flowers), holly, ivy and mistletoe. The displays are so overdone. It all looks so pagan and bacchanalian and the dark red roses have been arranged to look almost like splatters of blood. Is that on purpose? Is she so annoyed I'm marrying her daughter's old boyfriend?

I am hungover and disembodied as I walk down the aisle towards Calder, who is up at the front, stiff in his dad's dark suit and flanked by Hamish. Both of them look ashen.

I pass my bouquet of funeral flowers to Gina.

Calder doesn't take his eyes off me. His pupils are huge counters, just like when he rose from the sea.

How dare we go ahead with this marriage? An adulterer and a murderer.

'Friends,' Arran says, nodding to us both as I reach the front. 'We are gathered here for the wedding of Nancy and Calder. Calder has been sent back to us from the watery depths by God. One evening Jesus and his disciples were crossing the Sea of Galilee in a boat.' He gestures up to the stained-glass image of Christ in a boat. 'When a furious storm came up. Jesus was asleep on a cushion in the stern, and the disciples woke him and asked, "Teacher, don't you care if we drown?" He woke up and rebuked the wind, and said to the sea, "Peace! Be still!" Then the wind ceased, and there was a dead calm. He said to them, "Why are you afraid? Have you still no faith?" And they were filled with great awe and said to one another, "Who then is this, that even the wind and the sea obey him?" God ordered the sea to give you back, Calder. You are the embodiment of The Saved, walking among us. Your return is proof of God's love – he washed us all clean in that rescue, to do God's work, and so we celebrate this, your special union on the day of the winter solstice – that magical short day when we let go of the old and embrace the new.'

How does Arran know that Calder needs to be washed clean? What work does he think Calder is going to do for him? I glance over at Gina, who smiles and shoos my focus back to Calder.

'I gather that you have prepared readings for each other. Nancy?'

'Y-yes,' I stammer, un-scrunching my reading, from my fist. I take a deep breath and look up at Calder. 'I found this last night underlined in a book of your mother's. It's called "A Marriage" by Mark Twain.'

Arran flinches. Does he know this poem? It's quite an odd little piece. Strange that Isla underlined it at all, given that she was so scared of Douglas. Perhaps it was what she wished for? Last night, I thought it sounded romantic, and it would have a clever subtext for Calder and me, but now that I look down on my scrawl, it looks weird and cold. But I don't have anything else.

There's a long moment of silence, my chest tightening, my vision blurring. People are shifting in the pews, glancing at each other nervously.

I look up at Calder. 'You OK?' he whispers.

'Sorry,' I blurt and clear my throat. Here goes nothing. '*A marriage makes of two fractional lives a whole;*' I say hesitantly.

'*It gives two purposeless lives a work,*
And doubles the strength of each to perform it.'

I look up and Calder's frowning. I clamp my eyes back onto my scrawl.

'*It gives to two questioning natures a reason for living*
And something to live for.
It will give new gladness to the sunshine,
A new fragrance to the flowers, a new beauty to the earth
And a new mystery to life.'

There's total silence. Then I hear a few 'ahs' from the congregation.

I look up. Calder's smiling and nodding – thank God. He understands what I mean. That I'm declaring our pact. I'm accepting him, murder and all. And he's accepting me and my faults – even though he'll never fully know them.

Arran nods to Calder.

'Nancy. I love you,' Calder stutters out. 'I always knew that you loved me – but I've only recently understood how much.' Oh God, is he going to confess?

I laugh nervously.

'OK, well I'm not much of a reader,' he says shyly.

The congregation laughs.

'I'd had a fair few drinks last night when I thought this was a good idea, but here goes.

'*I'm Nancy's till I die,*' he sings hesitantly.

Everyone tenses and glances around.

'*I'm Nancy's till I die*,' he continues, slightly louder.

'*I know I am,*
I'm sure I am,
I'm Nancy's till I die.'

Of course! It's that Rangers fan song, but swapping my name for Rangers.

There's a huge volley of laughter, then clapping and cheers. Everyone joins in as he sings it again.

'*I'm Nancy's till I die,*
I'm Nancy's till I die,
I know I am,
I'm sure I am,
I'm Nancy's till I die.'

The awful tension of this moment is pierced. I laugh, tears pouring down my face, feeling split open with relief.

Calder's grinning. 'Shh everyone, let me get this out,' he says to the congregation. 'Nancy, when I was younger, I didn't think I could love anything more than Rangers' – big whoop from the back – 'but . . . here you are. And to quote the Rangers motto, I'm "Ready".'

There's more clapping and cheering.

Eventually Arran raises his hands to quieten us. 'Do you have the rings?' he asks.

Hamish blinks at me, then passes us our gold bands, with their swirling engravings wreathed around them. The curls in the gold look like the mist that wreathed around the island when we first arrived.

I slide my ring onto his finger. We are binding ourselves and our secrets together.

He slides his onto mine as we repeat the vows Arran reads.

'I give you this ring as a sign of our marriage.
With my body I honour you, all that I am I give to you,
and all that I have I share with you, within the love
of God, Father, Son and Holy Spirit.'

I am dazed as the service continues but finally, Arran reaches the end.

'In the presence of God, and before this congregation,
Calder and Nancy have given their consent and made their
marriage vows to each other.'

I look into Calder's kind, lovely eyes, and allow myself the faint hope that we can somehow weather all this.

'They have declared their marriage by the joining of
hands and by the giving and receiving of rings; I therefore
proclaim that they are husband and wife.'

Arran joins our hands together and finishes:

'Those whom God has joined together, let no one put
asunder.'

It's already getting dark when we step outside and Gina throws rice over us.

'Congratulations!' she cries.

'You did it,' Hamish says, clapping Calder on the back. He catches my eye and gives me a questioning frown, but I look away.

'And now to the beach,' Arran announces.

'The beach?'

'Yes, our winter solstice celebration is not to be missed. We have a huge bonfire, representing the burning embers of the past year and the wild flames of hope ahead. You have to come, to experience the magic.'

It all sounds a bit too pagan and hippy for me and I so can't face another church thing. 'Oh, thank you, but I think we're going to go home.'

'But that's the reason that I wanted you to have your ceremony today – besides fulfilling the wishes of your very persuasive friend.' He smiles at Gina and she salutes him back. 'The day when the sun begins its new solar cycle. Seeds that are buried in the darkness of the earth will emerge once again under the life-giving rays of the sun. You have to come.'

Calder shrugs and I nod.

I pull my discarded trousers and boots on under my dress and we're given two of the long grey church raincoats. I feel like we've entered the church's ranks and are putting on their uniform. We follow Arran and the crowd down to the beach. He and many of the congregation are now wearing the coats. We look like a flowing undulation of slate leading towards the beach. It's getting dark now and we're each handed a torch. Alison steps forward, her grey hood pulled up like a priestess.

'Put your torch into the fire,' she says, pointing to a metal brazier of coals.

I hold my heavy torch in and eventually it glows and catches, yellow flames licking around it.

'Now you, Calder.'

Hamish and Gina both take torches, baby Mason asleep on Gina's breast again, and we all join the procession of grey coats and bright flickering torches down to the beach. Calder holds my hand as we stride forward. I yank the hood of my coat forward, but my face is still blasted by the icy wind.

'You all right?' I shout as we trudge on. 'I loved your reading.'

He laughs. 'I'll always be all right now!' he shouts back, sounding upbeat for the first time in ages.

The procession of torches would be magical under normal circumstances, the line of yellow flames shimmering in the wind, but there's a strangely cultish feel to it all. I can make out a bigger light further down the beach. That must be the famous bonfire that Arran enticed us here with. Finally, we reach it: a huge mound of dark twisting branches glowing red, orange and almost white at the centre, with yellowy flames flickering and jumping in the wind. A blur of grey robed figures is circling the fire. I catch glimpses of various faces from the church, burnished with an orange glow. There's a weird frisson of excitement in the crowd and slowly, like a single organism, it parts organically and closes around us. We are engulfed and subsumed. As we reach the front of the crowd, I see Arran, on the opposite side of the fire, standing a head taller than his adoring flock, in his huge hooded grey coat, a long stick in his hand. He acknowledges us with a nod as he pokes at the fire with his stick. A flurry of glittering sparks leaps into the air and the crowd roars.

This wild sense of danger feels oddly right. Calder and I are off-kilter but in motion. Breaking through from the past and leaving our sins behind.

'We're going to be OK,' I call up to Calder, leaning into him.

He nods, his eyes wide, staring at the fire.

But then Janey suddenly appears beside me. 'I've checked Rob's WhatsApp again,' she says, so loudly that Calder can hear her, but she's clearly too overwrought to care. 'I've realised that my messages to him aren't even being delivered, there's only one tick.'

'So what,' I whisper.

'So, his phone must be off. None of my messages have delivered since I last saw him. He hasn't even logged on to WhatsApp since that night.'

Oh God, she's narrowing down the time frame of when he went missing.

'Perhaps he's changed his phone and number.'

'He'd go that far to avoid me?'

Calder is staring at the fire but listening intently.

'I honestly have no idea,' I say, fearing she can sense my two-faced cruelty. 'But people do do that sometimes.'

'Really?' she says desperately. 'I guess. Yes of course. Thank you. As long as he's OK, that's the main thing.'

Calder glares at me and then moves away around the edge of the fire.

The wood crackles. Laughter explodes. Suddenly, part of the huge wooden pile collapses and a blast of sparks jumps forth. The crowd roars.

Calder has reached Arran and steps in beside him, like

a faithful sergeant, his face lit up in the orangey flames. He glances across at me. I smile, as my chest constricts. I love him so much. Sparks fly away into the black sky, then the darkness envelops him. Arran stirs the burning embers and another swirl of sparks light Calder up again. I fear him too. I step back from the intense heat. I love him. And I fear him.

There is a wild feral energy surging in the crowd as a strange chant starts up. 'Washed clean. We are The Saved. Washed clean. We are The Saved.' But we're not clean. Is it safe to be closed into this circle of community?

Arran suddenly pulls out a bottle and holds it aloft to a cheer. I know that shape – whisky. I shudder as I remember Calder's chaotic drinking when we first met, but I know he'll swerve it tonight. He hasn't touched a drop for five years, promised me he never would again as it made him too wild.

Arran walks around the circle, sloshing the whisky into people's tumblers. Alison laughs as she knocks back hers in one gulp. Janey sips at hers, staring out at the water. Hamish refuses it. Arran's face is shiny, his eyes wild and bright. As he reaches me, he pushes a glass into my hands. As he leans in to fill it, his forehead touches mine, and I smell his herby sweaty scent. I hold my breath, to keep him out of me.

'Stop holding on so tight,' he whispers into my ear.

'What?' I blurt, inadvertently breathing in, just as he breathes out, and inhaling him.

'Accept the joy that Calder has been given back to us,' he whispers. He's obsessed with Calder, with pulling him into his strange congregation. His face is too close to mine.

I jerk my hand up, slopping the drink and catching his tooth with my glass.

'Calder has come back to us. He is The Saved. Let go,' he roars, his eyes flaring. 'Accept God's forgiveness and live!' Then he steps on round the circle.

I realise I'm trembling. I stamp my feet to try to ground myself. He's only a bloke, not a magician. But this all feels so . . . dangerous. Why is he always talking about forgiveness? What does he want with Calder? It's like he knows our secrets. I stumble, pushed from behind. Bodies are closing in on either side of me, behind me, pushing me towards the fire.

Arran reaches Calder with his near-empty bottle. He holds out a glass and the brown liquid sloshes in. I try to catch his eye, to warn him not to drink, but he's looking at Janey. What is he doing? He knocks the whisky back without hesitation, then stares into the fire, rocking forward, looking like he could fall straight in.

An old wooden cask on the top of the pyre suddenly falls apart and collapses down, sending exploding sparks upwards.

Everyone gasps.

Then there's a single scream from the shore.

We all turn and in the light of the falling sparks, we see something washed up onto the slates.

A body.

CHAPTER TWENTY-TWO

I knew the sea would take its revenge.

Whoosh. Drag. Whoosh. Drag.

The body is being slammed onto the beach by the breaking waves and then pulled back with the slates. The head keeps slamming onto the stones as everyone stares in shock.

People are holding their flickering torches up and creating a glowing arc of light over the body as it twists in the waters. I know that bald head. Oh God. I step closer. I see the capital C on the back of the neck. I saw it in the doorway at the back of Janey's shop.

A huge wave drags the body back once more, into the wet blackness.

'It'll get washed out!' someone shouts. 'We have to get it onto the shore.'

Several men step forward, wading into the freezing water, but then hesitate.

'I'll do it!' Arran shouts, stepping forward, so he's knee-deep in the water and staring down at the body, his back to us.

He gives a low moan, staggers back and falls into the water.

People start wading over to help but he rights himself and holds up a warning hand. 'Get back!' he shouts. 'I'm fine. I'll get him in.' He wades behind the body, going waist-deep, and reaches down to lift him in his arms. In the torchlights, water drenching them, it looks like some strange New Age baptism. But this is no rebirth.

Arran wades forward, pushing the body through the water. When it gets too shallow, he lifts it like a lover and strides out of the sea and up the slate, the water droplets glinting in the firelight.

'Get back,' he calls, as he lays the body down beside the fire and the golden light licks across it. It faces away from the crowd, towards the bonfire, draped in seaweed, a slippery grey hue to the skin, with obvious areas of decomposition. A crab scuttles out of the clothing and everyone gasps. It, he, looks like a Halloween mannequin that we are about to raise onto the bonfire.

I look across at Calder and give a small head shake, warning him not to react.

He is looking on in horror like everyone else, but to me, he stands out with his wild staring. I walk around and grip his arm tightly. 'Don't say anything,' I hiss.

'Who is it?' calls Janey as she runs around the crowd to get nearer. She falls to her knees, her face glowing in the light. 'Rob. Oh my God. Rob.'

I grip Calder tightly as he jerks to move forward.

Who? Who is it? Robert Walker? – I hear running round the crowd – *What's he doing here? Is it really him?*

Janey clutches Rob, but Arran steps in and drags her back. 'No, Janey, we have to be careful. We have to preserve evidence.' She fights him but eventually allows herself to be enfolded by a group of women.

There is a loud whispering and side glances – *Got what he deserved – karma – just deserts.*

'It's my fault!' Janey cries. 'He drowned trying to visit me. What are you all looking at?'

'We need to call the police on the mainland,' Arran says. 'Nobody should touch the body. I'll call them.'

'I don't think he drowned,' I hear one of the guys who carried him ashore say.

'He's got a rope tied around his neck,' another says.

I crane forward and see a thin dark rope sunk into his neck. How is that possible?

'Must have killed himself. Poor guy,' the first man says.

I look up at Calder. He's scrunching his face in confusion. Real confusion? Or . . . ?

'What are they talking about?' I whisper.

He shakes his head.

The fire is giving off a fierce heat, but I'm ice-cold inside.

'What? No!' Janey screams. 'Why? Why would he do that?'

The crowd is murmuring – *Killed himself. Caitlin. Guilty conscience.*

How can Rob have killed himself? Calder said he knocked him off the cliff.

As Arran finishes talking to the mainland police on his phone, he raises his hand for silence. 'Could I have your

265

attention, can everyone stop talking.'

Janey steps forward. 'Now? Now you want people to stop talking?' she screams at him. 'You got everyone talking about Rob with your meddling.' Then she rounds on the crowd. 'Still gossiping, are you? You all hounded him with all your ugly accusations. Made him afraid to be seen here.'

I make to move towards her, but Calder pulls me back this time.

'We have to get the body out of the elements,' Arran announces. 'We'll carry him up to the pub.' He tries to put his arm around Janey, but she shakes him off.

'If he did kill himself, it's because of all of you and your endless gossiping.'

'We're all just shocked,' Arran says.

'You all thought he was a child molester!' screams Janey.

'No, I—'

She pushes him in the chest and he stumbles back. 'You were the one who fanned the flames of gossip – having Caitlin over to the church all the time – wheedling away, trying to put words into her mouth. You turned her against her family and everyone against Rob.'

'No, that's not true!' he cries. 'I was just making sure she was OK. I never made any accusations. But I had to be thorough.'

'You gave it all credence with your pious doubting.'

Alison walks forward slowly, the crowd parting for her. She reaches Rob's body, and stares down, no expression at all. How can she look at her ex-husband, the father of her child, with so little care? With no reaction at all?

'Happy now?' Janey shouts at her. 'Those rumours about Rob were all a lie, weren't they Alison?' Janey walks over to her and shakes her shoulders. 'Come on, haven't you done enough harm. He's dead now, admit it. He never touched Caitlin, did he?'

Alison shakes her off, her face blank.

No one speaks.

'Admit it!' Janey screams.

'Got his claws into you, did he?' Alison says coldly.

'You knew?' Janey shouts. 'What did you do to him?'

'What did *you* do?' Alison spits, pushing Janey to the slates.

'Stop it,' Arran says, but Janey slaps his hand away.

Alison turns and walks back towards the village.

'You coward!' Janey shouts. 'Even now you can't admit your lies.'

Arran stops her from following. 'Janey, now's not the time. We'll carry Robert to the pub and wait for the police. Everyone else needs to go home.'

'I'm not leaving him!' Janey cries.

Arran nods. He lays out his sodden grey coat, gently lifts the body onto it and points to four men. They carry the body up the beach, towards the village, but struggle to keep him straight as they stumble over the slates.

'Calder, Fergus, can you help,' Arran calls, 'take the middle of the coat to keep the body stable.'

Calder walks forward and joins the procession, his face impassive.

The crowd stand either side, their torches lighting the way.

Calder is carrying the body of the man he killed. He

said he pushed him off the cliff. But Rob has a rope around his neck. Did he get caught up in netting, in debris in the sea? Or is everything that Calder told me a lie? Did he strangle Robert and throw his body into the sea? It surely can't have been the unlucky punch he described to me. But why? Because Rob had been sleeping with Caitlin?

Due to my own guilt, I've been naive, let myself become complicit in whatever he's done, and I'm caught up in his lies now.

As the body moves ahead of us, I follow at a distance, Gina carrying Mason and Hamish walking with me.

'Are you OK?' Hamish asks.

'I'm fine, just shocked, like everyone.'

'Let's go back to your cottage,' Gina says, 'I need to get Mason back in the warmth. And we all need to eat and warm up. I've bought a feast and whatever happened to that poor man, we should look after ourselves and not spoil tonight's celebrations.'

People often say that men will tell you who they are. And Calder said, 'I'm a murderer.' I thought he meant he felt guilty about an accident.

But is my new husband a cold-blooded killer?

CHAPTER TWENTY-THREE

The kitchen table looks like an altar. Gina has set up a row of night lights down the centre and placed the oval slates the church left here in between the flickering flames. She and Hamish have no idea that this dinner is so wildly inappropriate. And Calder and I can't draw attention to our part in what happened to poor Rob. They think he's an unfortunate stranger. The slates rattle as she lays the table.

I've put on all the heaters and am lying out our wet clothes to dry as Calder returns.

'What's happening?' I whisper.

'The body's at the pub and Arran's waiting for the police,' he says grimly.

'They're taking their time,' Gina says.

'There aren't any police here on the island itself,' Calder explains. 'They have to come over so it could take a while.'

'What about Janey?' I ask.

He shrugs. 'She won't leave him. Arran's trying to get her to go and lie down, but she's just sitting there, rocking back and forth.'

'Well, I'm sorry for the poor woman, but it sounds like he was a paedophile of some sort and his crimes caught up with him,' Gina says.

'That's not true,' Calder snaps, but catches my look.

'There was a lot of gossip about him when we were here,' Hamish says quietly.

'But that was all Alison, you know that,' Calder barks.

'We don't actually know that,' Hamish says.

'She was my girlfriend. I'd have known if . . .'

'Calder, you should change your trousers,' I cut in, 'yours are soaking, come back to the bedroom and I'll find you dry ones.'

Calder stomps back to the bedroom and I close the door.

'You lied about punching him?' I hiss.

'No, I told you exactly what happened.'

'But that can't be true.'

'You think that I, what . . . strangled him?'

'I–I don't know.'

'I have no idea what happened to him. I promise on my life.' He looks so desperately honest, wide-eyed at my reaction.

'We're opening champagne!' Gina shouts. 'Come on you two.'

'We shouldn't talk in front of the others.'

'Jesus, I don't think I can get through this dinner. Do you think they'll be coming for me?'

'Why would they? There's no connection to you. But perhaps they should?' I sweep up my little glass waterfall from the bedside table.

'No!' he shouts as I slam it towards the wall and it smashes into pieces.

I've kept this fragile ornament for five long years. And now I see it for what it is. A cheap bit of tat. Totally smashed. Like our relationship.

There's a sharp knocking on our door.

'You two all right?' Gina calls.

I drag the door open.

'What's going on?'

'We're fine.'

She frowns at me. 'I know this is all upsetting, but did you know that man well or something?'

'No, hardly at all, but it's a bloody bad omen on our wedding day,' I say, not looking at Calder.

'All right, come on now, let's try to have a nice evening. You need a drink. It is your wedding night after all.' She grins and play-punches Calder.

Calder strides out and I run after him.

Gina has brought in side lights from the lounge and turned off the overhead light in the kitchen. She's put out plates, cutlery and gleaming glasses. And a feast of dips, breads, salads and lasagne, so many colours, smells and textures. In the flickering gloom, it looks eerily beautiful. This is what would have once been my perfect wedding dinner.

OK. I just need to get through tonight, then I can decide what to do.

Gina stands at the head of the table and holds two

glasses of whisky aloft. She looks like a high priestess about to start a dark ceremony. Hamish is sitting at her side like her familiar, nursing a huge whisky.

'Here you go, you two, to warm you up,' Gina says.

We both take the glasses and down them in one. Who cares about whisky drinking now.

'That's the spirit. Now let's forget that sad discovery and celebrate your nuptials.'

'Is Mason OK on his own in the lounge?' I ask. 'I'll just check on him.'

'No, no, he's out cold in his travel cot,' she says, holding aloft a baby monitor. 'I'll hear soon enough if the fucker stirs.'

'Gina,' Hamish blurts.

'Oh come on, I love him, but let's be honest,' she says, making a yuck face.

'Fair enough,' he laughs.

These two don't know they're born – with their happy relationship, kids, little domestic annoyances. I want to scream at them: *Enjoy it, know what you've got, before it all gets taken from you.*

We all settle round the table. This almost feels like old times. But like we're acting out a play version. Calder starts pouring more whisky into our squat round glasses, then takes a huge swig.

'Let's have a toast to you two,' Gina exclaims. 'You've been through hell and come out the other side. Here's to Mr and Mrs Campbell.'

'Thank you,' I say, locking eyes with Calder as we all clink glasses and drink.

'Speech!' Gina shouts.

I drain my glass and stand, my chair scraping backwards. I feel the earthy warmth hitting my mouth, suffusing my nose and warming my stomach. 'Thank you both for coming to help us. You don't know how lucky you are. None of us do. Till it's all taken away.'

Gina frowns.

'I think I can honestly say – that Calder's accident changed us both. I see a new Calder now and I feel like a new Nancy.' I stare at Calder. 'There's no going back from here. To my new husband.' I pour some more whisky and knock it back.

'Short and sort of sweet,' Gina laughs. 'Calder?'

He waves her away, but she shakes her head. 'Come on.'

He stands and looks between us and then stares at me. 'To my wife, the best thing in my life, to whom I have and always will, tell the truth.'

Gina raises her eyebrows. 'Goodness, that's a high bar for a marriage. Eh, Hamish?' We all clink glasses and Hamish pours more for all of us. As he leans over, I find his physical presence so unnerving in front of Gina. How will we get through this night?

But gradually I'm oiled with alcohol and getting manic, playing my role, hearing about our London friends, about bad plays and good restaurants. Calder is a murderer. I am an adulteress. And we're discussing Argentinian steakhouses. I'm hyper with Gina, laughing with Hamish and staring at Calder as he stares back.

Elizabeth Frankenstein was murdered by the monster on her wedding night. What is Calder planning for me once Gina and Hamish go back to their cottage?

We open another bottle of whisky. Is that the second one already?

Calder knows that I know he lied.

The evening wears on. We nibble at the food. I can't eat but am drinking fast. I'm beyond caring, tired, almost hallucinating. Drink after drink. Mason only stirs once and Gina gives him a bottle, sitting in front of me, moaning about what a chore this lovely baby is. But of course they have an easy baby. Easy birth, easy baby, easy life.

'Aren't you breastfeeding any more?' I slur.

'God no. I survived a month of being suckled like a prize pig to pass on the antibodies or whatever they say is in the milk, but they sleep so much better with the formula.' I feel a deep stab of jealousy that she can so casually pass up that intense closeness.

'This table's got a really annoying judder,' Gina says as she puts down her glass and everything rattles. 'So, what's life really like up here?' she asks conspiratorially as the candles flutter. 'Are you bored out of your minds? Now Calder's recovered?'

'No,' I say sharply. 'We love it.'

'Oh well, each to their own, I guess.' Gina puts her glass down and it slides. 'Can someone put something under this table leg,' she moans. 'It's so annoying.'

'In the toolbox,' Calder drawls, pointing down.

She lifts a screwdriver and brandishes it like a sword. 'Are you two really not missing the cut and thrust of London?' Then she seizes and gives an awkward giggle. 'Oops, not that sort of cut and thrust obvs.'

Calder's face has gone deathly pale and I catch Hamish shaking his head at Gina.

They're all frozen in a tableau.

'What cut and thrust? What are you talking about?' I demand. 'Gina? Hamish?'

'It was nothing, poor turn of phrase,' she deflects, but she's dripping with meaning.

'Calder?' I demand. 'What does she mean?'

He stares at the floor.

'Sorry, but please can someone tell me what she means?'

'I didn't know that you didn't know,' Gina says innocently.

'Know about what?' I shout.

'The fight,' Hamish blurts.

'What fight?' I say incredulously, thinking that somehow Gina and Hamish have found out about Calder's fight with Robert, about the murder. 'How do you know about that? We haven't—'

Calder stands up abruptly, his chair legs bumping on the stone floor. 'She's meaning a fight I had in London,' he says with heavy warning, realising that I'm about to mention his fight with Rob.

'What fight, when?' I drawl stupidly. 'Will someone explain?'

'There was . . . an unfortunate incident,' Hamish says. 'An argument that got out of hand between Calder and Mike, our other sales rep. It got physical and Mike had to get medical attention.'

'What?' I stare at Calder, who looks away. 'What does she mean?'

'He ended up in hospital, 'cos of a screwdriver stab. But it was a flesh wound.'

'You stabbed someone with a screwdriver!'

'He was fine.'

'Well clearly not fine, if you put him in the hospital.' How many lies has he told me?

'Hey, come on, Nancy, don't take on,' Hamish says, reaching to touch me.

'Don't touch me.'

'All right, Nancy, no need to take it all out on Hamish,' Gina says sharply. 'He's done nothing wrong.'

'Ha,' I exclaim. 'Hasn't he?'

'What's Hamish done?' she demands, suddenly alert.

'Nothing, nothing,' I backtrack, feeling like I'm holding a heavy pan of water that's slopping all over. 'I just can't believe I didn't know about this. What was the fight about?'

'Babies,' Hamish says flatly.

'What?' Oh God, does he know about me getting pregnant somehow?

'It was stupid,' he says warily. 'All the other blokes have kids, so they were joshing Calder about him firing off blanks.'

'Jesus, Hamish,' Calder blurts. 'Enough already. They were being jerks, and I was pissed and overreacted. That Mike's a smug git. He had it coming.'

'And then your mum died very conveniently,' I blurt, 'and you said you wanted to move up here for the "quiet life".'

Calder rears up. 'I told you!' he shouts. 'You're better off shot of me. I'm out of here.' He sweeps out of the front door. Gina starts to follow.

'Leave him be,' I say dully.

She leaves the door open and turns back to me. 'I'm sorry I didn't tell you about it, but you were dealing with . . . so much at the time,' she says pointedly, clearly meaning my miscarriage.

And then I see a meaningful look pass between her and Hamish, and I know that she's told him about my miscarriage.

'You didn't?' I growl at Gina.

'Look, it's OK,' she says defensively. 'I know you said not to tell him, but he's my husband.'

Hamish is staring at me with such intensity. How long has he known? Has he worked out it was his? Of course he has.

'When did you tell him?'

'I held out,' Gina says. 'But it slipped out a month ago, when we had another pregnancy scare. It was the day before Calder's accident and I was going to tell you, but then it was all so touch and go for him, I just couldn't.'

'I told you not to,' I spit. 'But you just had to, didn't you. Because you two have such a brilliant marriage, you share everything. I'm the numpty who's moved her life up here for a man she barely knows,' I screech and then turn to Hamish. 'So, you know?'

Hamish stares at the floor. 'I was so sorry to hear about your trouble,' he mumbles. I can't bear that he knows about my lost baby. Our baby.

'It was very sad that you lost the baby,' Gina says. 'But it wasn't all bad. It proved that you and Calder can get pregnant. You just need to keep trying.'

'Oh yes, lucky me,' I say, catching Hamish's eye, knowing for certain now that he knows that the baby was his. 'Lucky me, losing a baby . . .'

'I didn't say that,' Gina says.

'Yes, you did. You're on to your fourth one, that you can't even be bothered to breastfeed, 'cos it gets in the way of your drinking.'

'What? I . . .'

'Shut up. All you've done since you got here is moan about your baby. You're so lucky. I've got no baby, and I'm stuck here with a man I know nothing about. Married to the fucker because of your meddling.'

Gina's eyes flare. 'Just because I have a lovely husband and we tell each other the truth about everything, doesn't mean I've done anything wrong. I'm sorry if your husband's lied to you.'

I stare at her, this fecund earth mother, who has the kids, the money, the job, and who doesn't doubt herself, and I want to smash it all up.

'Fuck you.'

She stands and narrows her eyes. 'I think we should get a taxi, Hamish,' she says icily. She picks up her bag. 'Come on, let's leave Nancy to her pity party.'

I fill my glass again and let the burning liquid slide down my throat. They are just walking to the front door when I speak. 'He's not what you think.'

'Calder's not my husband,' Gina says, wheeling back to me, 'I don't really care.'

'Not Calder. Hamish, your "perfect" husband.'

'No, Nancy,' Hamish warns, walking back into the room. 'Let's all get to bed before we say anything we regret.'

Gina looks at Hamish and then back at me.

'Oh, I see. He shagged you, did he?' she asks with a shrug.

When neither of us reply, she rolls her eyes.

'No one I know,' she snarls at him. 'That was my only rule. No one I know. Then you pick one of my best friends? No wonder you were so against me coming up here. Didn't want to be in the same room as the wifey and the mistress.'

'I'm not his mistress. It was only once. I'm so, so sorry Gina. One stupid, awful occasion when I was beyond smashed. After another failure to get pregnant. I didn't even remember it, just woke up with him. And I felt horrific about it.'

'Ah, did you? Well done you for feeling bad – after the event.' She swipes a plate off the table, which smashes operatically. Then she takes a deep breath and looks back at me. 'And where was your precious Calder when these shenanigans were going on?'

'He was in Birmingham doing the stupid build for that Airbnb.'

'In August,' she says incredulously. I immediately grasp what I've done. I can see her mind whirring about the dates. 'And then you had that miscarriage in . . . September.' She gives an ugly smile of realisation. 'Oh my, what a tawdry little secret. So, it wasn't just a little shag. He got you pregnant.'

Hamish looks down.

'That miscarriage didn't prove that you and *Calder* could get pregnant. It proved that you and my very fertile *husband* could.'

No one speaks. Gina reaches over, sticks her finger in

some taramasalata and slowly licks it off.

'So that's why you dashed up here?' Gina says to Hamish, in a steely voice. 'Not to help Calder, but to check on her?'

'Gina, I'm so sorry, we didn't mean for it to happen,' Hamish bleats.

I suddenly shudder and realise that the door's still open, letting in the cold wind. I stare out into the dark.

And see the red glow of a cigarette.

'Calder?' I shout as I rush towards him.

He walks slowly towards me, dragging on his cigarette. 'Well, that was all very interesting. No wonder you've been preaching forgiveness,' he says, his face an inch from mine, the smoke blowing in my face. He gives a tiny half-smile.

'I . . .'

He turns and strides off into the darkness.

CHAPTER TWENTY-FOUR

There's a sudden bang in the kitchen and I leap up from the settee in the lounge, hoping it's Calder returning. I must have passed out eventually because I've woken up here, dry-mouthed, scooped out and deadened.

But it's Gina and Hamish.

She's on the phone, barking instructions. 'Yes, I'm still here, have you booked it yet? Well hurry up. Yes, I'll hold.' She covers the phone. 'We're just collecting the stuff I left here yesterday,' she snaps at me. 'We've got a taxi waiting.'

'OK?' Hamish mumbles.

I shrug.

He glances at Gina who ignores him entirely. 'That's right, two seats – for one adult and one carrycot. First class. Glasgow to London, one way.' Hamish looks down. She frowns as she listens to the response. 'Thank you.' She disconnects. 'Keep going, Hamish. Get everything packed into the taxi, check I haven't left anything.'

'Have you seen Calder?' I ask. I'm unnerved by his lying, by that story about the screwdriver, but my fear that he's done something to himself overrides everything else.

'Are you talking to me?' Gina asks.

'Have you?'

'No. He will have taken last night's revelations very badly, I imagine. He doesn't have my fluid morals.' Little does she know how fluid mine have become. 'Painkiller?'

'Me?' I ask in amazement.

'If you feel like me, you'll need them,' she says, holding out a packet. I take three with the pint glass of water she hands me as we watch Hamish skulking past with the bags. He has Mason in his purple contraption, fast asleep. 'Ugh, keep him away from me. Babies and hangovers don't mix. I'm leaving Hamish by the way. Here and for ever. He's yours if you want him.'

'No, God, I . . .'

'I need to get off this godforsaken island and get to Glasgow for my flight. What you do with him now is your concern, not mine.'

Gina sips her water, assessing me.

'You knew that Hamish cheated?' I ask eventually.

She shrugs. 'Not with you, obviously.'

'I'm so sorry. I genuinely don't remember. I—'

She raises her hand to silence me. 'Yes, I know he cheats. Occasionally.'

'You've never told me.'

She raises an eyebrow. 'Well, it's embarrassing, isn't it.' Her voice falters and she looks uncharacteristically vulnerable. 'I don't like it,' she continues, shaking herself together, voice hardening. 'But I accept it. He has the odd meaningless fling and always comes back to me.' She sighs. 'But he broke the rules with you. Made me look stupid.'

'I . . .'

'Let me finish. I've seen you drunk. In the old days before you met Calder, I pulled you from strangers' cars, which you never remembered doing the next day. I know you love Calder. And I know you're jealous of me and my squalling lump of a baby.'

I open my mouth but she raises her hand again.

'But you are oblivious of the fact that I'm sometimes jealous of you. Hamish and I rub along, for the most part. But it's not what you two have. I've heard you on the phone these past weeks. Bereft. But God knows what he'll do with this new information. That's the problem with real love. It smashes. What Hamish and I have is leathery and can withstand all weathers, but yours is all or nothing.'

'I'm so sorry. I know that not remembering isn't enough explanation.'

'It's done, life goes on,' she says with finality.

'Can you ever forgive me?'

She shrugs. 'I have lots to sort out at home. But I imagine you may be coming back to London in the near future? Perhaps we'll talk then?'

'I . . . I don't know what's going to happen. I did love Calder. But now, I don't know. I had no idea about that fight in London,' I say quietly. 'About lots of things. He's not who I thought he was.'

'All relationships have secrets. None of us live up to

each other's expectations. Your problem is that you want the real thing. Much easier to compromise,' she says, motioning towards Hamish packing in the lounge. 'Till it isn't.'

I nod.

'Well, this taxi's going to cost a fortune as it is, better get on. Hamish!' she shouts.

He runs through with a baby blanket and a dummy.

'Nancy, we need to talk,' he mumbles.

'Oh my God,' Gina exclaims, 'can you tear yourself away from her for one moment to get me and your son back to our other three kids?'

He winces. 'I just wanted to check she was OK,' he mumbles.

Gina tuts. 'Get us on our way and you can check all you want.'

He gets baby Mason strapped into his car seat.

Gina turns back to me. 'I'm beyond angry with you. But I have to say this.' She frowns.

'What?'

'I liked Calder well enough. But I've always felt a slight, I don't know, something impenetrable in him. I should have told you about that fight in London. Hamish has many faults, but I know him, and weirdly I'd still fundamentally trust him in a crisis. But Calder . . . just be careful.'

She walks to the car and gets in the passenger seat. Hamish gives me a final glance and then gets in the back with the baby. The car finally crunches across the gravel, round the corner and I'm alone.

Where is Calder? I rush outside with the binoculars. No sign. He can't have stayed out all night, he'd be frozen. I don't know whether to be scared for him or scared of him.

I've always known Calder has a temper. We've had big arguments, but he was never, ever violent. And he was always sorry. But is that what stupid, oblivious wives say? Have I not allowed myself to see his darkness? I explained his temper away in the past because of his mother's harsh treatment. And now I know about his father's temper and violent death, perhaps at his mother's hand. What has Calder done? Strangled Rob? Because he slept with his daughter?

I try ringing him, but his phone goes straight to voicemail.

It was sunny when Gina and Hamish left, but I can feel the damp heaviness filling the air, see the light fading as the clouds descend, and know that we're in for a big storm. Last night was cold, but dry. Tonight will be wild and torrential.

Where is Calder?

There's no sign of him all day. He's either left the island or killed himself. I am blank and closed down as I register the possibility. I doze, topping up my painkillers and throwing up water. Each time I wake, I slide between cold fear and white-hot rage. I've put up with so much, lies upon lies, and I'm left alone again. I know it's not nothing, what I've done, and he found out in the worst possible way. But he's in another order of wrongdoing.

I go outside again, just as the light's fading, weighing up sins, unable to grasp onto any solid thought. Then I see a black blur moving against the bruised sky. The figure approaches down the dark slope of the hill. I watch his dogged gait, knowing it's him. Finally, all our secrets are out and we can face each other with honesty. I got pregnant by his best friend. He killed Rob for sleeping with Caitlin.

He's breathing heavily as he reaches me and stops abruptly.

The heavens open and we are soaked. But neither of us moves. We stand there, being washed by the heavy sheet of freezing rain.

We stare at each other.

Eventually, I turn and walk back into the cottage. As I'm coming back from the bathroom carrying some slate-grey towels, Calder shuts the cottage door.

'So, they've gone?' he says flatly.

'Yeah.'

'Good, I'd have fucking killed Hamish.'

I swallow. 'I'm sorry. It meant nothing. But I . . .'

'So, your boyfriend came up here for you, not to help me with my work.'

'No. I didn't even know he was coming. It was a terrible mistake, when I was beyond drunk – like you made a terrible mistake. If it was a mistake?'

He throws his head back and bellows. 'I told you the truth about Mr Walker. What you choose to believe me capable of is up to you.'

'How can I know what the truth is? You just keep lying.'

He narrows his eyes. 'How can *you* know what the truth is? Did I mishear? You didn't sleep with Hamish. Get pregnant by him. Miscarry. And not tell me?'

'Yes, but—'

He walks past me into the lounge. 'How do I know it's not been going on up here?'

'Calder,' I beg as I grasp his arm.

'Get off,' he says, shaking me violently away.

'I was off my head that day after yet another failure to get pregnant. You told me to have a drink with him . . .'

'Yes,' he bellows, 'a fucking drink. Not to get pregnant by him. And you didn't tell me.'

'I couldn't. Especially when I realised I was pregnant, and it must be his.'

'Why?' he barks, kicking a chair. 'Why must it have been his? We had sex before I left for Birmingham. Why couldn't it be mine?'

'Well, I guess . . . it could have been, but we'd been trying for so long.'

He sneers at me. 'Ah. I see. I'd failed you for two years but along comes big stud Hamish with all his children?'

'No, I didn't mean that.'

'You could have miscarried my child but didn't think that was something I should know.' He stares at me with such cold loathing. 'Poor old Calder,' he drawls sarcastically, 'who can't get anyone pregnant. Unlike that stud Hamish?'

'No, I—'

He leers down at me. 'Yes, be honest. That's exactly what you thought, isn't it?'

'I—'

The fat second of silence hangs in the air.

He smirks. 'And there we have it.' He swallows. 'Well, I may not have got you pregnant . . . but I got someone else pregnant.'

I widen my eyes.

He widens his back.

'Who?'

'Caitlin.'

I inhale sharply. No.

'Yeah. Happy now?' He throws himself back into a chair and aggressively picks at some nuts strewn across the table.

'Did she keep it?'

'I don't know,' he explodes. 'She said she wasn't going to. I would have supported her whatever. That's why I wasn't so surprised that she left the island without me.'

I sit down opposite him, unable to process this. 'So these are more lies. All those months when we were sharing our doubts about our fertility – and now you're telling me you got Caitlin pregnant? Rob's daughter.'

He falters in his white rage. 'That doesn't change anything about what I said happened that night with Rob.'

'Doesn't it?'

Calder slams his fist on the table, then recoils in pain. 'Fuck's sake. I didn't tell you about Caitlin being pregnant because I didn't want to upset you. Because I thought you'd think that if I was fertile, then it must be *you* who was the infertile one.'

I blurt out a cold laugh. 'So we're both fertile and we've both been hiding it to protect the other. So have you been in contact with Caitlin in London?'

He groans. 'There's no point in talking to you, you're deranged.' He's doing really well at looking shocked and affronted. But why are those postcards from Caitlin coming from the very area where we used to live?

'Is that why you killed Rob?'

He stares at me. 'What?'

'Because he was angry about you getting her pregnant?'

'Jesus, the punch was an accident. You said you believed me.'

'I don't know what to believe.'

'Well, it's just as well we never got pregnant, isn't it,' he spits out. 'Given what you think of me.'

We sit in silence, glaring.

'How are you so sure Caitlin's baby was yours – and not Rob's?' I say slowly.

'Don't be ridiculous.'

'All the islanders think Rob was sleeping with her and that he killed himself because of the guilt. But we know that you killed him.' I should stop goading him but I'm so angry about all these lies, I can't hold back. 'You either did it because he was angry that you got her pregnant – or you found out that he was the one who got her pregnant. Either way, you lied to me.'

'You're just making up stuff now. I told you what happened when I pushed him.'

'You didn't push him, you strangled him with a rope.'

Suddenly there's a massive crash above us and the whole cottage judders.

'What the fuck?' I scream as a fine spray of dust falls from the ceiling, making us choke.

'Get outside!' he shouts.

'Is the roof falling in,' I say as I dart to the door.

'No. It'll be a log or a dislodged rock from the hill,' Calder says, picking up a torch. We stumble out, coughing.

'What was that?' I say between retches.

He plays the torch beam over the roof. 'It looks fine,' he says, as we both crane up, searching.

'It felt like it came from the far side,' I say, pointing over. It's pitch-black outside, the usual lights from the piercing stars extinguished by heavy cloud. Calder is playing the beam across the roof as we circle the building, which looks intact.

'There's nothing,' he says.

'Well, something did that. We didn't imagine it.'

Then we hear a horrible agonised groaning. We both step back at this otherworldly sound.

'What's that?'

'Stay there,' Calder warns as he sets off behind the cottage. But I can't stay on my own, and I have to see what's making that awful sound.

As I turn the corner, Calder's torch reveals a large sheep, lying on its side, its eyes wide and staring, blood spouting from a gash across its eyes, moaning in pain. It's one of the fallen sheep Arran talked about the first time I met him.

'It fell from the hills,' Calder says blankly as we approach. When he lifts its head, it drops down and the sheep screams in agony. 'It's broken its neck and has God knows what internal injuries. Go in while I deal with it.'

'What d'you mean? What are you going to do?'

'I have to put it out of its agony.'

'What?'

'Nancy, it's in pain. We can't leave it like this.'

'No, no,' I plead, clinging to his arm.

'You want it to die slowly in agony?'

'I – no, but surely—'

The sheep suddenly gives a lacerating scream. Then it pants heavily, staring up at us, its eyes swivelling.

'It's fallen from the hill,' Calder says monotonally, 'hundreds of feet, it's beyond saving. Look at the poor thing.'

'But surely we should try?'

'We can't let it suffer. Go in,' he mumbles as he places the torch down at an angle so that it illuminates the sheep.

'No!' I shout.

He shrugs and pulls one of Isla's yellow-handled knives from his pocket. Why does he have that on him? He takes a deep breath, and bends down. The blade glints in the torch beam.

He looks over at me, his eyes black, then grasps the sheep's head.

'You shouldn't watch this.'

'Please . . .'

'Don't look,' he says, his eyes wide, his pupils the big black counters they were when his cold body rose from the sea. He lifts the blade, then slices down across the sheep's throat in a single movement, blood spurting out in an arc.

The straining sheep slumps. Dead.

CHAPTER TWENTY-FIVE

I run round the cottage, and start up the hills. It's stupid in the dark. But I don't care. My mind is a blank blur. As that blood spurted, I saw Calder's dead soulless eyes.

'Nancy,' I hear in the distance. I need to use my phone light to see, but I daren't alert him to my position. 'Nancy, come back, it's freezing!' he shouts. I register the fakeness in his voice, the wheedling attempt at control. But his voice is thin and getting quieter as I trudge up the initial incline of the hill. Suddenly, I stumble, jolt forward and slam onto the hard stony ground. The pain wakes me up as I rub my palms to dislodge the grit. I must concentrate.

'Nancy,' I hear vaguely.

The cold air sears my throat. The way ahead is virtually pitch-black. I trudge on. I can just about make out the outline of the next foot or so ahead, thick and inky, no depth – but I can see the path clearly in my memory.

I have to get away from that man back there. That liar and murderer. I need to be in numb action, till my mind can function again. When I was still in the agony of crucifying blame about my parents, a couple of years after their deaths, I signed up for motorcycle lessons, not caring if I lived or died. But somehow, facing life-or-death, I was forced out of my dull horror. I must push myself through the danger of this climb in the dark, to come out the other side.

I finally reach the wooden gate that takes me off the track and onto the hills. I visualise the path ahead. Forward and slightly to the right, clearly demarcated by bracken on either side. I feel the soft fans of fronds with my left hand and then my right, as I move tentatively forward. I know there's a ridge at the turning and I keep waiting to feel the shift in the incline. It takes for ever but I suddenly feel myself lurch up. I kneel in the dirt and breathe. It gets harder from here. I know it's a sharp left along the dirt track which hugs the hill. The panic that propelled me to here has receded, but I can't go back. I try to keep seeing the track in my mind, but this all feels so different in the dark. I know the track hugs the hill. It's smooth and gently inclined, and there's only one way across, so I can't get lost. It will bring me to the final rocky rise and then to the very top of the hill. I'll use my torch there to check my position and then climb and make my way down the easy path to the village.

But I have to get there first.

I've entered a tunnel in my mind. No backwards. Only forwards.

The wind is building and after edging forward for a few

minutes, I lie flat on the ground out of its reach. The rain is starting again. I lift my head and am lashed with a swirl of rain. I must keep going. It'll be safer over the other side. I'm too exposed here.

The wind is blowing sideways at me, but pushing me safely into the hillside. I keep one foot up against the hill and use the other to lever myself against it as I move. It's glacially slow progress. I step onto my inner foot and plant it against the hill, then drag my outer foot forward, keeping all my weight still in to the hill, breathing in the wet grass, before balancing momentarily on my outer foot again.

But suddenly there's a switch in the wind. I'm wrong-footed and wheel my arms in the air desperately, till I thud back into the hillside. I am nothing up here, buffeted over the edge with ease. I daren't stand up or I'll be blown off. So I crawl. There seems to be no end, when finally, I feel solid rock. I've reached the climb to the top.

I pull my phone out of my pocket and fumble with it, trying to keep it under me to stop the screen being washed by the rain. I finally get the beam on. I'm exactly where I thought I was, at the base of the rocky crest. The weather is unreal. I use the light to see where to place my foot, then angle it upwards to see the route ahead, but can't hold the phone and climb, so I put it away. I lever myself up the first big step then reach upwards, straining to feel out the angles of the rocks. I find the next foothold, rest my foot on it and pull myself up. Bit by bit, I drag myself up the rocks. My hands are numb and sliced. My face is raw. All my muscles are screeching with the effort. But finally, I'm at the top. I can barely see around but I'm through the worst. If I've got up this far, I can get down the wide path to the village.

But what am I going to do when I get there? No ferries now. I can't go to Janey or Arran. I haven't thought beyond getting away from Calder.

I take out my phone again and see I have service now. I know who to ring.

'Hello. Nancy?'

'Hamish, are you still on the island?'

'Yes. Are you OK? I wanted to call, but I knew you were with him.'

'I'm OK, but I need your help.'

'What? I can't hear you.'

'Hello, can you hear me?' The wind is so fierce, and the connection is terrible. I look at the phone and the line still seems to be open.

'Hamish?'

'Yes, hello, I can hear you.'

'I need your help.'

'Absolutely.' He sounds so childishly pleased. 'Shall I come and pick you up?'

'No, I'm fine. I'm coming over the hill.'

'What?'

'It's OK, I've done the hard bit. I—hello?'

I look down at the phone to check the reception and stumble. The phone leaps out of my hand and as I reach out to catch it, I fall forward, hitting the ground and rolling chaotically across stones and bushes, being scraped and swiped, till I smack into a wet undulation in the ground. I lie still, stunned by the fall. At least I didn't roll off the cliff. But then I feel myself moving involuntarily. Am I having some kind of seizure in the cold, muscles moving without me? But it's my body that's sinking, because the earth is moving below me. Slowly the soft spongy ground is falling in and then it gives way entirely and I'm sliding down between earthen walls, till I land with a thud. All my breath is knocked out of me and my head slaps backwards on wet soil.

I hunch in on myself, moaning at the pain flooding my body, and am engulfed in an overpowering stench of soil, leaves and rotting matter, earthy, resinous and fetid. I'm totally disorientated, in pain, blackness and stench. I'm out of the wind and rain, deep inside some sort of narrow gully. A rotting tomb of sticky mulch. What happened? I look up and see the faintest of lights above me, the pinprick of a far-distant star. I've fallen down one of those fissures in the grassland that opened up during the hot summer. It's black and disgustingly succulent down here and I'm entombed. I feel like the earthen walls of the gully are going to close in and squash me. I moan as I drag myself up to sitting, shrinking back from the soft gooey walls. I reach around in the dark, trying to find something to hold onto, and find a hard bit of rock above me and pull at it.

The rock comes away in my hand.

But it's not a rock. It's lighter, longer. A branch? A root? With my other hand, I feel the end. The bulbous end.

I know instantly it's a bone.

I drop it and scream, my voice slamming back off the walls, into and through me. There is a sprinkling of earth and insects over my head. I feel tiny legs scurrying across me and scream again.

I'm rigid. My hands pulled in. My head scrunched down.

The bone was above me. In the wall. I reach up tentatively and feel a woolly mass. Oh, another sheep.

Poor thing. The bone must be one of those stunted little legs of theirs – or a rib. Ugh. It must have fallen down here and got stuck. Moaned here. Weakened here. And died here. Long enough ago for the flesh to have rotted. To have been fed upon by whatever's down here with me, crawling over me.

I can't stay down here to die like this poor sheep.

I'm too scared to touch the walls. As if a skeletal hand will reach out and hold me prisoner here, as the fissure closes. No. This is real solid life. Nothing otherworldly has happened. The earth hasn't swallowed me up to the mercy of re-animated bones. It's a hot-weather fissure. It's a sheep's bone. Long dead.

I stare up at the faint glimpse of light above me.

Before Calder I couldn't find any solid ground in my life. I used work, drink, drugs, shagging to keep myself in motion, to feel something, however ephemeral. But finding Calder was seismic. He loved me. But it was all a lie. There was no solid ground. And now the fragile earth has fallen in. I am utterly alone, but at least I'm at rock bottom. I will not give in. It's freezing and I'll die here if I don't act. Think logically. Blank everything else out. I will make myself touch where the bones are first, rather than avoid them, so that I'm not shocked by mistake. They're sheep bones. Carbon. Nothing to fear. I reach into the blackness and feel wet gooey earth at first and then hard objects embedded in the wool. I tense and want to pull away, but I need to nerve myself to experience the worst. They're just bones. Bones like I have inside me. And wool. The shaggy wool of a poor sheep.

Then something larger than an insect runs across my hand. A mouse? A rat?

'AAGH!' I scream out loud, and bang the walls to scare off whatever is coming for me. The wall of earth above me explodes and showers me with rubble and bones. I slam back and freeze, trying to keep my head covered. What am I doing? This place is so fragile and I could be buried alive here. No more screaming and banging, whatever runs across me. I want to cough up the dust coating my throat, but I dig my fingernails into my palms and shove my tongue to the roof of my mouth, to stop my gag. I have to get out, right now.

The gully is narrow, so I should be able to wedge myself upwards between the sides. It's not such a great distance. Maybe nine feet or so. I can do this. I feel around and find a foothold. I test and step, clinging onto the wall. It's slippery from rain and God knows what, but I get a purchase. I reach about with my other foot and find a hard indent, a root – or a bone. I test and step. But it gives way immediately, rubble collapsing under me as I jolt down.

I try again and get a step further than before, before the wall collapses. I breathe, slowly, purposefully, trying to blank off the possibility that I won't get out, will be buried alive or freeze to death. I grunt at the irony that I will be the one to die of cold, when the cold was what saved Calder. I think of Arran, the pastor who leads back wayward sheep. This poor dead sheep couldn't get back to safety, but I will.

If the wall is too fragile for my full weight, then I'll distribute it. I push one foot flat on the wall and then push on the other equally. I push my hands out and try to share my weight between all four limbs. I slowly ease the pressure from one limb onto the other three as I move and then equalise again. I am sweating in the cold. Sliding and resetting. But I'm moving up my earthen coffin. The air is getting fresher as I reach the top. I will not fall.

Finally, I have my head and chest out of the hole. It's pitch-black up here too, but I can see shadows. The ground is wet all around me. This fissure is at the bottom of a water-filled undulation. It's slippery with no handholds. I keep edging myself up and slowly ease into the freezing pool of water, pushing myself away from the gap. I must not slip back. I try to slide across but I'm stuck in this muddy dip, the rain pouring down, and I can't get any purchase. I'm so close to escape, but simultaneously so far. I reach for the edge, only to slide back, swinging wildly. I jam my hands and feet out, so that I'm spread-eagled across the fissure and won't slide down again. I'm stuck.

Then I hear a thudding above me. I know that thudding from Calder's rescue. It's a helicopter. And suddenly I'm blasted with a spotlight. I've been found. Calder must have called the rescue services when he couldn't find me. I splay myself rigidly. I must hang on.

'Nancy?' I suddenly hear shouted nearby.

But it's not Calder.

CHAPTER TWENTY-SIX

'Hamish.' My voice is hoarse and being sucked up by the wind and rain.

'Nancy! Keep shouting,' he calls.

'Here, I'm over here, please hurry.' I'm so tired, but his voice gives me a bit more strength to lock myself in position, to keep myself from slipping back into the gully.

'Keep calling, I'm coming.'

'Hamish, I'm here. Hamish. Hamish.'

And after an eternity of shouting, he's suddenly right there, his shape silhouetted against the glare of the helicopter lights. I'm back trying to save Calder, but I'm the one being saved. Like a photo gone into the negative.

He lifts his foot to step towards me.

'No, don't!' I scream. 'Don't step forward.' His foot freezes in mid-air. 'Get back. The ground's too soft. It'll give way beneath you. I'm just about holding myself up, but I'm across a gully with a drop. If you step on it, the whole thing'll give way and we'll both be dead.'

'OK, don't worry, just stay still.' He's walking around the dip, sticking to the rock and gorse, assessing my position with a large torch. 'Hold on.'

'I'm trying, but I can't hold on much longer!' I shout. I'm freezing and my muscles are shaking. My body's giving in.

'OK, get ready to catch.' He stands on the rock in front of me, pulls a rope off his back, and throws it to me.

I swing for it, but as soon as I let one arm free, I start to slide, so I slam my hand back on the edge and wedge myself again. 'I can't let go. But I can't hold on any more.'

'Don't panic. You're OK, Nancy.' He comes around to my right side, tests the ground and then kneels as near to me as he can.

'I can't get to you. The ground's too soft. But I'm going to get you out. I promise you.' His voice is steady and strong.

'I'm gonna slide any moment!' I scream, my arms numb and useless.

'No, you're not. Don't you dare give up. I'm right here. Keep listening to my voice.' I feel our connection. He won't let me fall. He's scrabbling in the dark. I twist my head to try to see what he's doing, but the freezing rain is blurring my vision, filling my mouth as I gulp to breathe. He's crouched over his rope. Eventually, he stands and is holding a small lasso. He ties one end around something behind him, securing it tightly. 'Nancy, don't you dare give up. Stay with me. This is strong fibre rope from rock climbing – it can take your weight, I promise you. I just need to get it round you.' He's peering down at me. 'Can you use your elbow to keep the pressure up and then lift your lower arm and hand upwards, as a target for me to throw the rope over?'

'I don't know,' I moan.

'Come on. You can do this.'

I slowly edge my weight between my feet and left arm, till I've pushed my right elbow against the edge of the dip and raised my hand. I'm splayed out, a huge amount of pressure on the bony point of my elbow. 'Quickly! I can't hold this.'

He gets ready to throw. 'Don't move, even when I've got the rope over your hand.'

'OK. But hurry.'

He tosses the rope, but it hits my face. 'Ow.' I lose tension and start to slide.

'I'm sorry, I'm sorry. Keep the pressure up.'

I lock my arms again.

He pulls the rope back and throws again, this time not even reaching me. It just plops into the pool of water. He pulls it back again.

The pain in my elbow and all down my arm is excruciating. 'I can't hold it.'

'You can. You're so much stronger than you think. Hold on.'

My elbow is beyond agony, my arm shaking. My body dissolves and gives way. I let go, sliding sideways, just as the rope falls again and lands over my arm. Hamish pulls the slip knot as I slide, and it slams tight around my wrist. I jolt as I'm held firm by the rope, my body halfway back into the gulley.

'AAGH!' I scream at the agony of my full weight being supported only by my roped wrist. My hand will surely snap off.

'Nancy,' he calls. 'I've got you, I've got you.'

I'm a rag doll, beyond feeling. He pulls me up, agonisingly slowly, and I slide up through the freezing water and mud, scraped by rocks, till I'm finally out of the slippery indent and onto solid ground, my arm feeling like it has separated from its socket. The pain is all-encompassing. Once I'm near enough, he catches my useless floppy hand and drags me across the rough ground. I'm scratched by gorse and stones till I finally feel solid rock below me.

And then he gathers me up and I sob in his arms.

'You're OK now, you're safe.'

I cling onto him as we're lit by the blinding white helicopter beam. Hamish looks up and gives a thumbs up. 'Oh God, I thought I was going to lose you.'

'Now you tell me,' I choke out before arching in pain.

'The helicopter can't land up here. I have to get you down to them. I'll carry you.' He carefully lifts me onto his back and starts down the hill towards the village. The enveloping pain comes in waves. My right arm hangs down his back, numb. 'The poor sheep,' I moan, 'the poor sheep.'

'The sheep are fine,' he says, concentrating on every step.

'Ow.'

'Sorry, just a few more minutes.'

As he carries me down the rest of the hill, I focus on the lights of the village below and the pressure of his firm grip. I see the helicopter coming down in the field where it landed for Calder's rescue.

At the edge of the field, we collapse to the grass. Hamish sits behind me and hugs me, breathing hard.

'How did you ever make that throw?' I falter out.

He wipes my hair away from my face. 'Hoops.'

'What?'

'Hoops, you know, the kid's game. I played it for hours with Calder and Caitlin. We had these four coloured hoops and we would stake out sticks at various distances, more points for the further sticks.'

I squeeze his arm with my good arm.

Paramedics who look identical to the ones who rushed to Calder jump down from the helicopter. And as if we're re-enacting his rescue, I am laid on a stretcher, carried to the aircraft, and loaded in to be whisked to hospital.

'The poor sheep,' I mumble to the paramedics, knowing I only just escaped its fate.

I open my eyes to see my good arm lying along the bed, my hand still adorned with my new wedding ring. I'm in a hospital bed, surrounded by long blue curtains.

Hamish held my hand all the way in the helicopter as I experienced the same journey that Calder's lifeless body made. At the hospital I was treated for hypothermia and cuts and told that my right shoulder was severely dislocated, and it was reset straight away. I was watching the doctors moving around me, but from inside a blurry cocoon of painkillers. My wrist is broken in two places and I have metal screws to hold it in place, inside a cast. And apparently, I'm in shock. Yet I feel shock-free. It is utterly unreal that I am married to that man who chased me onto the hills, that I was with him for so long without ever knowing the real him, that I was totally unaware of what he's capable of.

I try to move my bad arm and feel dull waves of pain flooding across my body.

'Oww!'

A nurse walks over. 'I'll turn up your pain medication. How are you doing, Nancy?'

'I don't really know.'

'You're OK, everything's reset now. We kept you overnight to be careful, but all your vital signs are good.'

'When will I be released?'

'Soon. And your husband's outside, waiting for visiting hours at nine. But I think we can allow a little leeway and let him in.'

'No, don't let him in,' I moan as I throw the covers off and try to stand.

'Ah, here he is.'

The curtain rustles and pulls back to reveal . . . Hamish. I lie back and start to cry.

'Well, I don't usually reduce women to tears just by entering the room.'

I smile weakly. 'You're still here?'

'Of course. Sorry for saying I was your husband, but I wasn't sure they'd let me see you otherwise. I wanted to stay with you last night but got chucked out, so rode around on night buses to keep warm till I could come in.'

'Thank you, Hamish. Thank you so much. If you hadn't found me . . . thank you.'

'No bother.' He settles into a high-backed hospital

chair. 'That's two helicopter rescues you've been involved in now. It's getting to be a habit.'

'One I'm very ready to kick. I think I can get out of here soon.'

'I'll take you wherever you want to go,' he says and then sees my frown. 'Or not – sorry, I don't mean to presume.'

'Yes, of course, but I don't know where I'm going.'

'I don't want to pry, but I'm here to help you,' he says, taking my hand. 'I do care about you. But I know this is the worst time to tell you.'

I pull my hand away. 'Hamish, you are . . . were, Calder's best friend. You're Gina's husband. This can't . . .'

'Yes, totally. I've made such a bloody mess of everything. I'm the last person you need right now. A grubby philanderer. But I promise, on my life, that it was different with you.'

'I . . . I can't think straight at the moment.'

'Forget about me. Don't worry about anything. You need to focus on healing for now.'

'Excuse me,' the nurse says, looking confused, 'but I've got another man on the phone who says he's your husband.' She raises her eyebrows as she glances at Hamish.

'Oh yes, thanks I know who that is, but I don't want to speak to him.'

'He's sounding really distraught – insisting I put him through to you. He won't stop phoning.'

'Shall I talk to him?' Hamish offers.

'No, no, I'll deal with him.'

She passes a hands-free headset to me. 'Don't be too long. This is the ward phone.'

'Hello?' I say quietly.

'Nancy,' Calder says desperately. I glance at Hamish, who stands and walks away. 'No, it's fine—' I call, but he's gone.

'It's not fine,' says Calder down the phone. 'Thank God I've found you.'

'I wasn't talking to you.'

'What?'

'I'm OK.'

'Oh, Nancy. I'm so sorry, I didn't know what had happened. I thought you'd gone to him and I went home and got drunk. Then this morning I found out what happened. I'm so, so sorry.'

'I had a fall, I've broken my wrist, dislocated my shoulder. But I'm OK. I can't talk now. I'll call you when – I know what I want to say.'

'Don't go. Please. I've been out of my mind with worry. I'll come to get you right now.'

'No. Don't you dare.'

'But I . . .'

'I'll ring you as soon as I know what I'm doing. I have to go.' I disconnect the call and hand the phone back to the nurse.

Hamish returns. 'OK?' he says hesitantly.

'I think I've left him.'

He nods. 'Can I help at all?'

'What's happening on the island about Rob, I mean Mr Walker?'

'I gather they're investigating his suicide.'

'They think that's what it was?'

'Pretty certain, I think. Rumours about him and his

daughter have swirled for years. I guess coming back to the island brought it all back and the guilt finally got too much for him.'

How easily they've joined together rumour and fact to make a narrative. But they don't know the middle bit – when Calder killed Rob. Should I tell the police? But I've already withheld information. And what if I'm the one adding two and two to make five and there's a faint chance that Calder's innocent? I'd be sending him to prison for life. I need to get away to clear my head. I'm definitely not going back to that bloody island.

By the afternoon, I've been X-rayed again to check the positioning of my reset wrist, given painkillers and told that I may need to have the cast reset in a week. I'm told that I can get this done in a London hospital.

'You've got another call,' the nurse says as I'm getting my things together.

'I don't want to talk to him again.'

'No, it's not that man from before, it's the police.'

'Oh, OK.' They know.

I take the phone. 'Hello?'

'Is that Mrs Nancy Campbell?'

'Yes.' How long I wanted that name, and now it's grotesque.

'This is Detective Inspector Murray from the Police Scotland Major Investigation Team.'

'Hi, how can I help you?' They must know about Calder already.

'We're investigating the death of Mr Robert Walker.'

'Oh yes.'

'I wondered when you would be returning to the island.'

'I'm sorry. But I'm on my way to London today. Right now, in fact. What is this about?'

'I'm afraid that I have to insist that you return to the island as soon as you're able. We need to question you on an urgent matter.'

'Why? What's happened?' How do they know that I knew what Calder did – has he told them?

'When you were rescued from the hill on Langer yesterday, the paramedics reported that you kept talking about some bones you discovered up there.'

'Yes, that's right. Sheep's bones – the poor thing must have got wedged down there.'

'Possibly. Probably. But in the light of the body discovered on the beach this week and the likelihood of Mr Walker's suicide, our investigation has taken a turn. Locals have been speculating about him interfering with his daughter when she was sixteen and although we've tried to contact her, it seems she has no known address. We are considering the possibility that she never left the island and that perhaps the bones you found are related.'

'What. No, they were sheep's bones. I felt the wool.'

'You're probably right. But we're sending up a specialist unit, while we continue to try to contact Caitlin Walker, if that's the name she's still using. I have to ask you to return for questioning as we attempt to retrieve the bones.'

Oh my God. They were sheep's bones. Weren't they?

CHAPTER TWENTY-SEVEN

The mist is hanging low and is so thick that it obscures everything. The island is barely visible at all on this ferry approach. As if it's holding its secrets tight.

This time it's Hamish I'm standing next to. We are the only foot passengers and there's just one car in the base of the ferry. Calder is waiting for me on the island. He keeps phoning and texting but I'm ignoring him. I'm scared to be alone with him. Does he know what or who is buried up there? Is that why he killed Rob?

What do I say to the police? Tell them Calder's version of Rob's death, which doesn't make sense at all, tell them about his belief that Caitlin was pregnant by him? But given all the rumours, Caitlin might have been pregnant by her dad and so maybe Calder killed him because of that. Or did he kill him because he found out that Rob killed Caitlin? And so he was sort of justified? If Rob's dead anyway, should I let Calder keep his secret? Is all this another example of the islander conspiracy of silence, like when they turned a blind eye to Isla killing Douglas?

'You think they're sheep bones, don't you?' I ask Hamish for the thousandth time.

'I hope so.'

'Of course they are, I felt the wool.' This is all going to be resolved soon and then I'm off to London.

Hamish puts his arm around me and gives me a gentle squeeze. 'Are you warm enough?'

'I'm fine.' He bought me new clothes in Glasgow, including this huge purple coat, the shiny material of which slithers each time I move. It's big enough to zip up over my arm in its sling. Just as well, as it's freezing and drizzling. I did the same loving shopping for Calder, so I know why Hamish is doing so much for me. I'm relieved that he's with me, but I feel so guilty about breaking up his family. Perhaps now we're both free . . . ?

'I'm sorry Gina found out,' I say.

He shrugs. 'I'm not. I'm sorry I didn't leave her sooner.'

'Oh no, don't say that,' I say, turning to him.

He smiles. 'Honestly, I've never really been happy with her. It would have happened one day anyway. We were two people who wanted to be in a relationship and we found a way to coexist in ours. But that's not enough.'

'What a mess everything is,' I say. 'If only we hadn't got drunk that night.'

He touches my arm. 'I know I said it was a mistake. But I haven't been able to stop thinking about you since. And then when Gina told me about your pregnancy – our pregnancy—' He looks down at me with such warmth. I want to lean into him and let him look after me.

'Hamish, I can't think about us yet. I need to talk to the police, get my stuff from the cottage, and get back to London. Perhaps then . . .'

He nods. 'Of course. I've got a lot to sort out too. But I'm here for whatever you need.'

As we near the island, we're right in the middle of the swirling white mist. Nothing clear in front or behind.

'You don't think it is Caitlin buried up there?' I ask quietly.

'No, but . . .'

'What?'

'Well, everyone seems so convinced that Mr Walker was sleeping with her. So, who knows?'

'But you thought that Caitlin left the island?'

'Yes. She's been sending postcards from London ever since, according to her mum.'

'But why didn't she leave with Calder?'

'Well, they'd been arguing a lot in those last weeks.'

I freeze. 'They had?' Calder never told me that. 'What about?'

'I don't know. She was in a strange mood for ages, snapping at everyone, and then that last night they were really going at it – we were all drinking up on the hill and then I went home and left them to their squabbles. And the next day, Calder said he couldn't find Caitlin. Something must have really upset her to go off like that. I guess she wanted a clean break from him.'

'Or she never left?'

The mist is getting even thicker. God, how does the

boat know where it's going in this?

'What was Calder like before?' I ask quietly.

'When?'

'As a kid. Before he left the island.'

'He was, I dunno, quite a moody kid, short-tempered, but a good mate. He grew up on the other side of the island from the rest of the village and was an only child – so I guess that made him self-sufficient – a bit cut off. And his dad was – well, he was a drunk. An ugly drunk.'

'Did he hurt Calder?'

He shrugs. 'He would sometimes turn up with a black eye and some story about an accident. He didn't say much about his home life, but I think he saw a lot of stuff, violent stuff, between his parents.'

'And what do you think happened to his dad? Calder doesn't know much. He was with you on the mainland that night.'

'Err. No, he wasn't.'

'Wasn't what?'

'On the mainland that evening. Who told you that?'

'Calder did.' Oh God.

He shakes his head. 'No, he, Caitlin and I had bunked off school on the Thursday afternoon. We were all going to a gig, but Calder went off somewhere, so Caitlin and I went to the gig together. We never found out where Calder had gone.'

Yet another lie.

'I know this sounds like an awful thing to say,' Hamish says. 'But Douglas drowning was a lucky accident for Calder. He was an awful bloke. And Calder's life was certainly easier after he died.'

As the mist swirls across the boat, all the lies swirl in my head – the London fight, Rob's strangling, Caitlin's disappearance, Douglas's drowning. And the thing that connects all these things – is Calder.

As the ferry approaches the dock, I can just about make out his tall long-haired figure, standing on the edge of the sea wall. Watching for me.

The burly ferryman eyes me as he walks past for the docking. He waves the solitary car onto the land and then we foot passengers file off. We are walking through heavy mist and I trip but Hamish catches me.

Calder appears out of the white swirls, his eyes flicking to Hamish touching me and then up to my face. His face is drawn, his eyes dark and hooded.

'All right,' Calder mumbles.

We all stand together in a stiff silence.

'I guess I'll be going? If you're OK?' Hamish says finally.

'She's fine,' Calder snaps.

'Stop it,' I hiss. I turn to Hamish and give him a faint smile. 'Could you just wait for me up there, I'll be with you in a minute.'

'Thank you,' Calder says, stepping in next to me. 'For helping Nancy.'

Hamish nods and then turns to me. 'I'll be just over there,' he says and strides off.'

'I can't talk. I've got to go straight to the pub,' I say to Calder. 'The police are expecting me.'

'What are you going to tell them?' he says, taking my arm. I look down and he releases me.

'What should I tell them? You lied to me about what happened that night.'

'No. I told you the truth.'

'Really?'

'Look, I'm so sorry about what happened to you last night – I was in such a state but I should never have let you go up there on your own.'

'Because she's up there?'

'What?' He looks genuinely confused but I know not to let myself be tricked.

'That's what they're asking me about: the bones up on the hill.'

'What bones on the hill?' he says sharply, looking up towards where the hilltop would be, but for the mist. He seems completely wrong-footed by my statement.

'When I fell down the gully up there, I touched some bones.'

'What?' He blinks at me. He's either no idea what I'm talking about or he's a seamless liar.

'Is it Caitlin up there?'

CHAPTER TWENTY-EIGHT

'So, it was the feel of the wool that convinced you they were sheep's bones, Mrs Campbell?' Detective Inspector Murray says. He's a large man, with thinning hair, and tired eyes.

'Yes, exactly.'

We're in the pub, chairs stacked on tables and all the broken glass from my previous dramatic visit cleaned away. In the place of the fish I destroyed, there's now a map of the island. I couldn't get any sense out of Calder and had to come straight here. I'm being honest in my answers but not offering extra information.

'Could you make out the full skeleton?'

'No. I didn't feel around. I was focused on getting out of there.'

'But you definitely felt wool?'

'Yes, I thought, I still think that they were sheep's

bones. Sheep fall more often than you think round here.'
I'm horribly conscious that I'm parroting Arran.

'You may be right,' he says, pushing back his chair.
'This could be an expensive goose chase. Or it could be
something else. We'll know soon enough.'

A younger lanky officer comes over. 'Sir, we've just
had word that they've reached the top of the hill, but
the ground's very fragile, so it's going to take a while.
I'll keep you posted.' He walks to the back of the pub,
where several other policemen are gathered around a
table with radios. They've got specialist officers up on
the hill, being led by local climbers, investigating my
succulent tomb. Murray regards me in silence. Is he
giving me a chance to tell more? Should I? I worry that
as an outsider to the island he thinks I'm some sort of
weak link to whatever the islanders have done here. I've
seen the technique on a million police dramas but I have
to fill the silence.

'Look, a sheep had even fallen on our cottage only
that night, so I knew they were more accident-prone than
I'd imagined,' I babble. 'I'm sorry if I've sent everyone on
an expensive wild goose chase. I was really freaked out
by the bones and so told the paramedics. But I said they
were sheep's bones.'

I haven't lied. About the bones. But I haven't mentioned
Calder at all. And because I know that Calder killed
Robert, I feel like I'm directly lying.

'And why were you on the hill in the dark at all?' he
says evenly, like he's asking for the time.

'I'd had an argument with my husband and I was
taking the shortest route to the village.'

'In the dark?'

'Yes, which in hindsight was really stupid. But I was upset.'

'About?' Oh, he's cleverer than he looks with his innocent-sounding probing. I daren't bring suspicion to Calder, in case his murder of Rob was some sort of justified island retribution.

'It was just a tiff.'

'Must have been quite a . . . tiff?'

'Yes. But couples do argue you know. Are you married?'

'Divorced.'

I raise my eyebrows at him. 'So.'

He nods, like he's putting a pin in the subject, but just for now. 'You know Ms Muir,' he says, looking down at his notes.

'Janey, yes, a little, I met her a few weeks ago, when I arrived on the island.'

'But you didn't know Mr Walker.'

'No. Janey mentioned that she was his friend.'

'Boyfriend, according to Ms Muir.'

'Yes, that's what she said, but she didn't want it known.'

'Oh?' He looks up. 'Why not?'

'Because she was seeing him, and he was still married to Alison who lived on the island. And there'd been gossip about him being too close to his daughter Caitlin. It was all just rumour to me, I'd only recently arrived here. But that's what everyone's saying, isn't it. The real islanders would know more than me.'

'But you've never met Mr Walker?'

I hesitate and he inclines his head.

'Well, I saw him very briefly. Once. At Janey's, he was just leaving. We didn't speak.'

'When was this?'

'A few days before . . .' God, I've got to be careful. 'A few days before Janey said she last saw him.'

Murray frowns at me, picking up on my shaky intonation. 'But you have no idea what happened to Mr Walker?'

I have to force my breathing to stay slow. 'I knew Janey hadn't heard from him, because she told me on several occasions that she was annoyed, but she said they'd argued. I didn't know them well enough as a couple to know if that was strange. And then she said his mobile was off, or he wasn't picking up messages or something. She said she couldn't find him at his digs in Oban. I can't quite remember the detail as this was right before my wedding. And then his body washed up. That's all I know.'

'You seem to know a lot after only knowing her for such a short time.'

'She was a new friend, but she confided her fears. But I didn't know anything first-hand about what she was saying.'

He looks at me for a long moment and then stands. 'OK, well, we'll soon know what's really up there.' He moves to the bar to fill up his mug of coffee from the warming pot.

'Can I go now?'

'Yes, I've got your number. You're not leaving the island I presume?

'I was planning to—' He frowns. 'No, of course not.'

'This is an ongoing investigation and we may need to interview you further.'

I walk through the pub and join the group of islanders standing in the tiny town square, spread around the towering Christmas tree. Everyone is looking up towards the hill, which is wreathed in mist.

I see Hamish standing at the far side of the crowd and he gives me a small nod; Janey is sitting alone on a low wall; Arran is talking to Alison; no sign of Calder. They can't be human bones, can they? But if they are, they must be Caitlin. Murdered by Rob? I can't let my mind face what it's sliding towards.

'You OK?' says Calder, who is suddenly right beside me.

I glance over at Hamish, who frowns to see if I need him, but I give a small shake of my head.

Calder gestures me aside. 'What did they ask you?' he whispers.

'I didn't say anything about you.'

He swallows.

'They're not human. The bones. Right? They're not human, are they Calder?'

'I doubt it.'

'You don't know?' I say quietly, seeing Janey looking over at us.

He frowns. 'How would I know?' he blurts and people look round at us.

'Be quiet,' I hiss and give a weak smile to the onlookers, who turn back to the hill.

In the centre of the square is an old winch from the slate-mining days. It is a huge metal contraption, now completely obsolete. But something up there is being pulled free from the depths of the past. Secrets long buried.

'Nance, I—'

'Calder, I think you should tell the police the truth now – about whatever you did to Mr Walker.'

'No. That would make me look like a cold-blooded killer. I've told you the truth. It was an unlucky punch. Which I'll regret for ever. But they won't believe me now.' He sounds so plausible.

'Or was it some sort of island retribution?'

'What?'

'I–I don't know what to believe,' I say, walking away and over to Hamish.

'Everything OK?' he asks.

I nod and join the crowd in staring upwards for the first glimpse of climbers descending.

Janey pushes through the crowd to me.

'Is it Caitlin?' she asks, shaking my sleeve.

'I–I don't know.'

She looks over at Calder. 'You're both lying – about something.'

'I . . .'

She turns and walks away.

It suddenly starts to drizzle and there's a flurry of grey hood raising.

'Everyone come into the church while we wait,' calls Arran.

I walk up with the crowd, avoiding Calder's glare as he follows at a distance.

* * *

The church still has my wedding flowers in place but the white and red petals are curling and tired, and there's a musky scent of decay. People are strewn across the pews. Arran is giving out tea. Someone has made sandwiches, big doorstops filled with greasy margarine and hunks of cheese. I can't face eating anything. Calder and I sit apart on one of the hard-backed pews. I don't want to sit next to him but I don't want the stares if I don't.

The minutes tick by, everyone on their phones as the rain pelts on the stained-glass windows. If the gully is filling with water and the ground is waterlogged, the excavation of the sheep will be very slow. Heaters are plugged in, but the church still feels cold.

Calder keeps going outside, chain-smoking.

Arran comes over and pats my shoulder. 'Are you doing OK?'

'I couldn't have known they were human, if they are,' I say. 'Which they're not. It was so dark. You told me about the falling sheep and then one actually fell on our cottage. I . . .'

'It's OK. Take a breath. No one's blaming you.'

I so want to confess what Calder's told me about killing Rob. I feel so complicit. And as if everything is about to unravel. But what if it is sheep bones up there, or it is Caitlin, murdered by Rob, and I'm sending Calder to prison for an understandable crime?

'Maybe they should,' I blurt.

He frowns.

'Blame me. I found the bones. I feel like I've unleashed something dark?'

'We've all committed sins,' says Arran slowly. What

does he mean? 'None of us are totally innocent. But we can't hold our mistakes close every day. I've watched people do that, eaten up by their corrosive guilt. It burns you from the inside, till you're only a shell. If you confess your sins to God, he can wash you clean.'

'What are you . . . ?'

The big church doors swing open with a violent push.

'They're coming down,' calls one of the islanders.

We all rush out, wrapping our grey church raincoats tight. Everyone stares across at the fluorescent-coated figures as they make their way over. We watch in silence as they stride towards us, ropes coiled over their backs, bright light waterproofs, hard hats. Their faces are grim.

'Is it her?' Alison calls. Arran puts his arm around her but she shrugs him off.

Detective Inspector Murray walks ahead of the crowd and towards Alison, his eyes deadened. He lowers his head to speak quietly to her.

She nods, frozen for a moment, the flings her arm out. 'Tell them all, go on!' she shouts.

Murray faces the crowd. 'I'm sorry to inform you, but we now have it confirmed that there are human remains up on the hill.'

There is a shocked inhale from the crowd.

'We have to run tests, but it looks pretty certain that it's Caitlin Walker.'

Alison's face is white. 'All those years I stayed here to wait for those postcards,' she says dully. 'But she's been up there all this time. Rotting away.'

It was Caitlin's bones that I touched, Calder's sixteen-year-old girlfriend. His pregnant girlfriend. She's been lying up there all these years. Robert must have killed her. He came back to the island and couldn't deal with his guilt, so he killed himself? Please God let that be the explanation. Because if not . . . I look over at Calder, then at the other islanders, all sharing glances.

'It was a complete skeleton,' says one of the local climbers who accompanied the specialist team. We've all moved back to the church. Arran is giving out tea.

'It was so eerie,' the climber continues. 'The body was wedged into the ground in the side of the gully wall, lying flat like it was on a shelf – but face down.'

The listeners draw breath. 'A satanic sign,' I hear someone say. 'Makes it harder for them to return from the dead.' God, everyone's gone mad. But I look around this slate church, at the lights bouncing off that huge sheer slate altar, and anything seems possible now, in this sinister setting.

Alison is sitting stony-faced on a nearby pew.

'Alison, are you sure you want to hear this?' the climber asks.

'Just keep going,' she mumbles. 'I want to know. Every detail. She's dead now. Words can't hurt me any more.' She's so horribly calm in the circumstances. How is she not crying?

'OK. Well, the ground had cracked open right next to where she must have been lying all these years – as if to show her off. If the crack had come a foot or so to the right or left, no one would have found it. Only the leg bones had been disturbed,' he continues. 'Presumably that happened when you fell down there.' He gestures to me.

I nod.

'But how could they make such a definite identification so quickly?' Arran asks in an odd tone.

'They excavated slowly, brushing the soil back but having to keep adding supports to stop the ground above collapsing. And gradually they revealed the wee figure, long-haired. Because the ground was so peaty, the clothes and even the hair and some of the,' he glances at Alison but she waves him on, 'some of the face was still intact. And she was wearing a thick woolly jacket.'

The wool of a jacket, not a sheep. Those walls were so moist and soft – I was pushing my bare hands into the rotted flesh of my husband's girlfriend.

'I knew who it was straight away. I remembered that jacket she used to wear,' he continues. 'I told them. But the identification was confirmed from her flowered rucksack, which had been perfectly preserved. It had a name inside—'

'Lacquered in glitter,' Alison says dully, staring straight ahead. 'Capital letters, spelling out CAITLIN. I bought her that rucksack. She loved it, spent ages decorating it.' She shakes her head. 'Rob said over and over that she wouldn't run off like that. I should have believed him. Should have forced the police to investigate.'

The crowd are whispering.

'Before you all start up again,' she snaps, 'Rob didn't do this. I hated him with every fibre of my being. But no way would he have killed her.'

Arran walks up to Alison and kneels at her feet.

'You have to forgive me,' he says quietly. 'I know something that explains why he probably did do it.'

'What?' she exclaims, grasping his shoulders.

'I blamed myself for so many years after,' Arran says. 'I thought that what she told me was the reason why she left. But now I see it's . . . why Rob killed her.'

'No he didn't!' she cries. 'He couldn't have.'

'She came to the church that summer to ask forgiveness.'

'For what?'

'For . . . the abortion she was planning.'

Alison gasps and clasps her hands to her mouth.

'I told her I was there to support her. Said I'd help her with the baby or help her with an adoption, if that's what she wanted.' He wipes his eyes with his hand. 'But she said it was a bloke from the mainland. I didn't realise she was pregnant . . . by Rob.'

'She wasn't,' Alison says slowly. 'I lied.'

'What?'

'Rob never did a thing to Caitlin,' she moans. 'He never touched her. I was so angry, and I wanted him to suffer. So I spread those awful rumours. But it was all lies. He never killed her. I'd swear on my life.'

'But the pregnancy . . .'

She shakes her head. 'Rob had a vasectomy after we had Caitlin, it couldn't have been him.' She slumps down on the pew and finally I see a single tear fall down her flawless cheek.

'So who was she pregnant by?' Arran says.

There's a huge crash from across the room as a lectern smashes down.

'What did you do?' Hamish screams as he runs at Calder. 'You bastard. You murdering bastard.' He punches Calder hard in the face. He stumbles back and then launches himself onto Hamish and they fall to the ground, fighting.

I back away. I haven't let myself fully think it, but I suddenly know that it's true.

Arran and the villagers try to pull them apart.

'You were the last person to see her!' shouts Hamish, spittle flying everywhere as he fights against the men holding him back.

'You killed her?' Alison shouts. 'But she loved you.'

Hamish struggles to pull free again, kicking out at Calder. 'Poor lovely Caitlin. You killed her and left her up there to rot.'

Calder's shaking his head. 'I didn't. I promise I didn't.' His wild eyes find mine but I look away.

Alison starts hitting him with her fists. No one stops her. The islanders are converging in a circle around him.

The police suddenly muscle through the crowd and pull Calder free from the angry islanders. They drag him outside and down the church steps and bundle him into a police car.

Calder killed Caitlin because she was pregnant by him. The warmth of the heater next to me is too much and I lean back on the edge of a pew. He killed Robert because he found out that he'd killed her. My tongue unpeels from the roof of my mouth as I try to catch my breath. He stabbed a co-worker in a fury back in London. A drip of sweat drops onto my hand. And he started out by killing his own father at the age of fourteen. The flickering lights of the church fold in on me as if I am moving far away down a long tunnel. Poor Caitlin stuck down that gulley all those years. I can see Calder standing over Caitlin's body, using the toe of his boot to roll her towards that crevice and then kicking her in, letting her be swallowed up by the earth.

And then everything goes black.

As I come round, I'm lying across a pew, Hamish leaning over me.

'Nancy, thank God, are you OK?'

'Give her some space,' Arran says. 'Here, this is hot sweet tea. It'll help with the shock.'

I lever myself up, sip the rich sugary liquid and it brings me further into the room.

'It's no wonder you fainted,' Arran says. 'It's a lot to take in.'

Above me is the church's famous stained-glass window of the Virgin Mary. The church lights bounce off the glass, dappling my dirty jeans with coloured light. Mary looks beatifically down on me as she cradles Jesus.

The sea and then the earth have given up their secrets. And now the sky has revealed a secret from the stained-glass window.

I don't need the evidence. I already know it's true.

'I'm OK,' I say, struggling up. 'I'm going to have a lie down.'

'You can come back to mine,' Hamish offers.

'No. I'll take a taxi back to the cottage. I need to be alone.'

The battered taxi crunches away down the gravel, as I make my way into our slate-filled bathroom. I still have the last of a bumper pack of ten early pregnancy detection tests, from when Calder and I were trying for a baby. A lifetime ago. I hunch down and pee on the end of the stick, using my good arm, but getting pee all over my fingers. I finally manage to get the blue cap on with my injured hand and drop it on the side of the sink while I awkwardly wash my hands with the grey soap. Everything is bloody grey here. When I get back to London, if there is a life after this, I'm never buying anything grey again – coloured towels, bright soaps, white plates. Anything but grey.

You're meant to wait three minutes, but I look straight away. *Pregnant* has already appeared in the little rectangle. And there's no doubt it's Calder's this time. I'm pregnant by a killer. By a serial killer. Not only do I have to tell the police now because it is and has always been the right thing to do, but also because I cannot have this murderer anywhere near me and my child.

I brought Calder back from the dead. He should have died that morning in the sea – for killing Douglas, Caitlin and then Robert. I should never have let him come back.

He is the one who should be buried face down, so that he can never return.

CHAPTER TWENTY-NINE

I stare at the positive pregnancy test lying on the table. Attila jumps up onto my lap and settles herself into a curve, fitting herself across my belly as if protecting me. It's the first time she's ever settled on me. I can't believe the unbelievably cruel irony of being finally given what I have always wanted, to be pregnant by Calder, but for it to now be the most horrific thing imaginable. I have that violent man's baby growing inside me. And it would be the child of a violent man who is himself the son of a violent man. What kind of child would I be bringing into the world? I place my hands on my stomach. Calder's spreading through me from the inside. It is impossible that I, who have wanted a child more than anything, am now considering that I shouldn't have it. But if I have his child, I will be tied to that monster for ever, even if he's in prison for life.

My script work is lying on the table. I was on the latter stages of the film – using a quote directly from Frankenstein's monster when he's desperate for a mate: *If I cannot inspire love, I will cause fear.* Once Calder knows I don't believe him and am going to the police, what will he do to me? I've seen the darkness in his eyes. Thank God they've arrested him.

I doze intermittently through the night, waiting till it's time to walk round the island for the first ferry at nine. Whatever Detective Inspector Murray said, I need to get off this island now, as far away from Calder as I can. Then I'll talk to the police.

Suddenly, the front door swings open and Calder's silhouette blocks the space.

'Nancy, you're still here. Thank God.'

The curvy blue and white pregnancy test is lying on the kitchen table in front of me – in front of him – the word PREGNANT *still* clearly displayed.

'Calder. Are you OK? They let you go?' I hear the fakeness in my voice.

Attila hisses at Calder and I use the distraction to swing my shawl off my shoulders to drop it across the evidence.

He shrugs. 'They gave me a warning for fighting, and questioned me but couldn't hold me on all this madness about Caitlin. But I do have to return tomorrow to be formally questioned after the post-mortem.'

'I waited. But they wouldn't give me any information – so in the end I came back here.'

I walk around the table to him. He cannot know about the baby. He killed the last woman he got pregnant. *If I*

331

cannot inspire love, I will cause fear. I cannot show him that I'm afraid of him. But he's not stupid and knows me so well. I have to try to believe the lie that I still love him.

'It's ridiculous,' he explodes. 'They had zero proof beyond all those rumours and histrionics, so they had to let me go.'

'I guess they have to follow up every lead.'

He hesitates in front of me. 'You believe me, don't you?'

I blank off my emotions. 'Of course I do.'

He steps towards me, and I step back automatically. He registers my falter and looks at me warily.

'Are you all right?'

'I'm fine. Just shocked.' I step in and embrace him.

I am alone with him, in this isolated cottage. I have to convince him that I believe him. That I'm on his side. I have to dull my senses, erase Calder the killer in front of me and only see Calder from London. Who I used to love. I must be believable.

I look up at his old chickenpox scar above his right eyebrow, that I know so well, that I've stroked and kissed. I must be the Nancy that did that again. I reach up and caress the scar. I smile as my eyes sweep down over his mouth as I remember his smirk when he fished me out of Regent's Canal. I run my hands down his arms and stroke his hands that held mine as he taught me to skim stones. I mentally put back together my broken waterfall trinket and see it shining in the sunlight on our trip to the rapids. I lean forward and breathe in his musky scent as I play out the montage of our happy life together on fast forward, stopping abruptly when we arrived on the island, so full of hope. I am that Nancy now.

'I'll make you some tea. You must be exhausted,' I say gently.

'Thanks,' he says, throwing off his coat. 'This is a fucking nightmare.'

The whoosh of water shooting from the tap fills the room. As I pull over two mugs, I see the line of the endless mugs of tea he's made for me over the last five years, makes me, when he knew, knows, I'm stressed but didn't, doesn't, know what to say. I bang the kettle on the hob and light the gas. I think of the swirl of unsuitable earrings he's bought me, buys me, which I pretended, pretend, to love because of the pleasure he got, gets, when he sees he's made me happy. My back is turned to him. I hear him moving, his heavy breathing, the rustle of his clothes. I force my shoulders down, waiting for the punch, the push, the stab . . . but finally I hear him throw himself into a chair. I turn to see him smiling at me.

I am the old Nancy – who loves Calder.

'So what if I was the last person to see Caitlin?' he says. 'She was really hyper that night – saying she was trapped whichever way she turned. We were both drinking heavily, talking about her choices with the pregnancy, up on the hill and then . . . I guess I passed out. When I woke up a few hours later, she was gone and she'd left me a note saying not to follow her. The police have no proof that I was involved. Because I wasn't.'

I realise that he's rehearsing his story with me to tell to the police later.

The kettle starts to boil, a slowly rising wheeze, as I try to slow my breathing.

He sounds so plausible. But he sounded so believable before, when he was describing the 'accident' with Rob. And that was all a lie. And then he claimed he was away, when Douglas drowned. But that was a lie. And now he's crafting this story about Caitlin. Which is clearly a lie. He is a consummate liar. A psychopath.

The kettle is screaming. I pull it off the gas, the steam catching me across my arm and I drop the kettle, boiling water splashing out.

'What are you doing?' Calder shouts as he drags me towards the sink and runs my arm under the cold water. He's fast and violent – to help me – but I can't stop myself from fighting back and trying to escape his grasp. 'I'm trying to help you!' he screams as I yank my arm away. 'Are you mad?'

He stares at me and then takes a sudden sharp intake of breath.

'You're scared of me?'

'No, of course not. You were hurting me. That's all.'

He steps in too close and leers into me. 'What do you think I'm going to do?' he says in an odd tone.

'Nothing, I wasn't scared, it's my arm.' I swivel to the sink and shove the burn under the cold tap. 'It really hurts. Can you get some ice for me? Please.'

He seems to weigh something up and then moves to our huge coffin of a freezer.

I feel so vulnerable with one arm in a sling, the other burnt. How can I fight back?

He returns with a bag of frozen peas. 'Sit down and put this on your arm. I'll make the tea.'

I pretend to focus on my arm. But as soon as he turns

to the sink, I pull my shawl towards me and sweep up the pregnancy test, and hold the shawl and concealed test over the icy peas as if to protect my hand from the cold.

Calder makes us both tea. 'It's freezing in here,' he says, bringing blankets for us.

'Thanks,' I say, trying to sound like the old me.

'I'm sorry about everything,' he says slowly. 'I didn't mean to shout at you. It's just such a shock finding out that Caitlin's been up there all this time. But I had nothing to do with her death.'

'I know you didn't.'

He stares, assessing me.

I look back at him and our eyes click.

I think.

Or is he playing the same game?

'They didn't ask you about me and Mr Walker?' he asks.

'No, of course not.'

Calder's a clever bloke, though I always thought he was pretty straightforward, no dark layers. But has his whole personality been a creation for my benefit? Have I been played all these years? Was I some sort of cover? Were all my lovely memories just a facade? It sounds ridiculous. But serial killers have oblivious wives, making dinners, bringing up children, and everyone always says, *How didn't she know?* Isn't that exactly what a killer would do? Take on a compliant girlfriend to make himself look normal?

'This is a nightmare,' he says, shoving his hands into his hair. 'I can see how everyone thinks I'm guilty. But

I'm not. You believe me, don't you?'

'Of course.'

I put the ice pack down on the table and stroke his hair. He reaches out and clasps my waist, his head on my tummy. This is the tableau I always yearned for. Now it's grotesque.

'Thank you. I don't know what I'd do without you,' he murmurs.

He's so believable. How did I never see the darkness? I have to make sure that he's found guilty and locked up for ever.

'I haven't slept for forty-eight hours, I'm wrecked,' he says.

'Shall we lie down?'

'Yeah, good idea, come on.'

We make our way back to our bedroom and I pull off my wet clothes, pull on layers that I can survive the weather in later and lie down next to him. I slow my breathing and try to make my body go limp as if I'm asleep.

He curls into me, a heavy arm across me.

As soon as he's asleep I have to escape.

I'll scream if I stay still a second longer, but I think of the baby and I bear the wait again. I must get out of here. I think Calder is sleeping. His breathing has been slow and steady for a while. But I don't know if he's faking. To test me.

I can't leave it any longer. I have to get away. I use my good arm to grip the metal frame of the bed and painfully pull myself out from under his arm, inch by inch. As I finally pull free, his arm falls onto the mattress and I hold my breath, expecting him to wake. But his breathing continues slow and steady.

I sit up very slowly and pad out of the bedroom to get my coat and boots. I've just laced them when the overhead lights flare.

'Going somewhere?'

I straighten and we stare at each other. He knows I don't believe a word he's said. He knows I know what he's done.

Then all the lights go out.

CHAPTER THIRTY

'Power cut,' Calder calls. 'Don't move. I'll find my torches and Mum's candles.'

There's a massive bang above us.

'It's another sheep!' I scream.

'No, it's a thunderclap.'

We edge over in the dark to look out of the small window. A jagged crack of lightning breaks on the coastline, illuminating the churning sea. The wind is howling and rain is sheeting down.

'This is more than any usual storm,' Calder says. 'We had a storm like this when I was younger. It was devastating for the island. And we're really exposed on this side. We have to make the cottage as safe as we can. Keep the weather out as best we can.'

And keep me in?

The window we're standing at suddenly slams inwards,

cold air and rain blasting us as Calder fights to close it.

'We have to board up all the windows!' Calder shouts. 'I'll get the torches.' He bangs about getting to the cupboard and soon there's a strong beam of light across the room from a powerful torch. The window is flapping back and forth violently, rain pouring in. 'Here, take this,' he says, giving me the torch and taking a second smaller one for himself. 'I'll get the toolbox!' he shouts, 'you start gathering together any bit of wood you see lying about.'

His dad's rusty toolbox slams onto the ground as I pick up an old drawer. He smashes the sides off and then hammers the wood across the broken window.

There's a loud crashing above us.

'Is the roof coming down?' I shout.

'The chimney stack probably. I need to block the grate.'

We run through to the lounge. As Calder shoves open the door, my torch illuminates the room, covered in black soot and debris.

'I'll get the old newspapers and wood. We need to stop this up.'

He fills the column and hammers wood across the opening.

'Are you OK?' Calder asks suspiciously, as he shoves the torch glare in my face.

I shade my eyes. 'I'm just tired.'

'Sorry. Sit down. I'm going to light the candles. We need to conserve the batteries in the torches. God knows how long this will go on for, or how long it will take them to get the electric reconnected.'

It's freezing cold. The wind is howling outside, and the rain is slamming onto the boarded-up rattling windows.

He lights candles and places them on the table. The flickering light is eerie and bathes our faces in an odd glow. I hug my stomach. I'll protect you. I'll save you. From him.

'I need to wash some of this grime off me,' I call, walking towards the bathroom. As I step over, I surreptitiously pick up Calder's car keys as a weapon and slide them into my pocket.

'Nancy,' he calls.

'Yes,' I blurt, closing my fingers on the keys.

'Here, take this,' he says, giving me a candle.

'Oh, thanks.' I drop the keys into my pocket and take the candle to the bathroom

I wash some of the black soot and dirt from my hands and face. It's so much louder in here, the window rattling and the rain beating down against the side of the cottage.

'We need to be careful of all these open flames,' I hear him call. 'I'll clear the table.'

I suddenly remember my shawl left out there, containing the pregnancy test.

'No, I'll—'

As I open the bathroom door, I see Calder standing in the flickering candlelight, dropping my shawl onto the table and looking at my pregnancy test.

'You're pregnant?'

I nod.

'By Hamish?'

'What? No. Of course it's yours.'

'How would I know?' he spits.

'Because it only happened once – in London.'

'So that's where you were setting off to just now. To be with Hamish.'

'Oh my God, I'm not with Hamish. I'm pregnant with your child.'

'Like last time?'

I move away from him, around the table. 'You said you believed me. I told you, it was a terrible drunken mistake.'

'You cheated once. Why wouldn't you do it again?'

'And you killed once. Why wouldn't you do that again?'

He stares at me. 'What does that mean?'

'You say you killed Rob by pushing him over the cliff in a moment of anger.'

'That's the truth.'

I know I shouldn't say more, but I'm beyond any control now. 'And yet, he had a rope around his neck? You didn't kill him in a moment of madness. You garrotted him, then threw him into the sea. Because he knew . . . that you'd killed Caitlin?'

He throws his arms up and bellows. 'No, I didn't. And I had nothing to do with poor Caitlin's death.'

'Shut up, shut up, shut up!' I scream. 'Stop lying. You can't keep this up in the face of solid hard facts. You're a serial killer.'

'Oh my God. Who else am I supposed to have killed?'

'Your dad.'

He stares at me, open-mouthed.

Then the mended window flies open, the blast of cold air knocking the precarious candles over. We are in pitch-black.

I scream.

There's a sudden flare of light as the shawl on the table is ignited by the fallen candles. Everything catches so quickly. I see Calder's face, lit by the flames, his eyes huge. The whole table is alight now. The fire is between us and the door, the only way out. Black smoke is filling the room. We're both coughing.

'We've got to get out right now!' Calder screams, pushing me towards the back bedroom.

He slams the door shut and shoves blankets over the crack at the base. As the room starts to fill with smoke, he drags open the tiny window.

'Get out, now!' Calder shouts.

I clamber onto the chair he shoves in front of me and then squirm my way through the hole. I land heavily, grazing my hands and jolting my injured shoulder, making me scream in agony. I manage to roll onto my good side and lever myself up, just in time to see Calder forcing himself through the tiny window.

As he falls to the ground, there's an explosion inside the cottage.

'It's the cooker and the gas tank!' he shouts. 'Get back as far as you can. I need to move the rest of the gas canisters in the garden. The whole thing could blow at any moment.'

He runs out of view. I push my freezing hands into my pockets as I limp away and realise I still have the car keys in my pocket. But I can't drive. Never learnt. Though I've sat next to him when he's driving so many times. Thank God it's automatic. Keys in, turn the ignition, foot down and steer. I have to try.

I run towards the car, everything lit up by the yellowy

flickering. The driver's door is unlocked. I jump in and slam it shut.

'Nancy?' I hear in the distance.

I struggle to get the keys in the silver slot, having to use my injured right hand, which is all but useless. I edge round to use my better hand, squeezed up against the door, and finally turn the ignition. It doesn't start.

I look up, and see Calder running round the cottage towards me.

I lock my door and then swing round to lock the passenger door and heave myself between the seats to lock the back doors.

I'm screaming in agony as Calder reaches the car. 'What are you doing, Nance?' he shouts, banging on the window. 'Get out, you're too close – it's gonna explode – then the car'll go too.'

I turn the ignition, and this time it starts. I push down on the pedal. The car judders but doesn't move. The handbrake. I pull at it madly, but it doesn't budge.

'You can't drive!' Calder screams.

My hands are slippery with sweat, but I finally feel a button on the top of the brake.

'Get away from me!' I scream as I press the button awkwardly with my left hand, pull the handbrake and shove my foot down on the pedal. The car shoots forward, down the path, scraping along the wall with a horrible grinding sound, the wing mirror flying clean off. We won't be getting the deposit back on this rental. I pull my foot off just as I smash into the pile of slates covering Isla's ashes, and the car jolts to a stop on the very edge of the cliff.

Calder is running down the path behind me.

Where are the lights? There's just loads of buttons with symbols.

'Nancy – you'll kill yourself, stop.'

Finally, I see a little half-oval with lines from the blunt end. I stab it and the gloom ahead is lit up. I'm so much shorter than Calder, but don't have time to move the seat, so I sit forward to reach the pedal, drag on the steering wheel and press. The car turns and crawls forward at a snail's pace. I can't press too hard or I'll be tumbling over the cliff. I manage to pull on the wheel hard enough that the car veers back onto the track. I'm crawling along, sweating and peering ahead, when I hear a bang, as Calder hits the boot. I push my foot down and the car shoots forward again. This time I pull back gradually and I'm driving forward, Calder receding in the mirror behind me.

CHAPTER THIRTY-ONE

It's like driving in a black void. There are no lights outside anywhere, not even at the crossroads. The power cut must have affected the surrounding roads. The rain's lashing down. I should look for the wipers, but daren't stop. My right leg is cramping from the exertion of trying to control the pedal.

Suddenly, the wheels on the left clunk over a ridge. I've come off the road. The car is leaning at a precarious angle. I drag the wheel back towards the road with my good arm and press on the pedal, but the wheels spin without the car moving. I get out to see what's happened. In the dim glow spreading from the rear lights, I can see that the back wheel is sunk in thick mud. It can't get purchase. But I can't dig it out, in my state. I need to put something down for the wheel to catch on. Something hard that can take the weight of the car.

Slate!

The whole bloody island is made of the stuff.

I kick pieces of slate over, shoving them behind the wheel. And slowly, blanking to the pain, I pile up enough to give myself a chance. I glance back along the way I've come. No one yet, but he'll catch me up soon. I get back behind the wheel, release the handbrake and push down on the pedal again. And finally, the wheels bite and the car lurches up out of the mud and I'm back on the road.

As I get closer to the village, I'm confused that there are still no street lights.

But as I finally turn the corner that leads down, I understand. The whole place is plunged into darkness. It's like there's no village down there at all. There must be a power cut to the whole island. I carefully drive the car to the edge of the cottages, but daren't go any further in case I hit someone in the dark.

I look back but see no one. Or is Calder following in the shadows? If he is following, he's on foot and will be at least half an hour behind me – unless he's gone over the hill in the dark? Surely he wouldn't risk it in this weather? But I instantly know he would. He'll be here in fifteen minutes or so. I have to get help. Right now. As I walk down between the two rows of white cottages, I see torches and candles in some of the windows, dark shadows moving about. The weather is biblical and I'm utterly drenched. I don't know where to go.

Everyone thinks that Calder is a murderer, and I am his complicit wife.

I knock on Hamish's White House but there's no answer. I bang harder. Nothing. Where is he? I try ringing him, but it goes straight to voicemail.

Surely Arran will help me. I run up to the church, but the lights are out, the big doors locked. Then I see a flickering light in the vicarage next door. I run round and knock on the window.

'Nancy?' Arran says as he peers out. 'Oh thank God,' he calls and then gestures. 'Come round to the door.'

He drags open the wooden door and pulls me in out of the rain, into his musty hallway. 'Are you OK? What are you doing out in this?'

'Can I stay here till the first ferry?' I pant.

He frowns. 'To the mainland?'

'Yes. I . . . I need to get away.'

'I know this has all been very distressing, but why aren't you with Calder?' He hands me a towel.

'I–I can't explain now.'

He frowns. 'I'll get you some dry clothes. You wait in there.' He hands me a small spluttery candle from a side table and takes one with him.

I step into his low-ceilinged lounge. It's hard to see much but I can tell how austere it is. Simple hard chairs. A table. Almost monastic. I circle round then stop abruptly. In the flickering light I stare at the dresser. It's covered with framed photos: all of Calder. A young Calder in football kit, a teenage Calder with short-cropped hair, even a photo of Calder and me that we gave to Isla. And a photo of us from our wedding. I haven't even got wedding photos myself yet. What is going on with this obsession he has with Calder?

I hear murmuring and creep to the closed door. Arran's on the phone with someone in a back room. I inch the door open and creep into the hall.

'Yes, she's here now . . . No, I won't tell her . . . Don't worry, I won't let her go . . . I know . . . Of course I do. OK, bye, Calder. See you in a bit.' Oh my God, they're in league somehow and he's trapping me for him. What is going on on this island? Who can I trust?

I sneak back into the lounge, spinning in the doorway as I hear the creak of his steps.

'Are you looking for something?' he asks.

'No. I–I was just coming to find you.'

We eye each other. Does he know I heard him?

'So where are they?'

'What?' he asks, stepping towards me.

'Did you find those clothes for me?' He looks down at his empty hands and back at me. I tense, ready to resist his attack. 'I'm really cold.'

He hesitates, then turns. 'Oh yes, sorry, coming up. Stay in the lounge, you don't want to fall over in the dark.' He closes the door with a click. I have to get out of here before he comes back. God knows what he's planning. I walk over to the window and try the metal catch. But it's locked. I pull up one of the heavy wooden chairs, steady myself by holding onto the curtain rail and kick at the lock, smashing it and sending the window flying open. The noise is huge. I balance on the sill, considering the drop, but then the door behind me flies open.

'Nancy, stop.'

I jump down, landing in the wet flowerbed, shrieking at the jolt of pain on impact.

'Nancy, don't run!' Arran shouts, but I'm away down the little hill to the village before he can get to the door. I run fast, knowing I have to get out of sight. I see the bus shelter up ahead and duck behind it, gasping for air. So Arran is in league with Calder. Why does he have all those photos of him in his otherwise sparse room? More importantly, how can I escape both of them till the ferry arrives?

My phone tells me it's 8.20 a.m., and it's just starting to get light. At nine, the first ferry will be leaving the island. Thank God. I can escape this place for ever. Gina will help me find a lawyer, if I have to be interviewed further. I know she'll help once she understands the stakes. But where to hide till the first ferry? Across the road, I see the old-fashioned toilet block and stumble towards it. Never have I been so happy to breathe in the reek of urine and detergent. I fall in and sit on the cold tiles, crying with relief.

Half an hour later, I pull open the toilet block door. The rain's lessened, and the wind's lowered. I see the devastation the storm has wrought. Garden fences blown down, chairs and tables carried across the square, walls collapsed. Some of the boats have crashed into each other and are lying on their sides, half submerged in the sea. But there are men congregated near the ferry, getting it ready for the first departure of the morning. I'll be off the island in ten minutes, I'm going to be all right.

As I step out, I see Hamish running past. 'Hamish, over here.'

He turns, confused, then sees me and ducks into the toilet block.

'Thank God I've found you!' he cries, embracing me. 'Oh, you're soaked.'

'They're after me,' I say, pulling him in, behind the door.

'Who's after you?'

'Calder. And Arran. Calder killed Caitlin and then Rob because he found out. And Arran's helping him.'

'You're kidding.' He shakes his head in disbelief. 'But at least Calder's in prison for now.'

'No, they let him go.'

'What?'

'He said they had no solid evidence against him. So you see, I have to get off the island right now. I'm taking the first ferry out. Come with me.'

'No,' he says, with an awful finality.

That's it. I'm alone. He was my last hope. I thought he'd do anything for me. 'It's OK. But I have to go. I—'

'No, of course I'll help you,' he says, gripping my shoulders. 'I mean that the ferry can't get out of the harbour.'

'But why?'

'The storm's washed all the loose slates from the seabed into the harbour bay. Nothing's coming in or going out. It'll take weeks to sort.'

I lean back against the toilet stall. Exhausted. Trapped. Waiting for the inevitable.

'Trust me,' Hamish says, squeezing my arm. 'I won't let them get you, whatever it takes. My truck's just outside.'

I nod and feel a warm click between us. I can trust someone else. Maybe there is still hope. I lurch myself forward and peek out the toilet block door. I see Arran striding in the distance in his long grey raincoat. 'Arran's not far off,' I whisper.

'Nancy!' I hear shouted up from the beach and see Janey waving furiously at me. She's coming up across the slates . . . with Alison? They're both wearing the long grey church raincoats as they walk towards us in step. How are they even speaking to each other? Don't they hate one another? Janey waves over at Arran and gestures towards the toilet block, alerting him to my position. He nods at her and raises both his arms as if waving in others. I glance around and realise that there are more grey-coated figures surging towards us. What's happening? Are they all after me?

'They're all coming for us,' I cry. 'We have to move right now.'

'Nancy, are you OK?' I hear Arran shout. 'Have you seen Hamish?' I realise they can't see him in the doorway. Arran looks beyond me and shouts, 'Calder, she's in there.'

I swing round and look back up the street, where I see a single figure approaching. It's Calder. In a long grey raincoat. He *is* one of them.

'Oh God, Calder's nearly here.'

Arran is approaching.

Janey and Alison are crossing the road.

The host of grey figures are all getting closer.

'We have to run for it!' shouts Hamish, throwing open the door.

We launch ourselves out the door, into their view and dash down the siding to where Hamish's beat-up truck is parked. He yanks open the door and we clamber in.

Arran is nearly at the truck, as I slam the door. 'Go, go go!' I shout.

The truck lurches off.

But Janey and Alison are blocking our way ahead. They stare up at us, hands raised, grey coats flapping in the wind.

Hamish accelerates and at the last moment, the women throw themselves out of our path.

'We have to drive past Calder to get out of the village!'

shouts Hamish. 'We're nearly on him. Lock your door.'

As we reach Calder, he's shouting and gesticulating, his face thunderous. He bangs his fists on my door and howls as we shoot past.

We've escaped them. Thank God. I lean back and into Hamish as we accelerate away.

I look back through the rear window. 'Did you see they were all in those grey church raincoats – even Calder. It is a cult.'

'What?'

'That church, this whole community. They're a law unto themselves. Janey warned me. And Calder's one of them.'

'It's a closed shop alright, especially for the chosen one,' he says darkly.

'Calder?'

He nods. 'It was like that when we were children. He was the one Arran always doted on. The whole church fussed over him. I never fitted in here.'

Dark forces seem to be gathering. And Calder is at their centre. We have to get away, right now. 'What are we going to do? How can we possibly get off the island now?'

'We can take my nature-trip boat – if the storm hasn't got it. It's in a boathouse, in a protected cove, so it might be fine. But if they're following us, it's down a long dirt track, and there's no other route out from there. So we better pray it is seaworthy.'

I nod furiously and he accelerates again. We're either driving towards our escape. Or boxing ourselves in.

Easy prey.

CHAPTER THIRTY-TWO

We drive along the far side of the island, which I've never visited before, along a sheer clifftop road across wild brush land. The truck finally turns down a long dirt track, and we park at the top of a steep slope leading down to a small, deserted beach. There's only a light sprinkling of rain as we get out of the truck, but the sky is still filled with thick dark clouds. A large timber hut sits at the side of a small wooden pier.

I cry out as I get down from the truck, stumbling onto the ground.

'Are you OK?' Hamish calls, running round and helping me up.

'It's just my arm. Keep going, we don't have much time.'

'You're shivering,' he says, pulling a pile of clothes from the back of the truck as we set off.

'D'you think the storm's past?' I ask, looking up doubtfully at the massing clouds as we walk down.

'I never think of storms passing,' Hamish says. 'They just . . . let up.' It's an odd thing to say.

I'm clenching my teeth and hugging myself from the cold. This can't be good for my baby. *My baby*. That I know I'm keeping.

'Are you OK? Do you feel sick?' He's seen me touching my stomach.

'No, no. I'm just really cold.'

'You need dry clothes,' he says as he unlocks a heavy padlock on the huge wooden doors to reveal his bright orange nature-tour boat. 'It looks OK, but I want to be careful. Precious cargo! You put on those dry clothes quickly and then the tour overalls, while I get the boat ready. But hurry.'

In the tiny office, full of equipment and ropes, I change into Hamish's jeans, T-shirt and huge blue jumper. It feels so intimate putting on his clothes. The smell of him encircles me, holding me safe. I drag on the huge waterproofs and emerge, swamped in the get-up. 'Catwalk ready,' I announce.

'You look good in anything,' he says with an embarrassed smile.

He helps me put on a life jacket and checks the fastenings. 'I won't let history repeat itself, don't worry.'

'What d'you mean?'

'Calder killing his girlfriend. He won't get to kill you too.'

He jumps down into the boat and gives me a hand to board, then starts the engine. There is a far-distant crack of lightning on the horizon.

'Is this safe, going out in this weather?'

'Don't worry, that lightning's a way off and there's no thunder, so the eye of the storm is still far away.'

I sit at the back of the boat next to him and cling on tightly to the silver safety rail with my good arm, as Hamish starts the motor. We instantly shoot out onto the grey heaving sea. This boat is fast, and Calder has no idea where I am or where I'm aiming for. We're going to make it.

'Do you think all the others somehow knew about what Calder had done? Arran, Janey, Alison?'

'They protect their own, that creepy church – and Calder was always their favourite, so athletic, so attractive, so special.'

'Thank you so much, Hamish,' I say. 'You're doing so much for me. I feel like I've blown up your life.'

He shakes his head. 'Don't be silly. It's the opposite. You've freed me.'

I nod. 'And you me. Will you come with me to London?'

He smiles. 'Of course. I'll be with you all the way. If you want me.'

'Of course I do. God, Calder's a psychopath. How did I not see it?'

'Because you're a good person that he duped. I didn't see it either and I'm his best friend.'

'Thank you.'

'I'd do anything for you.' He hugs me awkwardly and I lean into him, looking ahead at our clear escape route to the mainland.

But as we swing out round the bay, I see another

boat coming around the headland, directly towards us. It's one of the boats from the dock, a small vessel that looks fragile on this wild sea. I peer at the driver and see his dark hair flying in the wind. It's Calder. He's waving manically at us.

'Oh my God, he's following us.'

'Don't worry, I can outrun him in this!' Hamish shouts. He speeds up and zooms past Calder, dousing him in white sea spray, and shoots towards the far coast. We're leaving him far behind. There's no way he can catch up.

My breathing starts to slow. We're going to make it.

Then suddenly, Hamish slows our engine, turns the wheel hard and starts back, aiming directly for Calder.

'What are you doing?' I scream.

'You'll never be free of him while he's still alive!' he shouts.

'Oh my God. Turn round, Hamish. Let's just get to the other shore, please.'

'No, we have to stop him once and for all.'

I lunge at Hamish, trying to pull his hands off the steering wheel, but he doesn't budge, just stares doggedly ahead. My right arm is all but useless and I'm too weak to move him. Lightning cracks on the horizon again, but this time I hear thunder following quickly after. It's getting closer.

'Stop it!' I scream. 'This is crazy.'

Our boat is aimed straight at Calder, as if we're going to ram him.

'Hamish, you'll kill him, what are you doing?'

'Do you think you'll ever be free of him if we don't do this?' shouts Hamish. He banks the boat and I let go of his arm to swing back onto the seat, clinging on desperately.

Calder's shouting at us, but I can't hear him above the motors, the sea and the increasing rain. We're driving straight at him so I brace myself for the collision. I saved him from this wild sea, and now I'm trying to help it finish the job.

At the last second, Calder swerves his smaller craft out of our way. And as his boat turns, I finally catch what he's saying.

'Hamish killed them all!' he screams.

'What?' I shout, but we're shooting out of earshot again. 'Hamish, what's he talking about?'

'He's deranged!' Hamish shouts. It's not possible. Hamish was on a business trip when Rob died. Wasn't he? I remember Gina saying he was away when I rang about Calder's accident. I'm swung violently as the boat banks for Hamish to ram Calder again.

'Stop it, Hamish, I'll fall in.'

He ignores me and speeds towards Calder. He clips the side of his boat, so Calder is almost thrown out. He's gesturing wildly. 'Be careful, Hamish!' he shouts. 'She's pregnant.'

Our boat slows suddenly as Hamish stares at me. 'You're pregnant? By him?' he screams.

I nod.

'It's just like last time,' he says, shaking his head and taking a step towards me.

Oh my God. What's happening?

'What d'you mean?'

He glares at me.

'Hamish?'

Then he steps back behind the wheel, revs the engine and aims for Calder again.

'Hamish, stop it.'

This time as he nears Calder, he slows the boat. Thank God. But as we pull alongside, Hamish darts away from the motor, jumps up onto the inflated rim of our boat and leaps across into Calder's boat, falling across the side but managing to scrabble on.

My boat is swinging wildly in the waves as it drifts away from them. But the engine is still on, so I take the wheel and turn it back to approach them.

What is Calder talking about? Is he still trying to manipulate me? But what is Hamish doing? I don't know who I believe. Who do I want to survive?

The sky is a dark bruised purple and freezing rain is now sheeting down, cutting my face, numbing my hands. I'm chanting 'No, no, no,' rhythmically, engine on full throttle as I circle back. But what am I no-ing? That Hamish will kill Calder – or that Calder will kill Hamish?

My motor suddenly splutters and cuts out just before I reach them, Calder with his long dark hair flying in the wind, half a head taller than the wiry flame-haired Hamish.

'Calder, Hamish!' I shout. But my puny screams are sucked away by the wind and sea.

They're facing each other, Hamish swinging at Calder.

They tussle, each straining to drag the other over. I'm struggling to stand as my boat rears and falls with the surging waves.

'Calder!' I shout, as I right myself.

He glances towards me and in that moment of loss of

concentration, Hamish pulls Calder down, out of sight into the base of the boat. I can't see anything. They're in the bottom of the boat as it rocks wildly, out of sync with mine. I try my engine but get no response. But I'm being washed further in with every second.

Our boats are tossed about like toys. I can't make out what's happening. Then suddenly, the whole scene is lit by a massive jagged crack of lightning, very close by. Everything goes white.

A single figure rises, but my sight is blurred from the lightning and I don't know who it is.

The flash of light is extinguished, and the scene fades to darker than before.

I squint desperately.

There's a crash of thunder very close, as if the headland rows of dark stones sticking up out of the water are the spines of sea monsters, re-animated and roaring.

My eyesight finally focuses.

Calder is the standing figure.

But behind him, a dark figure rises.

'Be careful!' I scream.

Calder's focused on me as Hamish launches himself onto him.

And then they're both gone – fallen overboard.

I scour the water desperately, trying to see either of them.

My boat is nearly hitting theirs and I'm terrified of squashing them.

Then Calder appears in front of me, spluttering as he fights against the waves.

'Calder, swim along to my steps.' He's struggling,

gulping water, but he manages to get across to the little steps and climbs aboard my boat. I hold an oar out to keep him back, unsure whether to trust him.

'He killed Caitlin!' Calder shouts, his body juddering with the cold.

'No. You did it,' Hamish snarls, crawling over the far side of my boat, ''cos she wanted to kill your child.'

I swing back and forth between them, not knowing who to believe.

'Her diary said you'd been pestering her!' Calder shouts. 'And the hair in Caitlin's fist was orange hair, like yours,' he says, advancing on Hamish. 'She grabbed it when you strangled her. The police informed Arran this morning – everyone's been searching for you ever since.'

They were all looking for Hamish? Not for me?

'It wasn't me,' he shrieks, backing away from Calder.

'They're testing the hair's DNA now. You know what they'll find.'

'Hamish?' I cry.

He looks at me in disgust. 'How could you have a child with him after everything I've done for us to be together?'

I poke my oar hard at Hamish.

'I'm sorry!' he cries as he falls back. Calder pulls the oar from me and thwacks Hamish in the side of his head. He slumps down and stays there, face down.

Calder brings emergency foil blankets from beneath the seats and wraps me in one, and then covers Hamish's body.

'They think he may have killed Mr Walker too,' says Calder.

'What?'

'The rope around his neck was similar to the rigging rope from his nature boats.'

The thunder is getting closer.

Hamish moans, rolls over and sits up.

'Stay down,' Calder threatens.

'Nancy,' he implores. 'Help me.'

Calder pokes the oar at him again. 'You might as well give it up now, Hame, the evidence is undeniable. You killed Caitlin and Mr Walker.

Hamish glowers but then gives a wild laugh as he rubs his head.

'Fair enough. You have no idea how much I've done for you, Nancy.'

'What d'you mean?'

'I came to the island that night to see you, set off straight after Gina told me about you miscarrying our baby. I knew it was a sign that we were meant to be together. I crossed in my spare nature boat that's tethered on the mainland. But as I approached the island, I saw something floating in the water – it was Mr Walker, half dead but still conscious. He'd swum round to the next bay from yours. I pulled him aboard but he was babbling about Calder knocking him off the cliff, and that we had to get the police up there. I couldn't have the police anywhere near that cliff, 'cos I knew Caitlin was buried there – 'cos I buried her. So I strangled him with boat rope and tossed him over the side.'

'Oh God, Hamish. But why did you kill Caitlin?'

'I didn't mean to. I loved her,' he coughs. 'I heard Calder and her arguing in the dark that night. When

Calder passed out, I showed myself and said I'd help her with the baby. But she still wanted that drunken oaf, wanted to go to London with him and leave me behind. When I tried to kiss her, she pushed me off. She was screaming so loudly – I was just trying to shut her up.'

I stare at Calder, realising how wrong I've been about everything.

Hamish pulls himself up and holds onto the safety rail. 'But I risked rescuing you from where I knew Caitlin was because I love you. It's not fair. I'm the clever one. Calder's a fucking oaf. But first Caitlin chooses him and gets pregnant by him and now you too.'

Calder stares at me, knowing how wrong he's been about me.

There's thunder and a crack of lightning right above us. We're in the eye of the storm. The boat starts to spin.

'We're too near to the whirlpool!' Hamish shouts.

The boat tips and we all cling desperately to the handrails.

'This boat's too big to be sucked down,' Calder says as he walks to the back of the boat to take the wheel.

I've turned to follow Calder but hear Hamish laughing behind me. He's moved to the prow of the boat and is brandishing a long knife.

'The boat's not so safe if it deflates,' he calls as he lifts the knife above his head.

If I cannot inspire love, I will cause fear.

'Bon voyage!' he shouts.

I throw myself forward and push him.

But he catches my arm and steps up onto the edge of

the boat, about to pull me in with him. Calder dashes across and catches my other hand.

I'm pulled between them.

There's another crack of lightning and we're all lit up for a second, Hamish's eyes pure silver in the bright light. Then Calder reaches across and pulls Hamish's fingers free from my arm. Hamish howls as he falls backwards into the grey churning sea. We watch as he's pulled towards the whirlpool. He swirls in the churning water, thrashing wildly, then he's sucked down.

Calder pulls me to the back of the boat, wraps me in the foil blanket once more and takes the wheel. He guns the engine and the boat leaps over a wave, bumps down and speeds towards the coast.

We don't look back.

CHAPTER THIRTY-THREE

'We killed a man,' I say quietly.

The words hang in the air. Unbelievable. But true.

'How can we ever be forgiven?'

Calder stares straight ahead.

It's New Year's Eve. We're sitting on separate pews, either side of the aisle in the cold slate church, a week after Hamish was sucked down into that icy cauldron, where he joined Douglas. The church is decorated for the New Year's Day service tomorrow – white lilies for purity and rebirth. But we feel anything but pure. After we got back to shore, Calder was treated for hypothermia overnight, but was otherwise fine. I had my shoulder and wrist reset and was kept in for observation for two days. By some miracle, we both survived and I'm still pregnant. Dr Viner said he didn't believe in miracles, just coincidences and luck. I'm not so sure any more. We've been caught up in forces beyond ourselves on this island, where Old Testament punishment has prevailed.

'Do you need forgiveness?' Arran asks in an odd flat tone. He's sitting on the steps of the slate altar in front of us. 'Forgiveness from whom?'

'From . . . I don't know, your God?' I say. 'Other people. Ourselves? Isn't that your big thing?'

'Anything can be forgiven by God,' Arran says, nodding as if to convince himself. 'If we are truly sorry.'

I shift sideways on the hard pew. My body is healing, though I'm still bruised and sore, but my mind is burnt out and slow.

I glance across at Calder on the other side of the aisle, thinking of that night when the cottage burnt down and we flung those awful accusations at each other. Can we ever forgive each other for what we said? For what we imagined the other capable of?

'I would have brought Hamish back in with us,' Calder says dully. 'But he couldn't bear to lose.' He coughs and then breathes deeply. 'He always hated losing to me, even when we were kids. He would practise hoops for hours and hours, so he could beat me.' He folds over and hugs himself. 'I killed my best friend.'

'Hamish was a very jealous man,' Arran says slowly. 'I caught him once bursting the new tyres on your bike, Calder.' He shakes his head. 'He said "it's not fair" in the strangest way, as if he was in the right. He wanted Caitlin 'cos you had her and then Nancy . . . I could see what was happening by the way he looked at you in the lane that day.'

'So, that's why you were trying to warn me off him.'

'I didn't know about him killing Caitlin then of course, but I saw the old darkness in his eyes.'

The police have confirmed that Hamish killed both Robert and Caitlin. The climbing rope Hamish used to strangle Robert was matched with the rope in Hamish's boathouse, the cut of the ends corresponding exactly. And the DNA from his hair clutched in Caitlin's fist and preserved by the peat burial proved her murder. Calder and I were questioned for hours after we'd received medical treatment. But our stories of Hamish's confession chimed with the evidence. Calder's tangential part in Rob's death was accepted by the police as an accident.

'I'm not sure if forgiveness is possible,' Calder says, looking up at the slate cross.

'We have to trust that the slate can be wiped clean,' Arran says.

'But we killed Hamish,' I say. 'And I accused Calder of killing Mr Walker, Caitlin and, oh God, even your own dad. I'm so sorry.'

'I accused you too,' he says. 'Of cheating, of lying, of our child being Hamish's.'

We stare at each other, stripped bare and raw.

Arran stands and steps up to the slate altar, facing away from us, running his hands over the smooth glossy surface. 'You can forgive each other if you truly want to, and be forgiven by God, if you are truly sorry.' He says it like he's chanting, his hands still glued to the altar, his knuckles white.

I shake my head. 'Can't you stop all that for a moment, Arran. It's just words. Empty advice. I know you mean well, but what have you ever done that really needed forgiveness?'

Arran's shoulders shake.

'I'm sorry, I didn't mean to upset you,' I say, standing up.

But then I hear that he's laughing.

'What's so funny?' I snap.

He looks up at the stained-glass window of the Virgin Mary, takes a deep breath, then turns towards us, letting go of the altar. 'You're right,' he spits out. 'What's the point of banging on about forgiveness.'

'I didn't mean . . .'

'Yes you did. And I am a hypocrite.'

'I didn't say that.'

'I preach it endlessly, have told countless others to "let go of their sins". What does that even mean?'

Calder looks up.

Arran steps down towards him. 'I promised her I'd never breathe a word to a living soul. But Isla is with her maker now and I . . .'

Calder shakes his head at Arran. 'No, I don't want to know. Let her rest in peace.'

'Please. I can't carry this burden any more.'

Calder lifts a hymn book and throws it at Arran, who just stands there and lets it hit him. A trickle of blood stains his cheek.

'Stop it, Calder!' I shout, leaping up to stand between them. 'Are you OK, Arran? What are you both talking about?' I ask, looking between them. 'Calder?' I see his clenched fists, knuckles white.

'If she murdered him!' he cries, 'she did it to protect me, for God's sake – let her memory be.'

Arran stares at him, then fumbles with his white dog collar, rips it off and throws it aside. He walks round the altar and stands behind it, crosses himself and speaks slowly. 'When Robert's body washed up on the shore at the bonfire

367

that night, I thought he'd come back for me.'

I remember the look of horror on Arran's face as he raised Robert's body from the water.

'Robert had come for you?'

'No. Douglas.'

'Stop it,' Calder mumbles.

Arran shakes his head. 'When I arrived here as a young pastor, Douglas was the big man on the island, ran all the building work, elder of the church. I didn't dare intervene when I saw Isla coming to church with bruises. Even when I saw you with a black eye, Calder, God help me. Then one day, she called me to come to their cottage.' He glances at Calder, who's looking down. 'There was blood everywhere.'

Calder gives a low moan.

'Isla killed him?' I ask quietly.

He nods. 'She said they'd been fighting and she'd knocked him backwards. He'd fallen back onto a metal boot scuffer bolted to the floor of the cottage – cracked his head open on it.'

I shudder. That awful boot scuffer that I've polished till it gleamed.

'She was hysterical – saying she'd be arrested and then Calder would have no one. I told her I'd defend her, explain it was self-defence. But . . . I knew she was right. You were only fourteen, Calder.'

Calder hangs his head and I walk over to put my arm around his shoulders.

'It was my pathetic fear of getting involved that had caused that tragedy. Douglas was already dead, so why make you and Isla suffer for my sin?' Calder shakes his head. 'So, when it got dark, we took Douglas down to the bay and put him in his little boat. Isla and I went in my boat and we pulled his behind. It was a full moon, so the whirlpools were especially deep. And we timed it so that we hit them at the height of the tide change. We'd weighted his body so that it would sink, and I was ready to scupper the boat.'

'So all you did was help her get rid of the body? I think that's kind of forgivable,' I say.

He shakes his head. 'What I did was unforgivable.'

Calder looks up.

'As we neared the whirlpool, I started to untie the rope and then . . . Douglas opened his eyes.'

Calder lurches forward, knocking prayer books off the pew, the clatter reverberating around the church.

'What did you do?' Calder shouts.

'I told Isla that we had to take him back,' Arran says, his voice strangled. 'But she was frozen, just staring at him. Then Douglas suddenly lurched up to sitting. He called her a fucking bitch and screamed "That soft boy's all mine now".'

I squeeze Calder's shoulder, but he shakes me free as Arran continues. 'We were nearing the whirlpool. Douglas had dragged himself forward to try to get onto our boat. Isla was in shock, seized in front of him. He was untying the weight we'd roped around his waist. Any moment he'd be free to leap across to us. I had a second to decide what to do.' He clenches his fists and looks up. 'Then there was a huge crack of lightning. Douglas and all his snarling hatred were lit up for me to see. God help me!' he cries. 'I drove my metal stake into the base of his boat and untied it. I watched it filling with water, being pulled into the whirlpool, Douglas screaming, and then suddenly it upended and he was sucked down.'

We're all motionless, the dust floating in the shadows. Arran seems to return to his body and looks at Calder. He steps down from the altar and walks over to stand in front of him. 'I murdered your father.'

Calder pulls back his fist, taut with anger for a long second. And then lets it fall.

Suddenly the clouds outside move and sunlight pours through the windows, bouncing off the polished slate altar to sprinkle the walls with light.

Calder sits down and I hug him.

'I tried to look after you after that, but I could never be a father to you,' Arran says quietly. 'I tried to get the whole congregation to support you.'

Calder watches Arran cry without speaking. As he finally calms, he looks up.

'So that's why Mum was so obsessed with the church after that?' Calder asks.

'Yes. She wouldn't go to the police, said Calder needed her and she'd go to prison as an accomplice. We both agreed to stay silent. She was grateful to me for saving you, but she found it hard to live with what we'd done. I had to help her, to stop her suffering further for my sin. So I talked to her endlessly about forgiveness, but she kept punishing herself and doing never-ending penance.'

'She made me sleep on the floor like her,' Calder says. 'I never understood it. We'd fast, learn passages of the Bible by heart . . .'

'I'm sorry,' Arran says.

'I still find the hard floor oddly comforting,' Calder says, glancing at me.

'It ate her up from the inside. I developed my whole

tradition of writing sins on slates and washing them clean, for her. But every time we wrote our sins in chalk, I saw her write MURDERER and had to wash it clean, as fast as I could, so that no one else saw it.'

Calder looks at me. 'I did bunk off school that day, like Hamish said, because Mum had rung to say that Dad was out of control again, drinking and angry. But I was sick of it all. I couldn't face going home to the screaming and fighting. I'll never forgive myself for staying on the mainland and getting smashed, instead of going back to help her. I got the first ferry the next morning, and she was cleaning the kitchen manically. Said she didn't know where Dad was. Just that he'd gone out drunk in his boat. I always thought that she'd killed him. And then when his boat drifted in, she went along with the story he'd drowned. She was always so obsessive about that damn floor. Always washing away the blood I guess.'

'You were a boy,' Arran says, putting a hand on his shoulder. 'I should have intervened much earlier. Afterwards, I kept looking for other tragedies to avert – which was why I worried so much about Caitlin and ended up running Robert off the island with my fears. I was terrified of missing another domestic horror. But I drove an innocent man from his family. Stopped Caitlin being found sooner. Do you want me to confess to the authorities about killing him?'

Calder shakes his head. 'Nothing would be achieved. You've done your penance. And you are what holds this community together.'

'But I'm a sinner,' Arran says.

Calder picks up his discarded dog collar and passes it back to him. 'Who better to help others?'

CHAPTER THIRTY-FOUR

Whoosh. Drag. Whoosh. Drag.

The waves are breaking on the beach and dragging the slates back into the sea. It's a month later and Calder is standing in the freezing sea, with just his head poking above the water.

'Only a few minutes,' he says nervously.

I'm halfway in, water up to my thighs – I'm not risking the cold on the baby.

'You're OK,' I laugh. 'Arran's "Icebreakers" swim here every morning for ten minutes. He says all ages and fitnesses do it. And we need to do this.'

'Actually, it doesn't even feel that cold,' Calder laughs. 'Not like . . .'

'What will we do with it?' I ask, as I look up to the remains of the cottage. It's a burnt-out shell, the windows blackened, the roof fallen in.

'Once we're settled back in London, we'll decide.'

I lean down and plunge my arms into the cold water, feeling tingly and alive.

'Once under?' I ask.

He smiles and nods.

'We have thought the worst of each other, we have to let it go,' I say.

'Washed clean. We are The Saved,' he chants with a smile, imitating the islanders and their chant at the bonfire.

'Washed clean. We are The Saved,' I join in sarcastically.

I lean forward and submerge my face, shoulders and my one arm without a cast into the freezing water as he bobs his head under. We scream as we surface, then wade back, falling chaotically onto the slate beach. We fumble around, our fingers dulled by the cold, rubbing each other with huge towels, our skin ruddy and sore. We stumble on the slate pebbles, laughing at our bumbling. Once we're dry, we pull on layers of clothes, Calder insisting on drying my hair over and over and then wrapping it up in a turban.

'I'm not fragile,' I laugh. 'Just pregnant.'

We sit down on the beach and drink the hot chocolate from the thermos that Arran packed for us. It's hot, sweet and delicious. My skin tingles and every part of me feels alive. I still feel disorientated, but I'm present. Here. On the slates. With my husband.

'We need to get going if we want to make the ferry in time for the train back to Glasgow and then on to London,' Calder says.

'Just give me five minutes.'

He packs up while I walk along the beach, looking

down at the slates, every one different in shape, size and colour, looking for just the right-sized pieces. I'm warm inside and ruddy and alive on the outside.

I see that someone, probably a child, has built a construction on the ridge of the beach, stacking slates into a three-sided fortress. I crouch inside it, looking out at the sea, where the bodies of Douglas and Hamish still reside. Since my parents' deaths, I've kept a slate fortress around me to protect me. I leapt into the safety of Calder and pretended we were perfect; I tried to hide from what happened with Hamish by coming up here; I tried to get round what Calder did by justifying it; and then when I believed he was a killer, I tried to find some new safety with Hamish and then boomeranged back to Calder. I have to stop ricocheting to the next fantasy safety and let myself be open and honest.

Calder berates himself that he could have saved his mother. I berate myself that I caused my parents' crash. No wonder we had that deep wordless click when we met. Two guilty people, trying to find peace. I've stacked the guilt about Hamish and Calder on top of this deep seam of guilt that runs right through me to my core. Heavy on my chest. Curling my edges. I cannot imagine an existence without it. I felt so lost when I considered letting it go at that slate washing church service of Arran's. But Isla was hardened by her guilt; Arran became overly controlling; Hamish justified his and kept going. We came to this island of forgiveness for a reason. We have to forgive ourselves. Finally.

As well as the cautionary tale that Isla left us, she did something concrete to help us. She insured her cottage at a huge premium and we have enough money to start again in London. Calder will find building work. That *Frankenstein* reboot will give me a nest egg but will be my last editorial work. I will brave doing some writing of my own. Enough of my behind-the-scenes tinkering with other people's creations; I have to stand up and take the risk of finding my own voice.

I see two perfect-sized slates in the fort battlements and carefully slide them out without destroying the structure. They are flat and oval, with smooth curved edges. And they're flecked with dots, splodges and lines of glinting gold. But it's the fool's gold of pyrite that has tricked so many people in the past. I will not fool myself any more with made-up fears and past guilt. They aren't real, however much they glimmer for my attention. I walk back, hearing the Jenga-block clinking of the slates, and know I'll miss that sound. I give one slate to Calder, hand him a piece of the chalk that Arran gave us and take my own.

'We have to let go of our guilts,' I say. 'Once and for all. Let's write them all down.'

I write, *By distracting Dad I killed my parents. I doubted my husband. I killed Hamish.*

Calder writes, *By deserting Mum I killed Dad. I doubted my wife. I killed Hamish.*

We look at each other and nod.

I hope we can forgive ourselves and each other.

We walk down to the sea and kneel. We slowly wash the slates in the sea water and see the white words melt away into the grey. Then we throw the slates and they smash apart. Impossible to put back together.

'Ready?' Calder asks.

I nod, as I slide one small slate pebble into my pocket and stand.

I take Calder's hand and turn away from the beautiful, shimmering sea.

We drive back into town and drop off the stuff that Arran's lent us, and hug our goodbyes.

'You'll come back one day?' Arran asks.

'Maybe, one day,' Calder says.

Janey stands at a distance and waves. She's wary of Calder but has accepted the truth that he didn't kill Rob. She had joined Alison that awful morning along with the other church members to search for Hamish and save us from him.

'I was going to give you more slate tincture for healing irreparable damage, but—' She glances at us. 'I don't think you'll need it. I'll be in touch to forward your . . . special delivery, in a couple of months' time.'

After we returned to the cottage to assess the fire damage, we discovered that Attila had given birth to four kittens in the burnt-out ruins. That was why she'd suddenly turned aggressive to Calder – nothing to do with him, only her self-protection. Attila herself refuses to leave the wrecked cottage, looking after it for us. Arran, Alison and Janey will each have a kitten. We'll be taking the fourth, once it's ready to be separated from his mother, of whom he's the spitting image. We've already named our kitten Prince Csaba, the name of one of Attila's sons, who was rumoured to have ridden down a pathway from the night sky to fight invaders. That's the kind of strength I need now.

I hug Janey and Arran and we walk down to the ferry and step back on.

The ferry manoeuvres its bulk awkwardly as it pulls away, and then we're off to the mainland and from there to London. My left hand caresses the slate pebble in my pocket. I'm carrying it with me to remind myself that slates can always be wiped clean and life can move forward.

I stroke my belly and Calder puts his hand on top of mine, as we watch the island receding slowly, enveloped back into the swirling mist, until it disappears entirely.

NOTE FROM THE AUTHOR

I was inspired to write this story after reading about the unusual medical phenomenon of being clinically dead in freezing temperatures, but where there is still a window of opportunity to be brought back to life. I've read many accounts, including on: Anna Bågenholm, the Swedish radiologist, who survived after a skiing accident in Norway in 1999 left her trapped under a layer of ice for eighty minutes in freezing water, whose heart didn't beat for many hours and who had the lowest ever recorded accidental hypothermia temperature in an adult who survived; the 2011 saving of seven Danish teenagers from a group who were on a school trip when their boat sank in the freezing Præstø Fjord off the island of Zealand, who were clinically dead and whose hearts stopped beating for six hours before they were brought back; and English teacher Audrey Schoeman, who was hiking in the Spanish

Pyrenees in 2019 and got trapped in a snowstorm, her heart stopping for six hours before it beat again.

All were clinically dead – no heartbeat, no breath. Their brains and organs would normally have been injured beyond repair from lack of oxygen for even just a few minutes. But they were all extremely, hypothermically, cold. As one of their doctors said: 'You're not dead, till you're warm and dead.' These were extreme experiences for them, and for their families and for the amazing medical staff who brought them back.

These events and the work done by the doctors to bring them back have led to great advances in medicine, and the use of extreme cooling for many patients to preserve organs after cardiac events, until the heart can be restarted. It is a hugely exciting field which is pushing the very limits of what we define as the moment of death.

ACKNOWLEDGEMENTS

Huge thanks to my fantastic and very supportive editor Lesley Crooks and everyone at my brilliant publisher, the wonderful Allison & Busby, including Publishing Director, Susie Dunlop; Sales and Marketing Executive, Libby Haddock; Head of Sales, Daniel Scott; Publishing Assistant, Fiona Paterson; Copy Editor, Sara Magness; and thanks for the marvellous cover design by Christina Griffiths.

Massive thanks to my wonderful agent Liv Maidment for all her support throughout the whole process of writing this book, from first idea to final drafts; and to everyone at the Madeleine Milburn Literary, TV & Film Agency, especially to Madeleine Milburn herself; to Liane-Louise Smith, Georgina Simmonds, Valentina Paulmichl and Amanda Carungi in International Rights; to in-house editors Georgia McVeigh and Rachel Yeoh; and to Hannah Ladds in Film and TV.

I could not have written this book without the amazing support from my writing mentor Sarah Clayton who teaches 'The Write Wild Method for Writers', which uses being in nature to expand and support creativity (https://write-wild-books.cademy.co.uk/). I first visited the slate islands of western Scotland on one of her wonderfully inspiring writing retreats. She and her lovely husband Mike Clayton took me on a second trip to research the Scottish slate islands once I was writing the book, and they drove me all over the stunning area and introduced me to so many brilliant people.

On both trips we stayed at the wonderful Garragh Mhor B&B in the village of Ellenabeich, which I cannot recommend highly enough; we were looked after brilliantly by hosts Jan McSkimming and Darren Ainsworth. Jan is a brilliant cook of healthy delicious food and a healer, and Daz is an amazing creative blacksmith. They were both so inspiring and knowledgeable about the area and provided an utterly unique and life-affirming place to stay.

Also thanks for local colour from: The Baron of Bachuil, Chief of Maclea; Robert & Iris Smith from the Explore Lismore Land Rover Tour; Seafari, Ellenabeich, the Corryvrecken Tour; Norman Bissell, the brilliant author of Barnhill who lives on Isle of Luing; and the staff of The Oyster Bar, Ellenabeich.

Thanks to all those who have written about and given interviews on the experience of being brought back from cold weather heart stoppages. And thanks to the brilliant doctors who have treated them, and spoken about the ever-expanding science around the phenomenon and their experience with their patients. All these amazing accounts and observations were invaluable.

Huge thanks for all the incredibly helpful editing notes I received along the way from: Sarah Clayton my mentor; my brilliant and ever-supportive writers group Jo Pritchard, Katherine Tansley, Marija Maher-Diffenthal and Sarah Lawton; the wonderfully perceptive and ever-encouraging editor Jon Appleton; my intuitive and supportive Faber reader Laura Marshall; stunning historical mystery writer Beth Underdown; brilliant thriller writer Holly Seddon; and wonderful editor Anna Barrett from The Writer's Space.

I am ever grateful to Sophie Hannah and her Dream Author programme for keeping me grounded through the ups and downs of writing.

Thanks to my website designers Naomi Adams and Faith Tilleray from 'A for Author', and photographer Ben Wilkin for my headshot.

Huge thanks to Berry Beaumont for her support; to Sue Cowan-Jenssen for all her ongoing kindness; and to writer Claudine Toutoungi for her friendship and laughter about being a writer. Oh and thanks to brilliant playwright Andrew Viner whose name I nicked, with permission, for the cardiac specialist.

And finally, endless thanks to my lovely supportive husband Andy and my wonderful son Archie, for all their patience, encouragement and love.

LIZ WEBB originally trained as a classical dancer, then worked as a secretary, stationery shop manager, art class model, cocktail waitress, stand-up comic, voice-over artist, script editor and radio drama producer, before becoming a novelist. She lives in North London.

lizwebb.co.uk
@LizWebbAuthor